The Last Day
I Saw Her

The Last Day I Saw Her

LUCY LAWRIE

BLACK & WHITE PUBLISHING

First published 2016
by Black & White Publishing Ltd
29 Ocean Drive, Edinburgh EH6 6JL

1 3 5 7 9 10 8 6 4 2   16 17 18 19

ISBN: 978 1 78530 014 1

ALBA | CHRUTHACHAIL

Typeset by Iolaire Typesetting, Newtonmore
Printed and bound by Nørhaven, Denmark

For Arlene

Acknowledgements

I owe a huge debt of thanks to my friends, Jane Farquharson and Lesley McLaren, who helped me at every stage. Second novels can be tricky and I couldn't have got here without their writerly advice, insight and enthusiasm.

Thank you to the wonderful team at Black & White Publishing, in particular to Karyn Millar for her sensitive editing of the manuscript, and to Janne Moller for holding my hand through the whole process. Thanks also go to my agent and friend, Joanna Swainson, for her constant support and encouragement.

I want to thank my sister, Katherine, for letting me read her teenage diaries when I was trying to find Hattie's voice – that was above and beyond the call of sisterly duty!

This book also has an older sister – *Tiny Acts of Love*. I was overwhelmed by the amazing response of the book-blogging community when it was released, so heartfelt thanks go out to them. I want to thank each and every one of my readers, too. A story doesn't come to life until it is read, so thank you for finishing what I started.

Thanks also go to my mum and dad. And to my daughters, Emily and Charlotte, who inspire me every day.

Finally, I have some incredible friends who have gone out of their way to support me, and my writing journey, over the last couple of years. I will never forget your belief in me, and all the ways you helped me. Most of all, *The Last Day I Saw Her* is a book about friendship, so this one's for you.

1

Janey

I can't even remember what I was thinking about, walking along that corridor to the classroom in those last few moments before everything changed. Pip's meltdown over his supermarket-brand fish fingers, perhaps. Or the fact that he needed a new coat, now that the weather had turned. Did I have an inkling of what was coming – a tingling in the skin, or an adrenaline swoop in the stomach? Surely there must have been some part of me that knew.

Room 12 was the last on the right, brightly lit after the gloom of the corridor, with paintings and collages crowding the walls, and a stretch of windows overlooking a rainswept playground. Twisty wire creations hung low from the ceiling, casting filigree shadows on the surface of the large square table that stood in the middle of the room.

Four people were sitting round it already.

'Oooh, hello!' said the woman nearest me, who looked vaguely familiar with her rounded cheeks and long front teeth. 'Are you new? Sit down.'

She motioned to the stool beside her.

I edged my way round, past a lifesize papier mâché goat and a row of newly painted Punch and Judy-style puppets, gazing from a shelf.

The woman shot me an appraising look. 'You're very smart.'

I was wearing my one still-presentable work suit – grey with a faint pinstripe through it. I'd thought, since it was a course on 'How to Write a Killer CV and Ace that Interview', I might as well look the part.

This woman, however, was dressed in pink hotpants and a running vest. Odd choice.

'I'm Jody,' she said. 'This is my husband, Tom.' She gestured to a short man in jeans and a Megadeth T-shirt. 'We can't *wait* to get started. Last week's session was mindblowing.'

Gosh, she was keen. Maybe she was putting a brave face on it – how unfortunate that both she and her husband should be looking for work at the same time.

Suddenly, I placed her. 'I – I think I know you. You go to the Jungle Jive class, don't you – the one in St Matthew's church hall on a Friday morning?'

'I take *Vichard* to it, yes,' she said, as though I'd accused her of attending for her own pleasure. 'Do you have a child?'

I failed to answer for a moment, caught up wondering why anyone would name their son Richard if they couldn't pronounce the letter 'R'.

'Oh – oh, yes I do. Pip. He's two and a half. And I'm Janey,' I added.

She nodded, narrowing her eyes, as though she wasn't quite ready to accept my status as a Jungle Jive member.

'I've only been a couple of times . . .'

'You'll *vecognise* Molly too, then,' she said, pointing across the table to a small woman with dark curly hair, sitting next to a smug-looking man. They seemed to be fiddling with bits of green card and a box of pipecleaners.

'Oh yes, I do. Her wee boy plays the violin, doesn't he?'

But surely they shouldn't be playing with the art supplies – that wouldn't help them write killer CVs.

And why were we in the art room anyway? The corridor I'd just walked along had been lined with empty, *normal* classrooms. I glanced behind me at the Punch and Judy dolls, their heavy heads lolling on bendy necks.

'Don't you have a partner?' Jody asked, her face twisted into an expression somewhere between pity and bewilderment.

My heart sank. She'd pegged me as a lonely, tragic single mother – was it the pinstripes? Did they look desperate? Or was it just my face?

'Who will you practise the techniques with?' she persisted.

Oh God, the interview techniques. Eye contact and firm handshakes, and how to command a room. 'Oh. I didn't know you were supposed to bring a partner. I assumed the tutor would pair us up.'

Jody snorted. 'Oh, you're a hoot!'

I felt like a schoolgirl, shrinking against the wall bars in the gym because nobody had chosen me. I should have probably left right then – the idea of me with a proper job was farcical anyway. But Murray would know I'd bottled it if I arrived home two hours early, and would raise a knowing eyebrow at my pathetic little bid for independence.

'Suit yourself. Anyway, it looks like Steve's late. Again.' She hopped off her stool. 'Come on, Tom. Let's get started.'

She shot him a challenging look, as though she was about to start firing questions at him: 'When's the last time you led a team to a successful outcome?' or some such horror.

'Maybe we should wait,' said Tom.

'No. We can at least start the greasing-up process.'

She slipped off her shoes and walked over to the other side of the room where, I now noticed, there was a large plastic sheet laid out on the floor. Tom squatted down at her feet with a resigned sigh, and unscrewed a jar of Vaseline.

'Do it properly,' said Jody, 'or the plaster could tear my skin off.'

I whipped round to look at the other couple. Molly was twisting green pipecleaner-and-card leaves into the man's hair, her tongue protruding in concentration.

I jumped down from the stool, my sensible court shoes clacking loudly on the floor.

'I've got the wrong class,' I announced to nobody in particular. 'Oops. I'll just go now.'

Nice one, Janey. All dressed up in your pinstripes and you can't even book an evening class.

'This is "The Art of Love",' said Jody. 'An *art workshop*,' she went on, slowly. 'For couples. Every Tuesday.' She flicked a glance down to my feet and up again. 'Bring your own bottle.'

'Right.' I wanted to slap her, standing there with her nice dull Megadeth husband and her air of entitlement. But I nodded politely. 'See you, then . . .'

'Stay,' said a voice.

I turned. A man stood before me, his forehead beaded with rain, or sweat, unstrapping a wide across-the-shoulder bag. I wondered for a moment if I'd met him before. Short dark hair, mussed up into a peak in the middle. Boyish around the mouth, but lined around the eyes. Glasses with square black frames. No, he must just have one of those faces.

My legs felt heavy, suddenly, aching to sit down again.

'I'm Steve. You're welcome to stay. This is my class.' He had a trace of a Northern accent – from Leeds, or Sheffield perhaps, exotic here in New Town Edinburgh. He was taking off his jacket now – a cracked, brown leather jacket – which rattled as he threw it over a stool.

4

'No, really . . .'

'We're down a couple.' *A coopell.* 'The Smythes have dropped out.'

Oh well, if the Smythes have dropped out . . .

I took the form out of my bag. 'Um . . . I was looking for "How to Write a Killer CV and Ace that Interview".'

He peered at it and shook his head, frowning. 'That's C808. That runs from November sixth. This is C806. "The Art of—"'

'Yes. Yes, I know.'

'The admin staff aren't the best. They can't work the new website. Sorry about that.'

'It's fine, honestly, I'll—'

He gestured towards Jody and Tom, cutting me off mid-fluster. His hands seemed too big for his body, white and knuckly.

'We're just playing around with materials today. Would you like to stay? Sorry, I didn't catch your name?'

'Janey.'

He looked me straight in the eye then, and something happened. It was as though there'd been a buzzing in the room, through my body, my mind, so constant that I hadn't noticed it. For months. Years. A whole weary lifetime, maybe. And he'd just flicked a switch and turned it off. Stillness. Silence. Just my own heart beating.

And now I think about it, maybe that was it: the stillness made way for what was about to happen, letting it rise like a bubble to the surface.

But in that moment, all I could do was watch as he crossed the room, reached into a cupboard and came back to the workbench with a sheet of A3 paper and a packet of colouring pens.

Already I knew that I wouldn't be leaving. I wouldn't be walking out of this warm, brightly lit room into the night. I wouldn't be going home to the flat, where Pip lay sleeping and Murray frowned over legal reports at the kitchen table, and shadows pooled in the corners of the rooms. Not yet.

But it was the pens that made me sit down. They were brand new – a perfect rainbow held lightly in my two hands. The gummy smell of the clear plastic packet transported me to the first day of a dozen autumn terms: the sweet, pink-sharpened wood of new pencils, the clearly labelled ruler and Pritt Stick. Trimmed hair and shiny shoes.

I drew out the black pen, nestled in at the far right of the pack. My hand hovered over the cool white sweep of the page, reluctant to mark it.

'Steve,' called Molly. 'I want to make roots, sort of twisting and clustering around Dave's calves.' She paused to make twisting and clustering movements with her hands. 'I want to show how I really *get* him, from an eco perspective. I was thinking papier mâché? Could you come over?'

It was a while before he returned. I'd been enjoying the benign schoolroom bustle: Steve's thoughts on root-making, delivered in the serious tones of one brain surgeon advising another, and Jody's critique of her husband's plastering skills. But my sheet of paper was still blank, apart from my name, and the date.

'I couldn't think of anything to draw,' I said to him.

'Try drawing with your left hand,' called Jody, now wrapped in soggy white bandages up to her thighs. 'That's what we did last week. Just to, you know, loosen us up.'

Steve shrugged. 'Sometimes it can be useful if you haven't done any art for a while. The idea is to be playful with the materials, not get hung up about the results.'

'You bypass the rational, language-based part of the brain,' announced Jody bossily. 'And access the inner child. Pass my wine, would you, Tom, m'darlin'?'

Well, if Jody could access her inner child, I bloody well could too.

Using my right hand, I positioned the pen in the grip of my left.

'Look,' Steve said. 'Stop there for a sec. What's happened?'

I shot a glance down my front, half expecting to see buttons undone at my cleavage, or a burst zip.

'You just tensed up. Can you feel where you're holding your tension?'

I released my lip from between my teeth, expelling the breath I'd been holding high in my chest.

'That's better. Try loosening up.' He stretched his arms in front of him, flexing his fingers. I had the sudden urge to reach out and touch him, to wrap his fingers round mine. 'Sounds a bit weird, but let your mouth go soft. The tension goes from your jaw into your arm, and your hand, and into your work, which is the last place we want it to go.' He drew the pale blue pen from the pack and held it aloft, gritting his teeth as if to demonstrate.

Was this right? Should this man be telling me to make my mouth go soft, in a room of Jungle Jive couples celebrating the art of love?

'I don't know what to draw.' I glanced over at Molly, who was taping a large strip of bark to her husband's torso.

'What do you feel like drawing? When's the last time you drew something just for the hell of it?'

'Probably at school.'

'What would you have drawn?'

With my wavering left hand, I drew a figure with stick arms and legs, a lollipop head, curly hair, and added three dots, to be the three dark moles on my left cheek.

'It's me,' I explained. 'My hair used to be curlier.'

He gave a sideways nod, as if to say *fair enough*, and nudged his glasses up where they'd slipped down. For a second, I imagined a comedy plastic nose attached to the square, black frames. Pip had one at home, a 'free gift' from the front of his Thomas the Tank Engine magazine.

What to draw next? After a moment's hesitation, I added a big smile. But somehow, I couldn't get the curve right – it remained crooked and tight, however much I went over it. The eyes looked startled, black holes in that sea of white, so I added eyebrows, which only made the curly-headed figure look anxious. With a flash of irritation I added a skipping rope, trailing off snake-like towards the right of the picture. It looked odd, unfinished.

'Su-perb,' he said. 'That's you started.' But he didn't move away. He hovered by the side of the bench.

Unsatisfied with the figure I'd drawn, I lifted the pen again.

'Going to draw something else? Go for it. Try and free up that hand. There's loads of research on this, by the way.' He reached up his own hand and ran it over the top of his head, nudging his little peak of hair to the side.

'Mmm.'

'Basically, it's about accessing the right hemisphere of the brain, things like feeling, intuition, creativity . . . All the stuff that gets knocked out of us at school, by the so-called education system.'

His voice deepened on the last three words. I smiled – he sounded like my grandpa. Any minute now he'd start talking

8

about 'this bloody government' and how they'd single-handedly ruined the country.

I looked down. What was this I'd drawn? Another figure, a black scribble, stood at the end of the skipping rope. She was smaller than the first, with straight hair, and a wavy line where the mouth should have been.

A little crawling sensation down my neck.

'Oh,' I said.

There must have been something in my voice, because the half-mummified Jody stepped off her plastic sheet and moved, haltingly, over to my bench. She stood close enough that I could smell the gluey tang coming from her bandages.

'So if that's you,' she said, pointing to the first girl. 'Who's that other one?'

I gave a tight little laugh. 'I have *absolutely* no idea. I didn't mean to draw this.'

Steve craned his head round to see the picture straight on. And then he moved, right round beside me so his shoulder was almost touching mine.

I stared at the paper.

'Hey,' said Steve, tapping my arm gently with the end of the pale-blue pen. 'You might want to breathe.'

My left hand lifted the pen and stiffened as I tried – and failed – to take control of it.

'Who *are* you, little girl?' boomed Jody.

'Thanks for that, Jody,' began Steve. 'I think—'

'Who are you?' I repeated, in barely a whisper under my breath.

My hand wrote five spindly words:

YOU KNOW WHO I AM

I gasped, jerked back from the workbench.

'Okaaaay,' Steve said. 'Don't panic, Janey. When we unleash our creativity the results can be . . . unexpected. Especially if it's the first time you've done it in a while. Take it easy. Stop if you want to.'

'Who are you?' I asked again.

No, no. I know who you are and I can't bear it.

The pen moved – quicker this time:

HATTIE. HATTIE. HATTIE.

Steve stepped back, banging into a stool, scraping it across the floor.

The room filled with silence again: deep, underwater silence. Steve, Jody and the others seemed to have melted away.

You. It's you. It can't be you.

My hand – my treacherous, traitorous hand – scribbled two words, then in one last, convulsive effort, a third, before it fell, dead still, onto the paper:

LISTEN JANEY LISTEN

*

'Wait,' called Steve. 'Hold up a sec!'

But I was gone. Out of the classroom, clattering down the stairs and out onto the street. The quickest way to get home was to cut through the Colonies, with their neat rows of tiny terraced houses, and walk through Stockbridge. I stopped to catch my breath on the bridge over the Water of Leith.

What had just happened? Had those little black words

really crawled onto the page from my subconscious? Had my inner child just been unleashed by a packet of coloured pens and a blank sheet of paper? That might have been easier to accept if I'd had any sense of being in charge of my hand, in that moment when it began to write. But I could still feel that hot rush of panic at the loss of control, like the moment you knew you were going to vomit.

My lungs were too tight, the air wouldn't come. Pinpricks of light burst into my field of vision.

Calm down.

I closed my eyes and let the rush of the water fill my head. For a moment, I was back in Glen Eddle, aged nine, standing calf-deep in the stream, the water pressing cold through the thin rubber of my wellies. I'd learned that if I closed my eyes, the imperative of keeping my balance would make thinking impossible, and the roar of the water would wash my mind clean and cool.

Hattie.

It had to be Hattie Marlowe, I reasoned. But why would my hand pretend to be her now, twenty-five years after I'd last seen her? I'd become quite comfortable with the idea that she was getting on with her life somewhere, probably now with a clutch of gorgeous, tyrannical children, or a slick city career. In fact, I realised now how much I'd relied on that assumption. The world had always been that little bit warmer, lifted a semitone into a sweeter key, because of the thought that Hattie was in it somewhere.

Could she – the actual Hattie – be trying to reach me?

Ridiculous. Even after everything that had happened back then, it was ridiculous.

And anyway, there was Facebook. Or the St Katherine's

Alumni Association. She'd be able to find me. No need to communicate through left-handed writing via 'The Art of Love'.

Unless.

No. Not dead. Please.

★

Later on, at home, in the quiet of my bedroom, I pulled a blue cardboard folder out from the bottom of my sock drawer. A folder with one word – 'Hattie' – written on the front. I remembered how strange it had felt to write her name there in permanent marker, as though I was laying bare some fragile thing no one was meant to see.

I slid the pictures out and laid them on my bed. And I peered into them as though they might, just this one time, awake from their hidden half-life and start talking back.

But no. This could never do any good. If Hattie – my oldest, dearest friend Hattie – wanted me to listen, then there was only one thing to do. I put the pictures back into their folder, telling myself I wouldn't look at them again.

On a deep shelf in the box room, high up by the tiny window that let in a little light from the tenement stairwell, I found a red and white Woolworths bag. It was still where I'd put it when I'd moved in.

And inside it, Hattie's diary. I sat down cross-legged on the box room floor and started reading.

2

Hattie's Diary, 1989

Authorised readers: Janey Johnston

Unauthorised readers: STOP and think how you would feel if an unauthorised person read your most private, intimate thoughts. YES JUST STOP.

Thursday, September 7th

My new piano teacher, Miss Fortune, gave me this notebook today. It's meant to be so I can record moments of musical inspiration. So if I hear something interesting, going about my everyday life, I can write it down and make up a musical composition about it later. The examples she gave were (1) a blackbird singing in the garden, and (2) a man dropping stones in a well.

But I don't want to be a composer. So I'm going to write about strange happenings in everyday life. Starting with HER.

The lesson didn't get off to a good start, because I heard Mum being rude about me when Miss Fortune was showing her out. They'd left me in the music room – a big room at the front of the flat that smelled of cigarettes and cats. Miss Fortune said something I couldn't hear, and then Mum laughed and said, 'I'm not expecting miracles. She's not going to be another James, we know that. Just do what you can. Thank you *so* much.'

Then the door of the flat clanged shut and Miss Fortune came back into the room. She was wearing a dress with flowers on it, kind of belted in at the waist with a long, sticking-out skirt. She's quite old-fashioned, looks like she should have oven gloves and be smiling and taking a pie out of the oven. That kind of old-fashioned.

I suddenly thought of her sitting on the toilet, having to hold that big skirt out of the way. The wheesh-wheeshing sound.

I stared down at the music case on my lap and tried to think of Amadeus with his hairball, dying in surgery. But in fact I didn't even have to think about that, because I hate my new music case so much. It's brown, with a leather handle that feels like a rat's tail.

Miss Fortune sat down next to me and lifted her eyebrows.

'So! You are Hattie. *Ha-ri-e-tta*. You and I are going to have the most wonderful time. While we're in this room, we're on a flying carpet. It will take us wherever we want to go. All around the world! Back in time for tea! Anywhere! All we need is our imaginations.'

She raised her hands, as though to say, 'What are you waiting for?' And that's when I noticed it. Her right hand was all withered. Some of the fingers were too small, and twisted inwards.

I looked away quickly – down at the rug, which didn't look anything like a flying carpet. It was green with gold stripes through it, faded at the end nearest the window.

'What can you play?' she said.

'I did my grade four last year. I did pieces by . . .' They were all so boring, I couldn't remember. 'They're in my, er, music case.'

14

I looked up to find her eyes fixed on me. And not in a good way.

'*Sorry*,' I whispered.

I could hear the clock on the mantelpiece, ticking away. Miss Fortune breathed in deeply, and the hairs inside her nostrils quivered. They were darker than the hair on her head, which was a sort of apricot colour, arranged in stiff-looking waves.

She nodded in the direction of the grand piano. 'Sit! No, don't open your music case. Just play what comes into your head.'

That's when I noticed the metronome. It was made of dark wood, in a tall pyramid shape, with a picture of an eye – a horrible, staring eye! – attached to its swinging arm.

I sat there, paralysed. I could hear children shouting in the playground across the street, and the time ticking past on the clock, but I couldn't touch that piano, not with that *thing* sitting on top of it.

Eventually she sighed and came over. She put a hand on my chest, and the other one – the horrid clawy one – at the bottom of my back. She straightened me up.

'Thaaaat's it.' Her breath smelt of tomato soup. 'Feeeel the music coming up from here.' She jabbed the middle of my stomach. 'From here! Now try!'

She stepped back triumphantly, crossing her arms. One leg stayed stuck out in front, the high heel of the shoe planted on the ground, toe pointed up towards the ceiling. She looked as if she might be about to do Scottish country dancing. The long up-and-down bit in Strip the Willow, maybe.

I realised there was no getting out of it, and quickly

15

played 'I Know Him So Well'. It wasn't too hard to pick out the top line in C major, and add some broken chords underneath. My face felt hot when I'd finished.

The corner of her mouth kinked up in a snarl. 'Banal,' she said, under her breath, but loud enough for me to hear. 'We'll do listening for the rest of the lesson.'

She went over and put an old-fashioned record on the record player, then sat down in one of the armchairs and lit a cigarette.

'Sit down, dear,' she said. 'Would you like a biscuit?'

Friday, September 8th

Sadly, our biology teacher this term is Mrs White.

But at least Janey is sitting next to me. Nobody seems to have told Mrs White that we aren't meant to sit next to each other because of the talking – ha ha!

I told Janey about Miss Fortune while we were supposed to be looking at pollen under the microscope.

She looked at me, all wide-eyed and mischievous, and dropped polleny water on her skirt.

'D'you think she's a witch?' she said.

I knew Janey was only playing, but it was the first time she'd smiled all day.

'Ye-ees. I think she could be.'

But just then the fire bell went, and we had to file out of the building and stand in the playing fields in the rain. It was only a practice, but they said afterwards that we'd done very badly, so there'd be another practice before half-term.

Note of musical inspiration: fire bell, plus stampede of feet.

Thursday, September 14th

When I arrived for my piano lesson, she already had music playing – I could hear it from out on the street. Something big and orchestral. She let me in without speaking. Then she sat down in her armchair, closed her eyes, and her mouth stretched. It stretched into a long, dry, orange lipstick smile. She didn't move the whole lesson, except that she sometimes did conducting with an imaginary baton – the way Dad does sometimes when he gets carried away. I didn't want to close my own eyes, because I had this feeling she might have been sort of lying in wait, waiting for me to do that. I watched the needle quivering, lifting and falling, as the record spun round and round. It made me feel a bit dizzy.

When the clock reached five past five (my lesson was meant to finish at five!!), the music stopped. She sat there, with her eyes closed, for another four minutes.

Her eyes popped open, wide between her spidery lashes.

'Sublime,' she whispered. 'No?'

'Yes!' I nodded earnestly.

'Next week, same time?'

'Yes.' I grabbed my music case.

'A moment, please.' She held out her hand.

I stared. What was I supposed to have done?

'Music case.'

I handed it to her, and she looked through the stuff in it. My grade four pieces, mostly. Then she picked up one of her own music books from the top of the piano, and slid it into my music case.

'I've given you a book of finger-strengthening exercises. *Fun for Ten Fingers.*' She laughed, as though it was a very

17

funny joke, though I don't see what's funny, personally, about making a poor talentless girl struggle with finger exercises. 'Let's see what you make of that. Goodbye, my dear.'

It was fish fingers for tea. And then Mr Kipling individual apple pies with custard. I had a second apple pie, but Mum drifted off upstairs to lie down and told me to get on with my homework. It was just French tonight – some boring thing about cheese-making, but I had to do it properly because me and Janey got into trouble today for saying *quelle dommage* too often in the conversation exercise. Madame Malo seems to have twigged that it's her catchphrase.

It was about eight o'clock when I heard it. Somebody playing the piano at the top of the house. Not the Steinway in the first-floor drawing room – that's always locked – but the upright on the top landing, outside my bedroom. Someone was just playing the same three notes up and down, up and down, near the bottom of the piano. When I walked out into the hallway, and peered up the stairwell, it stopped. The cupola was dark, and the dark seemed very thick. Like paint. As though the night was pressing against the glass, trying to get in.

It can't have been Mum. She never touches either of the pianos. And once she's gone for a lie-down it's hours until she gets up again.

The other option is Mrs Patel – could she have been dusting the keys? But in fact I saw her leave before dinner so I don't even know why I thought that.

When I was finishing the last cheese-making sentence, I thought I heard the piano notes again, but I didn't go to investigate. The logical explanation is that it is just mice running over the keys or something.

I didn't want to go up to bed. This house is far too big, especially with just Mum and me living here now. The footsteps echo on the chessboard tiles in the hall. They make me think of *The Hound of the Baskervilles*. That old film version. And the banister makes strange shadow patterns against the walls.

If there is a nest of mice living inside the piano, then I suppose that might be quite good, as it might make it dangerous to practise.

Friday, September 15th

No biology today, so I wangled things so I was in the same cross-country running group as Janey. It was freezing and my legs were tingling – no trackie bums allowed until after half-term, said Miss Partridge. Janey made me laugh by saying her legs looked like big raw sausages, all blotchy and pink.

We walked all the way round, except when Miss Partridge was watching, so I was able to tell Janey the story. When I got to the bit about the piano playing itself, she kind of twisted her lip between her teeth, the way she does when she's thinking, and she said, in a very serious voice, 'We'll discuss this in the pavilion.'

The pavilion smells of wet wool and sweat and old boots, and there are always chunks of grassy mud all over the floor that people have trailed in. It's a pretty disgusting place.

While we were sitting on the bench, leaning down low to unlace our boots, Janey turned her face to mine and said, in a very quiet voice, that she thinks Miss Fortune probably has psychopathic powers and is somehow responsible for what happened with the piano.

I wasn't sure, because after all it was only three notes.

'But don't worry,' she said, laying her hand on my boot for a second. 'I've got a plan.'

She said her granny has agreed to her having piano lessons as long as she doesn't get any silly ideas about it (they are trying to stop Janey from going the same way as her mother, whose life has been ruined by having too much creative spirit). Her plan is that I should get Mum to phone her granny and recommend Miss Fortune. Janey could then go to lessons, and since she's not interested in learning the piano, she could be sort of like undercover, building a case against Miss F.

'But I'm not interested in learning the piano either,' I said.

'Well, we can both be undercover, then.'

'Do you know what you're getting yourself into, though?' I asked. 'You'd have to do scales and sight-reading and stuff.'

Janey's never been very musical. Miss Spylaw put her in detention last term for 'wilful deafness' – though it wasn't her fault, she just had the chime bars lined up the wrong way.

She kicked off her left boot and sat up. She shrugged her shoulders, not caring, eyes shining.

I said, 'I mean, I *have* to do it, because of Dad and everything . . .'

'Why? Because your dad's a composer?'

Janey never seems to have grasped that Dad is actually quite famous. His last two musicals sold millions of tickets.

She's funny, the way she's sometimes just not that impressed with people. Take Maddie Naylor, for example, whose dad owns Naylor Construction. They have a mansion in Easter Belmont Road, like in *Dynasty* or something. Most people suck up to Maddie because she has these amazing parties – the last one actually included a helicopter ride. But Janey won't talk to Maddie because she snatched her crisps at break one time, staining her character forever. Because it wasn't like Maddie needed crisps. She gets crisps every day. Whereas Janey only had crisps once last term.

I did try and practise tonight. I wish I hadn't because now I have the added problem of TL.

3

Janey

'Ooh, is that Daddy?'

I thought I'd heard the low rumble of a taxi idling outside, and sure enough when I got to the window I saw Murray crossing the street in a couple of quick strides, his overcoat flapping behind him.

'Pig of a day,' he announced neutrally, unwinding his scarf as he stepped inside. 'Where's the Pipster?'

'I hiding!' A giggle emanated from the sitting room, followed by a volley of light thumps as the little feet set into forward motion.

'Daddyyyyy!'

Murray grabbed Pip and whooshed him up high so that he screamed in delight, his legs flailing.

'Hide-e-seek,' said Pip, fixing Murray with an urgent look as he was lowered to the ground. 'I hide.' And he ran off into the sitting room. I nodded towards the shadow visible at the hinge of the door, and Murray shot me a wink.

'Where's Pip?' he called. Then he turned to me. 'God, I'm bushed.'

'I'll make tea.'

'Where's Pip-squeak?'

'I hiding,' reminded Pip, in a sing-song voice, from behind the door.

'Fee-Fi-Fo-Fum . . . Is he in . . . the bathroom? No . . .'

A peal of giggles, strangled and mischievous in Pip's attempt to repress them.

It was a short game, lasting only until I got to the kitchen, when squeals rang out through the flat: the sound of Pip being caught, dangled upside down and tickled.

'So, what was so bad about your day?' I handed Murray his tea and sat down against the wall by the door, so I could see Pip playing with his trains in the hallway. Our conversations usually descended into work chat pretty quickly: his work, that is. His job as Managing Partner of McKeith's solicitors involved high levels of intrigue and drama, which is more than could be said about my work proofreading legal textbooks, and working from home meant I didn't even have colleagues to gossip about.

'Oh, just the usual bollocks about bonus allocation. A couple of the associates are saying they'll walk if they don't get something substantial this year. Lemmings off a bloody cliff, as far as I'm concerned. But some of the partners are weighing in on it as well. It's the same old story. They have no idea how tough it is to keep the business afloat in this climate.'

'And how did the tender go for the new hospital project?'

'Beatty let some junior associate loose on the pitch and he ballsed it up spectacularly. We didn't have a chance anyway, Bodkins have undercut our rates by thirty per cent.'

'Oh dear. And how's Gretel?'

He shot me a sideways look. 'She's good. She's off to Brussels next week to head up a taskforce. The Working Time Regulations, and the impact on small employers.'

'God, that sounds even more boring than the last one. What was it, age discrimination and the opening hours of recycling centres?' I blurted it out, so eager to sound animated, clutching at anything other than the polite 'oh really?' response.

23

Murray frowned. I'd ignored the unspoken Gretel Rule.

'Sorry. I mean, it's not boring. Just quite dry. Legal.'

He sighed, and sprawled backwards on the squashy sofa, his feet planted wide apart on the floor. He still had his brogues on. With their little pattern of dots, they looked faintly ridiculous, like the clumpy brown school shoes I'd had to wear in primary one. Or like Mr Men shoes.

He tugged his tie loose, craning his neck to one side as though it was sore.

For a moment, I almost slid onto the sofa beside him. I could have rubbed the knots out of his neck. He turned to me suddenly, as though he'd guessed my thoughts, and I dropped my gaze to the carpet, and its nubbly lines of oatmeal wool.

'And what have you been up to this week?' I loved the way his voice went quiet – almost tender – as he asked the question, the Managing Partner bluster melting away.

For a moment I wanted to tell him the truth, that I hadn't been able to stop thinking about Hattie, and had been trawling the internet for the merest glimpse of her. How I'd telephoned St Katherine's, only to be told they couldn't release any details of former pupils. And how I'd joined Facebook and friended a bunch of old classmates so that I could ask them if they'd heard from her. One of them still had an old class list from primary six, and bless her, she'd scanned it and sent me a copy. I'd phoned round all the telephone numbers on it, hoping I might be able to reach a few parents still living at the same addresses. This had yielded four further phone numbers. I'd followed up each of them, with a faux-friendly, 'Hi! I'm Janey. We were at school together?' But nobody had heard anything of Hattie since she'd left.

Most of all I wanted to tell him how those first few entries in her diary had made me feel – as though I was seeing my old self again through her eyes – bold, funny, merciless in my judgements, single-mindedly loyal. I'd never realised how much of me had disappeared along with Hattie, on that terrible December day when she'd failed to turn up for school.

'Oh yes, my day was good, thanks. Pip almost ate a slice of cucumber with his fish fingers.'

Well, he'd stabbed it with his fork and thrown it on the floor, which I thought was progress.

'That reminds me. I thought maybe Pip and I could do some baking. I cut out a recipe for gingerbread men.' He drew a square of newsprint out of his jacket pocket and waved it around, looking slightly embarrassed.

He must have read one of the same articles I had, which recommended involving reluctant eaters in messy, fun food-making activities.

'Pip?' I called into the hallway. 'Do you want to bake?'

Murray project-managed the production of the gingerbread men, or women, as it turned out, since Pip was determined to stick stodgy gingerbread skirts over their legs. He was always softer – almost reverential – with his son, but from time to time I could hear his boardroom voice ringing out from the kitchen.

Leaving dishes piled in the sink, and the kitchen coated in a fine icing-sugar dust, they emerged with the look of men who'd achieved something great, and flopped on the sofa to watch *Grandpa in My Pocket*. Pip copied Murray's stance: arms crossed, chin pressed onto his chest. They were the picture of father–son bonding until Murray started glancing at his watch.

Please don't go.

'You could stay and help with his bath, if you like?'

A few times, when Gretel had been out socialising with clients, or 'out with the girls' on a Friday night, he'd stayed on after Pip's bedtime and we'd talked over a glass of wine, or watched telly together. We could almost have been a couple, albeit an odd one, me in jeans, T-shirt and a Masterchef apron, him in his Savile Row suit and Cartier cufflinks, a full thirteen years older than me.

Not that I wanted to be in a couple: not with someone who'd once been my boss, and had knocked me up at a drunken client event at Gleneagles, before hooking up with a scary uber-lawyer called Gretel. But company ... company was nice. I didn't like sitting in the flat alone after Pip had gone to sleep. I didn't like the feel of the minutes ticking away until it would be time to go to bed myself ... time to fall asleep and give myself over to The Dream again.

'Sorry. No can do. Gretel's expecting me back tonight. She thinks I'm at the gym doing Body Combat for Men ...'

He paused, watching me with a raised eyebrow, as though waiting for me to approve his choice of imaginary exercise class.

My cheeks felt hot. 'D'you think maybe you should tell her? You know, that you come here on Friday afternoons?'

'Yes, I should probably bring her up to speed. Leave it with me.' He stood up, holding out the uneaten gingerbread person Pip had foisted upon him.

'I'll take it.' His fingers brushed against mine as he handed it over.

Pip and I followed him into the hallway, where he shrugged on his overcoat and put on his scarf.

He hunched his shoulders. 'Cold out tonight.'

He gave Pip a growly hug, nodded a goodbye to me, and turned to open the front door.

My left hand was tingling. The fingers tightening involuntarily.

What? No ...

My left hand snatched the gingerbread person from my right, aimed and threw it, hard, at the back of Murray's head.

'Ow!' He swung round, shooting an accusing glance at Pip, who was staring at me open-mouthed.

'Oops! Off you go, then.' I managed to keep my voice light, fighting down the surge of panic. I ushered him out into the cold night and shut the door after him.

Hattie's Diary

Friday, October 20th

There's something wrong with my music case. Mum said it was a bad dream, but it wasn't that at all.

This happened last night. I'm writing this in the safety and comfort of school (wet break). Janey is collecting old tennis balls from the holly hedge because she forgot her PE kit again.

So basically, I'd done my homework (Spartans, and how they let their babies die on hillsides to see if they were strong enough, also how they played flutes) and gone to bed. I was just going to let myself have a little think about AR (see old diary: the ceilidh with St Simon's on 17th June), and snuggled down under the covers.

But then I started thinking sad thoughts. About Dad and how he hasn't been back from New York since Easter, even though he promised he'd come back every couple of months. He's supposedly working on some amazing new idea he's got for a musical, but I wonder if he and Mum have actually split up and just not told us. It was so lonely here over the summer. James was on summer camp for most of it, and Mum kept saying she was too tired to have my friends over, because they'd run riot over the house. We did a few nice things like baking madeleines, and putting new wallpaper up in my room, and once she put on some music and taught me how to waltz. But she had long naps in the afternoons, which didn't leave much time for going out. I read a lot, curled up on the window seat in the kitchen.

So I was thinking about all this, and that's when I heard it. A shuffling, bumping noise, coming from the cupboard by the door.

My first thought was that it could be mice again. I put on my slippers, because I didn't want mice running over my bare feet, and put my ear to the cupboard door, listening until I felt brave enough to pull it open.

My music case – *which I'd put at the back of the cupboard* – flopped out and landed on the carpet. I put it back in, right at the back, underneath Cluedo and Risk.

I woke up later to the sound of more thumping. I put on my Walkman but the only tape I have is the one Mum gave me to go with it – a Haydn string quartet – and it wasn't loud enough to drown out the noise. Something with a beat would've been much better, but my parents, like Miss F, think that pop music is 'banal'. (Nobody is allowed to say that some of the songs in Dad's musicals are basically like pop music, but with violins and stuff to disguise it.)

At ten past midnight there was another huge thump. I got the music case out and took it down to Mum. Her room was pitch dark, so I just hovered in the doorway and said 'Mum' a few times.

When she sat up and put on the bedside light I actually got a bit of a fright, because she was still wearing her eye mask, and it looked for a moment like a great black hole in her face.

She yanked it down and sank back down onto her pillows with a sigh. Then, tilting her head to one side then the other, she pulled out her earplugs. One of them pinged off the bedside table and landed on the carpet by my feet. I pretended not to notice: I didn't want to touch the horrid, fleshy thing.

'Hattie.'

She looked so pale without her make-up. Her eyelids drooped as I told her about the music case, and she said it was 'jussabadream'.

She pulled on her mask and rolled over. I turned off the light for her, then very quietly put the music case down beside her bed before tiptoeing out.

There was no mention of it this morning at breakfast (Weetabix).

5

Janey

'We have to wade through a sea of *mud*?' Murray's nose wrinkled as he surveyed the car park. With a sigh he opened the boot of his Lexus 4x4 and carefully changed out of his Mr Men shoes into a pair of pristine Hunter wellies.

'No, Pip, wait!' I shouted. He'd pulled his hand out of mine with a wild shriek of 'Thomas Tanken!' and was running towards the ticket office, taking the most direct route through a puddle that was more like a small pond. 'Nope. Too late.'

Murray strode into the puddle, grabbed his son and flipped him sideways so his muddy shoes were held safely away from Murray's checked Burberry raincoat (his Sherlock Holmes coat, as I privately thought of it).

'Can't keep Thomas waiting, can we?'

Pip practically expired with delight at the sight of the steam train with a big plastic Thomas the Tank Engine face stuck on the front.

'Sit dere!' he shouted in his most imperious voice, pointing at a table seat at the front of the carriage.

I hurried over to secure the seats, but when I looked back at Murray his face had gone rigid with shock. He bared his teeth and jabbed a finger towards the party sitting across the aisle: a woman and a young boy who were busy looking out of the window.

The woman turned. Murray raised his eyebrows and tried to twist his grimace into a smile.

'Gretel!'

And oh *God*, she looked like she'd walked straight out of a film. She was Truly Scrumptious with her long blonde waves and lacy white blouse. She was Ingrid Bergman's Ilsa with those cheekbones and the wide chin. I blinked and looked again.

'Hi, Murray.' Her expression was bright, her tone even and unsurprised.

'Gretel!' he said again. 'Hello. I thought you were taking Mutti out for lunch today?' He turned to me and said, rather formally, 'Gretel's mother is sixty today.'

I smiled and nodded.

'There was a change of plan,' said Gretel. 'I told you I was taking Gulliver out for *his* birthday tomorrow.'

Oh yes, this was Gretel's fabled godson Gulliver, who'd known all his phonics from the age of two and who liked to snack on small bowls of olives.

'Well, Jill was planning a day out with Gulliver today. But her mother was meant to be going to Bathgate with Aggie McCrae to look at mother-of-the-bride dresses because Aggie's daughter Cat is getting married in September – they've had to bring the date forward – it was going to be a spring wedding but then Cat got pregnant and she wanted a proper white wedding dress, you know, not a pregnant meringue-style dress, so they've arranged things with the hotel – the Baldounie – you know that one where Richard and Jess got married? Apparently the hotel wouldn't change the booking, and they'd paid a £5,000 deposit, which I thought seemed like a lot. Mind you, I'm sure Annette Quigley paid

£7,450 as a deposit for her wedding, because remember that was around the time her credit card got stolen, and the bank queried it as a possible fraudulent transaction. But they agreed in the end, as long as the new date was a Tuesday, which she doesn't mind because she's feeling awfully sick. She thinks eighty to a hundred and ten guests is about the right number.'

There was something old-fashioned about her voice, with its received pronunciation but with slight German stresses on certain words . . . It made me want to lay my head back on the red velour headrest and close my eyes. I had a sudden, sharp memory of one rainy Boxing Day afternoon, curled up on the sofa with Grandpa watching *The Sound of Music* on the new colour telly . . . Even Granny had tapped her foot along to the music as she'd darned socks.

But now Gretel was looking at me, evidently expecting a response.

'Oh, yes.' I said quickly. 'Eighty sounds about right.'

'They've had to take the pâté off the menu too. But Jill's mum has sprained her wrist and can't drive to Bathgate. She slipped on some fox mess in the garden. Anyway, Aggie had this mother-of-the-bride appointment and Jill is very kindly driving her to it, and is going to advise her on the outfits too, which, let's face it, is a better outcome than Jill's mum doing it.' Gretel winced at the idea. 'So she asked if I could look after Gulliver today instead. I thought he might like to see Thomas the Tank Engine. Thanks for giving me the idea, Murray.'

'Er . . .'

Gretel flashed him a bright smile. 'I saw the tickets in the drawer of your dresser. Three tickets for the Thomas train. Unusual choice of activity for a client away day – that's what

33

you said you were doing today, wasn't it, Murray? But hey, I thought, don't knock it till you've tried it. So here we are. And these are your clients, are they?'

'Gretel, er, meet my son, Pip.'

'Hi Pip,' said Gretel. 'Oh look, that man's got a hat on like the Fat Controller! See, Gulliver?'

'And I don't think you've met Janey either. She's . . . um. Well, she used to work at the firm.'

She's the one I shagged at that completion dinner just before we started going out together? That awkward situation with the pregnancy and everything? Remember, darling?

'The famous Janey. So we finally meet.' She exhaled loudly and looked at her watch. 'When do you think the train actually starts moving? We've been sitting here for ages. Just as well Gulliver had his sudoku sticker book in his rucksack. He's very easily bored. He goes to a forest nursery.'

'Oh?' I said politely. 'What's a forest nursery?'

'They don't have any inside premises. Just an awning, if the rain becomes torrential. But they're worried about him making the transition to primary one, in a non-forest school.'

'Ah . . .'

'They were going to ask whether he could have a vegetable corner in the classroom. Space might be an issue, though.'

'Or those . . . erm . . .' I actually wagged a finger, in my eagerness to contribute. 'Erm, growbags. You know, the ones you can grow strawberries in . . . and things.'

Why was I trying to please her? It wasn't that I'd warmed to her, exactly: with her perkiness and the little 'ta-da' movements of her hands when she was speaking, she exuded a sort of spoilt girlishness. But perhaps it was that: the air of brightness and total certainty about her that made you feel nothing could go wrong when she was at the centre of it. Maybe that was why she was such a successful lawyer.

What would she be like as a friend?

A silly thought, given the circumstances. It was Hattie's diary that was making me think like this, as though there was suddenly a friend-shaped hole in my life that needed filling.

And of course Hattie had had that too . . . a knack of making you think everything would be okay. It had almost pulled me in when reading those first few diary entries: I'd been lulled into believing that the phantom piano playing would turn out to be mice after all, or that Miss Fortune, the evil villainess, would receive her comeuppance in a breathless, Secret Seven-style denouement. Hattie and Janey, brave storybook heroines, would be best friends forever, skiving cross-country and passing notes in biology.

I put a hand to my mouth, caught by a stab of pain at the thought of it.

Gretel frowned, and shot a look down to my feet and up again.

'Fat 'toller!' Pip lifted a wavering fist in the direction of the window and beamed his wide-open 'love me' smile at Gulliver.

'The Fat *Con*troller,' corrected Gulliver, blinking slowly. 'Gretel, can we move over there?'

★

'Is she always like that?' I asked Murray on the way home.

He sighed. 'Look, I'm sorry she was there. I screwed up, leaving the tickets in the dresser. Leave it with me, okay? I'll sort it.'

'Does it need sorting? Actually, I was amazed. I'd always assumed she was very possessive about you. But she seemed totally unfazed about meeting us.' I paused, trying to work it out. 'Perhaps she was trying to hide her true feelings, though. Maybe the inane chattering was just a reaction to extreme stress.'

He gave a short grunt of a laugh. 'If that's the case then it's a worry.'

'Yes,' I agreed, putting a serious look on my face.

'Because she must exist in a *permanent* state of extreme stress.'

He shot me a sideways glance, like a naughty boy checking whether he'd got away with something, before returning his eyes to the road.

6

Hattie's Diary

Monday, October 23rd

Today was the first day of 'Plan Shapiro'. The name was Janey's idea. She's read this book by a ghost hunter called Dominic Shapiro, who goes to people's houses and sorts out their supernatural things for them, a bit like Scooby Doo. It has checklists and stuff. She found it in her granny's attic.

We went to the old fire escape during break, the one that leads down from behind the chemistry lab. She asked me again about the music case. Apparently Dominic Shapiro had a case about a haunted pair of ballet shoes once, which is a bit like a music case. She can't remember what he did to solve it, but she's going to bring the book to school tomorrow.

She did say that he always looks for scientific explanations first. So, for example, he might call a piano tuner to check the piano outside my room, in case the wires of those bottom three notes are faulty. Janey says I should definitely suggest that to Mum, especially since the notes have woken me up twice now, and could be the reason I failed that history test so badly (tiredness). She's also going to lend me her A-ha tape for my Walkman. She says it's really banal and really good.

The Shapiro book also has some good suggestions for

covert investigations, like a drop-box for messages between operatives. I've got an old red metal cash box, which we're going to bury up in the bank of trees behind the hockey pitch.

I've asked her to come round for tea tomorrow. And to stay the night, though the adults don't know that yet. I knew she'd want to, since James is home for his half-term.

Tuesday, October 24th
When we got home from school, James was in the drawing room practising the violin. We could hear the music floating down the stairs.

'Shall we go up?' Janey asked, her eyes all bright.

'No,' I said. 'Let's have some fun with him. You haven't seen him for ages, have you? Not since you've grown your hair long. He might not recognise you. You could pretend to be Dominica Shapiro, a ghost hunter come to investigate the house.'

'What . . . in my school uniform?'

We went to Mum's dressing room. She was there, in fact, sorting through her shoes, and she laughed when we said what we were doing, and pulled out some of her older outfits for Janey to try on. We chose a black Chanel suit and high heels. It was all a bit on the roomy side, especially the skirt, which we had to belt in quite severely. But luckily Mum is quite small. It wouldn't have worked, for example, with Janey's granny's clothes.

I suggested make-up next, and Mum nodded towards her dressing table, all cluttered with powders, and creams, and lipsticks. Janey pretended to hesitate, saying it was 'over the top', but was secretly very keen and didn't take much persuading. So she sat there like a queen on Mum's red cushioned seat, and I put lipstick and mascara on her, and a subtle hint of blusher. She wasn't pleased, though, when I sprinkled talcum powder through her hair, to achieve a greying effect (a tip from the Shapiro book).

I suddenly thought that a clipboard would be a great finishing touch, and remembered that I had one in my room from the Neanderthals trip. When I came back, Mum was putting eyeshadow ('emerald crush') on Janey, stroking it across her eyelids with a little brush. Janey was sitting bolt upright, with her eyes tight shut and her hands clenched, looking as though she was barely breathing from the joy of it. Then Mum patted Janey's shoulder, said she looked 'adorable', and went back to her shoe counting. And I took Janey out of the dressing room and propelled her across the landing towards the drawing room. James was in the middle of a passionate cadenza, which I think she found off-putting, because she insisted on hanging back until he'd finished and was about to start the slow movement.

She went in, and hovered just inside the door, biting her lip.

'Oh God,' I heard him groan.

'I'm Dominica Shapiro,' she said, fearfully.

'Have you two got some kind of vendetta against me? Don't you know I've got a recital tomorrow at the Queen's Hall?' His voice wasn't really annoyed, but he was pretending to be sort of indignant, his voice squeaking up on the word 'recital'.

'Oooooh, the Queen's *Hall*!' I came into the room behind her. 'Ooooohh! James! Can we get your *autograph*?'

He marched over and grabbed me by the waist, turning

39

me upside down. He carried me into Mum's room and dropped me on the bed.

Janey looked on longingly, no doubt wishing he'd do it to her.

'Ugh!!' I shrieked. 'What terrible B-O! You'd better have a proper wash before your recital. Otherwise the audience will all go unconscious in their seats.'

Janey put her hand over her mouth in shock; she doesn't have any brothers. As James stalked past her, on the way back to the drawing room, she shook out her curls, in a timid but obvious way.

After tea – awful ravioli – and homework (rivers in Greek mythology) we went to my room and set up everything we needed for our vigil. We each had a notebook to record anything. We put the music case in the middle of the floor, and Janey said we should sit cross-legged on either side of it, with our hands resting, palms uppermost, on our knees.

Then she said something she'd learned from the Dominic Shapiro book.

'Spirits in this house, please make yourself known.'

We stayed silent for a while until Janey said '*quelle dommage*' very sadly, and that set us off.

We're going to stay up until midnight and then call it a night.

Wednesday, October 25th
I'm in biology right now. If I start writing about tadpoles, it will be because Mrs White has come over.

So Janey and I fell asleep quite quickly in the end. And when I woke up again it was 3.08 a.m. according to my digital clock.

It felt like something had woken me, so I stayed still and listened. And yes there *was* an odd sound coming from the hall. And it wasn't the usual piano notes either.

Janey was dead to the world on her zed-bed. She just grunted and rolled over when I prodded her.

The walk over to the door seemed to take a hundred years. I opened it bravely, and looked out.

This is what I saw: a black shape crouched down beside the banister, the one that runs the width of the galleried landing. I thought I could make out the paler shapes of hands, clinging to the bars.

And there was a noise coming from it. It could have been singing. A thin, high, drawn-out note, wavering at the end, dropping down a semitone. And again. Over and over again.

I put my hands over my ears.

The noise stopped, and the shape froze for a moment. I held my breath as it unfolded itself to its full height. A grey blur of a face turned towards me.

'Mum?' My voice was strange and weak. I could hear my actual heart thumping inside my voice. 'What are you doing?'

She was wearing her navy-blue silk dressing gown, the one Dad gave her for Christmas last year. That's why she looked like a dark shape.

She pressed the heels of her hands against her eyes, and then swept them quickly across her cheeks.

'Back to bed, darling,' she muttered as she walked past, trailing a hand so that it almost touched my arm.

She must have been sleepwalking. It was only Mum. Nothing to be scared of. Nothing to be scared of at all.

41

7

Janey

I wasn't entirely sure why I'd come back.

Partly, it was because I wanted to attempt left-handed drawing, or writing, again. I'd tried it at home, sitting at the kitchen table when Pip was in bed, and nothing had happened. My left hand lay limp across the paper, a useless, dead thing. But maybe it would work again in the classroom, with Steve there. He'd emailed me after the first session, saying he was concerned about me rushing off, and asking me to feel free to come along another time.

The sight of the email from him, unopened in my inbox, had sent a kick straight through me. There was something there, dancing in the pixels that made up his name . . . some sort of energy. That half-hour spent in the art room shone in my memory, a bright spot in the string of dreary autumn days.

And partly it was because I'd seen Jody and Molly at the last Jungle Jive class and they'd asked me to go for coffee afterwards. Oh, how nice it was not to be the one walking out of that church hall alone. And it was a relief, in a way, to share my worries about Pip's fussy eating, and haphazard bedtime routine, even if they did rather pounce on my parental inadequacies, proffering advice with almost indecent eagerness. Then they'd gone on to discuss the workshop, so easily, so comfortably – as though it was a class in yoga, or upholstery, or breadmaking – that it seemed entirely natural that I should go back.

'And oooh, that Steve's quite dishy,' added Jody with a little wriggle. 'In a geeky, Jarvis Cocker sort of way. You should ask for his number, Janey. Haha!'

I resented the 'haha!' and gave Jody a hard stare that she didn't even notice.

But now we were back in the art classroom, sitting round, taking turns to write words on a flip chart, brainstorming ideas that resonated with us as individuals, as couples, and as human beings in the world. We were each to choose one of the words and create a piece of art about it. Over the next few weeks, each couple would produce a pair of canvases that would complement each other when hung together. Hopefully.

Jody and Tom were both doing 'womanly', agreeing, with coy smiles, not to look at each other's until they'd finished.

Molly was doing 'sustainable', and immediately went off to the materials cupboard to look for anything that might pass for fish hooks. Dave, in a bold move away from eco themes, was doing 'marketing'.

It was quarter of an hour or so before Steve came over to my bench, and all I'd done was set out my paints and paper on the workbench.

He didn't comment on my dawdling. 'So. Your word is "safe"?'

I nodded, suddenly embarrassed.

He frowned, and rubbed his jaw with the V of his hand. 'Any thoughts on how you're going to do that?'

I took a deep breath. 'Hattie. The girl who . . . spoke, through the left-handed writing . . . you know. Well, she was my best friend when I was at school. I've been trying to find her.'

He nodded.

'I just want to know she's okay. That she's safe.'

'Okay.' He pulled out a stool and sat down, knees apart, hands holding the front of the wooden seat like it was a horse. There were heavy, whitish creases in the denim of his jeans near the crotch. 'So what might that look like? How can you tell if someone is safe?'

I thought of the tall, stone house in Regent's Crescent, the ornate railings and rows of blank windows.

'You can't, always. But I hope she's found a safe place.'

'Okay . . . a safe place. So, think about what it feels like *inside*' – he stretched out his hands and planted them on either side of his torso, below his ribs – 'when you're in a safe place.'

'Oh . . . I don't know.'

'Yeah, but your body language changed when you thought about it. Your shoulders relaxed.' The room seemed to have gone quiet. I could hear the in and out of his breath. 'Were you thinking of somewhere specific?'

How did he know?

'When I was nine. The last summer holiday we had at Glen Eddle. Hattie's parents had a house there.'

He shrugged, and jumped down from the stool. 'There you go, then.'

I lifted my paintbrush.

Slowly, awkwardly, I painted a forest, dark on a craggy grey mountainside, and a rushing stream, appearing now and then between the trees. In my mind I was seeing Scots pine, larch, birch, shifting in the wind and sunlight, but they appeared on the page as green and brown splodges.

I found the finest paintbrush I could, and painted in a bridge over the river. Then I added a little orange-raincoated figure with navy wellies, standing in the middle of the trees.

Me. But I wouldn't have been alone in the forest. An odd little rush of panic came over me. I closed my eyes.

Where are you?

'I'm here, you idiot. Get down.'

It's James, and he's crawling along at my feet. He grabs my arm and pulls me down onto the forest floor. We lie on our fronts, elbows dug into the pine-needle mulch.

I hold my breath as we listen for signs; a twig cracking, the wheeshing sound of low branches sweeping over a cagouled shoulder. The forest is silent, though, except for the stream trickling in a ditch nearby. The smell of wet moss rises up from the earth.

'D'you need more ammo?'

I nod. He reaches into the pocket of his cagoule and hands me three pine cones and a couple of twigs, lacy with grey lichen.

A scrabbling noise from the ditch; someone is creeping through the tunnel that diverts the stream underneath the forest path. James nods and we move forward, commando style. I move to the right to avoid a crop of ripe toadstools, and brush against him.

There's a flash of orange by the tunnel.

We jump up. 'CHAAAAARGE!' shouts James as he starts chucking pine cones at the small figure of Hattie, emerging from the ditch. And Graham, following close behind in his CCF camouflage gear.

Hattie laughs and runs towards us, feet flapping in her Mickey Mouse trainers. She pelts a pine cone at James. I retaliate with a couple of twigs, but they don't fly well.

Graham retreats into the ditch, randomly flinging out pine cones.

'You wuss, Grey!' bellows James. 'Come out and fight like a MAN!'

A huge red toadstool arcs towards us and lands by my feet, splitting into white mush on contact with the ground.

'Aaargh!' shouts Hattie, who is standing beside us and now seems to be on our side. 'Biological weapons! James – do something!'

James eyes the toadstool crop doubtfully.

'You shouldn't touch them,' I say. 'You could die an agonising death.'

James pulls his raincoat sleeve over his hand and, mouth set into a straight line, grabs the biggest toadstool by the stalk, wrenches it from the ground and runs towards the ditch so he can get a closer aim.

'He's so brave . . .'

'Do it again, James,' Hattie demands. 'With just your bare hand this time.'

He looks unsure.

'No, Hats,' I say. 'We'd better get back for tea. Mrs Patel said it was sausages tonight.'

'Janey, you look like a real soldier! You're covered in mud.' She brushes at my cords with a pine frond.

We walk back through the dimming woods. I'm trotting, trying to keep up with James. Hattie and Graham amble along behind us.

'Shall we just keep the same teams for tomorrow?' I suggest. James grunts, scuffing his boots into the gravel of the path.

'But I think we'll need to change our tactics,' I add. 'Those twigs are not very aerodynamic.'

Hattie snorts. 'Not very aerodynamic!' But then she runs ahead to catch me up.

'And shall we play Pictionary again tonight?' I say. Hattie nods and all of a sudden I stop, and stare round at the forest, cradled by the mountains on all sides, the grey corries stretching

46

high and forbidding. And it is a perfect moment. Wet with mud, with pine needles stuck in my wellies and twigs in my hair; sausages for tea and a game of Pictionary. Maybe we'll even open the bottle of Irn Bru that Hattie's mum bought at the petrol station on the way up.

But when I look along the path again, they've gone. They've all gone. And it's dark.

My eyes snap open.

It hurts. Oh, it hurts.

'Janey? What's up?'

It was Steve, standing beside me. I looked around the classroom, trying to reorientate myself. Molly and Dave had gone, and Jody and Tom were clearing their workbench. How long had I been lost in the world of Glen Eddle?

'It was such a lovely scene, and then it went dark. It was like a big black cloud just moved across.' My words were spilling out, sliding into each other.

'Tell me about the cloud,' said Steve.

'It's everything that's going to happen next. Grandpa getting ill . . . The whole bloody mess with Miss Fortune . . .'

He bent close to the painting, holding his chin in his hand, then straightened up and adjusted his glasses. 'I'm wondering. What would happen if you just let that cloud drift on past?'

'No. Everyone's gone. I'm *cold*. I want to go home.' A tear darted down my cheek.

I looked down at my painting again, my eye drawn to the group of figures gleaming wetly in the wood. I was the one in the red coat, straggling along at the end, holding . . . *oh God no . . . please.*

I was holding a hammer.

Suddenly it was happening. I'd gone into that strange,

47

underwater place, seizing breath after breath that couldn't reach my lungs. Pinpricks of light burst into my vision.

'Janey,' said Steve. 'Tell me what's happening to you.'

'D-drowning.'

He took my arm, sat me down on one of the stools. 'Stop fighting,' he said. 'Your body knows how to float. Let yourself float to the top.'

He stood there in front of me, watching quietly, just waiting, a hand hovering near my arm. This was so ridiculous, a teenage thing. I hadn't had panic attacks for years. And he was right, it would pass. It would pass if I stopped fighting.

'Okay?' he said finally.

I nodded. Looked at my painting again and managed a smile.

'Sorry.' I stood up. 'I'm a bit wound up. I haven't been sleeping very well. I thought I'd drawn a hammer, but look, it's clearly a stick. That's what we were doing that day. Throwing sticks. We were playing soldiers. Anyway, I must go . . .'

'We could give you a lift home if you like?' Jody had sidled up to me, placing a heavy, sympathetic hand on my shoulder. Oh *God*, she'd seen the whole thing.

'No, no, it's fine. I'm only five minutes away. I could do with a walk.'

'Okay. Take care, babe.' And they left, Tom nodding awkwardly in my direction.

I began to gather up the paintbrushes on my workbench.

'I can do that,' said Steve.

'No. You shouldn't have to clear up everything.'

'Put them down.'

I turned to protest but then he was beside me, pulling me

round towards him. Adrenaline surged through me, blazing a trail from my chest to my fingertips.

'Look at me,' he said. 'Janey, look at me.' But I couldn't. I knew those eyes would see straight inside me. I focused instead on the pores on his nose, and the grooves down to the corners of his mouth.

I gave a tiny shake of my head.

Then he folded me tight against him. No, he *clung* to me.

I rested my face, just for a moment, against the soft cotton of his shirt. I couldn't remember the last time anyone had held me. Possibly the night Pip had been conceived. Possibly not even then.

And then came the most extraordinary feeling. Hurt – held in every part of my body, so quietly, for so long – uncrystallised, flowed through me in a sickening tide, then ebbed away into his arms.

He rocked me. Rocked it all away. Almost . . . almost.

I slid a hand down, and pulled the full length of his body against mine. I wanted to press him into every curve, every dip and angle, to let my body lose its shape to his. He held me tighter.

Then I imagined my white, dimpled thighs, wobbling as he thrust into me.

He lowered his head, breathing into my neck.

'Oh Jesus. You're trembling. I'm sorry. This is all wrong. We can't do this.'

He straightened up and pushed my shoulders back, trying to look into my face.

'You all right?'

I disengaged myself. 'I just need a minute.'

In the bathroom down the corridor, I tried to wipe away my smudged mascara with a bit of dampened toilet roll.

What are you doing? I demanded of my white-faced reflection. *Get a grip. Get a grip.*

★

When I returned to the room, he motioned to the stool next to him.

'Shall we talk about it?'

His voice was low, and its gentleness was unbearable. It made me want to spill out my soul; made me want to push against him.

'Well you *did* it,' I said petulantly. 'Maybe *you* should talk about it.'

'Janey, this can't happen. I'm an art tutor. You're a student.'

'I'm sorry. I just got upset for a minute.'

'Yeah, I know. Look, Janey, it's probably best you don't come to the class any more.'

I felt as though somebody had cut a little cord, a lifeline that I hadn't even noticed I'd had. And I was drifting out from the shore.

'But I need to.'

'We've crossed a line. All sorts of bloody lines. I shouldn't have even let you do that work today, after what happened last time. I'm not trained in art therapy.'

His face had gone closed. He sat with his arms crossed, one foot tapping on the ground.

'Well, can we meet as . . .' I wanted to say friends, but realised how stupid it sounded. As if he'd want me for a friend.

'I can find you another class, if you like. I can give you

some leaflets and stuff about art therapy, too. You might find it interesting.'

'I wanted to do more left-handed drawing. What about that? What about Hattie?'

'You'll get there,' he said, fixing me with those fathomless eyes. 'I'm sorry I won't be part of it. But I'm sure you'll get there.'

8

Hattie's Diary

Thursday, October 26th

Another piano lesson today. We've wangled it so that Janey's lesson is first and mine is straight afterwards. Janey convinced her granny she only needed a short lesson, because she's not really interested in learning piano. (Well, she didn't say that to her granny, but said something like beginners only needed short lessons.)

So when I went there today, Miss F came to open the door, and told me to sit on the sofa while she finished off with Janey. She was wearing her green and olive dress. Bad sign.

She was making Janey do finger-strengthening exercises, going up the keyboard with her left hand, playing three notes up and down again with her pinkie, fourth and third fingers. NB: when she was right at the bottom of the keyboard, it was the same sound that comes from our piano at night.

Janey slowly stuck out her right hand, so it was just below the level of the piano stool, and made a 'thumbs down' sign with it, raising it and lowering her fist three times. It confirmed what I already knew: Miss Fortune was in a bad mood.

'Since you're both here, let's talk a little about harmony. We need to understand music from the inside, girls.'

She started playing some sort of piece, all hoppy and skippy like a Scottish reel or something. It's amazing how she can play quite well, even with her withered hand, but if you look, she's only using two of the fingers. 'Hattie,' she said loudly, without stopping, 'I want you to tell me what key this is in.'

I looked at Janey in alarm but she just bit her lip anxiously.

'I – I don't know . . .' I said. Her fingers were touching as many black keys as white.

'Ah, but how can you find out?'

'Er . . .'

She suddenly stopped in the middle of the piece, and told Janey to sit down and finish it off.

'I'm sorry, I don't know this piece.' She'd gone bright red.

'So make it up,' said Miss F, flapping her non-withered hand. 'Improvise.'

Janey sat down and picked out the melody with her right hand. She even managed to add in a few left-hand chords. I was amazed – she's only been learning a few weeks. Then she lost the tune but made up another bit, a bar or two perhaps, and then stopped.

'Tell me which chord you've finished on.'

Janey looked down at her fingers. 'It's G major.'

'Exactly,' purred Miss Fortune. 'You've found your way back to G major because the key of the piece is G major. You may have noticed the modulation into D in the middle – a little *flirtation*, if you will – but you've come back to G, which is the *tonic note*, in this piece. The G major chord is the *triad* formed from the *tonic* note.' She spoke all in ups and downs as if she was reading a nursery rhyme.

'The tonic chord is the root chord, or the home chord. A tune will always find its way back to the tonic. Melodies behave just like us. They always find their way back home. Let's sing it, girls, let's sing *geeeeeeeee*.'

'Geeeeee,' sang Janey, her voice quavering.

I pressed my chin onto my chest and frowned deeply. 'Geeeeeeeeeeeeeeeeeeeeeeeeeeeee.'

Janey's G turned into a giggle. 'Geeeeee-he-he-hee.'

Miss Fortune sighed heavily, and sent Janey away, telling her to do finger-strengthening exercises for twenty minutes each day. This was a kind of punishment, as she usually says ten.

Then she made me play that awful pavane thing. After I'd finished, she took a deep breath, and sighed it out very slowly. She made me sit down on the couch and then she spoke to me in a voice that started off very quiet.

'Tell me, my dear,' she said. 'Because I'm interested. What is it about you that makes you so special? So worthy of attention? What is it about you that means I should waste my time, week after week? Why should I make *every effort* to bring you on when you clearly take on board nothing that I tell you?'

I was itching to take out my notebook and record what she was saying. I could smell raw meat on her breath.

'Is it your father, is that it, Hattie? You think, perhaps, that because your father is the famous Emil Marlowe, you have the right to waste my time? Not to practise? To assume that different rules apply to you than to everybody else?'

'No,' I said in a small voice. 'But it's actually James who's the musical one. He's got a scholarship at Ramplings, you know, the famous music school.'

It felt like we were having two conversations at once. A weird sick game, when we both knew I'd seen TL.

'Yes, I'm aware of Ramplings,' she said. 'Well perhaps you could bring *James* to see me one day, when he's home for the holidays. It might relieve the godawful tedium of having to teach you and your mousy little friend.' She laughed a high, tinkly laugh and patted me on the knee.

'Now, I've got some custard creams just opened. I'll bring them through. Shall we do listening for the rest of the lesson?'

Dinner: sausages again.

9

Janey

'Now, Richard ... Richard!' Miss Margot was trying, but failing, to sound firm over the din of the music.

Vichard had shoved one drumstick up his nose, and was bashing a dark-haired little girl around the head with the other.

Jody, sitting beside me, was oblivious, busy updating her status on Facebook. She was obsessed, at the moment, with building up 'likes' for her garden design business page. She didn't really look old enough to be in charge of such a venture, with her red rosy cheeks, and bunnyish front teeth.

Behind Miss Margot, another stray toddler crouched over the iPod dock, dripping Ribena onto it from the straw of his carton, his face a picture of scientific enquiry. His mother had nipped outside to take a phone call for work, and I knew I should have alerted Miss Margot to the imminent demise of the sound system, but a big part of me thought it would be a blessing if the music had to stop.

'Okay, boys and girls – ready for the chorus?' She nodded enthusiastically, a manic grin pasted onto her face.

'The *MONKEY* jumps to the JUNGLE BEAT! Diddle-diddle-DOO! Diddle-diddle-DOO!'

'Hmmph,' said the girl next to me, as we were getting ready to leave. 'I'm more into the classics, I must admit.' She pulled a face, a froglike expression of doubt. 'But it was nice and jolly, I suppose.'

She had a large, beaky nose and crooked front teeth, and her hair was a bushy dark brown that snaked and bounced around her shoulders.

'Are you new?' I asked.

'Oh! Yes, I'm Cleodie. This is my niece, Rose.'

'Is she okay, after the drumstick incident?'

'Yes, I should think so. Is that par for the course, would you say, for Jungle Jive classes?'

'Pretty much, yes. Sorry.'

'Oh well, not to worry.'

'It's nice of you to take your niece.'

She considered. 'Yes, it is rather, isn't it?'

'This is Cleodie,' said Jody loudly, appearing at the froglike girl's side and laying claim to her with a hand on her arm. 'And Vose. They're coming for coffee.'

We manoeuvred our buggies out of the church hall and across the rain-soaked street into the coffee shop, where we shrugged off our wet coats and released our children into the play corner. There was an almost empty box of Stickle Bricks, a squeaky giraffe and one naked, rather raddled-looking Barbie doll.

'So,' said Jody when our coffees arrived. 'We've missed you at the art class. Don't say you've dropped out. Steve will be *gutted*. His funding may be cut.'

'I'm sure Steve will pull through,' I said. 'I'm not sure I even counted towards the numbers. It's a class for couples, remember? It felt a bit odd doing it on my own.'

'Oh *hon*,' Molly said, squeezing my shoulder. 'You'll find someone. Won't she, Jode?'

Jody raised a noncommittal eyebrow, taking a long sip of her caffè latte.

'Just look at Paul,' added Molly, as though this were a case in point.

'Paul from our antenatal class,' said Jody. 'A year ago his life was in bits. Bits! His wife, Shona – she's a high-flying lawyer – ran off with a human-rights barrister. Left him holding the baby, quite literally. They've sorted things out now, though: he has Elgin all week, and she swans in at the weekend and takes him away for all the fun bits.'

'Oh . . .'

'He was on the edge of a breakdown,' Molly told me with wide eyes. 'We had to physically drag him to see his GP. But he's fine now. He's found someone! Paul has found someone.'

'Geoff,' added Jody quietly, stirring more sugar into her coffee.

'I could go with you to the class,' offered Cleodie. 'We could pretend to be a couple. I must say, I'm curious. It sounds *wild*.'

I looked up sharply. What had Jody and Molly been saying?

'Well, er . . . it's difficult to get away in the evenings,' I said. 'Murray can't always look after Pip.'

'How *is* Pip? Any change?' Molly leaned forward to make this enquiry, with a slightly pained expression, as though Pip was an elderly aunt who was not long for this world.

'Ah,' said Jody, holding up a finger. She pulled something out of her rucksack and pushed it across the table. It was a recipe.

'Fish fingers?'

'Mackerel fish fingers. Vichard can't get enough of them. You wrap the mackerel in spinach leaves before coating in egg and breadcrumbs. I *say* breadcrumbs, but they're made of rolled oats and crushed bran, with some flaxseeds for extra crunch.'

'That's very kind.' I pretended to study the recipe. 'Thank you, Jody.' No need to say that Pip was unswervingly loyal to Captain Birdseye, and now insisted on pulling the packets out of the freezer cabinet himself, after the dark day that I'd attempted to serve up Sainsbury's own brand.

'Oooh, lovely,' said Molly. 'Could I copy that down?' There was a long interlude while she searched in her bag for a pen, then we all searched for pens, then Molly went up and asked the counter staff if they had pens. Finally, she typed the recipe into her phone, laboriously with one finger, muttering each ingredient under her breath.

I was itching to donate the hard copy of the recipe to Molly, but knew this would be frowned upon when I'd been singled out as the deserving recipient. Instead, I placed it reverently in my bag.

Cleodie, sitting across the table, raised an eyebrow at me.

'But he eats jam sandwiches?' said Molly brightly, finally tucking her phone away into her bag. 'Oh *well*.' She shrugged, and smiled.

'Yes,' I said. 'At least he's getting the benefit of the strawberries.'

Silence, as we sipped our drinks. Molly looked round to glance doubtfully at Pip.

And then she said, 'Have you thought of making courgette jam?'

★

Afterwards, I walked home with Cleodie – Molly and Jody were going straight on to a baby sign-language class. It turned out her flat was in the next street along from mine.

59

'God, I thought I was going to die of boredom in there,' she said, swaying to the side as though she was about to expire. 'All that yummy-mummy chat. At one point I nearly told Molly I couldn't give a fuck about colloidal oatmeal. I nearly shouted it out loud. But you seem a bit more fun. Come in for a coffee. This is me here.'

I stood for a minute, twisting the strap of my bag.

What? Fun? I should probably decline, terminate the encounter while she still seemed to think this was the case.

But Cleodie didn't look to me for confirmation. So I lifted Pip out of his buggy and followed her inside.

'I've got a main-door flat too,' I said. 'It's so nice not to have stairs to worry about.'

Cleodie led me into the kitchen, where the work surfaces were covered in dirty dishes and there was a strong smell of overripe bananas. She poured water into the kettle, holding it nearly horizontal because a large saucepan and a wok were soaking in the sink. 'See, that's the problem with parenthood. You start worrying about stairs and things like that.' Turning to me, she did the frog expression again and pushed her glasses further up the bridge of her nose. '*I* don't. Which is not very good, since I'm looking after Rose full-time just now.'

'Does her mum . . .'

'Oh! She's got this terrific job. Her big break. A part in an STV drama thingy. So I've stepped in to help with Rose. But she's going to start nursery soon, which is just as well, because I need to get on and finish my novel.'

'A novel? How exciting.'

'It's a drag at the moment, I can tell you. Full-time childcare knocks every creative impulse out of you. I always put it off all evening, then end up writing well into the wee small hours and being shattered the next day! Quite often,' she added, dropping her voice to a whisper, 'we just slump in front of *Dora the Explorer* in the mornings.'

'Oh, everybody does that,' I said with a wave of my hand.

'Yeah, but I'm not great with kids,' she said. 'I could never be a mother. I like being able to hand Rose back and get on with my own things. How on earth do you do it? Spending all your time with Pip, I mean. Day in, day out.'

She carried the mugs through to the sitting room and placed them on a battered stool that served as a coffee table.

Had I found someone, I wondered. Had I found someone who wouldn't judge me if I were to confess how lonely I felt most of the time?

'The days can feel quite long,' is all I said.

'Oh well, you and Pip can always hang out with me,' she said in a dull, puddleglum sort of voice. 'And Rose,' she added by way of an afterthought.

'She'd be a nice friend for him,' I agreed. Rose was kneeling on the rug, bent over some toy farm animals, feet sticking out behind her, wiggling her toes. Just like Pip. With their milky skin and fine, nut-brown hair, they could almost have been twins.

'Old McFarmer had a pig,' sang Pip softly, clumping a stray T. Rex across the brown plastic farmyard. 'Ee-a see-a toe.'

Rose joined in, her voice robust. 'Old McFarmer had lots-of-animals.'

'What a nice song,' I said, touching Pip's head lightly.

'It's funny how they have an innate singing thing,' said Cleodie. 'Rose was singing before she could talk.'

'But don't you just hate Jungle Jive?' I said in a guilty rush. 'The diddle-diddle-doos and all that.'

'I'm tone deaf,' she said with a grimace. 'But I should think that anyone with an ounce of musical capability would feel their hair standing on end. Is that you? Are you musical?'

'I was once.' For a moment I felt like elaborating, opening a conversational door into the world of Miss Fortune, and the Marlowes and Hattie. But then Pip cried out – a single peal of distress – and vomited all down himself.

'Oh God! Pip, are you okay? I'm so sorry, Cleodie, there's a bit on the floor there.'

'Oh yuck,' she said, wincing. It was a refreshing response. I'd noticed that Jody and Molly never missed an opportunity to demonstrate their complete ease with bodily fluids. Last week Molly had sat through the entire Jungle Jive session with yellow vomit all down her top, like some kind of Brownie badge of motherhood, as she sang and clapped to the jungle beat.

'I'll get a cloth,' said Cleodie doubtfully. 'The bathroom's along the hall. There's a bunch of wipes and stuff in there. Do you need to borrow some of Rose's clothes?'

'It's okay,' I said, grabbing Pip's changing bag and slinging it over my shoulder. 'I've got spare clothes in here.'

'How organised of you,' sighed Cleodie. 'When Rose was sick in the Botanics last week I had to wrap her up in my scarf like a little Egyptian mummy. Whereas you, you're the perfect mother.'

'Far from it,' I said as I lifted Pip under the arms and carried him to the bathroom. 'Believe me.'

10

Hattie's Diary

Thursday, November 2nd

I wasn't feeling well at school today, and went to see Mrs Potts after lunch. She let me lie down in the sick room, in the little bed with smooth white sheets. She felt my forehead and took my temperature with a thermometer, its little metal endy bit poking under my tongue. I must have been hot because she gave me a white plastic cup with some water and two tablets to take.

She left me alone to rest. I kept thinking about her cool hands, the way she'd stroked the hair back from my forehead and tucked me into bed. I heard her on the phone, in her office next door, and thought maybe Mum was coming to collect me. But nobody came. I fell asleep, and missed the bell by miles. By the time I'd got to Miss Fortune's I was late and Janey had already gone.

Her hair was a slightly darker shade of apricot today. She already had the eye metronome going and she motioned towards the piano. I guessed that she wanted me to play that awful pavane thing, so I got it out of my music case, trying not to touch the rat's tail music-case handle.

When I'd finished, she sat watching me for a long time as the metronome ticked on.

'Hattie. Do you know the meaning of the term "pavane"?'
I looked at the floor and shook my head.

'It's a stately court dance, popular in the sixteenth and seventeenth centuries. *Stately*, Hattie. Do you think you played that in a *stately* way?'

Her voice was quiet but dangerous. I bit my lip and thought about it for a minute.

'Or did you play it like a herd of elephants falling down the stairs?'

'Sorry.'

'Have you practised even one iota since our last lesson?'

'Um, well you see, I've had a really difficult history project this week . . .'

She stepped over and thrust her withered hand at me, between my face and the piano keys. I tried to look away but she clutched the back of my head with her other hand and held it there so I had to look.

'I practised several hours a day for twelve years,' she said. 'I studied at the Conservatoire in Paris. I was one of the lucky few for whom a career as a concert pianist was a real possibility and not just a distant dream. Then one stupid night after a stupid party I got in a car with a *stupid* man who'd drunk half a bottle of whisky. It took them three hours to cut us out of the wreckage. My right side was crushed. Nerve damage in the shoulder. And the result was this.'

She dangled the hand in front of my face.

'And a lifetime of drudgery in a damp flat in Edinburgh, teaching spoilt brats with no talent, but who are at least blessed with a pair of hands that ACTUALLY WORK!'

All of a sudden I felt this great 'whoosh' through my head, and I ran to the bathroom because I knew I was going to be sick.

It's a horrible bathroom: no windows, and the walls are

painted yellow. The stink of carbolic soap made me feel even worse.

I was sick into the toilet. After the initial panic, I noticed that Miss Fortune was standing there behind me, breathing loudly through her flarey nose, arms crossed, one toe pointing out in that way she has.

'Come on,' she whispered. 'Get it all out.' And then she whacked me on the back with the heel of her hand, so hard that I fell forwards and had to catch hold of the toilet seat.

Then: 'Oh, you poor wee scone! Get up and I'll make you some orange squash.'

Dinner: crackers and cheese, not feeling well.

REMINDER: Sandra Bowes-Green's birthday is on Monday. She got me a pencil for mine, so I shall get her something small.

11

Janey

'Okay, sweetheart. Into bed.' I shifted in the chair, preparing to lift Pip off my lap and into his cot. I could feel the tension leave my body, the ache behind my right eye ease down a notch, as I anticipated collapsing on the couch with a cup of tea. I could give myself half an hour off before starting work.

'No. Blue Babar.' He leaned towards the floor, reaching for one of the books in a pile by his cot.

I stifled a sigh. 'But we've done Yellow Babar, and Green Babar already. Blue Babar is very long. It's bedtime.'

'Blue Babar!' There was a stern frown now.

So I read Blue Babar, struggling to add some expression to my voice, forcing myself to pause and involve him: 'How is Celeste feeling now?' 'How many candles are on the birthday cake?' 'Can you see Cornelius over by the trees?'

When I finally deposited his struggling form into the cot, he changed tack.

'Milky, Mamma. Milky for Pippy.'

I ruffled his hair and went into the kitchen. I'd decided earlier that week to try to get him off his night-time bottles; he was two and a half after all, and bottles were supposed to be dreadful for all sorts of reasons. All of my parenting books agreed on this. I was hoping that cutting down on milky might encourage him to eat something other than jam sandwiches and fish fingers. But with this headache, the withholding of milky was surely a battle for another day. With a heavy sigh, I took two clean bottles out of the steriliser and filled them with toddler milk. I put one on the top shelf of the fridge – for when he woke up in the middle of the night – and took one back through to his bedroom. Grabbing his milky in both hands, he wiggled his fingers in a goodnight wave and shuffled onto his side. He looked so small against the length of the cot.

I went to bed at around eleven, and a couple of hours passed in the darkness. I tuned in to the noises from outside: the gentle roar of buses from the main road, the low chatter of people walking past on the pavement. The heavy tenement door swinging shut and footsteps echoing up the stone steps to the flats above. Murray had always asked how I could stand the noise, living on the ground floor, but I liked the sense of other people being around, especially at night.

★

I woke in blackness, jaw clenched, head pounding, slick with sweat. It always took a minute or so for my waking mind to take control, to remind me what was real. I rubbed my eyes, trying to dispel the dream. It was just nonsense.

Nonsense, fifty-seven nights in a row.

I snapped on the bedside light and ventured into the bathroom to find some paracetamol.

But I'd woken Pip; a wail sounded from his bedroom. I made for the kitchen, rubbing my eyes as I pulled open the fridge door.

What?

On the top shelf, Pip's bottle of milky. But lying in front of it, a kitchen knife. The middle-sized one in the set, with a black curved handle and a five-inch blade gleaming against the frosted glass of the shelf.

What?

I was probably still dreaming.

But I knew I wasn't.

I must have done this. Last week, while making Pip's dinner, I'd put a packet of digestive biscuits in the fridge, and this was just that kind of mistake.

Except that I hadn't used any knives tonight. I'd hardly even been in the kitchen after fetching Pip's bedtime bottle, only once to make a cup of tea. I'd been reading Hattie's diary at the same time, though, leaning over the work surface to pore over the tiny writing as the kettle had boiled. So I'd been distracted. That would be it.

But I shuddered at a sudden notion that the 'strange happenings', as Hattie had called them, might have somehow shifted and transferred themselves from the past to the present, might have peeled off the page as I'd read.

I stood there for a while, unsure what to do, the cold of the tiles seeping into my bare feet. Was this an emergency situation? Should I be telling somebody about it?

But who? I couldn't call Murray, not at two o'clock in the morning. He might be lying in bed next to Gretel for all I knew, if this was one of her nights for staying over. Or he might even be in the office, presiding over some corporate takeover. Maybe Jody or Molly, or one of the mums I knew from the nursery? Definitely not. They'd be grabbing every precious minute of sleep before their charges woke at the crack of dawn. My mother, crashed out after a busy day's filming? One of the students in the flat upstairs, who I'd never bothered to introduce myself to? The police? And what would

I say anyway? *My Jamie Oliver chef's knife – last used to prepare butternut squash soup yesterday – has moved out of the knife rack and materialised in my fridge?*

There was no one I could call. No one.

But Pip, why wasn't he still crying for his milky? With a shock of fear, I ran through to the bedroom only to find he'd fallen asleep again, his face soft and pinky in the glow from the nightlight.

I checked the doors – the front door onto the street, the side door that led into the tenement stairwell – both were locked. What about the windows? I remembered opening the deep sash window in the kitchen this afternoon when I'd burnt toast, but I was sure I'd closed it later because it was freezing outside. I climbed up onto the work surface by the sink and reached up to check the catch. It was fastened tight.

Looking out at the darkness, I suddenly wondered if I could call Cleodie. Her flat, in the next street along, backed onto the same patchwork space of shared back gardens, or drying greens as people still called them. Maybe I'd be able to spot a cosy lighted window about halfway along the block. She'd said she liked to write at night.

But no, only five lights were on, three on the top floor and two on the first. Maybe they were mothers too, roused from their beds to warm up bottles of milk or tend to sick children, laying cool hands on damp foreheads and carefully measuring out Calpol.

I pulled the duvet off my bed, dragged it through the hall and curled up on the floor beside Pip's cot. I lay quietly, watching for the first hint of grey to creep in through the cracks around the shutters. And comforted, somehow, by the thought of those sleepy, tousle-haired mothers, awake too through the lonely hours of the night.

69

12

Hattie's Diary

Friday, November 3rd

We had to do circuits in PE because of the extreme weather conditions (rain). On the plus side, Hilary Grogan called Janey a spasmo when she fell off the vault box, and Miss Partridge heard, and she got put out.

We seemed to be slower than the others at getting round all the stations. Janey said we shouldn't count how many step-ups etc. we were doing, because it gives an oppressive feeling of competition.

'I think I might have something to report about Miss Fortune,' she said, when we were at the rings and cones station (we hung on there for quite a while, as it is the least strenuous).

'What?'

'When I was on my way back from the toilet yesterday, I noticed something.'

(We both take two toilet trips per lesson, any more than that and she cracks down.)

'I glanced into the kitchen,' she went on, 'and the end bits of the kitchen table had been pulled out to make it bigger. And it was set with *two* places.'

'So?' I chucked a ring in the direction of the nearest cone. 'Hey look! I got one over.'

'She lives ALONE!'

'Hmm. I suppose she could have been having a friend round for tea. She was wearing her green and olive dress.'

She stopped and turned to face me. 'And afterwards, when I was playing that sonatina thing, I heard *thumps*. Coming from the kitchen. Or it could have been the back bedroom. I think someone was there.'

'So what are you thinking?'

'What if she's kidnapped someone, Hattie? A child?' Her voice shook with earnestness. 'I think the time has come for you to *grill* your mother about Miss Fortune. We need to step up a gear with the investigation.'

'I think we should. Janey . . .' I turned to face her, and opened my mouth to tell her about TL. But something else came out instead. 'I need you to tell me something honestly. Do you secretly *like* piano now? You're actually getting quite good at that sonatina.'

She flushed a little bit, and looked down at the yellow ring she was holding.

'We-ell,' she said. 'I hate *her*, of course. But, to my surprise' – she looked up and gave a wide-eyed, startled look, as though we were sharing in the moment of revelation together – 'I think I quite like playing the piano. Is that okay?'

'Of course it's okay.'

She solemnly placed the yellow ring on top of my head.

But Miss Partridge noticed us then. 'Hattie and Janey!' she shouted. 'Move on to sit-ups, NOW!'

Monday, November 6th

This afternoon, while Mum peeled the carrots for tea (mince and potatoes), I tried to talk to her. It was cosy and warm in the kitchen. The basement is nicest when it's dark outside. During the hours of daylight it is gloomy and pointless.

'Where did you find Miss Fortune?' I kept doing my drawing – a picture of the Trojan Horse – so she wouldn't realise the question was important.

'Where did I *find* her? Where do you think I found her? Under a rock in Queen Street Gardens?' She did a little trilling laugh.

'How did you find out about her? Do you know her? Was it through Dad?'

'One of the masters at Ramplings gave me the name. That new one, Mr Hickory, that James likes so much. She's on their approved list.'

'So why doesn't she work at Ramplings, then, if she's so great?'

'Because she lives *here*, Hattie. In Edinburgh. And don't be cheeky. You'd do well to follow your brother's example. You've got a lot of work to do if you're going to get up to speed. He'd already done his grade eight violin – *and* flute – by the time he was your age, remember.'

'So what does Daddy think about Miss Fortune?'

She turned the tap on almost full, and held a carrot under the stream. But it was a carrot SHE HAD ALREADY WASHED. And peeled. Idiot.

'Mum?'

It took another twenty seconds of tap-gushing for her to come up with this feeble answer: 'Daddy would be more than happy, I'm sure, with anyone on Ramplings' approved list.'

'So Daddy doesn't know about Miss Fortune, then.'

Scanning back in my mind through my last few phone calls with him, it began to make sense. 'Does he even know I'm having lessons?'

'Yes, *of course*, darling, we'd been talking about setting it up for ages. We talked about it at Easter, didn't we?'

So she hadn't even bothered to BLOODY mention it to him, in other words. When James had started the violin, aged four, Daddy (so the story goes) personally interviewed twelve different teachers, and sat in on the first few lessons to make sure. And then when James took up piano, Mum had taken him on the train to Glasgow every Saturday for his lesson. I'd had to go too, with my princess colouring book and a pack of scratchy old colouring pens that didn't even work.

The cheek of it! But I could see the opportunity.

'Mum, she might have been put on the approved list ages ago. She might be a bit past it now. She probably is, actually. I think you should check with Dad.'

She sighed, and thunked the carrot down on the draining board. She didn't turn round, but just sort of leaned forwards onto the heels of her hands.

'You can finish this off yourself, Hattie. I've got one of my headaches. I'm going to have a lie-down.'

'But don't you want to see my Trojan Horse once it's finished?'

'Just do your practice, darling. The pavane. I'll be listening out. Promise.'

13

Janey

I stood lost in contemplation of the yoghurts, trying to decide if it was worth buying the Thomas the Tank Engine kind again. A few weeks ago, Pip had seen Vichard tucking into one at the coffee shop, and he'd reached over, dipped his finger into the bright-pink gloop and licked it. I'd been buying them in hope since then, even though they always ended up splatted on the kitchen tiles.

Pip, sitting in the trolley seat, kicked me with a socked foot. He'd propelled both of his shoes across the floor before we'd even got through the fruit and vegetable section, and they were stuffed into my handbag now.

'Just a minute, Pippy.' I picked up the yoghurts and put them in the trolley. Then, on a mad impulse, I picked up the organic, sweetened-only-with-fruit-juice kind, and put them in too.

Waste, I seemed to hear my grandmother say.

'Janey,' said a voice.

Steve.

The grooves in his face seemed deeper, as though he'd worn a permanent frown since we'd last met. He was carrying a basket, which contained a packet of beansprouts, two raw beetroot and a large pack of Solpadeine, the logo visible through the thin white plastic of a pharmacy bag.

'Oh, hi! Are you looking for yoghurts?'

Shut up. Next I'd be recommending the Thomas the Tank Engine variety.

He looked me straight in the eye.

'How are you? How have you been?'

God, he was lovely. It felt like I was melting. My edges softening and blurring away, like soap in warm water.

'Oh!' I laughed, and shook my head a little, as if thrown by the change of subject, away from yoghurts. 'Fine! Yes, fine. Just getting a bit of shopping. This is Pip.'

He bent down and held out a hand. 'Pip. Nice to meet you, mate.'

Pip studiously ignored him.

'Come on, Pip. Say hello.'

'Nah, leave him,' said Steve. 'He's all right.'

'He's a bit tired today, aren't you, baby?' I stroked his silky hair, holding the curve of his head under my palm.

'I was worried about you,' Steve went on. 'After the last class. Your forest painting and all that. A bit of a cock-up on my part.'

I couldn't think of a single thing to say. I turned my attention to the items in the trolley, searching for inspiration.

'Have you tried pak choi?'

Oh no. He might think I was inviting him round for dinner. 'I mean . . .'

'Are you sleeping? You said you hadn't been sleeping.'

What was it about this man? He looked at me, and he *saw* me. He saw me, when I was all but invisible to the rest of the world.

I became aware, suddenly, of the blood flowing hot and fast under my skin. Of the air flooding my lungs as I took a breath. As though I'd been a drawing, flat and grey, that had leapt off the page into three-dimensional life.

'Erm . . . am I sleeping? Am I sleeping? Well, Pip's not sleeping too well, so I guess I'm not either. He's started coming into bed with me, though. That makes life a bit easier.'

I'd always been strict about making Pip sleep in his own cot, but the previous week I'd read a new parenting book – *Your Toddler, Your Way* – that said it was fine for a toddler to share the parental bed. In fact, not allowing it could result in a catastrophic 'mother wound'.

But Steve raised an eyebrow and gave a wry smile. 'Doesn't that mean you won't get a decent night's sleep till he's eighteen or something?'

'It's a big bed.' Why was I talking about my *bed*? I dropped my eyes to Pip, looking bored in the trolley. 'Isn't it, Pippy? It's a nice bi-i-ig bed.'

For fuck's sake.

Silence, except for the distant, tuneless bleeps coming from the checkouts and the hum of the chiller cabinets. Steve looked at his watch. The brown leather of his jacket creaked as he moved his arm. 'D'you want to grab a coffee?' he asked.

'Oh! I thought we weren't supposed to see each other. You being the tutor and all that.' There was a hint of challenge in my voice, a teasing note. Where had that come from?

His gaze slid past me, over my shoulder. Then it flicked back onto me, and he gave a tight, awkward smile.

'Come on, Janey. Help me out here.'

I felt a tiny surge of . . . something. Power?

'Well,' I began, airily. 'I suppose there's nothing to stop us meeting as . . . *friends*.'

His expression didn't change. Oh God, he could see through my pathetic attempt to flirt and thought it was ridiculous. 'Or

76

not!' I continued. 'Not friends, I mean, if that's too much. You could be a . . . benevolent observer.'

Silence.

'Or if that's inappropriate we could both be benevolent observers of each other. D'you want to come to my flat? For coffee, I mean.'

He pressed his lips together, as though he'd decided against saying what he'd been going to say. Then, lightly – ever so lightly – he touched his hand to the small of my back, directing me down the aisle towards the checkouts.

It was as though I was walking for the very first time. I could feel the muscles in my thighs, my calves, my feet. And in my arms, and down my sides, as I pushed Pip in the trolley. All tensing and releasing in perfect time to carry me to where I needed to be. He'd set my body singing. And it was all so ridiculous. The craziest thing in the world.

★

'So do you teach art full-time?' I asked once we'd got back to the flat and I'd poured him a glass of water; he'd declined my offer of coffee, as though he'd thought better of it at the last moment.

'Yeah, I teach at the local college. I'm doing a few classes with the adult education programme on the side.'

'Oh. That must be . . . interesting.'

'It's okay. I've signed up for a Masters in art therapy next year, so I'm trying to get experience of working with a more diverse range of people.'

I pictured Jody, wrapped in her bandages, and nodded thoughtfully.

'Do you have family in Edinburgh?' asked Steve.

'No. I've just got my mother. She lives in London.'

I slipped off the sofa and settled cross-legged on the floor beside Pip, who was kneeling over his Lego Duplo zoo. His feet peeped out behind him, toes wriggling in the soft grey socks.

'Are you in touch much?'

'She's an actress. She used to be in the West End and all that, but she managed to move into TV. She's got a part in *Small Miracles* . . . you know, that soap about the maternity ward. Maybe you've seen it?'

He gave a noncommittal nod.

I had a sudden vision of Steve, sitting at home eating his beetroot salad on a tray, solemnly watching the drama unfold. *I need a lovely big push, Mrs Jones. Oh no . . . oh no, Nora, get Dr Stevens, we've got a shoulder dystocia!*

'Or maybe not. I mean, it probably isn't your thing. But she's very happy about it.'

She was like a gushy, fake friend, phoning occasionally to dump her news on me then disappearing off to her own life with a 'must dash, darling'. The pattern hadn't changed since I was a child, except that then I used to sit by the phone every Sunday night, my stomach twisting in anticipation; would she or wouldn't she call? To this day, the music to *All Creatures Great and Small* brings on indigestion.

Steve sipped his water, his face unreadable.

Pip broke the silence with an elephant noise. I clicked the zookeeper into his 4x4 and wheeled him round in a slightly frantic circle.

'Does Pip go to nursery?'

'Yeah, three mornings.'

'So what do you get up to?'

'Well, oh, goodness, what do I get up to? I usually start with a couple of hours of proofreading, then I quickly whizz round doing all the things I can't when Pip's around: cleaning, ironing, tidying . . .'

Do you have to sound so tragic?

'And I've been going swimming.' As if that would elevate me from domestic drudge to yummy-mummy-about-town. I'd only been twice.

'Swimming's cool,' he said softly.

'Right. Well, I might make myself a cup of tea after all. Sure you don't want anything? I've got some Jaffa cakes.'

'Janey. What's wrong?'

'What?' I looked up. Behind the glasses, his eyes were as black as crows.

'Anxiety. You're buzzing with anxiety. You're . . . I just can't . . . sorry, but I can't keep talking like this, pretending I don't see it.'

As in the supermarket, he'd cut through my small talk. It was impolite, somehow, as though he'd walked through the middle of the Duplo zoo, scattering its carefully placed occupants.

But close behind that came an unravelling sensation somewhere in my chest. What would it feel like, to confide in him?

'It's just Hattie. My old friend Hattie. I've been trying to find her. I've been reading her old diary and it's . . . it's sort of stirred everything up. In my head.'

He frowned. 'How come you have her diary?'

I shrugged. 'It was in a cardboard box filled with all her stuff. I found it on my desk when I came in on the last day of term.'

'Last day of term?'

'Yes. 14th December, 1989.'

Her diary had been tucked inside her history folder. There had been art work too – this mosaic thing of a waterfall she'd spent ages doing, and a clay model of a squirrel, as yet unpainted. Her music case was at the bottom of the box, with books of piano music inside. She'd even left the script of a play she was due to be in next term, with all of her lines highlighted.

It felt as though she'd given me her life, frozen at that moment in time, and for a while I found that comforting. Perhaps I was just supposed to keep it safe for a while, until one day she'd appear back in the art block to finish off her mosaic, or sweep up on stage at the last minute, resplendent in Tudor costume, to star in the play.

I'd scoured through the diary, of course, those Christmas holidays, thinking she might have left it for a reason, that it might contain some sort of clue that would make everything clear.

'Bit strange,' said Steve. 'Why leave you a box with no explanation?'

'I don't know, because I never heard from her again. And I've tried everything I can think of, the St Katherine's Alumni Association, the—'

'I was at St Simon's,' he said softly.

St Katherine's brother school, just across the playing fields.

'Which year?' I'd thought I'd recognised him, that day of the first art class. Maybe I'd seen him – even danced with him! – at one of the infamous ceilidhs.

'Oh, I'm a few years older than you, I think.'

'You didn't know Hattie?'

He shrugged. 'I wasn't exactly big on the whole social scene. But have you tried the obvious things to find Hattie? Have you tried finding her parents?'

'Her dad was the composer Emil Marlowe.'

'He did *Dark Side Spectacular*, didn't he?'

'Yeah. He hit the big time in the 1980s. He was living in New York when Hattie left. But he died a few years ago. I tried phoning the lawyers who seem to be in charge of his copyright and stuff, but that was a total dead end. I even tried phoning some charitable trust that he'd had set up. I found it on the internet, some thing for disadvantaged musicians. I asked if they could pass my details on to a member of the family with a request to contact me.'

'And?'

'She pretended to write down my details, but I bet she didn't. She probably thought I was a disadvantaged musician trying to bypass the official channels.'

Steve nodded and frowned. 'I might be able to help. I've got one or two contacts.'

'You?'

'I have a friend who works with the homeless. He'll know about missing persons, or how to find people who don't want to be found. I'll have a word with him.'

I thought of the rows of grim faces staring out of the missing-persons pages in *The Big Issue*. Hooded shapes huddled in shop doorways. Then I thought of Renee, coming to collect Hattie from school, driving the Bentley right through the school gates and up to the main entrance, even though you weren't supposed to. And Emil, on television a few years ago, holding up his latest award – last award, as it turned out – for the cameras, displaying his perfectly symmetrical smile.

'I don't think . . .' I began. But who knew, with that family. 'Yes,' I said. 'That would be great. Thanks.'

He paused, and shot me a careful look. 'Another option, I suppose, would be to explore the non-dominant hand technique a little more.'

As soon as I heard the words, I knew I wasn't going to be able to say no. A hand seemed to take hold of my heart and squeeze it.

Don't go there, I told myself. Walk away from this. It's smoke and mirrors, a stupid parlour game that can't ever help you. Focus on the real world.

A scream of frustration from Pip. He was trying to fix a Duplo tortoise onto the back of a police motorbike.

'It's okay. Mummy help you? But the thing is,' I said lightly, pretending to be absorbed in tortoise-fixing, 'the non-dominant hand thing is supposed to access my inner creativity, isn't it? Other aspects of myself? Not another person.'

He shrugged. 'But that's how this all started, isn't it? Maybe there's something there that might help you find her. Or at least shed some light on why you've got this thing about finding her.'

I didn't need anybody to shed light on that.

'Of course, as I said, I'm not an art therapist. I need to be very up front about that, after . . .'

After our frenzied hug, our stolen moment in the art classroom. I felt myself blushing.

'Oh, *no*.'

'It's an ethical minefield. But you could do it by yourself. I could give you a book with some exercises to work through.'

'Of course. No, I wouldn't ask you to . . . to compromise yourself . . .'

82

To *compromise* himself? I pictured him in my bed, naked in a tangle of sheets, as a dark-suited person – an art tutors' ethics inspector? – peered round the door and marked something on a clipboard, shaking his head.

'I mean, it's absolutely fine. It would be great if I could borrow the book.'

But then I remembered the inky scribble of a girl. Words bleeding across the white paper. If I was going to do this, I couldn't do it on my own. I might drift away from the real world and never come back.

I sat back on my heels and looked him in the eye.

'But what if something bad happens? I know you can't advise me, but maybe you could just . . . be here?'

He shot a furtive glance at Pip.

'Shall I come back later? When he's gone to bed?'

Yes. Yes, please come back. Don't leave me in this flat alone. I can't bear another night of it.

'Okay then. He should be down by eight, but leave it until—'

'Actually, no. Let me drop off the book. You should read it through first. I'll come back on . . . how about Thursday night?'

'Thursday night is fine.'

'Mummy! Do chairs!' Pip blindsided me with a green Duplo base plate that was almost as tall as him. I took it from him, absently.

'Maybe, if you're going to get into all this, you should think about talking to someone. Someone neutral, I mean. Dragging up the past can be . . . What's that look for?'

Mad. He thought I was mad.

But then he smiled. He thought I was *funny*. What was this? I felt naked with this man for some reason – totally stripped back. But across that came that little surge of something again – power? For a moment, they seemed like two halves of the same thing.

'Nothing,' I said. 'I wasn't looking like anything.' Realising I was hugging the base plate against my chest, I put it firmly down on the carpet. Whatever was going on between me and this man, hiding behind a large green Duplo base plate wasn't going to help matters. 'But okay, I'll think about it.'

14

Hattie's Diary

Saturday, November 11th

London trip!!! For Janey's birthday, her mum – *Martina* – sent her two tickets for *Cats* the musical, because she's in it just now. Mum drove us all the way down to London. We left at 5 a.m.! And she arranged for us to stay in the biggest suite on the top floor of The Blenheim . . . Janey could barely believe it when she saw it, and practically died when she saw the chocolates on the pillows. I reassured her that this was quite normal for me, because of my grandfather owning the hotel chain, that they were only Ferrero Rochers and she shouldn't be intimidated by them.

'So you're an *actual* Ferrero Rocher by blood?' said Janey in an awe-inspired voice.

'What?' I said.

Turns out she thought it was a famous family, she was getting mixed up with the Rockefellers. She threw one of them at me to punish me for laughing. (A Ferrero Rocher, not a Rockefeller person.)

Cats was at 2.30 p.m. Mum dropped us off early, because she wanted to go up to Ramplings to see James. She gave us £20, so we had an ice cream first, and Cokes, and we were in a fair old state of excitement when the curtain went up.

But Martina, oh my goodness, she was gorgeous with her

dark smoky eyes, slinking around the stage in her orange and grey stripy suit. During some of the songs, the cats came off the stage out into the audience, right behind our seats, and when she pounced up to us and flexed her claws, I thought I'd stop breathing – she was just so – I can't even describe it. It was like she was larger than life, more than human, with ten times the impact of a human. I don't know if it was the music, or the costume, or the sleek, cat-like movements. I just don't know.

Sadly, I could quite understand why she would have decided to abandon Janey if it meant she could do this instead. In some ways it's just as well Janey's father died early on, as he wouldn't have stood a chance against it either. Not with him just being a pest controller. *Anything* else looks weak and washed out in comparison.

There was a standing ovation at the end, and the audience were all singing along. Dad would've hated it. He is so jealous of Lloyd Webber.

We went backstage afterwards, but Janey said if Martina mentioned my dad, I was just to pretend I hadn't heard her. She's worried her mum might ask to meet him, so she could pester him for a part in one of his musicals. Not only would that be embarrassing, because she is past it, Janey says, but she wants her career to fall flat as soon as possible so she will come home.

As soon as we went into the dressing room, though, I couldn't stop thinking to myself, she won't ever come home, she won't ever come home. It was buzzing through my fingertips. I knew it as surely as I know my own name.

At first Martina was all mwah-mwah kisses, and she gave Janey a present – a gold Estee Lauder powder compact – which she said she'd bought at Harrods. Then she asked us how school was. Janey went red and started telling her, in a voice you could hardly hear, about the play we're doing next term. Martina nodded and listened with a frozen smile, as though she was suspecting that Janey wouldn't be very good in a play.

Then she grabbed Janey's face in her hands and said, 'Oh, look at you, with those solemn grey eyes. You're such a good girl. A steady girl. NEVER let anyone take that away from you. Passion . . . creative spirit . . . they're all very well. I can't help the way I am. But sometimes it's like a curse.' She gestured wildly to the walls of her dressing room. 'Look at me, living this life . . .'

But then Macavity the Mystery Cat appeared looking for some paracetamol, and Martina's attention drifted. I don't know how she could flirt with him like that. He has practically no hair, which you only notice when his cat-head thing is taken off. Janey just sort of shrank into the corner, twisting the plastic belt on her new C&A coat, and looking like she might cry.

Later, Mum took us out to Sorrento's, an Italian restaurant, and we had pizza with oozy mozzarella cheese, with grassy bits on top which were called oregano. Mum was all smiley for once, teasing us because of the way we wolfed it down. Janey told her that Mrs White says that too about us, whenever she's on lunch duty. She says we eat like a pair of criminals on the run. This was a daring thing for Janey to say, as she doesn't normally do chit-chat with adults. But Mum threw her head back laughing.

'You're a treasure,' she said, patting Janey's hand, her rings glittering as they caught the candlelight.

Then it was back to the hotel. We walked along the street

all holding hands, with Mum in the middle, and we sang 'Memory'. Mum told us that it had always been a favourite of hers, and not to tell Dad! Once we got to the room, we raided the mini-bar for more Cokes, and stayed up to chat for a bit, but not too long; Mum said she wasn't going to stand for any nonsense. She had a twinkle in her eye, though.

Janey started crying when she was brushing her teeth.

'It's okay, Hats,' she said. 'I'm crying for happiness. I feel like I've had TWO mothers today, as opposed to the usual none.'

I didn't say the obvious, that Mum is hardly ever like this, and usually only when there's an audience. I suppose I didn't want to break the spell.

'Did your mum never want you to live in London with her?' I asked.

She shook her head. 'She says Granny and Grandpa's is the best place for me. They'll always look after me because of my dad. And they can give me a good steady life without any cursed passion, like she's got.'

Janey's gone to sleep holding her powder compact. What she doesn't know is that an Estée Lauder powder compact should come in a box, with cellophane wrapped around it. That is half of what you're paying for.

15

Janey

Dr Polson was the oldest doctor at the practice, with a reassuring manner and a furrowed brow that suggested he *really cared*, whether or not that was true. He checked the rash on Pip's tummy and declared in a jolly voice that it was a spot of eczema.

My heart was still racing, as it had been since I'd made the appointment that morning. I'd half made up my mind to mention the sleep situation to Dr Polson, and to casually drop in a mention of my nightmares. But maybe the more important thing would be to mention the knife in the fridge?

Or the other thing I'd been trying to put out of my mind: the jar of damson jam I was sure I hadn't bought, standing proud and crimson on the kitchen shelf last Saturday.

Was it just absent-mindedness? Or something worse? What would Dr Polson do if I confided in him? Scenarios ran through my head: psychiatric referrals, a visit from the social work department. Oh God.

'How are you getting on?' Dr Polson asked as he typed something into the computer. 'They can be a bit of a handful at that age, can't they?'

'Oh,' I said, forcing a smile into my voice. 'We're fine.'

Pip slid off my knee and pulled at my hand. He wanted to leave. His fingers were cold in mine, I'd only been able to find one of his gloves that morning. I'd been scolded by

Mrs Paxton when we'd got to nursery. She'd told me that the children needed to be properly wrapped up for the cold weather: 'A hat, a scarf, and *two* gloves next time please, Miss Johnston.'

Every day, another small failure adding up to . . . what?

'He'll be needing constant attention, I daresay?' He gave a wry little chuckle.

I pictured long rainy days in the flat, doing my best to raise a smile when Pip wanted to get out playdough for the fourteenth time in a day, or empty out my bedroom drawers again. How could it be possible to adore somebody so much, yet be so drained by spending time with them? I could lose myself in watching him, the faint trace of an eyebrow, the roundness of a cheek, or the whorl of an ear, and yet at the same time dread the prospect of a day alone with him.

'Yes. He goes to nursery three mornings.'

'But other than that, he's with you? He's a lucky boy. Time with Mum's the best thing at that age, eh?'

Not necessarily. He'd probably realise that when he was older. *She was like a wet weekend, lost in her own world half the time.*

'We're not getting much sleep.' I blurted it out.

Dr Polson frowned at the computer. 'Now, why has it done *that*?' He shook his head, pressed a few more keys, and the printer on his desk started whirring.

'Sleep,' he said, reaching over for the prescription, 'or lack of it, is the bane of all parents' lives. The health visitor can help with sleep-training techniques. Ask at reception. And meanwhile, try and get at least one or two decent nights' sleep a week. That's where Dad comes in. Make sure he takes a turn. Boot him out of bed if need be!'

Gretel would be delighted about that.

I drew Pip closer, and he nudged his silky head into the crook of my neck. It centred me for a moment, and I felt quite certain that I'd be able to sort things out, pull myself together. Pip would grow up the happiest of boys, and he would know that I loved him – how could he not? It would be a truth he wouldn't even have to think about, as warm and certain as the sun in the sky.

'Well,' said Dr Polson, handing me the prescription. 'Don't hesitate to come and see us if you've any concerns.'

I stood up. The knife. Should I mention the knife? Would I one day look back at this moment and wish, with every shred of whatever might be left of me, that I'd sought help?

'Okay, Pip? Say bye-bye to the doctor?' I lifted his wrist and swirled it in a limp little wave.

What kind of person hides behind a two-year-old?

It started raining on the way home, sleety drops pelting the roof of the car. As usual I had to park miles away from the flat – there were never any spaces during the day. I carried Pip, tucking him inside my coat as much as I could. His cold, damp cheek bobbed against mine as we walked.

'Here we go, darling. Let's go in and get dry.'

I opened the door. He clung to me as I tried to lower him down, lifting his legs so I couldn't set him on his feet.

'Cold,' he said. 'Want Mummy.'

'Okay,' I said, kneeling to peel off his coat and his wet trousers. 'Let's get these wet things off. Oh look, there's your blue train jumper drying on the radiator. Do you want to wear that? It'll be all cosy. It will warm your tummy up.' He squealed as I rubbed his tummy, my hand still cold from outside. 'And let's get a towel for that rainy hair!'

I went into the bathroom, found a towel and turned to walk out.

No. It was impossible.

Pip's missing glove was stuck over the shower head that extended from the wall above the bath. The navy-blue fleece was stretched taut around it, the fingers splayed out in a way that somehow made me shudder.

Whatever noise I made must have frightened Pip, because he started crying.

I tugged his wet trousers back onto his protesting legs, grabbed the blue train jumper from the radiator and got us out of there.

I phoned Murray from the car, saying I thought there'd been a break-in.

'Janey, I'm just going into a meeting. What do you need? The police? Locksmiths? I'll get Sandra to send someone down.'

'Someone's been messing with Pip's stuff.'

He appeared ten minutes later in a taxi, and told me to wait in the car with Pip while he checked the flat. Somebody could still be in there, he said, frowning.

'Should we call the police?'

'Let's just take things one step at a time,' he said, holding his hands up in a 'slow down' gesture.

When he returned, he opened the car door and bent down to speak to me. I could smell the sharp tang of coffee on his breath. He probably hadn't had any lunch.

'There's no broken windows, no forced doors. Nothing to suggest a break-in. The front and side doors were locked. What exactly did you think was missing, Janey, because I've got the board of Robertson Cathcart twiddling their thumbs back at the office.'

Once back in the flat, I made straight for the bathroom.

'It's his glove. Pip's glove.' I pointed to the shower head. With Murray in the room now, the glove, so threatening before, merely looked tiny and comical.

Murray gave a soft sigh and crossed his arms.

'Someone's put it there. It wasn't me. And it wasn't Pip. He wouldn't be able to reach.'

'Well,' he said, after a long pause. 'It's one of life's mysteries, I suppose. Look Janey, if everything else is okay, I'll get back.'

'Yes, of course. I'm sorry.'

'I'll get Sandra to send down a locksmith. Cover all the bases, hmm?'

My mind flashed back to Hattie and all the things that had happened in that dreadful house. The way nobody had believed her either.

Nobody except me, and even I had treated it like a game. I'd been taken in by her 'oh well' shrugs, by the way she'd played her part as the level-headed one in that family, rolling her eyes at the creative whims of James and her father, and at Renee's unpredictable moods. I hadn't listened properly. Hadn't seen.

'Okay then.'

He stood looking at me for a moment, frowning.

'Are you all right?' he said gruffly.

I nodded, and walked him towards the door, anxious that he should leave, giving me time to place Pip safely in front of CBeebies before I fell apart.

16

Hattie's Diary

Friday, November 17th

When I sat down next to Janey in biology this morning, I knew there was something terribly wrong. Mental torment was pouring off her in waves.

I asked her what the matter was and she pressed her lips together and shook her head.

'Buck up, girls,' said Mrs White. 'It's the day we've all been waiting for. The frog has arrived, and you're going to watch me dissect it.' She handed round the frog worksheets. They were still warm and purple-inky-smelling from the copying machine.

'Janey. You can tell me *anything*.'

She placed her pen on the worksheet, then swivelled it round like one of the hands on a clock, so that it was pointing at Hilary Grogan, at the end of the row in front of us.

'Her again?' I said. 'What has she done?'

'Come up to the bench please, girls,' boomed Mrs White.

Honestly, it was disgusting. The frog was a yellowy-grey colour, not green at all, and pickled in some stinking preservative solution. When Mrs White made the incision right up its front, Janey began to cry.

'What's wrong?' I asked, when we'd been allowed to go back to our seats.

'I felt so sorry for the frog. Just lying there, all dead and useless.'

'But you looked terrible before that. Please tell me. It's Hilary Grogan, isn't it?'

It took me another five minutes to get it out of her.

'She called me sourface,' she said finally. 'It's just . . .'

'I know.'

Of course I knew. It reminded her of the day of her grandpa's funeral, the first day back to school last January. She wasn't allowed to go to it, because her granny said it was adults only, and she cried all the way through lunch. Hilary Grogan called her sourface, as she was coming back to the table with seconds of pudding, and Janey – this is very unusual for her – whirled round and slapped her, sending the jam sponge clattering to the floor.

They both got sent to Mrs Waverley's office. Janey didn't come back for ages, and I realised she'd probably been put in the pink room to reflect on her actions. And halfway through French I suddenly knew – I just knew – that she hadn't told Mrs Waverley about her grandpa, or the funeral, or any of it. So I said I needed to go to the loo, and went over there. I lost my nerve a bit, just before I knocked on the door, but then I closed my eyes and pretended I was Janey's mother – not useless Martina, but a sort of imaginary one – and that I had every right to stand up to the authorities if Janey's happiness was at stake.

So I went in, and I said this: 'Janey would never normally have done this. She's upset because her grandfather's funeral is today. Please let her out of the pink room and give her a chance to explain herself. Think of her human rights.'

Mrs Waverley raised her eyebrows. 'What about Hilary's

human rights? Should I stand by and condone an act of violence?'

'I don't care about Hilary Grogan's human rights,' I said.

That made the eyebrows go up again, more sharply this time.

'Janey's grandpa wasn't just a normal grandfather. He was like her dad. She once told me he was the only person in the world who loved her. He was her *one person*. Apart from me.'

Mrs W stood and looked at me for ages.

'In that case,' she said eventually, 'I think you'd better go into the pink room too.'

My heart sank, but then she reached into a cupboard behind her desk and piled my arms with Scrabble and a bashed-up box of Cluedo, and a box of silvery-red Tunnocks tea cakes on the top.

Janey and I sat in there all afternoon, safely boxed away from the world inside those pink walls. She cried, then played for a bit, then cried, and played a bit, and ate tea cakes. I remember the way it made me feel when she finally smiled at quarter past three, at my impression of Colonel Mustard. It just made my heart swell up, like I'd coaxed a freezing, half-drowned kitten back from the brink of death.

And today Hilary Grogan did it again. I couldn't believe it.

'How about I come back to your house after school?' I said. 'You can show me all the photos of your grandpa.'

She shifted in her seat. 'Or why don't I come to yours, and you can put on that tape of Chopin, and we can meditate to it. And maybe burn one of your mum's scented candles? Get that horrible frog smell out of our noses.'

This is her new thing, meditating. We've tried it a few times. She closes her eyes and lies very still and imagines her grandpa is sitting beside her on his wickerwork chair, listening to the music too, and reading his newspaper.

So Janey came home with me. Mum drew the line at giving us her scented candle but we put an old Victoria Plum soap on top of the radiator.

We sat on the floor face-to-face and tried to think about her grandpa. The funny thing is, it seemed to work better for me than for her. At one point I swear I heard him flick his page over and say, 'Bloody government.'

Janey gave me a funny look when I told her. 'That's what I was thinking,' she said. 'Can you read my mind or something? Get a piece of paper and a pen.'

She made me sit at my desk with my eyes closed, holding this pen, and she stood behind me with both of her hands on my head and tried to convey her thoughts to me. Nothing happened so I decided to try and spark it off with something.

'Oh Grandpa . . .' I wrote.

Janey gasped. 'Keep going!'

'I miss the sprouts you used to grow.'

'Oh GOD!' This was very unusual for Janey, who never swears.

'What?' I said, opening my eyes. My writing had trailed off towards the bottom corner of the paper, looked a bit spidery and weird like a mad person's. 'Were you actually thinking about sprouts?'

'No.' Her eyes were so wide I thought they might pop out of her head. 'But I was thinking about my granny's HAM AND LENTIL SOUP!'

'Hmm. I suppose they're both foods.'

We tried it for a while more but nothing else happened.

When we were lying in bed later, trying to get to sleep, Janey's voice sounded out of the darkness. 'Hattie?'

'What?'

'The piano in the hallway. Why have you taped the lid shut with all that black tape?'

I couldn't think what to say. It was embarrassing. 'Oh. Just the, you know . . . I thought I could hear it playing again. At night and stuff.'

She was quiet for a while and I thought she'd fallen back asleep. 'What did your mum say? I mean, the tape might pull off the varnish or something.'

'Oh. Mum hasn't been up here for a while. Not since she had that sleepwalking thing.'

'Oh right,' said Janey. She asked me why my voice was all shaky, and I said it wasn't, and that she should go to sleep.

Monday, November 20th

This morning, as I was going downstairs, something happened. I'd had my breakfast (boiled egg) and was all ready to go, but suddenly remembered I had to go up to fetch *The Lord of the Flies*. If I get another disorder mark this term it'll be a detention.

When I was on my way down, about halfway down the top staircase, I heard something behind me. It was like something falling through the air, down through the space in the middle of the stairs. As if it had been dropped from the cupola right up above. Just a slight 'whoosh'. I turned round, but there was nothing there. And no sign of anything having fallen onto the chessboard tiles down below, either.

Maybe it was the whoosh of my ponytail as I swung my head. I'd done my hair nicely, with the new scrunchy that Janey had got me.

I really don't think this whooshing has anything to do with the music case. I checked, and it was in the vestibule where I'd put it, wedged against the wall behind the umbrella box. I'll have to touch it at some point to get out that awful pavane, because Mum is nagging me to practise it. The rat's tail handle will be very cold, and possibly a little bit damp from the umbrellas, as it has been raining a lot this week. The pavane itself might have got damp.

Dinner: dressed fish.

Wednesday, November 22nd

I heard the whoosh again this morning. Only this time, it was between the first floor and the ground. Janey asked me what was wrong, during cross-country. She grabbed my arm and pulled me to a halt behind the holly hedge.

'It's safe to tell me things,' she said. 'It's just like telling yourself.'

And when I did, she said she thought maybe I had a whooshy ear. And then I remembered that I did go swimming at Glenogle on Saturday, so maybe there is water stuck in it. That must be it.

Too tired for dinner. Dizzy.

17

Janey

I took the pen in my left hand: a nice, normal black Biro. And we had mugs of tea, and a plate of syrupy homemade flapjacks. The kitchen was quiet, apart from the swish of the dishwasher, and lit softly by just the cabinet lights, gleaming off the worktops.

Steve sat watching me, his arms crossed and his chair pushed out from the table. His jacket was slung over the back of the chair, as though he might need to depart at a moment's notice. And he'd accepted his tea only under duress, as if he could see straight through my cosy scene-setting and didn't want any part in it.

I met his eye and was struck with a sudden urge to snap the main lights on. What if he thought I was trying to lure him into bed, with my rose-sprigged mugs and Nigella flapjacks?

Ridiculous.

'Okay, so what do I do? I can't remember what to do.'

'Don't think about it. Just let your hand do whatever it feels like.'

I drew a little stick figure. So far, so predictable.

With a box round it.

And another box, harder and blacker.

And another.

My hand ached. I pulled the pen off the paper. 'Are you Hattie?' I asked.

Another box.

'Keep talking,' said Steve softly.

Another box.

'Where are you?' There didn't seem to be enough air in the room. Each word came out tighter and thinner than the last. 'Where did you go?'

My hand stopped. There seemed to be no answer to that. No answer in this whole wretched world.

I thought of the pictures in my 'Hattie' folder, spilling over the bed after that first art class. Face after face.

'Are you . . . okay, wherever you are?'

The hand shifted and drew a sharp upwards spike, with a scribble at the top.

I shot a glance at Steve. 'What do you think that is?'

He was staring intently at the paper, half of his face in shadow. After a moment, he shook his head. I looked at the paper again.

'A tree?' I said. 'You've drawn a tree. Is it?'

The pen started to write.

THE TREES OF GLEN EDDLE

'No, no,' I said, turning to Steve and shaking my head. 'This can't be real.'

A lurch of dizziness. I closed my eyes.

'What does it mean, "The Trees of Glen Eddle"?'

'It's a piece of music.'

Neither of us moved. The air seemed to crackle and whine. I thought of Grandpa, with his portable radio, turning the dial to find the right frequency as he carried it out to his vegetable garden.

But this wasn't Grandpa. This feeling was little-girl-shaped, and standing so close I could feel her breath on my neck.

'I wrote it, *The Trees of Glen Eddle*, I mean. My music teacher, Miss For—'

'Tell Hattie,' said Steve.

The pen flew out of my hand and skittered against the floor tiles.

'Okay,' he said. 'You know you can stop any time you want to.'

'Yes.' The atmosphere in the room had changed now. I forced a laugh. 'I think that's quite enough from you for one night, Miss Hattie.'

He sat for a few moments, watching me. 'Finished?' he said. 'You're sure?'

And then: 'Are you okay?'

'Yes. Oh yes. I'm fine. Absolutely fine.'

Don't ask me. Just stay.

'Thanks for the tea.' He stood up, reaching for his jacket, which emitted a breath of stale, leathery air as he pulled it on. Would it feel cold, I wondered, against the cotton warmth of his shirt. I wanted to slide my hands around his waist, feel the muscles of his back, the nubbly bones of his spine under my fingers.

'You're going?'

'Yep, I'd better head. Early start. I'm bushed.'

I felt small, a nuisance, for dragging him out on a rainy Thursday night, forcing him to watch as I drew stick figures and black boxes.

But when we reached the front door, he handed me a business card with a number written across it. 'You can call me. Any time.'

'Oh. Thanks.'

He eyed me: detached, evaluating. 'You look done in. Will you be okay? I could get hold of something to help you sleep, if you like.'

I shuddered. The thought of being stuck inside a chemically induced sleep wasn't appealing.

'No, no. Thanks. I've got *Christiansen*.'

'Aha! I quite like that.'

It was a subtitled Danish series about an educational psychologist, the latest big thing, just going into its fourth series on BBC 4.

'I've only got the first series, so I'm watching them over and over again. But when I close my eyes it doesn't really matter. I usually just drift off to sleep. I'm hoping I might become fluent in Danish.'

He smiled politely.

'And maybe even be able to diagnose Asperger's syndrome and stuff like that.'

Don't go.

Because the dream would be waiting for me, in the still of the night when the Christiansen DVD had finished and those soothing, confusing voices had given way to the stubborn silence of the flat.

How I wished I could ask him to lie down beside me. Stay with me until I fell asleep.

'What?' he asked.

Maybe he could stay all night and I could just lie there, breathing in and out, still and safe. Warm and calm. Next to someone who'd known Hattie, even if only for a moment, as a scribble on a sheet of paper.

'Nothing. See you sometime.'

His hand rose and hovered by my arm, and I braced myself for his touch. But he pulled it back, shuffled in his pocket for his car keys, and left.

18

Hattie's Diary

Thursday, November 30th

Since last week, the whooshing has been happening every time I go down the stairs. I'm ready for it now, though, and have been practising turning my head just as I hear it, to see if there is anything behind me. There isn't. Not really. Except today I saw a fluttery streak of dark. Just for a millisecond. It might be my eyes are going funny. I told Janey about it in biology. We were taking turns to look at a water flea – *Daphnia* – down the microscope.

'Such a beautiful name,' she said as she peered down the microscope, her left eye all screwed up. 'For such a disgusting thing. It's totally still but if you look carefully, its heart's beating away really fast. It's got a little secret life that none of us know about. I wonder if it's *thinking*.'

'I saw a sort of dark thing, falling down the middle of the stairs.'

Janey lifted her face and looked at me. Perplexed. That's what she was. Not disbelieving, but perplexed.

It's funny, because to begin with she was really into all this stuff, the strange goings-on and everything. It was she who suggested Miss Fortune could be a witch. But now she looks perplexed any time I mention something weird.

I wanted to tell her about the other thing. The music I

heard last night – a waltz or something – ringing through the house at three o'clock in the morning. It started off cheerful and then went off into a minor key, all sad. I went out into the hall to check the piano and the noise stopped dead. But I could still hear it ringing around, echoing off the walls and down the stairwell. Echoing round my own head. Even now.

'Do you think I'm going mad?' I asked her.

She reached her hand across the desk and touched her pinkie against mine. Mrs White was looking out like a hawk, so we had to pretend to be discussing *Daphnia*. But she was trying to let me know she was there.

I was about to tell her about the waltz, and even about TL, because it's like being sick, sometimes it's better to get it out. But then something dreadful happened. Janey's face disappeared. I could see the biology lab, and Mrs White at the front, and hear everything that was going on around me. But when I looked at Janey, her face was just a circle of nothingness. Not even grey, or white, or black, just kind of background coloured.

I looked over to the window. Everything to the left of it – Fiona and Rebecca – dissolved into nothingness.

'What's the matter?' I could hear her voice, though I couldn't see her.

'Janey. Don't panic, but I've gone blind.'

'What?'

'*Don't* tell Mrs White.'

'Okay, but Hattie . . .'

'Have you got that mirror? Your gold compact?'

She did, of course; she keeps it in her schoolbag, even though it's against the rules.

I looked in it, and it confirmed my fears. My face had disappeared.

So I just sat quite still for the rest of the lesson, pretending to write in my folder. Janey pretended to examine the tadpoles, too, but she kept whispering 'are you okay?' and she wasn't really concentrating.

When the bell went, she took my arm and led me out of the classroom.

'You two are like a couple of old ladies,' said Mrs White. 'A couple of old dears. Girls, I want your diagrams finished for next time, please, and six characteristics of *Daphnia*.'

Janey wanted to take me to the nurse, but I wouldn't go, so she took me to the fire escape and just sat with her arms around me. When I closed my eyes, I saw a bright zig-zaggy thing crawling across the blackness inside my eyes. I leaned against her because I felt too awful to do anything else, and fell asleep.

I woke up when the bell rang for the end of break, and I could see again.

'It might be stress,' said Janey. 'Or maybe it's *hormones*. Maybe you're going to start your periods!'

I moaned in horror.

She laid her cheek against my shoulder. 'Don't worry. I still have a free sanitary towel in my schoolbag from that talk last year. It's a bit fluffy but it's yours if you want it. If it's not that, maybe you should go and see the doctor.'

'I can't go without telling Mum.'

'Hmm,' she said. Even though Janey kind of worships my mum, she knew it would be impossible to tell her about the whooshing and everything.

But suddenly my head started hurting horribly like someone was stabbing me behind my eye, and Janey pretty much dragged me to the school nurse. She offered to pretend to be ill, too, so she could stay with me, but I said no. It was English next, and she likes English.

Mrs Potts put her cool, plump hand on my forehead again, and took my pulse with the little watch thing fastened to her dress. I loved her so much, just for a second, that I asked if she would phone Miss Fortune and cancel my piano lesson. She looked at me for a moment, curious, as though she was trying to guess what I was thinking.

'So will you?'

'It's not my place to do that, as you well know, young lady. But I'll put it to your mum that you'd be best off going home to bed.'

I was allowed to lie down in the sick room bed, then. She pulled up the covers for me, and stroked a bit of hair back from my forehead, and looked so kind that I nearly told her about the blindness.

In the end, she wasn't able to get Mum on the telephone, but I left at quarter to four, saying that I felt much better and that I'd go to my lesson. I didn't go, though. For the first time, I skived. I went to one of the rooms behind the school hall, full of bits of scenery and rails with costumes from plays. It had a comforting musty smell like old warm wood and polish. I curled up in a corner, on a big red furry dragon's tail, and closed my eyes.

Hattie's writing ends. The rest of the diary consists of blank pages.

19

Janey

On Friday afternoon the sun appeared for the first time in weeks, so when Murray came round we took Pip for a walk round Inverleith Park. He loved visiting the duck pond, and counting the dogs that walked past with their owners: 'One, two, 'leven, sixty-eighty . . .'

'Is he still enjoying nursery?' Murray asked, nudging a loose stone off the path with his golf umbrella.

'Oh yes. He's made friends with a little girl called Sophie.'

He nodded. 'It'll do him good to spend some time with other children. He can do some more mornings, if you like. Don't worry about the cost, I'll cover it.'

'No, I like to have him with me. I can work in the evenings.'

'Look, just do whatever you think is best for him. I've told you, you don't have to worry about money. It's because of me that you lost your job, I know that, and I want to make my contribution. Do you need me to increase the direct debit?'

'Thanks, but we're fine. I've still got some of the, er, the settlement from the firm.'

They'd paid well over the odds to get rid of me without a fuss, after Gretel – whose father was the head of the Frankfurt office of McKeith's – had decided I shouldn't work at the firm any more.

'But I want to help. What the hell am I doing all this for if I can't support my fam— my son properly. I want him to have his mum around.'

He mumbled the last part, clearly embarrassed by the word he'd almost said. Something about the autumn light, and the shouts of children in the playground nearby, made me think of the family we might have been. If only I could take his arm and walk by his side, closing the space – the polite, careful space of eighteen inches or so – that we always left between our bodies. And if only I could confide in him, as I would if he were mine, about the Hattie questions that were looping round my mind.

But why shouldn't I confide in him? It wasn't as though I'd be using up something that belonged to Gretel. It was hard to conceive of her asking his advice on anything, especially not lost, longed-for best friends.

So I told him about my search, editing carefully, keeping it light. He listened without interruption, eyes following Pip as he meandered ahead of us.

'So I've drawn a blank. But Steve thought he might be able to track her down.'

'Who exactly is this *Steve*?'

'Well, he's an art tutor. I met him at his workshop thingy, "The Art of Love".'

Murray looked as if he'd bitten into a rotten apple.

'Oh, I didn't *mean* to go to it. I was trying to go to a class about how to write a killer CV. I saw some fliers at the nursery, and I just thought it would be a good idea to think about, you know, workplace skills and all that kind of thing. For when Pip's a bit older. And I must have put in the wrong course number because . . .'

' "The Art of Love".' Murray shook his head.

'Really, I had no intention of going to an art class. Ha!'

Although that wasn't entirely true. The flier had caught my eye because of the Monet thumbnail on the front and the advert for an art appreciation class: 'A Riot of Light: The French Impressionists'. And I'd thought why not? Why shouldn't I do something like that? Something for myself, for once.

But that perky little burst of enthusiasm hadn't lasted long. Later that night, when I'd gone home and looked up the website, I'd been assailed by the list of sensible, practical courses on job skills. Shame had come over me, for what good would the French Impressionists be to a jobless single mum? I could almost see Granny, sighing and shaking her head, as Murray had just done.

'So this *Steve* is some New Age, beansprout-eating freak, no doubt.'

'No! It wasn't like that at all. I only went to two of the sessions but they were really . . . interesting.' I fought down an image of Steve's body, pressed against mine, the hardness at the crotch of his jeans. 'And then we ran into each other and he came over for coffee.'

'Has he met Pip? I hope bloody not.'

'Honestly, it's fine. Jody and Molly from Jungle Jive go to all his workshops. They swear by his techniques.'

He muttered something that sounded like, 'I'll bet they fucking do.'

'What was that?'

'So he's in with all the yummy mummies then? Hmm. Well, tell him thanks but no thanks. I'll look into this Hattie business myself. Should be able to track her down. I've got a few contacts.'

110

He pushed his bottom lip out slightly, just the way Hattie used to when she was feeling stubborn. Suddenly I felt like the me I'd been back then.

'What, are you going to ask around at the next Law Society dinner? What is it with you men and your "contacts"?'

'The firm uses PIs all the time. For litigation cases. I could get one of them on to it. Don't worry, Janey. We'll find her.'

We.

I wondered what Gretel would say if she knew that Murray was embroiling himself in a search for a wild-eyed, giggling girl-ghost when he was supposed to be playing golf with an overweight property lawyer named Brian.

'You know, it might be easier if you just tell Gretel about our Friday afternoons.'

'Look, Janey. After the Thomas train I explained to her about having tea at yours on a Friday. She accepted that gracefully, as I think I mentioned to you before.'

'And it only took a weekend in Paris and a Tiffany bracelet.'

'Exactly,' he said. 'But she wouldn't like it if she knew I was spending every Friday afternoon with you, Janey.' He gave a slight shudder. 'She really wouldn't like that at all.'

'No. That would seriously cost you.'

'Look!' shrieked Pip as we reached the top of the steps near the pond. He'd seen an old lady down at the water's edge, with three cocker spaniels straining at their leads.

'Stay close to Mummy,' I said. 'We don't talk to dogs unless we know them, remember?'

Murray cleared his throat. 'Oh yes, we're off to Dumfries first thing tomorrow. There's a litter of puppies for sale and we're going to take a look.'

'Puppies? Why?' Was Gretel in need of a fur coat?

'Well, I didn't want another dog so soon after Bailey. But Gretel thought Pip might like a puppy.'

Pip? Gretel had never shown the slightest interest in him. Now she was buying dogs for him?

'We had a long chat about it all, and Gretel's keen to be involved. She thinks she's ready to make the move. To set up home together.'

Oh brilliant.

'We've got our eye on a house in Morningside. A family house. Gretel's mother is on that side of town too, so it makes sense. She can keep a closer eye on her.'

And a closer eye on Murray, too.

'Gretel thought the Puppy might be something for her and Pip to . . . to bond over.' He winced slightly.

'Lovely.'

That's when I saw them, sitting on a large picnic rug on the grass to our right: Jody and Vichard, Molly and Cameron, Cleodie and Rose. Should I pretend I hadn't seen them? Too late, Jody was waving.

I walked over. 'Hi, everyone.'

'Hi!' said Molly, over-brightly.

'Hi Janey,' said Jody, stretching her face into a smile. 'We're having an inky-dinky picnic.'

'Just a complete spur of the moment thing,' said Molly. 'I made some cupcakes with Cam this morning and we made about a *million* too many.'

'Ah right,' I said nodding vigorously, as though there was clearly no option, in such circumstances, other than to have an emergency picnic. If they had neglected to invited me that was entirely understandable, in the drama of it all.

But – oh God – why should this *hurt*? I felt like I'd been

shoved back into primary six again, when I'd been the only one in the class not invited to Hilary Grogan's birthday party.

Molly reached into a Tupperware container and thrust three gloopy greenish cupcakes into my hands. 'Here, have some. They're courgette and buttermilk.'

I stood awkwardly, clutching the cupcakes. What was it about this woman and courgettes?

Cleodie budged up, all elbows and knees, flipping a Tupperware lid across the rug and knocking over Vichard's milk. 'Sit down here, Janey.'

I lowered myself and Pip into the space next to Cleodie and Rose, trying to avoid a splodge of green icing. Murray remained standing, grimly surveying the park like a secret service minder in his dark suit and overcoat.

'This is Murray,' I said, gesturing to him with my cupcake-filled hands. 'Pip's dad.'

'Dad,' said Rose. She looked shyly across at me and climbed onto my lap. Oh, she was gorgeous. I wanted to wrap my arms around her and squeeze, to lay my cheek against her warm little head.

Stop it, Janey.

Jody craned her head round to talk to Murray. 'So, you're a lawyer, I hear?'

'I'm at McKeith's,' said Murray, quietly, as though it was slightly embarrassing for Jody that she didn't already know.

'I nearly went into law,' she said, wrinkling her nose. 'Just as well I didn't, or I'd never have started my garden-design business.' She sighed, and hugged her knees into her chest. 'I mean, they say women can't have it all. But *I* have. Vichard comes to work with me every day – he just pootles around the gardens. He has his own little trowel and fork, and we're out there in the rain and shine, breathing the fresh air whatever the weather. It's so much better for him than any boring, stuffy old nursery, isn't it, my love?'

So we weren't mentioning the trip to A&E a few weeks ago when he'd shoved a yew berry up his nose. Or the three bouts of bronchitis last winter, each of which required hospitalisation. One of Jody's favourite conversational topics was how Vichard practically *lived* at Sick Kids.

Vichard certainly didn't look convinced about the benefits of his outdoor lifestyle. He stuck his thumb in his mouth and eyed his mother balefully.

'Oh, part-time working's the answer, for me,' said Molly, and launched into a monologue about her job, saving sick owls. We heard about the adopt-an-owl scheme she'd masterminded to help fund the sanctuary, and the joy of introducing recovered owls back into the wild. There were some downsides to the job too, such as the reams of paperwork that had to be filled in when a new owl was admitted.

'Proofreading's quite good too,' I piped up. 'I can do it when Pip's in bed.'

'You'll need a proper job, though, sooner or later, won't you?' said Jody. 'What did you do before Pip?'

'I was a legal secretary,' I said. 'And a PA to, er, to Murray.'

I glanced at him, but he was staring, solemn-faced, down towards the duck pond.

Molly looked excited, all of a sudden. 'Paul's looking for people. Isn't he, Jode?'

Jody stretched out her legs and yawned, as though it went without saying that *I* wasn't the sort of person he was looking for. 'Any more of those rice cakes left, Moll? I just can't stop eating today.'

'He *is*,' persisted Molly. 'He's setting up this charity. A music charity or something. He got a big bung of funding from somewhere and he's trying to get it off the ground. He's looking for administrator-type people. He's an actor, really, but that's on hold for the moment because the hours are so tricky and the income is so uncertain.'

'Well, I'm on benefits,' said Cleodie happily.

Jody and Molly froze, as though she'd announced she was an international heroin smuggler.

'I did my back in last year and had to leave my job. Hopefully when my novel's published I'll be self-supporting again. In the meantime, Rose's mum pays me cash in hand.'

Silence, except for the wind riffling through the trees behind us, and the sound of Cam's little teeth crunching on a carrot stick.

Jody just stared, as though she'd encountered a new species. Molly made a low owl noise by blowing into her cupped hands.

'Backs can be such a nuisance,' I said.

What a stupid thing to say, as though we'd be better off with our heads attached straight onto our legs, like the people who populated Pip's paintings.

But Cleodie winked at me.

Murray sighed audibly and looked at his watch.

I lifted Rose onto the rug, dropping just a tiny kiss on the top of her head, then rounded up my family – my almost-family – and took them home.

Janey

It had been a strange experience, reading Hattie's diary of that autumn term. It was as though those few months of my life had been excavated, cleaned and polished, and given back to me again in a little bright string of moments. We'd been so . . . not exactly happy perhaps, but *spirited*. I began to see how our friendship had kept the harsher realities of life at bay, whether that was Grandpa's death, my mother's indifference, or Hattie's family beginning to collapse in on itself.

But it couldn't do so forever. The time came when I realised that things were very wrong with Hattie. What she told me, during lunch break on one dank Friday afternoon in December, never faded in the years that followed; it stayed fresh and red, stamped into my mind.

We were supposed to be doing choir. The carol service was fast approaching and Miss Spylaw had been so horrified by last week's rendition of 'The Holly and the Ivy' – a complicated four-part arrangement that she'd composed herself – that she'd scheduled extra practice sessions. But Hattie had steered me firmly past the double doors of the school hall and out into the grounds.

★

She took a shuddery deep breath. 'I had to get out.'

'You don't look a hundred per cent,' I said, shaking my

head gravely. We used to love fussing over each other in this way, one of us coaxing the other to miss games or go to the nurse for a lie-down at the slightest excuse. But today she really didn't look well: her face was pinched and thin, her hair stringy and dull. She was probably coming down with a cold. I offered her a cherry Tune.

Arm in arm, we walked over to our secret place. Behind some trees, on a bank at the end of the hockey pitch, we had found an old school sign, abandoned on the mossy, crackly ground. We'd decided it was probably Victorian, or at least from another era, more resonant and mysterious than the 1980s. It was underneath this sign that we'd buried the Shapiro drop-box, although there'd been nothing worth hiding in there yet.

We sat down on a low stone wall that marked the school boundary at that point. There was a belt of trees beyond it, which we liked to imagine was the edge of a vast and ancient woodland. It probably would have been, in olden times, Hattie had assured me.

But now, she sat and stared at her shoes. 'Something's happened, Janey. At the house. I wouldn't normally tell anyone. But I know it's safe to tell you things. It's just like telling myself.'

'Was it the strange whooshing again?'

'I saw what it was, Janey,' she said, twisting her fingers. 'The whooshing thing, I mean. I got the feeling it was going to happen, just as I was reaching the first floor landing, and I swung right round, and I saw it. The black, fluttery thing was her hair. It was a woman, falling.'

'Falling?'

'Yes, through the gap in the middle of the stairs. She landed on the tiles. With a terrible sound.' Her voice tightened into a squeak.

'It's okay,' I said, not at all sure that it was.

'She's still there, Janey. Lying face down, with dark hair spread out all around her head. Her neck is at a funny angle to her body.' Her eyes darted under closed lids, as if she was seeing it in her mind.

'Sh-she's still there?' My heart was beating hard. 'Have you told your mum?'

'Mum doesn't seem to be able to see her.'

'Oh.' I should have been excited, reaching for the Dominic Shapiro book, arranging séances and vigils and marking things in notebooks. But it felt different this time, there was no 'oh well' shrug, no wide eyes to tell me she was relishing the drama, and that we were, on some level, playing a game. And now that I thought about it, the piano lid, taped shut, hadn't been a game. The music case jammed under the umbrella stand – as far away from Hattie's room as possible without actually being out of the house – hadn't been either. She'd done those things because she was terrified. Terrified of things that weren't even there.

A cold, leaden feeling settled around me. It felt like a dreadful worry that couldn't be solved – like when Grandpa was diagnosed with lung cancer. A sense that the only way out of this was through it, and that 'through it' would turn out to be an appalling place.

'What did your mum say?'

'When we were leaving for school I said casually, "Mum, what's that in the middle of the floor?" and she just glanced over her shoulder and gave me a blank look. "What's what?" she said. So I just left it. She's very angry with me, anyway,

118

because of not going to my piano lesson yesterday. I didn't want to push it.'

After break, she fretted silently through double maths, staring out the window and chewing the end of her ponytail. I made some notes on the back of my jotter, and I came up with three possible explanations:

1. The body was real, and Hattie's mum was lying.
2. The falling woman was a ghost.
3. Hattie was seeing things that weren't there, which meant that something was wrong with Hattie.

I felt a little better after that: I was unconcerned about the first two options, and there was only a one-in-three probability that the third was true.

After school we took the bus together to her house. Her hand trembled as she unlocked the black front door. I held on firmly to her arm as she pushed it open and we went inside.

There was nothing there, no body in the hallway. Hattie stood and stared at the floor, her mouth set into a grim line, as though it was half likely that something would materialise there.

Then she sat on the bottom stair, wrapped her arms around herself and began to cry.

'It's okay, Hattie. I'm here.' I patted her arm, a little desperately. 'D'you think it was real? Or could you have imagined it, because you're so stressed and everything? I mean, if your mum couldn't see it?'

She buried her head against my chest and sobbed, her body shaking in my arms.

Oh, Hattie.

I laid my cheek against her hair. She smelled of school, the fug of mince that had lingered in the dining hall that lunchtime, and the lemon soap they'd always used here at Regent's Crescent in the sparkling-white porcelain bathrooms. She smelled of laundry folded into warm, neat piles on the Aga when Mrs Patel had been ironing.

A sense of peace came then, so soft, so unexpected that I almost forgot to breathe. I didn't *need to know* any more. If she was mad, I would be mad too. If she was ill, neglected, haunted, lied to, or misunderstood, then I would be too. It didn't matter about probability, and options 1, 2 and 3. There were no options other than to stay there with her, clinging to her on that bottom step, one still point as the world tipped and spun around us.

When she stopped crying, she wiped her nose with her sleeve and took a pen out of her schoolbag. She'd just drawn an outline, on the black and white tiles, of where the corpse had lain, when her mother walked in.

★

And the next day, my world fell apart.

French had finished late – *quelle dommage!* – and Hattie and I had to queue up for our lunch, which was cold roast pork with roast potatoes. Mrs Peston, the teacher on lunch duty, had a go at Hattie because of her untidy ponytail – locks of dark hair had escaped, snaking down her back. Hattie, normally robust about being told off, seemed to shrink into herself. She looked thinner than she had even the day before, her shoulder blades sharp beneath the thin cotton of her blouse.

We sat down at one of the long wooden tables, a little way apart from the others. She was just staring down at the grey disc of meat on her plate, her bottom lip nudged out slightly.

'Hattie, what's the matter? Is it your mum? Was she angry about you drawing on the floor yesterday?'

'No. She didn't say anything about it.'

That was a relief. Renee had surveyed the hallway and suggested that maybe it was time for me to be getting home. She'd said it calmly, but something in her voice had made the skin on my back crawl.

'Well, that's good!'

'But I've got something to tell you.' And she closed her eyes.

My first thought was that she had cancer. That was what all the headaches and the being sick was about. It wasn't just old people like Grandpa who got it. A girl in our year was in hospital with leukaemia and I'd been thanking God, every night in my bed, that it wasn't Hattie. Maybe this was my punishment.

I put down my knife and fork. 'What?'

'I'm leaving. Mum's arranged for me to go to boarding school. At Ramplings.'

'But that's in England, isn't it? All the way down the bottom, near London?'

'Yes.'

'When?' Maybe she meant that she'd be going in a few years' time, for her GCSEs or her A levels or something. Or maybe it was like a finishing school, where you went after normal school to learn ballroom dancing and flower arranging.

'I'm leaving at the end of term, Janey.'

Panic coursed through me. I searched around for any chinks of light.

'But you'll still be here over Christmas.' I made it a statement, not a question. 'And Easter, and the summer holidays.' Nine long weeks.

121

She shook her head, and a single tear plopped down, onto the little slick of grease where her potatoes had slid across the plate.

'We're leaving as soon as term finishes. We're moving to Suffolk.'

It just wasn't possible. 'But why?'

'I don't know. She went on about making other friends. Being near James. Say something.'

Other friends? This couldn't be right. Hattie's mum *adored* me. Hattie's mum thought I was a treasure. Hattie's mum . . .

'Oh Janey, don't cry.'

Somewhere across the dining hall, somebody dropped a tray. Crockery and cutlery fell to the floor with a clatter. It wasn't the sort of school where everyone cheered if you dropped something, but there was a silence, punctuated by a few giggles, before the noise rose back to normal levels.

Normal. How could all these people go on as if nothing had happened, as if the world hadn't just cracked down its centre.

We pushed our plates to the side and held hands across the table, weeping until the hall emptied and one of the kitchen staff came past with a broom, whistling as he swept away the detritus of the busy lunch hour.

★

The next couple of weeks flew past with dizzying speed, crashing to a halt with the last day of term and the carol service that evening.

My nerves jumped in my stomach as I proceeded with the rest of the choir into the darkened cathedral. Because it just didn't make sense, her missing the last day of term like that.

I'd accidentally told her yesterday – it was impossible to keep secrets from Hattie – that I was planning to make a Victoria sponge, so that we could cut it in the form room at break and have a goodbye party for her. I'd brought in lemonade, too, and paper plates and cups from Woolworths, and an oversized card saying 'We'll Miss You!', and these items had wiped out nearly all my pocket money. I only had five pounds left now to buy all my Christmas presents.

And then there was the box, that box with all her stuff that gave me such a funny feeling when I saw it. I needed to ask her about that tonight, because she'd be coming, surely. Even if she'd been too busy to come to school, packing up her room, maybe, or getting measured for her new Ramplings uniform, she wouldn't want to miss 'The Holly and the Ivy', not when I was the understudy, with a real possibility of singing it, on account of Sarah Lyon-Darcy having just recovered from tonsillitis. Not when she knew there'd be no one else to bother about it, what with Granny being at the bridge club Christmas drinks.

We had to walk very slowly, in step behind the tall sixth former who was singing the first verse solo of 'Once in Royal David's City'. In theory, this should have given me plenty of time to scan the faces in the rows of pews. But it was dark in the cathedral, and my candle flame swooshed and leapt in front of my eyes, leaving a burning afterglow that made it impossible to see into the shadows.

Nine Lessons and Carols, but it seemed like a hundred or more. There was no last-minute collapse by Sarah Lyon-Darcy. The phrasing I'd practised so carefully, the knife-sharp diction – thee Holleee anD thee Iveeee – was surplus to requirements. I didn't care. I longed only for the whole thing to be over so I could look for Hattie. And even after the minister had dismissed us, we had to stay in our places for an age, singing some Bach thing until the cathedral emptied.

I thought I saw her then, a smaller figure in a group of upper-fifths, her white face bobbing in and out of view as they filed out of the pews and mingled with the people crowding the aisle.

The moment Miss Spylaw nodded and put down her baton, I squeezed past the others and ran out, out, out: past the enormous Christmas tree in the vestibule, down the stone steps, onto the street.

Groups of parents were standing around chatting to one another, waiting under golf umbrellas for their daughters to appear. Some families, already reunited, were scurrying off to their cars.

The noise of the chatter against the rain and the traffic seemed to fill my head, and my vision lurched as I turned this way and that, trying to catch sight of her. Cars zoomed past, one after another after another, swooshing on the wet road, and a taxi pulled up at the pavement, rain glittering in its headlights.

Courage flooded through me, warm and strong and shocking. I opened the taxi door and got in, feeling in my pocket for my last five-pound note.

*

Regent's Crescent, so wide and impressive in the daytime, was gloomy in the dark and wet, only dimly illuminated by the pale globes of the Georgian street lamps.

Most of the houses had Christmas trees in their windows,

with multicoloured lights, and extravagant displays of tinsel and baubles. I felt a surge of envy: Granny's lights had been broken since 1985 when I'd twisted them too enthusiastically back into their box, and our tinsel was threadbare and, frankly, embarrassing.

At the Marlowes' house, the chandelier in the drawing room was lit, bright against the high white walls and corniced ceiling, but there was no tree in evidence. Why would there be, when they were leaving before Christmas?

My heart contracted for Hattie. She loved decorating the tree. Last year she'd spent a full ten minutes gazing at a blue-green glass bauble, and the way it captured the light, until Renee had come in and told us to get on with it.

I rang the doorbell.

No answer. I stepped back and looked up.

There was a quick dark flash at the drawing room window before the curtains were pulled across.

I waited. Rang the bell again.

Perhaps it wasn't working. Or maybe Renee was simply in one of her moods, and didn't want Hattie to be distracted from her packing. Either way, repeated ringing seemed unlikely to get me anywhere.

So I resolved to sneak into their back garden. It was a simple matter, I told myself, of finding the little close at the end of the terrace, with the steps that led to the private communal gardens behind the house – more like a private forest – and climbing over the garden wall. Hattie and I had spent hours exploring the area on long summer evenings, skittering along earthy paths gnarled with tree roots, jumping softly over walls like a couple of young cats. But doing it on my own on a black December night, with just the light from the back windows of the terrace, was a rather different proposition. By the time I dropped onto the flowerbed at the top of their garden I felt like the unfortunate man in 'Rapunzel', stealing cabbages, about to bring down some dreadful judgement upon myself.

I crept right up to the patio by the basement kitchen window. The light was on, pooling on the large wooden table where dinner was set for two, with a bowl of salad at each place setting and a quiche on a board in the middle. Oh joy! Hattie would be coming down soon to eat her dinner, and I'd be able to signal to her to let me in.

I knelt there for ages, the cold of the flagstones numbing my knees, waiting for her to come. But in the end, Renee came in alone, pushed the meal to one side, and sat, head in her hands.

I lifted my hand, poised to tap on the window. I'd explain that the doorbell wasn't working, and she'd call Hattie down. Or better still, I could persuade her she was wrong about moving away. It was ridiculous, for so many reasons, not least *me*. I was practically family. They couldn't leave me behind. I could talk to Renee, woman to woman, and make her see. I began to rehearse the words in my mind.

But my hand stayed where it was. That inch of space between my knuckles and the glass could have been a thousand miles. The long hand on the kitchen clock inched on towards the half hour.

Eight thirty? Granny would be livid. I was building myself up to scale the wall again and go home when Renee stood up. She unhooked a coat from the back of the door and felt in the pocket for her keys.

126

21

Janey

Pip shrank against me in horror as I tried to move him towards the fish counter. I'd been reading yet another article about making children eat. The notion of involving reluctant eaters in the preparation of food was now old news. This article said you had to go further and get them engaged with the sourcing of seasonal, local produce. It had recommended getting up early and going to visit a fish market at dawn, and afterwards make a wall display with photographs and recipes with hand-drawn pictures. I'd compromised with a visit to the fishmongers at Bruntsfield after nursery, and a recipe cut out of the Sainsbury's magazine. We were going to try making our own fish fingers, as I'd explained to a sceptical Pip.

'Let's just have a look.' I bent down towards the counter, holding Pip's hand. 'Ooh look at that big one.' A monstrosity with enormous bulging eyes and a mouthful of piranha-like teeth gazed out dully from behind the glass. I was surprised to read the sign saying it was only a monkfish.

Pip peered closer, a look of fascination coming over him sure enough.

'Where fish fingers?' Seemingly in reply, one of the lobsters lifted a nasty-looking pincer. Pip screamed, and clung to my hips, lifting his feet off the ground like a monkey trying to wrap itself round a tree trunk. I felt my jeans slipping down – I'd lost a bit of weight during the last few weeks.

'Pip, it's okay. Come on, let's have another look.' I scanned the counter for anything that didn't have pincers or eyes. 'There's a nice piece of haddock there.'

'Birds Eye! Birds Eye!' wailed Pip.

There was a loud sigh from an old lady behind us in the queue, which was now reaching out of the door. A smart yummy-mummy type glanced at her watch.

With one hand on the back waistband of my jeans, and one trying to stop Pip falling off me, I whispered an apology to the fishmonger, in his white rubber apron, and waddled out of the shop.

'I'm *hungry*,' sobbed Pip as we struggled along the pavement towards the bus stop, him dragging off my arm now. My heart sank. Pip's fussiness meant that eating out was impossible: even a sandwich at Starbucks was out of the question. Unless . . . the day wasn't that cold, and there was a Tesco Metro across the street. We went in and I bought a loaf of white bread, a jar of strawberry jam, a packet of forty paper plates, and picked up a little plastic spoon that would have to serve as a knife.

'Want to have a picnic at the playpark, Pippy?'

I knew there was a playpark in a nearby side street, because it was opposite Miss Fortune's flat.

Pip sat beside me on the bench, swinging his legs as I prepared his sandwich, sighing with relief as he sank his little white teeth into the soft, spongy bread.

I stared up at the tenement across the road, a four-storey wall of stone stretching the length of the street, its windows like rows of eyes.

Behind the net curtains, in Miss Fortune's flat, someone was moving around.

I felt a strange little tug in my chest area, and became aware of my pulse quickening slightly. The pull intensified as Pip finished his sandwich and put his sticky hand in mine, leading me towards the slide. By the time we left the playpark, clanging the red metal gate shut behind us, I'd made up my mind.

'Ah'm jus' wunn o' the carers,' announced the large woman with the plastic apron who opened the door. 'Mabel. If yous're lookin' for Esme she's in there.' She gestured towards the living room.

Esme? Miss Fortune wouldn't have liked the informality of first names. And a carer?

Pip had tensed as soon as we'd crossed the threshold – the musty smell, perhaps, or the oppressive atmosphere in the narrow hallway with its wine-coloured carpet and dark wood sideboard. Now he gripped my hand tightly with both of his as we proceeded into the living room. I looked straight ahead, avoiding glancing at the doors into the kitchen and bathroom.

The thing that had been Miss Fortune sat slumped in an armchair, eyes fixed forwards and downwards, almost but not quite in the direction of the small television in the corner which was showing *Cash in the Attic* at nearly full volume.

It was the same flower-patterned, wing-backed chair that she used to sit on, eyes closed, during our listening sessions. Then, she'd sat straight, chin lifted, as though she could actually smell the music curling through the air like smoke. Now, her head lolled to the side, and her arms trailed listlessly along the arms of the chair. Her right hand – the withered one – looked the same as always. Her left had seized into an arthritic claw.

I stood in front of her, feeling like an awkward twelve-year-old again.

'Hello, Miss Fortune. I'm Janey Johnston. Do you remember

129

me? You used to teach me piano. And you taught my friend, Hattie Marlowe, too. It was back in the eighties.'

As if she'd forget.

'I was wondering if you knew anything about where the Marlowes had . . . Oh Pip, no!'

He'd toddled over to the Steinway, and was pulling himself up onto the piano stool.

Not there, not there.

As I crossed the room it seemed to ripple, as though I was underwater.

'No no, darling.'

He wriggled off the stool and away from me, and tried to slide his fingers under the piano lid.

I drew his fingers away and kissed them, lifted him, and turned back to Miss Fortune again.

'Do you mind if I turn this off for a sec?' I waited politely for a response that I knew wouldn't come, then lifted the remote from the wheeled invalid table that stood by her chair, and silenced *Cash in the Attic.*

'I just wondered if you had any idea where the Marlowes went, after they left. Or if you'd heard anything about them recently. I know you had connections at Ramplings.'

Oh, it was hopeless. As if they'd have been exchanging Christmas cards all this time. It was utterly ridiculous. And in any case, there wasn't even a flicker behind those eyes.

From the primary school up the road, a bell rang, and the sounds of children shouting and laughing drifted over. Pip turned his head toward the bay window.

'She has good days an' bad days,' said Mabel, waddling into the room with a disgusting-looking meal – shepherd's pie, perhaps – in a foil tray.

She placed the meal on the table and wheeled it round towards Miss Fortune's knees.

'There you go, luv,' she wheezed, her face red with the effort of leaning down.

'Does she ever, you know, communicate? At all?'

'Some days she's more compus mentus, like. It depends on her medications an' that.'

'I think we'll get going,' I said, setting Pip back down on his feet.

'Right you are.' Mabel didn't seem fazed by the shortness of our visit.

Just as we were leaving the room, I swung round and said, 'Do you know how to use the record player? It's just that she loves music.'

I moved over to the bookshelf where all the records were. Pip followed, his finger looped into one of the belt hooks on my jeans.

'This one,' I said, holding it out. 'She'd love this.' Chopin.

Mabel gave it a suspicious look and slapped it down on the arm of the sofa.

'Aye, right then, I s'pose. I'm only meant to get her washed and fed, mind.'

'Here, I'll show you how.' I switched on the power, placed the record on the turntable and carefully lowered the needle.

The opening chords spilled out of the machine into the room: Nocturne in C-sharp minor, the posthumously published one. I'd forgotten, at some point over the years, that it was almost unbearable to listen to.

Mabel gave a slow, disdainful sniff and crossed her arms over her bulging middle.

'I'll see you out then,' she said.

We'd reached the door to the hall when a voice rang out behind us.

'Practise the Mazurka on page seven, my dear.'

'Will do, my sweet,' sang Mabel in a conciliatory tone, not bothering to turn round.

But I stopped, overwhelmed suddenly with a sense that Hattie – my beloved Hattie – was in the room behind me, watching me leave.

I went back in, and knelt down on the rug in front of Miss Fortune, watching carefully.

'Miss Fortune?' It came out as a whisper.

'Mu-mmeeee,' whined Pip, tugging at my coat.

Her eyes shot wide open. I started, jerked back. But it wasn't me she was looking at.

She made a noise – halfway between a groan and a word.

'What? Sorry, what was that? I didn't quite catch . . .'

The eyes stayed fixed on Pip, unblinking. All the hairs down my arms stood on end.

'It's Janey Johnston here, Miss Fortune. Do you remember me?'

And then they closed, like shutters going down. Or a switch going off.

'Come *on*, Mummy,' demanded Pip.

'Did you hear what she said?' I asked Mabel.

'It sounded like "Janey". That was your name, wasn't it, luv?'

'Yes . . .'

'Ye're not lookin' too well. Ye've gone awfie white.'

★

As I sat with my arm round Pip, jolting homewards on the top deck of the bus, it occurred to me that I didn't know what was worse: the notion that the Miss Fortune I'd known was still in there somewhere, trapped in a decaying body, or that there was nothing left of her at all, just a tangle of dying neurons firing in the dark.

But there had been something – a change in her – after the Chopin had come on, ringing through the dead air of the room. I'd seen it as I crouched before her.

Her left arm had lain on the arm of the chair as before, but her thumb and forefinger were held together, moving incrementally, keeping perfect 4/4 time.

22

Janey

I don't know what made me go to St Katherine's. It was trespassing, really. But when I walked past the back gates, on the way home from dropping Pip at nursery, I saw a couple of mums trundling buggies along the path round the playing fields, no doubt heading back from dropping their older children off. So I thought I wouldn't be noticed.

I made for our 'secret place', moving quickly along the sidelines of the hockey pitch and up the bank of trees. The old school sign was still there, weathered and rotting at one end where the wood had split. I lifted it and heaved it over to the side. A few woodlice scurried away, and a millipede wriggled on its back. Hattie's red cash box was still there in its hollow, with the key attached on a bit of string. Dominic Shapiro would have been shocked by such lax security. My fingers trembled as I wiggled the key in the lock.

It was empty, of course. I lifted the box – so very cold from being in the earth for so long – and cradled it into my chest.

★

'What's the matter with her?' said a thin little voice.

I jerked upright. How long had I been sitting there on the ground?

Two young girls, about eleven, stood before me. I wiped my wet face with the back of my hand – a muddy hand, as I realised too late.

'Come on,' said one of the girls, holding out a confident hand. 'You don't look very well. We'll take you to the nurse.'

They stood either side of me, one blonde and one redhead, each firmly holding an arm, and they marched me into the building, past the assembly hall, and the maths and English classrooms, into the medical room. I let myself be led, a child again, with a muddy face. I was beyond embarrassment.

It couldn't be, after all these years . . . Yes, it *was* Mrs Potts, sitting at her desk with her navy uniform, with white bands on the sleeves.

'Oh my Lord!' She stood up and came towards me. 'It's Janey Johnston, isn't it? My goodness, girl. You haven't changed one iota in . . . I don't even want to think about how long!'

It was a strange feeling to be recognised. To meet somebody who'd known me as a girl.

'She's not well, Mrs Potts,' announced the blonde girl.

'I'm fine,' I said. 'Just feeling a bit light-headed. I should be going . . .'

'Stay for a wee minute first. I don't want you keeling over in the corridor! Thank you, girls. Off you go.'

'Thanks,' I called after them, but they'd disappeared in a flurry of chatter and quick footsteps.

'Come through here and sit down.' Mrs Potts led me through to the side room with the cot. 'I'll get you a drink of water.'

And when she'd come back with the white plastic cup: 'What brings you here, Janey?'

I looked round the little room. And suddenly, it was deluged in red: the sheets of the cot sopping with blood, splashes of it on the floor, frantic footprints smudged on the lino tiles.

I wasn't well, that was all. The room was darkening to black.

'I think I'm going to be sick.'

She pursed her lips and reached into a cupboard for a grey cardboard basin.

'Sorry,' I said, when the nausea had passed. 'I should go. I just came here for a stroll along memory lane.'

Mrs Potts eyed me thoughtfully, perhaps wondering what part of that stroll had involved quite so much mud.

'Could I?' I nodded towards the wash basin.

'Oh, yes, yes. You get yourself sorted out, dear.'

'I shouldn't have come,' I said, wiping the mud off my face. 'It was an impulse thing.'

Mrs Potts's face, which I could see reflected in the mirror, was all calmness and understanding.

'It's your old school, Janey. You're always welcome here.'

'My friend Hattie. You might remember her. Hattie Marlowe. The thing is, I've been trying to get in touch with her again. I just can't seem to get any news of her.'

I tried to make my voice light and casual, as though getting the mud out from behind my fingernails was my main priority and definitely not tracking down a lost girl. But my heart was beating fast. It was just possible that Mrs Potts had access to alumnae records, perhaps just one click away, on the computer on her desk.

'I remember Hattie very well. Such a lovely girl. And what about you? What've you been up to? You went off to . . . let me see, was it one of the music schools?'

'Er, no,' I said quickly. 'It didn't really work out. I trained as

136

a legal secretary. I did that for quite a few years and I enjoyed it a lot. But now I've got a little boy. Pip. He's two.'

Ever so gently, she smiled.

'Well now. How about that. Things have a way of working out at the end of the day.'

Something wrenched inside me. If I let her go on like this I'd start crying again.

I dried my hands carefully on a scratchy blue paper towel and turned round to face her. 'Well, I'd really better go. I feel a lot better now. Honestly.'

As I was heading towards the door, she touched my arm.

'Do you know, a friend of mine is looking to buy a new flat.'

What was she on about?

'She went to view one the other day, in a very smart apartment block not far from here. She said it was very nice. What was it called again?' She tutted softly. 'Oh yes, Sutcliffe Heights. I'm sure it was that. Sutcliffe Heights.'

She shot me a meaningful look.

'Really?'

'Yes. You'll see the for sale sign up if you pass it. I'd say it was definitely worth a viewing, if you were looking for somebody. I mean, something. If you were looking for a new flat.'

'Oh,' I murmured.

'Anyway, dear. It was lovely to see you. Do take care. And come back and visit when you're feeling better. We'll get a couple of girls to take you on a proper tour. That would be fun, wouldn't it?'

I turned and enfolded her in a hug, gratitude transcending my awkwardness for a second. Then I hurried away before the spell could be broken.

23

Janey

Sutcliffe Heights. It was the penthouse that was for sale.

A woman opened the door. Petite, with neat curves swathed in black trousers and tunic, big eyes with dark lashes. A pointy chin like a little girl's.

The dark-toffee highlights threw me for a moment. And the nose looked different: the little bump near the top was gone.

'Hat – Hattie? Hattie.' The words teetered between a question and a statement.

She blinked. She had traces of crows' feet, just soft ones, which lifted in the moment that her eyes widened. Stepping forward, she held out her arms. She'd always been a toucher.

'Holy moly. Just give me a heart attack, why don't you? Janey Johnston! Janey-Janey-Johnston! Come here right now!' She squealed as I stepped into her embrace.

She released me, then took hold of my hand and dragged me inside, across a vast expanse of dark wood flooring into the living room. I felt tall, ungainly, walking behind her. Curves? Since when had Hattie had curves? But then again, I hadn't seen her since we were twelve, our bodies straight up and down.

'What the hell have you been up to, Janey-Janey-Johnston? Come right in here. I'm not letting you *move* from this couch' – she pushed me down into it and plonked herself next to me – 'until you tell me *everything*.'

I gave a nervous laugh. 'You're not an easy girl to track down, you know.'

She blinked, still smiling.

'I wrote to you,' I went on, hearing a shake in my voice now. 'At Ramplings, after you left. Time after time.'

Where did that come from? Sitting there, on her plush sofa, in her beautiful flat, I was horrified to find I wanted to hit and shake her.

She stretched her hands out on her lap, staring at them. They were small and perfect, the nails painted a clear coral pink.

'Letters? Did I get them? No. And it seems you never got mine, either. That'll be down to Mother Dearest, no doubt, and her henchmen at Ramplings. I should have known. She did the same thing to James.' She shook her head and assumed a sad expression for a second or two before her face brightened. 'But what have you been up to? What are you doing these days? Did you become a horse physiotherapist, like you wanted?'

A memory flashed into my mind: a wet break spent in a corner of the careers library with Hattie, finding the most outlandish fact sheets we could, and daring each other to ask solemn-faced Miss Hatton to photocopy them. Hattie cracked up when she handed over 'Sewage Process Plant Operator' and we both got a disorder mark.

'Er . . .' I tried to focus my thoughts. 'No. I trained as a legal secretary. But I'm doing proofreading at the moment.'

'Married?'

For some reason, I wanted to tell her that I'd *almost* married someone once, that I'd gone out with Simon, a pale, thin physics PhD student and practising Christian, for nearly five years. We'd even had sex once, befuddled by Cava, on the night he proposed. But he was married to a girl called Ruth now, with three daughters, and twins on the way. Or so he'd said in his last Christmas card.

'No. But I've got a little boy. Pip. He's two years old.'

'Oh!' she whispered. 'A little boy. When on earth do you find time to do your proofreading, then?'

'He goes to nursery a few mornings a week. Little Goslings Nursery actually.'

'Awww,' said Hattie, because it was the nursery where we had met as toddlers, before we could even remember. James had been a Little Goslings child too. There'd been a photo of him in a teddy bear jumper, lined up with his nursery class, on the wall of the Regent's Crescent kitchen.

'And how's the family? I was sorry to hear about your dad.'

'Yeah, thanks. Mum's still in New York. James is an investment banker, drowning in more money than he knows what to do with. He lives in Maidenhead with Simone, his wife. She's—'

'And what about you?'

'Me? Mostly, I've just been toiling away. Building up my business.'

'Oh? What kind of business?'

'Luxury skin clinics,' she laughed, getting up and heading to the ice-white bank of units that was the kitchen. 'Want a drink? Tea? Coffee? Vino?'

'Oh, something cold, thanks. Water's fine.'

'Right-oh.' She turned on the tap and splashed some into a purple-tinted glass, soaking the granite surround. She kept talking, while she reached into the fridge and poured a glass of white wine for herself. 'I did loads of things in my twenties, and I was in nursing for a while, but then I fancied something a bit different. So I got myself trained up in medical aesthetics and it just went from there. We started in London and Bristol, but now we're up here too! We opened one in Stockbridge six months ago. Botox, dermal fillers, acid peels. All that malarkey.'

I tried not to look too bewildered. This just didn't sound like Hattie at all.

'Who's "we"?' I asked.

'Oh, my business partner Ernie. We were married actually! Hence the name change. Should've made him change his name to mine, really. The Marlowe Clinic would've sounded a lot better than The Wilson Clinic. Ah well, you live and learn. The divorce was completely amicable, we're still fabulous as business partners. He runs the London side of things.'

She slid onto the sofa beside me, folding her legs underneath her, and launched into a long monologue about the Edinburgh clinic: the new leather chairs she'd sourced from Italy, the high-profile clients whose visits were shrouded in secrecy, the clients who were on benefits but came regularly for their injections.

'It sounds great,' I said. 'I've been wondering what you were up to.'

'Well, here I am.'

'Yes,' I murmured. 'Here you are. But you're moving?'

'Ooh. Yes. I should probably take that sign down now. We concluded missives on this place weeks ago, and I'm moving out on Monday!'

'Where are you going?'

'Well, that's a real bugger. I'd found this fabulous double

upper in Eglinton Crescent, but the sale's fallen through. So, ha! You're going to love this! Guess where I'll be staying till I find something?'

'Where?' Surely not.

'Only the Regent's Crescent house! Woo-hooo!' She made a ghostly sound and wiggled her fingers. 'Oh, it's a bit of a bind but it saves me having to rent somewhere. Mum's keen on the idea, because she's coming back from the States later in the year. She's involved in planning a big retrospective thingy for what would have been Dad's seventieth. She wants me to oversee some work that's getting done, decorating the hall and so on. It's a mess. Nobody's been looking after it since Mrs Patel died and the last tenants left.'

I sat back, stunned.

'I'm going there on Monday to pick up a spare set of keys for the workmen.'

Drawing in a silent, deep breath, I let my gaze drift across to the big picture window, and its view over to the Pentland Hills in the distance. The tops were dusted with white and I suddenly wished I was up there walking, breathing the sharp clean air.

'I know,' she gushed. 'Fab view, isn't it?'

I gave the most cheerful smile I could muster. The last twenty minutes had shown that this wasn't my Hattie. My Hattie, the one I'd been longing for all these years, was only a ghost in my imagination. I was glad that the woman I'd found seemed happy and healthy, but as the conversation had progressed, I'd been preparing myself for the faux-friendly parting of ways and disingenuous promises to keep in touch: '*Bye, it was so lovely to catch up. Let's meet up for a coffee soon.*'

But now, some long-forgotten version of myself stepped up

in my mind, and stood stoutly, arms crossed, between me and that casual goodbye. Because the sleek, elegant woman beside me had once been my Hattie, with her socks fallen down and her ponytail hanging askew, and there was no way she was going back into that appalling house by herself.

'If you really must go there, I'm coming with you.' And for once, I spoke in a voice that brooked no argument.

Hattie

Janey is back. I knew it would happen one day, and now it has. Although it hardly seems real, that she was here just this afternoon sitting on my sofa, in her trailing skirt and moss-green cardigan, working the ends of her sleeves with her fingers. Nervous fingers. She always had nervous fingers.

And *excavating* me. With those stubborn grey eyes. Trying to work out what I'd turned into.

It seems that she's a single mother, and a lapsed legal secretary. She looked pretty gloomy about it, to have lost her career, so I tried to lighten her up by talking about the clinic.

The thing is this. If I let Janey in again, what else will come in along with her?

I can feel it now, as I lie here. I felt it the moment I saw her, a staticky feeling at the tips of my fingers. A zing through my brain.

She wants to come to Regent's Crescent. I said yes, because it was hard to resist. But I don't want to see her kid, this Pip she talks about. She can come with me on Monday and we can have a cup of tea, and laugh about the teachers at St Katherine's, or whatever. But then, that's it. It'll be a little bright spot, a little sweet spot, and then everything will go back to how it was before.

Time for a glass of wine. I'll put on some music. One of those

143

chill-out albums. As banal as possible! I need to do my nails again before tomorrow, and top up the gradual tan. Nobody wants a beautician who doesn't look the part, but it never ends. It's like painting the Forth Bloody Bridge, I swear it. As soon as you've got everything looking presentable, something else starts peeling or flaking or just generally looking crap and you have to start all over again.

24

Janey

How strange that the flat should radiate *home* so much more when Murray stepped in the door. I'd worked hard to make it comfortable for me and Pip, with nice food in the cupboards, deep carpets and pale-cream walls that softened the light. But still, a certain uneasiness lingered in the shadowy corners of the rooms, and in the way Pip's small voice and mine seemed to disappear into the high-ceilinged spaces above us if the TV wasn't on. When Murray came in – throwing his coat across the hall table, asking if the kettle was on – he dispelled that unease as though the lights had come up on a cosy sitcom.

'Doughnuts!' he exclaimed, when he saw the box on the kitchen table. Pip had chosen them in Greggs that morning, his fingertips held lightly to his chin as he contemplated the cakes in the glass cabinet for a full five minutes. 'How did you know they were my favourite? And all six for me? Fantastic.' Murray reached out both hands to grab the lot.

'Noooooo!' shouted Pip, lunging forward.

Murray's mobile rang, and he stepped away. Pip grabbed the doughnut box off the table, sending the contents bouncing onto the floor. He reached down and picked up two, clasping them protectively against his chest.

'Gretel! Hi!' Murray shot me a glance, holding up one finger to silence me. 'What, the guarantors on Project Ferrera? No. Absolutely not. The heads of terms are quite clear.'

I had a sudden flash of twelve-year-old Hattie, in fits of giggles over my Ferrero Rocher mistake. It was funny how I still thought of her as the 'real' one, despite yesterday's encounter.

Pip banged his head off my legs to remind me he was still there, and I crouched down in front of him, feeling sugar crunch under my feet. 'Want to try one?' I released one of the squashed doughnuts and took a bite. 'Mmmmmm. Yummy.'

But why was I whispering? Why should I play along with the Gretel game and become invisible like some thirty-something Soren Lorensen? Was I so in awe of this Ferrera deal, whatever it was, that I shouldn't make a noise in my own kitchen? The old Hattie would've had something to say about that. So would the old me, for that matter. I gave Pip a little tickle under the ribs.

He gave a long screech like a rainforest parrot.

'What? Oh, that's just Brian. He's just hit the ball into the, er, pond.'

He frowned and shook his head.

'Yes. He's not having a great round.'

He nodded, half-consciously, towards me, as though I was the balding, overweight Brian.

I pressed my jaw down towards my neck and frowned, trying to re-create Brian's jowly appearance. Pip copied: a mini-Brian.

'Yup. I'll be home around eight. Do you want me to pick anything up for dinner? Oh, okay. Samphire.'

Bitch.

I took a wooden spoon in both hands and swung it wildly at one of the fallen doughnuts, imitating Brian's legendary poor swing.

Murray's face creased and his voice broke up with the effort of trying not to laugh.

'Yep. Have to go. Bye.'

He shook his head as he stowed his phone in his pocket, trying to signal that he was above my juvenile antics.

'Stay,' I said, as bold as I'd ever been with him. 'Don't go home for eight. Don't get the flipping samphire.'

'I have to,' he said. 'And talking of Gretel, we need to have a word.'

'What?' I said, leaving Pip to his doughnuts and propelling Murray into the hall with a daring hand on his back.

'We got the keys to the new house yesterday,' he said. 'Honestly, you'll love it. It's a Victorian villa in Morningside, with a big sunny bedroom for Pip, and a magnificent garden for Trixie.'

Ah, so the blasted puppy had arrived.

'Pip's going to love Trixie,' he went on in deep, confident tones, as though this was so obvious it hardly needed to be stated. 'She's so great with kids.'

I let an awkward silence fall.

'In fact, we're very keen for Pip to see the house, and we were hoping that he could come to stay for a night. Next Saturday.'

Every instinct flipped onto red alert. Pip, go and stay by himself in some house in Morningside that I'd never seen before, which might not even have stair gates or socket covers, with some unknown dog rampaging around the magnificent garden?

Breathe.

'Pip's too young for sleepovers. He'd get upset without me.'

'Please, Janey. Gretel really wants to be involved. In time,' he went on, 'we'd like Pip to think of the Morningside house as a home from home.'

I thought I might vomit.

'Has Trixie been fully vaccinated?'

Murray gave me a hard stare. 'Janey, please be reasonable about this. This house, we've bought it with Pip in mind. It's not as if we're going to have any other kids.'

I shrugged. Not my fault if Gretel had never bothered to take time out of her schedule to have children.

'She couldn't have any, Janey,' said Murray as though he'd read my mind. 'She tried with her ex-husband for years but she had some kind of problem.' He winced, clearly uncomfortable with the way the conversation was steering into gynaecological territory. 'So just, *please*. Please don't be difficult.'

There was a hint of warning in his voice. The unspoken message was all too clear. *Because Gretel can be very, very difficult indeed.*

25

Janey

Hattie was late. Pip had found a way to amuse himself by climbing up and down the front steps, and peering down through the railings into the little basement yard below, which was half in sunshine and half in shadow. The windows were dark, grimy on the outside, impenetrable.

'You'll get your head stuck, silly.' I gently pulled him back so his head was clear, but he clung to the railings and swung back on his heels, letting his hands take the weight of his body.

With a clatter of heels, Hattie appeared.

'Hello! Is this Pip? I didn't know you'd be bringing him!' She bent down and held out a hand to shake his. He glanced up at me, unsure what to do.

I ruffled his hair, and stroked it back into place. 'Pip, this is Mummy's friend, Hattie.'

Pip turned and buried his face in my skirt.

'Right!' she said, with a mischievous flick of an eyebrow. 'Here goes. Are you up for this, Janey? Ready to confront the dark side?' She turned the key in the lock of the big black door.

I lifted Pip and held him close to my chest as Hattie opened the door. There was a sweeping sound as a pile of letters and junk mail was pushed aside. The air smelled of damp stone.

'So far, so gooooood,' said Hattie, her voice sliding up as she unlocked the inner glass door.

We walked through the vestibule into the main hall, our boots mussing the fine film of dust on the chessboard tiles. To the left, doors opened onto vast, half-remembered formal rooms. To the right was the staircase, its ornate black banister coiling up to the first floor landing, and then on up to the second, far above. The cupola stared down like a great eye.

'Shall we go downstairs?' The basement kitchen had always been the least daunting room, with its worn wooden table, and the toasty smell of laundry warming on the Aga.

'Brrr,' said Hattie. 'I'll need to get that thing fired up if I'm going to move in. It's Baltic in here.'

Pip clutched at my coat as I carried him across the room and scrambled his feet against me as I tried to set him down.

'It's okay, Pippy-pips,' I whispered, stroking a strand of hair back from his forehead.

'Tea?' said Hattie.

She filled the kettle while I rinsed dust off a couple of mugs and unpacked the Sainsbury's bag I'd brought with me, containing tea bags, sugar, a small carton of milk and some biscuits, and a small Tupperware box of cars for Pip to play with.

'Custard creams, Janey? Very 1980s.'

They were the biscuits Miss Fortune had always had, of course. I'd bought them as a tentative joke, wondering whether Hattie would pick up the reference.

We'd sat down at the table, with Pip playing on the rug with his cars, when I decided to take the plunge.

'What do you really think happened, back then? All those strange things.'

She didn't stiffen exactly, but there was a tiny pause in her stirring of the tea, a silence before the chink of the spoon against the mug resumed.

'Oh crikey, Janey. What a pair we were!' she smiled, chin pointed downwards, looking at me through her lashes. 'What was it, some malarkey about my music case?'

Some malarkey?

'And the falling woman.'

'Just a ruse to wind up my mother, wasn't it? I didn't want to get packed off to boarding school, wasn't that it?' She shrugged prettily. 'Anyway, we should take a look around upstairs. Mum wants me to make a note of anything that needs touched up while the decorators are here.'

She brought out a notepad, which sent a twinge through me. She and I, creeping around the house, making notes of the manifestations, crouching at a certain bend in the stairs, creeping behind the piano, our ears pressed to the wood to listen for scratchings (mice?), creaking or, once – we'd been convinced – a *sigh* that sounded like it was coming from the depths of the wood itself.

'Do you get any sort of *feeling* being back here?'

'Feeling? Oh come on, Janey, you're trying to wind me up and it *won't work*! What do you think we should do, go round the house with this notebook, and make notes of anything strange? Draw pictures of the little black marks on the skirting board, perhaps?'

So she did remember.

'Hey, Toots, what's up?'

Pip had stopped playing and was staring past us – through us – over towards the window, eyes fixed on something, something at his level, or just a bit higher. A smile on his face,

151

totally unselfconscious, caught in a moment of surprised pleasure.

'What's up, darling?'

'Dend,' said Pip, turning his smile onto me. He raised a stubby finger and pointed towards the window.

Hattie rubbed her forehead, briskly, with the back of her hand.

'You okay?'

'Headache,' she said. 'Come on, shall we do the upstairs quickly and then get moving?'

But by the time we were halfway up the basement stairs, she seemed to have changed her mind about seeing the rest of the house. I could sense it in her, a trajectory of intention towards the front door.

'You're right, I'll come back and do the rest another day,' she said, once we were at the top, seeming to agree to a suggestion I hadn't made.

'Yes, best get home if you've got a bad headache.'

Pip twisted round in my arms and looked up the stairs. He pointed, kicking me in the groin with a hard little boot. 'Don't my dend?'

'Not today, my love,' I soothed.

'Right,' said Hattie after we'd exited. '*So* lovely to see you again. Let's do coffee some time!' She blew an air kiss that reminded me of my mother and off she went, heels echoing down the empty street.

26

Janey

When term started again in January, I went back to Miss Fortune.

1990. Every time I wrote it down it looked wrong. A stark, blank new year to be faced without Hattie, or so it seemed now; something had prevented her from getting in touch with her new address. Nevertheless, I felt it was important to carry on as normal, to keep compiling evidence. It was what she'd have wanted.

I'd telephoned Regent's Crescent every day since the carol service, in case they'd decided not to move at the last minute. I knew, deep down, that there'd be no answer, that there would be nobody there to hear the ringing echoing up the empty stairwell. But for those few moments each day, standing in Granny's sitting room, twisting the curly telephone cord round my fingers, I let myself imagine a house full of noise and homework and the smell of Findus Crispy Pancakes cooking.

I held my breath as I rang Miss Fortune's buzzer. It was a bitter afternoon with snow in the air, the cold catching at the back of my throat. I wondered whether she'd answer – it seemed quite possible she'd have vanished off the face of the earth too.

For once, she opened the door before she'd stuck the smile on her face. There was a drawn-out moment before it appeared, in which the flesh-coloured splint on her hand seemed the main thing about her, grubby against the vibrant green and pink of her floral dress.

'Well well, it's you!' This was delivered in a gust of spearmint, with undertones of raw meat.

I breathed out and smiled back. It wasn't so bad, after all. This was a teacher, not a monster, and I could do this. The thing was to keep on the right side of her. If I practised hard and listened intently, if I accepted the custard creams and orange squash with due reverence, then everything would be fine.

It was almost as though Hattie could sense my resolve. I could feel her there with me, in the lesson, doing the 'thumbs up, thumbs down' signals in my peripheral vision, trying to make me laugh.

'So it's just you and me now, my dear,' she said as she motioned to me to sit down at the piano. 'And I want to talk to you about something important.'

My heart thudded.

'The dimensions of music. The melody is the horizontal dimension: it moves forward in time, can only be expressed *in* time and *through* time. Harmony is the vertical dimension. The sounds, the chords, underneath the melody. *Supporting* the melody. But do you know what a counterpoint melody is?'

'Another tune happening at the same time?'

'Yes. Two or more independent melodies that overlap. I was going to let you hear one of the Bach prelude and fugues.' She looked at me and wrinkled her nose. 'But just for fun, how about an example from popular music? This might get the point across.'

She went over to the bookcase that held her record collection and leaned far down, looking for something on the lowest

154

shelf. Her flower-upholstered bottom bobbed and swayed in the air for a full minute.

'Here, then: "Je t'aime", sung by Jane Birkin *et* Serge Gainsbourg. Listen for the melody of the strings in the chorus. Let them transport you.'

The song sounded okay at first, but the woman's whispery voice grew breathier and breathier, until I was barely able to follow any of the melodies, contrapuntral or otherwise, for the increasingly frequent sighs and gasps. This could barely even be described as a song: it was clearly two people *having sex*.

Horrified, I fixed my eyes on the keyboard and didn't look up again even when the music had stopped.

'In counterpoint, the melodies are independent but they can form a temporary vertical effect: filling in the harmonies for the other melody, and then moving away to become separate again.' She sighed, and I looked up, fearing that I didn't appear sufficiently transported. But she was staring out of the window, looking dreamy. 'And sometimes there's darkness, dissonance in there, and it shouldn't work, but it does; it's beautiful, for reasons nobody in this world could ever explain. Each melody brings out the *gorgeousness* in the other, in ways you couldn't imagine till it happens, till they come together. Rather like lovers, in fact, which makes that example very illustrative.' She smiled, and kinked an eyebrow at me.

I could feel the red rising up my chest and face. I'd have to throw my beetroot-coloured self onto the mercies of Bach. 'Do you know, I've always wanted to hear a prelude and fugue?'

On the walk home I imagined Hattie so hard that I could almost hear her laughing: 'The having-sex song was bad enough, but did you see, she hasn't trimmed her nose hair for at least three weeks!'

'Come on,' I whispered. 'She wasn't that bad. I thought she was going to make me *play* the fugue thing when I pretended to be so interested in it.' But my words disappeared into the cold empty air and when I listened for her again she was gone.

★

As the weeks went on, I began to dread my lessons less and found that I no longer felt sick with nerves on the long walk up the hill from school. I caught myself looking forward to the moment when I'd turn on to her street and see the music room window up ahead, glowing amber in the grey chill of the afternoon.

She always gave me a few minutes to warm my hands by the hissing gas fire.

'No point trying to play until the blood's flowing properly,' she'd say. 'And what about gloves, child? Where are your gloves?' She'd shake her head and tut, lamenting, as my grandmother sometimes did, the careless ways of young people.

Then she'd give me a creamy blob of Vaseline Intensive Care to work into my chapped fingers. And the air would grow rich with the smell of it, and it made me think of mothers, somehow, and I'd almost not mind about the ordeal to come. The critique of my playing was always delivered in bright tones, always with a Cheshire cat smile, always devastating.

'I'm in a sentimental old mood today,' she said one day. 'A nostalgic mood. Shall we do listening? Yes, I think so. Grieg's Piano Concerto in A minor. We'll be wicked things and skip to the second movement.'

There was a faint thud and a squeak. It sounded as though someone was moving furniture in the back room.

Miss Fortune paused on her way over to the shelf where the records were kept and closed the door firmly. Then she gestured, in exaggerated hopelessness, at the ceiling.

'Those wretched students. Forever making a racket. I'll turn it up extra loud. See how they like it.' She chuckled as she wheeshed the record out of its sleeve and placed it on the turntable.

The Grieg *was* relaxing. Relieved of the prospect of having to play my difficult sonatina, I started thinking about the end-of-term play I was going to be in. I was only a non-speaking servant called Clara, but at least I was a female this year. I began to drift: costumes, the smell of thick pan-stick make-up, the after-show party, Mrs Williamson . . .

Suddenly a voice boomed through my imaginings: '*Argenteuil seen from the small arm of the Seine!*'

I jerked awake. Oh God, what was this now?

She was standing in front of me, one foot stretched out in front, an arm pointing to the picture that hung over the fireplace.

'Monet. A man gave me this print a long time ago. He was the love of my life. We were at the Conservatoire together . . . Paris.'

My heart sank. Was she going to play 'Je t'aime' again?

'You know what happened in Paris, yes? The accident?'

I did know, because Hattie had told me. Did Miss Fortune know that we'd compared notes about her? I glanced across at the metronome eye and suppressed a shudder.

'But before that, it was a precious, precious time,' she went on, still gazing at the picture. 'It shines in my memory, Janey.

Shines! A career as a concert pianist still seemed very much within my reach. We used to dream together, to walk, some weekends, by a tiny village on the Seine, not far from Giverny.'

The spider eyes shot round at me. I nodded earnestly, and sat straighter in my chair.

'I was beautiful then,' she added, in a matter-of-fact tone.

Oh no! What was I supposed to say? That she was beautiful now, too? It would hardly be true. I frowned at the painting, pretending to be so absorbed in it I hadn't heard the comment.

'Blossom, my dear. By a river. A riot of light, and springtime and sheer joy. That's what this slow movement says to me. What does it say to you?'

I thought quickly. Grieg was Norwegian, wasn't he?

'Er . . . Fjords?' I said, instantly regretting the question mark in my voice.

Her upper lip kinked momentarily, but then she put back on her enthusiastic, Julie Andrews face.

'It could be somewhere in Scotland, Edinburgh even,' she offered. 'It also makes me think of the pond at Inverleith.'

A giggle caught at the base of my throat.

'Yes,' she insisted. 'In springtime, too. Cherry blossom. Ducklings. Where I used to walk on Sunday afternoons with the other love of my life.'

I was still trying to think of other Norwegian things.

Vikings?

*

Time passed; even without Hattie, time passed. And without quite knowing why, I was practising the piano at every opportunity, squirrelling myself away in the smallest, furthest-away music room every break time, and for hours after school. Perhaps, to begin with, it was a way of avoiding the girls in the playground, in their tightly closed groups, or delaying my return to the dark, cabbage-smelling house in Trinity. But as time went on I found that, through music, I could wrap myself in something that felt like love.

I began practising a Chopin nocturne; someone had left photocopied sheets on top of the music room piano one day, with fingering instructions marked on in fierce red pen. It was too difficult for me, and I invariably fluffed the notes. But I'd seized on it when I'd recognised it as one my grandpa had used to listen to. Once it had come on his transistor radio as he'd been watering his tomatoes, and he'd stopped and closed his eyes.

And something about the piece let my sadness out. The longing for him, so tightly furled in my chest, my shoulders and my neck, would loosen and flow down my arms, my fingers, onto the keys. And afterwards I'd go back to class with my arms warm and shaky, my vision swimming.

One day, months later, I told Miss Fortune, in a tiny voice, that I'd brought a piece I'd been practising, and that I wanted to play it for her.

She sat still through my performance. If she noticed the too-difficult bars that I skipped over, or the chords I'd thinned out in places, she never said anything.

'It's unusual, Janey, especially in the case of such a young player, for a piece to channel emotion like that. It's a gift, in its own way. I've known professional pianists who'd be able to fly in the air sooner than they could convey those depths of emotion. But technically, you've a long way to go. Such a long way to go, with your execution.'

159

My execution?

'Until what comes out of those fingers matches what's in your head.'

'Oh. Should I stop practising it, then?'

I was rushing to please her, anticipating her response. But why did I say such a thing? To give up the nocturne would be like packing Grandpa into his cold, dark grave all over again.

She gave me a strange look, filled with something like longing.

'If you feel that way about a piece, I don't think you *could* stop practising it, dear. I'll give you some more finger-strengthening exercises, though. And we can go over the fingering together.'

'That's brilliant, thank—'

'Oh, but that sounds like hard work,' she said throatily. 'Let's do it next time.'

I nodded.

'How about a spot of Rachmaninov, for the last ten minutes? I treated myself to a new recording of the second symphony.'

27

Janey

Hattie surprised me by phoning the following week, just as I'd got in from the nursery with Pip.

'Well, I've moved all my stuff in to the House of Hell.' She sounded breathless, as though she was climbing stairs. I pictured the staircase at Regent's Crescent, banisters twisting up like a great wrought-iron centipede.

'So you're staying there tonight?'

'I am. Would you like to come over for dinner? A little house-warming? Nothing elaborate, mind. But I can knock up a mean spaghetti arrabiata.'

'Sorry. I don't have a babysitter.'

There was a long pause, then a noise like a door being creaked open.

'Oh, just bring him with you,' she said finally, in a 'what the hell' kind of voice. 'Put him to bed upstairs, and stay the night. Then you can have a glass of wine and not bother about driving.'

'Right,' I said. 'Tell me what ingredients you need and I'll pick them up on the way.'

*

'Right, toots,' said Hattie, ushering us into the hall and taking hold of Pip's hand. 'Want to see where you and your mummy are sleeping? Right at the top of the house?'

He tilted his head back, his throat milky against the blue ribbed neckline of his jumper.

She led him carefully up the stairs, and I followed behind with our overnight bags. On the first-floor landing we passed the double doors into the cavernous drawing room where the grand piano stood, its black bulk reflecting off the polished wooden floor, and then, towards the back of the house, the master bedroom suite where Renee had slept away so much of Hattie's childhood. Maybe, if we were to open the door, we'd find her sleeping there still, black hair stark against the white pillowcase.

On the second floor – Pip's gaze kept drifting down the stairwell, as though in terrified awe of the distance he'd climbed – they stopped at the first door on the left, dark mahogany and tight shut.

No. For God's sake not in there.

'Hattie, I think it might be better if—'

But now she was leading him past it, on to the next door, the room adjacent to her old bedroom. She gestured inside. Double bed, bedside table, lamp. Otherwise empty. Fine.

Hattie kept up a monologue about Farrow & Ball paint colours, and the difficulty in sourcing Victorian baths, all the time she was making dinner. She didn't pause for breath until we were halfway through our pasta, or rather, I was halfway through mine, as she'd barely taken a mouthful.

'But look at me prattling on! I want to hear all about *you*!' She tilted her head winningly to one side.

In truth I'd barely been listening. The process of feeding Pip, bathing him in the high-ceilinged, echoing bathroom, and settling him in a strange bed had left me feeling strung out and distracted. Sitting at the table now, I was acutely aware of the black square of window behind me, and preoccupied with the question of whether Hattie was going to close the blind or not. Or whether I should move round the table so I'd have my back to the solid wood sideboard, but on what pretext?

Stop this right now. Say what you've come to say.

'Hattie, there's something I need to tell you.'

She picked up the wine bottle – in fact, grabbed it – and reached across to refill my glass. 'Oh really?'

'Well. Oh God, this is a bit embarrassing. A few months ago I went to this art workshop. Kind of by mistake.'

'Mmm?' She twirled her fork in the spaghetti, then lowered her face towards the bowl to shovel it into her mouth. She ate in a way that was completely at odds with her elegant persona and it was achingly comforting.

'And in the first session, this odd thing happened.'

'Oh crikey. Don't tell me you're in love with the art teacher!'

'Er, not exactly. But he got me to try writing with my left hand.'

'Oh no, not some awful inner-child thing, was it?'

'I think that was the intention, yes. But it wasn't how it worked out.' I stared down at my pasta, the red twisted clumps on my plate, and felt suddenly sick. 'No, because, you see, it was another person who came through. I drew a picture of her, and then she started speaking. She said I had to listen to her. And she called herself Hattie.'

I looked up at her then. Her eyes were fixed on me, her fork suspended halfway to her mouth.

'Oh come *on*, Janey.' Her tone was warm, rich, affectionate, laced with a smile that hadn't quite made it to her eyes.

'And I was just wondering whether it was actually you.

163

Whether you did want to, you know, tell me something.' My voice trailed off to a mutter.

She looked charmingly bemused.

'Janey, no. No, I don't think so.'

'I asked who was there, and the writing said, "Hattie. Hattie. Hattie".'

'Oh how *delicious*! Like Mr Rochester crying out, "Jane! Jane! Jaaa-aaane—"'

She flung out a theatrical arm and crumpled over the table, a tendril of expensively tinted hair landing in her spaghetti.

'You sound like a dying sheep.'

'Ja-aa-aa-neyyyyy . . . Ha-att-ie-ee . . .'

'Yes, I suppose I could have been channelling a sheep of the same name.' I wiped my mouth with a piece of kitchen towel. 'I'll put that to Steve the next time I see him. Right, I think I'll just go and check on Pip.'

I made my way up the basement stairs, and up the staircase to the second floor. Viewed through the banister, the chessboard tiles seemed to warp and bend. I'd need to lay off the wine and drink some water.

On the way, I paused outside the door of the room next to Pip's.

Don't. What good would it do?

I grasped the round handle and twisted it to the side. Then the other way. It was locked. The house swayed under my feet. Dropping to my knees, I held my head in my hands until it passed. Alcohol. Just alcohol.

In Pip's room, the bedside lamp was still on as I'd left it, an ugly thing with a tassled, pollen-yellow shade. Pip was lying flat on his back in the middle of the double bed, arms splayed, mouth open, cheeks flushed. Too warm, maybe. I pulled the duvet down to his waist.

'He's fine,' I said to Hattie when I got back downstairs. She was eating salad leaves out of the plastic bag they'd come in.

'Is he a good sleeper? Or is he an utter nightmare?' she added ghoulishly.

'He's not too bad these days. Sometimes he wants to come into bed with me, but I don't mind that.'

'What about when he was a baby?'

I pictured Pip in his first soft blue babygrow, curled like a comma against my chest. After getting home from hospital, we'd retreated to my bed for a week or so, to feed and sleep and cry and stare at each other. I got up from time to time to make soup or toast, one-handed, as he slept against my shoulder. Or to answer the door, dishevelled and blinking, to the midwife.

'He was—'

On the table, the baby monitor interrupted with a loud burst of static. Hattie frowned at it, and gave it a shake.

'Oh, the battery must be going,' she said.

Should I go up?

Hattie put her hand over mine. 'Leave it. We know he's fine, you were just up there. It's just —'

From the monitor came a sound, a sob tailing off into a desperate little whimper.

My baby . . .

The noise came again, barely audible this time. But something made me take the stairs two at a time.

Pip hadn't moved – he was lying spread-eagled in the same position.

I lay down beside him, tuning into the rhythm of his

165

breathing, only just perceptible as a slight movement of his pyjama collar against his neck. Was he dreaming? I watched his closed eyelids, tracing the faint pattern of pearly blue under the skin, where the veins branched up and across towards his temples. I leant in close to inhale his salty, sleepy smell. He didn't stir.

Then came the thump of someone coming up the stairs. Someone running.

Hattie swung open the door, out of breath.

'What is it?' she cried. 'What's wrong?'

'Shhh,' I whispered, getting up and ushering her out into the hallway. 'Nothing's wrong. Why?'

'I heard you through the monitor. There was this thumping. I couldn't work out what you were doing. I thought you were trying to move the bed around or something. And then there was crying. Really *horrible* crying.'

'Well, Pip only cried out a couple of times. He was fine by the time I'd got upstairs.'

'It wasn't Pip.'

I grabbed the banister.

She stared at me, eyes swimming with panicky tears. 'It sounded like you.'

★

'Could the thumping have been me running up the stairs?' I said, once we were down in the kitchen again.

Hattie handed me a steaming mug of tea and sat down, hooking the arches of her neat little feet over the strut of the chair.

'No. I heard you going upstairs, and the sound of Pip's

door opening and closing. Which was when you went into the room. Presumably. Then it was quiet for a while before the thumping started.'

'Maybe it picked up the wrong frequency. Maybe it's coming from next door. Maybe Lady Smythe is babysitting her grandchildren tonight.'

'Yeah, maybe.'

The monitor burst into staticky life again.

'What *is* that?' said Hattie.

I strained to hear. Were there deeper, darker shapes – words? – flickering behind the white noise?

'My God. Is that . . . someone talking?'

'No, Hattie. No. Your mind's running away with you.'

But I scraped my chair back and went upstairs again. Just to check.

Once again, Pip was fast asleep and the house was silent, other than the static hiss and spit from the kitchen.

Hattie was hugging herself when I came back down, her knees drawn up in front of her.

'It's going doolally,' she said, twirling a strand of her hair round her finger and sucking the end of it, as she used to do in lessons. I'd always used to poke her arm, trying to pull her gaze away from the window and the blue Pentland Hills in the far distance. And on the back page of my jotter I'd write—

'Hairballs! Yeah, I know. There were words coming through, by the way. When you were upstairs. I couldn't hear most of them but—'

'There were no words, Hattie. You're imagining it.'

'I definitely heard something.' Her eyes drifted back to the hissing monitor.

I sighed. 'Okay, what did you hear?'

'Danger Mouse.'

She closed her eyes and laughed silently, harder and harder until she was gasping for breath.

I smiled a tight little smile, wishing I could laugh with her.

The static noise stopped abruptly. The green light – the one that showed the monitor was working – had gone out.

'It's dead,' said Hattie, picking up the monitor and giving it a shake. She opened up the back of it, took out the batteries and turned them over to examine them, then slammed them onto the table with an irritated shake of the head, as though the evening's disturbances were all attributable to the battery manufacturer.

And with that she flicked back to her sophisticated self. How could I reach through it and bring her back? What would the twelve-year-old Janey have done? What would she have said?

'Defective,' I said in the deepest voice I could muster, with a correspondingly deep frown.

'Oh Janey,' she drawled. 'You're such a *hoot*.'

'Hmm.' Suddenly, I didn't want to stay up with her, drinking wine and pretending into the long dark night. I just wanted to lie next to Pip and breathe him in. 'Better get to bed, then.'

'Indeed.' It was only half past nine.

But as I followed her up the stairs, something about her – about the way her shoulders seemed to droop when she'd forgotten anyone was looking – made my heart twist in my ribs.

'Are you okay?'

'Pig of a headache,' she said. 'Don't worry, Ernie gave me some of his uber-painkillers last week. So I'll be dead to the world tonight, once I've taken a couple of those. If old Danger Mouse puts in another appearance I'll snore right through it. Sorry!'

28

Janey

Steve had just popped round, he said, because he was in the area. He hovered in the hallway, swinging a slim Waitrose bag.

'Stay,' I urged. 'I can put your shopping in the fridge, if you like?'

'Cool,' he said, handing the bag to me. There was a plastic pack of Swiss cheese in there, a grapefruit and a small jar of capers.

Now he sat against the living room wall, a bottle of Murray's Amstel Light on the carpet within reach of a languid hand.

I perched on the edge of the sofa, jingling a soft Iggle Piggle ball that Pip had been flinging around the room earlier in the day. I hadn't had the heart to tidy his toys away.

'Pip's gone to stay the night with Murray and Gretel,' I said, in a tone I might have used to discuss imminent root canal treatment, or the melting of the polar ice caps.

'Oh, the dreaded custody issue.'

'What dreaded custody issue?'

'Well, it was bound to come up sooner or later, wasn't it?'

'No. Murray and Gretel just want more time with Pip, and I'm being very reasonable about it, so that everyone can stay calm and friendly. There won't be any need for any drama.'

I'd decided there was nothing to be gained from digging my heels in and antagonising Gretel. And everything to be lost, potentially, if she started throwing child-custody lawyers at the case. There were sure to be several at her beck and call, within the legal dynasty that was her family. So I'd agreed to Pip's visit. I'd even bought housewarming presents: a Jo Malone scented candle for Gretel, and a shiny nutmeg grater, chosen by Pip for his father. He'd also insisted, going round Sainsbury's, that we buy a jar of bone-shaped dog biscuits with a red ribbon round the lid for Trixie. We'd wrapped the gifts carefully and he'd put them at the bottom of his overnight bag, hiding them under his pyjamas, 'for be surpwise, Mummy'.

'Yeah, that sounds sensible,' said Steve. 'Keep everyone onside.'

'What about you? What have you been up to?'

'Oh, just work stuff.'

'But, what do you do in your spare time?'

'Dunno. Just madly busy with work, mostly. Nobody showed for my last class today, though, so I went up to town. I'm looking for a really good thick doormat for the front door.'

'Oh? Do you live in a muddy area?'

'No.' He took a long drink of his Amstel Light, his gulps sounding loudly in the quiet of the room.

I sensed that I'd crossed an invisible line again. You probably weren't supposed to ask art tutors where they lived.

'It's a flat down near the Shore. It's near Leith.'

'So guess what. I found Hattie Marlowe.'

'You found Hattie?' His face lit up. 'Hooray! That's big news! Why didn't you tell me?'

I felt wrongfooted. Should I have phoned him, or texted him? It was natural, after all, that he'd be interested, after his involvement in the non-dominant-hand drama. But I wasn't sure if we counted as *friends*, the type who texted each other over such things. I should have told him, though – maybe his friend who knew about missing persons was still scouring the country looking for her.

Or maybe I hadn't told him I'd found Hattie because . . . well, I didn't really feel as though I *had*.

'Was everything okay with her?' he asked. 'Did you tell her you've been worried? Did you tell her about the non-dominant-hand exercise?'

'Yeah, she thought that was very funny. It doesn't sound as though she was trying to send me telepathic messages.'

Steve's forehead creased into a concerned frown.

'In some ways I wish I'd never found her at all. She's not at all like she was at school.'

He opened his mouth to speak, but then sighed, as if he didn't even know where to start.

'Do you think our personalities stay the same?' I blurted out. 'The same as when we were children? Or do we change into different people?'

He blinked slowly, and his expression seemed to say 'not again' as though people had been trailing in and out of his workshop all day, all asking this same tedious question.

'Hey,' I said lightly. 'You'll have to know about this stuff when you're an art therapist, surely?' I threw the Iggle Piggle ball up, but fluffed the catch. It tinkled onto the floor, only just missing the glass of red wine at my feet.

'We could debate it forever. What do you mean by "personality" anyway?'

'Well, who we are.'

He sighed again, and downed the rest of his drink.

'We're a product of our environment. What people think of as a personality is just a pattern of learned responses. So, yeah. People change all the time. You have an idea of "Hattie" in your head that you've consolidated over the years, but what's that based on? A mish-mash of memories from decades ago. All subjective. And selective, too, though you probably don't realise it. If you asked ten people what her defining characteristics were, they'd all say slightly different things.'

His analysis tended to back up what I'd felt, after meeting her again: that my memories must have played tricks on me. But something in me kicked against this notion.

'Which ten people, though? Which ten people would have known Hattie as well as me? She was my friend. I loved her.'

'Which is why you can't be objective. Out of the ten people, your account would be the least reliable.'

'That's rubbish,' I said. 'And so like a man.'

If Steve found this remark cutting, he gave no indication of it.

'Think about it,' I went on. 'What would any of us ever be, if you only asked the people who didn't love us?'

'Well you tell me, then,' he said. 'You tell me what she's like. Not what you remember about her, but what she's actually like now.'

'Okay. She's got this incredible flat, all dark wood and chrome. It has a view right over to the Pentland Hills. And she's very interested in Botox and glycolic face peels.'

Even as I said it, I was aware how ridiculous it sounded. I seemed to hear a little giggle: the old Hattie mocking her well-groomed successor.

'It's tough to accept when people change.' His voice was softer now. 'What is it that you wanted to happen, though? To pick up where you left off? Carry on like you're twelve again?'

'No. We don't have much in common any more. I – I hardly even want to spend time with her.'

'Well, that's not so surprising, is it, if you think about it? This was a friendship that met your needs as a twelve-year-old. Why should it still meet them now? Why does it have to?'

'Meeting my needs?' I said. 'It's not like I'm buying a new washing machine, or some life-insurance policy.'

'Why would you compare your friend to an insurance policy?'

'I don't know. Why would I compare her to a washing machine?'

'Fair enough.' He let a long silence fall. He looked at his watch.

'Oh, sorry,' I said in icy tones. 'Am I *boring* you?'

He shrugged. 'Maybe. A bit.'

'Well. Maybe you should go then.'

He looked me straight in the eye. 'I was wondering if we're going to talk about what's really on your mind.'

'*What?*'

'It's as if there's something else you're thinking about, almost all the time. Sometimes I think it's Hattie, but at the same time it's not Hattie. It's like a script running constantly in the background. Or a song on repeat. It's exhausting just watching you.'

What?

'Look,' I said. 'I know you arty types probably like to sit around on beanbags analysing each other but—'

Steve rose to his feet. 'I should go.'

'Why?'

'I'm not interested in playing games, Janey.' Unfolded, he looked alarmingly big against the wall.

'What do you mean?'

'You draw me in, with your words, and those looks you give

173

me, like you want to be real with me, and then you kick me out. You want me to be the sensitive, arty type when it suits you, and then you turn it around and take the piss. What's that all about?'

'I was just . . . That's unfair. You caught me off guard, that's all.'

'Talk straight, Janey. Talk straight or not at all.'

He was shrugging on the leather jacket. He was rooting in his pocket for his keys. He was turning. He was leaving.

No.

'Do you believe in ghosts?'

He stopped, his back outlined in the frame of the door. As seconds slipped past I found myself wondering about the expression on his face: would it be impatience, sympathy, professional concern? For a horrible moment I was convinced that when he turned round, his face would be nothing but a blank, an oval of smooth skin.

But when he did turn, he merely looked worn, and tired. He came and sat down beside me.

'I'm listening.'

So I told him about the knife, and the glove. I told him about the baby monitor, hissing and shrieking while Pip lay upstairs asleep.

'Oh, *Jay*,' he sighed. The shortening of my name felt so intimate, sent shivers over my skin.

He looked at me for a few moments, his eyes heavy.

'I didn't mean to take the piss before,' I said. 'You just . . . I just . . .'

'Come here,' he said.

He pulled me into his chest. I could feel his hands, one spread high on my back, the other reaching right round me, spanning the side of my ribcage. He held me as I might have held Pip, containing me, as though I was infinitely precious. As though he needed me, somehow, like I needed him.

But when he spoke his voice was matter of fact. 'You don't have to go through this on your own. There's help if you need it.'

What sort of help? I wondered. A priest or a medium? A psychiatrist? Social workers? Assessments? A whole army of other problems. But for now, it felt so good just to be held.

'Who're you gonna call?' I murmured. 'Ghostbusters?'

He laughed. I felt it as well as heard it, a throaty vibration where my ear was pressed against his chest. He dropped a kiss, an affectionate little kiss, onto the top of my head.

I had to have this. I had to have more of this. I pulled him against me. Decisively, so there'd be no mistaking my intention.

Then he was kissing my forehead, and my face. Tentatively – like it was a question – finding my mouth. And I was kissing him back.

The rush of it drowned everything else out, swept me clean. I didn't want his concern, or his taskforce of helpers. I wanted him inside me. The sooner the better, the harder the better. I stood up, took his hands and pulled him up. Standing so close, he seemed to tower in front of me. I hooked my fingers into the waistband of his jeans.

He exhaled, a deep, shuddery breath. 'Oh God, Janey. Oh God, do you want to do this?' He pulled back to look at me. 'Are you sure?'

'Let's go to my room.'

But when we got there, it started to go wrong. He pulled my T-shirt up over my head, skimming his hands down my sides, and then moved in to kiss me again, pressing his weight against me so that I moved backwards and let myself drop onto the bed.

'What's up?' he whispered, flipping my belt out of its buckle.

'Nothing.' I stroked the side of his face, feeling the pull of his stubble against my palm. I wanted him. I wanted him . . .

But suddenly I was hovering near the ceiling, watching us: my body splayed pale on the bed, his hands, pushing and exploratory. What a strange thing to want to do: to put this body part there, the rubbing, and writhing. A biological function, an evolutionary drive designed to produce offspring.

Right on cue, Steve paused. 'On a practical note, I've come a little unprepared.' His voice was deep, and suddenly polite to the point of being formal. 'Have you got any . . . er . . .'

Condoms. A memory flashed into my head: easing myself out of the bed in that plush suite at Gleneagles and finding that the condom had burst. Taking the morning-after pill the next day, because I was a responsible adult, wasn't I? Learning three weeks later that I'd become a statistic. A failure-rate statistic.

'Oh yes.' My voice had tightened, turning polite to match his. 'I think I've got some. I'm not sure if they're . . .'

. . . out of date.

Did condoms go out of date? Only if you were a sad case who nobody wanted to fuck.

He was kissing, kissing, kissing, working down my neck, back to my mouth again, his nose digging against me like a beak. I needed air. I was spinning.

I was going to be . . .

'What? Janey.'

176

I ran to the bathroom.

After a minute, he knocked. 'Janey? Can I come in?'

The door handle turned. I'd taken the lock off, because of Pip.

He'd wrapped my dressing gown around himself: Cath Kidston roses.

'Very fetching.' I attempted a sparky tone of voice, wishing I was wearing more than a faded old bra and unbuttoned jeans.

'Are you okay?'

'I'm sorry. I just thought I was going to be sick, but I'm fine now.'

I winced at the way it sounded, given what we'd been doing. But he came and sat down on the floor next to me, against the side of the bath, and put his arm round me.

'Come here, you.'

'Sorry.'

'Hey, don't.' He rubbed my shoulder. 'You okay now?'

'Yes. Sorry. I don't know what happened there. Maybe it was the wine. I'm not used to drinking these days.'

He pulled a warm towel off the towel rail and wrapped it around me. I laid my head against his shoulder, feeling the boniness under the padding of the dressing gown.

'It's my fault,' he said. 'I shouldn't have.'

'No, no, it's . . .'

'No, I *really* shouldn't have.' He gave a gusty sigh. 'This is nice, though. We can chat. Would you like to chat?'

'Mmm.'

'Would it help if we agree to be friends, and not take things any further? It seems like you, I don't know, that things are complicated for you. You need some head space, not me wading in. We can just talk, if you like.'

So I laid my head against his shoulder and let him in just a little bit more. I found myself telling him about the year when I was twelve, and Grandpa's death, and Granny's tight white face, and Mum flying up for the funeral and back again the same day. The long summer with a bright, shining week at Glen Eddle. Then Hattie's ghosts in the autumn term. And how it had felt when I'd lost her too, like love itself had fallen off the edge of the world.

And then we went to bed, me under the covers and Steve stretched out on top of them next to me, still swathed in Cath Kidston roses, his big white feet crossed at the ankle. I put on *Christiansen*, and we watched episode seven – which we both agreed was the best of the series – the Danish voices rising and falling in a perfect, muddled counterpoint to the sound of Steve's breathing next to me.

*

The doorbell woke me.

It couldn't be Murray and Pip back already – could it? He'd said he'd drop him off around ten, and it was only . . . oh no! Ten to ten.

Steve lay on the other side of the bed, frowning in his sleep. I'd gone to sleep – velvety dark and dreamless – with his hand, still and heavy, on my shoulder.

But Murray! What would he think? My first night without Pip and I'd taken a strange man into my bed.

Pip flew into my arms when I opened the front door, clinging like a koala as I ushered Murray past the closed bedroom door and into the kitchen.

'Tea?'

Please say no.

'Thanks. And I'm starving too, if you could make some toast or something.'

Really? I'd imagined them having a leisurely breakfast in their sunny Morningside kitchen, with freshly ground coffee, home-squeezed orange juice and warm blueberry pancakes whipped up by Gretel.

'So how did you all get on?' I asked.

'Very well. Though, Janey, he woke up three times in the night.'

He spoke in a slightly accusing tone, as though he was a customer and I'd fobbed him off with a defective product. Honestly, one sleepless night – just *one* – and he looked grey and exhausted, and clearly hadn't found time to shave. I had a pleasing image of Gretel, flat-haired and slumped on the sofa in the £2-million Morningside house, too exhausted to plug in her heated rollers.

'*Poor* Pippy.' I nestled my face into his neck. He detached himself and when I lowered him to the floor he scurried off to the corner and dragged out his small red plastic table and chair and put them in the middle of the kitchen floor. Then he slipped out into the hall. I was right behind him, praying that Murray would stay in the kitchen. To my horror, the bedroom door was ajar, but – oh, thank God – the room was empty, the dressing gown flung across the back of the chair.

Pip came out of the bathroom dragging his step-up stool. Absently, I carried it to the kitchen for him.

'Gretel and I have decided to set up a playroom for him,' said Murray, as though he was announcing a stock exchange flotation, or a joint venture between two multinational corporate giants. 'What do you think he'd like?'

179

Ha! They'd obviously struggled to entertain him, as well as to cope with his erratic sleep patterns.

Murray screwed up his nose. 'Gretel wants to get him some wooden gubbins made by Scandinavian elves or something . . . but Lego Duplo's his favourite, isn't it?'

'Duplo is good,' I agreed. 'But be sure to take out any green bricks. He hates them. They remind him of peas. I found a whole load of them down the toilet the day after his last birthday.'

Oops. Should I have told Murray that I'd left Pip unattended – even for a moment – with Duplo and the toilet?

Perhaps Murray saw the shadow of doubt cross my face. 'It's not easy, keeping him entertained. I don't know how you manage on your own.'

'We muddle along, don't we, Pippy?'

I looked down.

He was sitting on his step-up stool, pulled up to the little red table, pattering his socked feet on the tiles and fixing me with an urgent look.

He'd set the table for two, with mismatched plastic plates and cups pulled out from his toy box in the corner.

'Samwidge,' he said, gesturing to the empty red chair opposite him. 'Pip and Dend want samwidge.'

'Oh yes,' said Murray. 'What is this "dend" he keeps talking about?'

I thought for a moment. I'd heard him say it before, but hadn't paid much attention. Now there came a hollow sensation in my stomach as I realised what it meant.

'He substitutes "d" for sounds he can't pronounce, especially at the start of words.'

'So what's he saying?'

180

'In this case, I think he's substituting "d" for the sound "fr".'
Friend.

Pip had a friend we couldn't see, who was sitting opposite him at the red Ikea table.

★

'It's common for children to have imaginary friends,' said Murray later, when Pip and Dend had finished their samwidges and were playing in the living room.

'I know, I know. Perhaps not when they're this young. But yes, I know.'

'So what was the matter, just then? You were shaking.'

I said nothing.

Murray leaned forward on the sofa, clasping his hands. 'Are you happy enough, living here on your own?'

'It's fine.' I'd already gone through this with Steve last night and simply couldn't face it again.

'Is it to do with that time when you thought you'd been broken into? Has something else happened?'

'I'm not sure,' I said carefully. 'Sometimes I get the feeling that somebody's been in the flat.'

Murray stood up. 'Get me a list of everybody who's got keys to the flat.'

'Nobody does. Nobody has got keys. And I got the locks changed, remember? After the, er, glove thing.'

'What about the arty-farty chap. That . . .' he paused and wrinkled his nose as if trying to remember the name. 'That *Steve.*'

'What? No! Why would he do something like that anyway?'

His cheeks went pinker. 'Search me. Maybe he gets a kick out of it.'

181

I sighed. 'How can you possibly say that? You've never even met him.'

'I don't need to,' he said darkly. 'Look, just be careful.'

Be careful who you let near my son.

The unspoken words hung in the air.

'Fine,' I said sharply.

'Good. Right, better get back, Gretel's got a lunch thing. But, er, before I do, there's something I wanted to mention.'

'Oh?'

'You might get a letter from our solicitor. Mine and Gretel's, I mean.'

'Why?'

'Oh, it's just a formality, but Gretel thought it might be a good idea to have a written agreement in place. You know, about access to Pip.'

'*Access?* I let you have him for the night, like you wanted. And isn't it about time you told her about Friday afternoons?'

'We were thinking it might be good for Pip to spend some more structured time with us.'

'Us?'

'Yes. Gretel and me. Maybe every second weekend or something, Friday to Sunday?' The words came out in a rush.

'Fridays? But you both work Fridays.'

'Gretel's mother's keen to have Pip on Friday afternoons.'

'Gretel's *mother*? I've never even met the woman.'

'Well then, you can meet her, can't you? What's the big deal? Don't get so worked up about it. Gretel wants to do it through the lawyers, just to make it clear.'

'This is about when she saw us on the Thomas train, isn't it? That's when it started. She couldn't stand to see us out together.'

182

'As I say, it's just a formality, so let's get it sorted and move on. Right! Bye Pip-squeak. Hug for Dad?'

Pip scampered over to him, and tears, hot and stinging, filled my eyes. Tears of anger at myself, for being lulled into a false sense of security with the Friday games of happy families, into thinking he might actually have been interested in *us* being a family. And what could I say? I didn't have any room to be unreasonable. If Gretel wanted to she'd set an army of lawyers on me and anything could happen.

But when Murray had left, my anger gave way into something more complicated. Because how must it have felt for Gretel to see Pip, that first day on the Thomas train? To see Murray's genetic legacy – his hair, his eyes, his chin – expressed in a child that wasn't hers? Maybe she'd thought of the children she'd never been able to have, with their half-imagined faces she'd never been able to see. Wasn't it quite possible she'd fallen in love with Pip – my beautiful, newly formed, baby-scented Pip – there and then?

I lifted Pip and clung to him till his legs began to flail and he told me, in his sternest voice, to let him go.

29

Hattie

I was so happy today, going to meet Janey. I practically skipped down Dundas Street, nearly broke one of my heels.

When I got to the coffee shop and saw her, sitting there all fresh-faced, in her cream dress and her cardigan with the wool unravelling at the hem, oh God, I felt overdone, like I'd dressed up in my mother's clothes. Or been snared for a makeover at a department store beauty counter.

Pip was hanging off her arm, pestering for a sachet of jam. She was saying no because he'd already had three, and she was trying to get him to eat a carrot and beetroot muffin, but also looking like she'd quite like to throw it at the wall. She nodded in relief when I suggested we leave because I wanted to show her something in a shop nearby. I suppose she thought I wanted a second opinion on a coat or something. The sort of girly shopping trip we'd never had a chance to do together.

They'd moved the piano to the front of the shop, and tied an enormous white ribbon around it as I'd asked. I touched her arm to make her stop in front of it, and she drew in a breath.

'This is for you, Janey. I've got a fair few birthdays to catch up on.'

And it'll have to cover all her future birthdays too, not that she knows it. I can't risk staying around, for all our sakes. Because what would I do? What would I do, if I saw something? Something swirling into the glow of her and Pip. Blooming red, like blood in warm water.

I'd settled on a gorgeous upright, with a satin cherrywood finish. It was for selfish reasons, really. If she isn't going to be in my life, it will make me happy to think of her playing it, getting lost in a Chopin nocturne or playing 'Nellie the Elephant' as Pip thumps around the sitting room.

'Oh!' she kept saying, holding her hand over her mouth.

'Don't worry,' I whispered. 'Dad did loads of business with them, so I got a very good deal.'

She turned slowly towards me, eyes fixed on the ground, then shook her head.

'Do you like it? Will it be an okay size for the flat?'

'Yes,' she whispered, still looking at the ground. 'Yes.'

And she reached out for me, with a stiff, awkward, trailing-sleeved arm, and folded me into a hug, burying her face against my shoulder.

'I've got a night out next week,' she said, when we'd gone back to the café. She said she needed another cup of tea to get herself together after the shock of the piano. She'd even bought another carrot and beetroot muffin for Pip, on the basis that at least he'd *touched* the previous one.

'Oh, who with?'

She blushed and looked at me through her lashes as though we were twelve and dissecting the ceilidh with St Simon's.

'Steve. He's the person I was talking about the other day. The, er, art tutor type person. It's just as friends.'

'Shall I babysit?' I heard myself saying. 'I'd love to spend some time with Pip.'

Before I go.

'Do you know, that would be brilliant! I was going to ask

Murray but it would be a bit awkward actually. He doesn't like Steve. He wouldn't understand that we're just friends.'

'Fab. Just tell me when and where, hon. Pip and I will have a ball.'

'Did you hear that, Pip-squeak? Auntie Hattie's going to babysit!' She ruffled his hair and picked out a dried-up lump of jam.

'I've got some news, too.' I said. 'James is coming to stay at Regent's Crescent next week! With his wife, Simone, which is a bit unfortunate admittedly but she'll probably just stare miserably into her phone most of the time. So what do you think? We could all meet up. It'd be just like old times.'

I honestly thought she'd be chuffed to bits. She'd adored James when we were little. I suppose I'd even been hoping that, with the three of us together, it might draw him out of himself a bit. Maybe he'd chat with us and laugh and have fun, instead of droning on about investment banking and then drinking himself into oblivion as he normally did at family get-togethers. I might see the old James again. The James that I hadn't really seen since he got sent away to Ramplings. I had a sudden image of him, standing by the door at Regent's Crescent with his trunk and his violin case, his legs thin in shorts and long socks, his skull bumpy under a harsh haircut. His freckles standing out on his face as he struggled not to cry.

'Janey? What do you think?'

She didn't make any sign of having heard me. I thought perhaps she was annoyed with Pip, who was now throwing chunks of muffin on the floor, and chanting, 'Don' like it,' over and over again.

I stooped down under the table to pick up the muffin fragments.

'Won't it be fun, though?' I said. 'We could even go on a trip to Glen Eddle, play soldiers in the forest with Pip. What do you think?'

But when I sat upright again and looked across at her I did a double take. She sat with her arms in a cross against her chest, staring at some point in the middle distance behind me. Her eyes glassy, her face the blank white of a winter sky.

30

Janey

Steve had suggested meeting in a bar in town.

Walking in, I was nervous to the point of distraction. Which Steve was he going to be? The art tutor turned cautious but well-meaning friend? The Steve who'd stripped my T-shirt off and pushed me onto my bed? Or the one who'd listened to me talking late into the night, the lines of his face creased into an expression that looked like love?

He was sitting at one of the tables, turning a coaster round and round. He stood up when he saw me, and hovered awkwardly for a moment, before placing his hand lightly on my upper arm. I moved in for a quick hug and he groaned softly as I released him.

'What?'

'You're just . . .' He shook his head. 'Just so gorgeous. Sorry, sorry, I know . . .'

It felt like the sun itself, flooding my skin with warmth. It was such a long time since someone had wanted me. Since someone had looked at me and seen anything other than a mumsy blob with doughy arms and a worn-out, papery face.

He scanned the bar, seeming unsure whether to sit back down. The door from the street swung open with a burst of noise: a crowd of office workers coming in for their after-work drinks.

'Do you want a drink?' he asked. 'Or do you just want to, you know, walk, talk? Drive somewhere?'

Back to his place?

'Don't worry,' he said with a hint of a raised eyebrow. 'I know we've got to behave.'

'Let's drive, then.'

We walked down to where he'd parked his car in Heriot Row, and we drove away out of town, through Corstorphine, out onto the city bypass then the motorway. He'd put Leonard Cohen on the stereo, quite loud, and it didn't seem right to speak, only to let it flood over me. I laid my head to the side and closed my eyes.

When the engine stopped, I found that he'd driven to the coast, to the tiny village of Blackness. He'd parked just along from Blackness Castle, a great block of a fortress on a rocky promontory jutting into the Forth.

'What do you think?' He stretched out his legs a little, but made no move to get out of the car.

'It's a gloomy sort of place,' I said, pulling my coat around me. The car was cooling quickly, now that the heater had gone off with the engine.

'It's called the ship that never sailed,' said Steve. 'If you see it from the seaward side, it looks like a huge stone ship that's run aground.'

His words – the way he said it – set something aching inside. A ship of dreams, petrified in this cold sea.

'So,' he said finally.

I found, to my panic, that I didn't know what to say. We had no comfortable in-jokes, or shared history to fill the gaps. Only that cut-open connection, whenever he looked me in the eye.

'Why did you bring us here?' I asked. Then softened it with, 'Do you know this area well?'

Do you come here often?

I cringed at myself.

'Not really,' he said softly. 'Though I've always quite liked it.'

'We came here on a school trip, once,' I said. 'We stopped on the way back from P5 Camp. We had to sketch the castle so we could write a pretend newspaper article when we got back. Then it rained, so we had to sit on the coach to have our sandwiches. We all ended up in hysterics, because someone said they'd seen a white shape at one of the windows. Mrs Peston had to get Maddie Naylor to breathe into a paper bag.'

How come I knew, beyond a doubt, that he wouldn't respond with any of his own school reminiscences?

'Was that with Hattie? Have you seen her again?'

'She's babysitting! God knows how she's going to cope with Pip.'

'Is he being a handful?'

I sighed. 'He seems a bit fragile at the moment. He keeps going on about his imaginary friend. He insists I lay out clothes for Dend each morning. Last week in Sainsbury's he had a screaming fit because I wouldn't buy a Rapunzel costume that Dend wanted. I had to abandon my trolley and carry him out to the car. It took half an hour to calm him down. He actually went *blue*.'

'What did you do?'

'I followed the advice in one of my parenting books.'

'What was that?'

'Er, use a loud, excitable voice to match his, and exaggerated facial expressions, and try and reflect his emotions back in, um, in a loving way.'

'So what did you say?'

'Pip very *angry*! You want dress! You want it nowwww!'

Steve raised his eyebrows.

'Yes. Over and over again. There's no use just saying it once.'

'Hmm.'

'Yeah. It was an interesting shift for the man collecting the trolleys.'

Steve gave a soft laugh and fidgeted in his seat.

Was there anything I could talk about that didn't make me sound like a neurotic, haunted wreck or a struggling single mother? I tried to think of a safe subject. The history of Blackness Castle, perhaps. With effort, I cast my mind back to my newspaper article. It had been very thorough, I'd got three house points for it, whereas Hattie only got a tick.

'Did you know that the Earl of—'

'And what about you? Are you sleeping? Still dreaming?'

It was as though he'd reached a hand into my chest and taken hold of my heart.

I looked away. 'Hmm.'

'Still don't want to talk about it?'

'No.'

'Oh, Jay,' he said, his voice deepening into my name.

I stayed very still, the air tight in my chest.

'I think the dream is just . . . I think I'm a bit tense at the moment, that's all.'

'Why?' He spoke so softly he was almost whispering.

'I, I feel like I'm standing on the edge of my life. That it's just blankness ahead of me. I've got Pip, he's my life, but he won't need me forever.'

'Pip's only two,' said Steve. 'He'll get more independent as he grows up, but with that will come more freedom for you.'

'Freedom to do what?'

He threw out his arms, palms upturned.

'To do whatever you want to do. Be whoever you want to be. You're so amazing. You're ridiculously attractive. I mean, look what you reduce me to – some bloody gawky-eyed teenager.'

'Oh come *on*.'

'You're resourceful. You've managed on your own – *incredibly* well – with Pip.'

Only because Murray was bankrolling it all.

'And you're fun. You've got that something that makes people want to be around you. Charm. That's the word I think of when I look at you.'

For a moment I nearly laughed. I thought of Jody and Molly's pitying looks, the healthy recipes they nudged across the table to me every coffee time, the way they talked over me in conversation without even realising they'd done so. I thought of Murray, stepping carefully in and out of my life every Friday, drip-feeding me information about his own on a need-to-know basis. And Gretel, trying to stage a hostile takeover of my child as though he was a business interest and I was some kind of underperforming CEO.

But then, a new picture flashed into my mind, so clear, so unexpected, that I almost forgot to breathe.

Maybe I *was* doing a good job with Pip. Maybe I was funny, and warm, and even beautiful, and somebody would want me again. Maybe I could be part of a proper family, a family with me at its strong, beating heart.

It was as though I'd suddenly caught the other picture in an optical illusion, seen the old crone morph into a beautiful young woman, marvelling that it had been there in front of me all along, marvelling that none of the marks on the page had changed.

I turned to Steve, trying to find the words to explain what had just happened.

'Relax, I'm not going to make a move,' he said in a low voice. 'I'm happy just to be here with you. You're important to me and I don't want to screw that up.'

And so we sat there, side by side, staring out of the window into the dark, him telling me how he'd like to paint Blackness Castle, if he could come on a summer evening, in exactly the right kind of light, me aware only of the sound of his voice, and the breath rising and falling in my chest, feeling quite brand new.

Hattie

Okay. Just back from babysitting.

The first weird thing is that the layout of the flat is the same as Miss Fortune's old flat, except the bathroom's at the back, between the back bedroom and the kitchen.

'You've even got that same odd little side door!' I said. 'Do you remember we used to pretend it led into a dungeon where she kept her victims? You heard thumping sometimes.'

Janey laughed. 'It only leads into the tenement stair. It's very boring.'

'Are you suuuure?'

'Yes! That's the way we get to the back garden. Well, the drying green, really. It's just a patch of grass.'

'Dog poo,' said Pip, in the tone of someone relaying very bad news.

'Yes,' she said. 'Some old lady upstairs lets her dog out there and never picks up after him. Poor Pippy fell over last time we went out there, and he got it all over his trousers and his coat. So we go to the park when we want to play, don't we?'

'Pa-rk?' said Pip in a sing-song voice. 'Now-w?'

He had a tantrum when Janey said no, we weren't going to the park, not when it was dark, raining and time for his bath. I was ready to say yes – anything to stop the noise – but she must've known what she was doing because he stopped. This mother-child thing is like a dance. He kicks off and all his feelings shoot out everywhere, noisy and bright and kind of nerve-shredding, like fireworks, and she lets that happen but somehow contains him at the same time. She encircles him, moves with him, until he slows, breathes and stops. How did she learn this?

She took ages fussing around, asking if I was sure we'd be okay, and writing her mobile number on three different bits of paper.

'Oh, and before I go, I thought you might want to take *this*.'

She went into a cupboard and brought out a cardboard box.

'It's all your stuff. Your diary and everything. School bits and pieces. You might as well have it now. Look, I'll phone you around nine, okay, and check things are . . .'

I told her to leave, to have a good time. 'He's only two,' I said. 'How hard can it be?'

There was a wild cackle from the sitting room, and a massive thump.

'Oh God,' she said. 'He likes launching himself on and off the sofa. Don't let him do that, will you, Hats?'

I nodded firmly, trying to look as though I could do that encircling thing if I needed to.

'Don't go, Mummy!' wailed Pip, appearing in the hall, knowing by some weird toddler telepathy the exact moment she'd turned to leave.

After I'd given him a bath, and put him in his cot, I went back to the kitchen to make some tea. But The Box was there on the table.

I couldn't have it just *sitting* there all night. I turned the contents onto the table, just about smashing a lumpy grey squirrel sculpture in the process. I flicked through my school jotters, and opened a page of the diary, when a little hand appeared on my knee and just about made my heart stop.

'Pip! Did you climb out of your cot? That was dangerous!'

He looked doubtfully down at his Spider-Man pyjamas.

'Don't worry, don't worry.' I didn't want him bursting into tears. 'Hey, would you like a story?'

He knelt down, beside a book of piano music that had fallen on the floor. And he pointed a solemn finger at a photograph of the composer on the glossy back cover.

Esme Fortune, according to the thick black script underneath. Esme Fortune, with an over-powdered face and a slash of orange lipstick, and that smile.

I remembered her giving the book to me: a suite of German folk melodies arranged for piano and violin. She'd suggested that James and I could practise them together over the Christmas holidays.

'Owd lady.'

I shivered. Something about the little soft finger and that face.

'Hungry,' said Pip, sensing a moment of weakness.

I told him that it was too late for snacks, that we'd already brushed his teeth. A step I was not in a hurry to repeat.

'Firsty.'

'Let's get you back to bed.'

'I *firsty*!'

195

So I made him a fresh bottle of milk, but as I was carrying him back through to bed, he clamped the bottle teat in his mouth, and I can't have put the lid on properly because it came off, soaking me in milk.

'Don't wowwy,' he shrieked, scrambling down me and darting off into the hallway.

'Where are you going?'

'Get Mummy cloves.'

I followed him into her bedroom.

Bursting to show how helpful he could be, he ran for the chest of drawers near the window and pulled one of them open.

'Oh no, Pippy. That's her underwear.'

He pulled open the second drawer down. It was socks this time, all folded into neat pairs. But there was a glimpse of blue underneath. I pushed the socks aside and there was a cardboard folder. With 'Hattie' written on the front. I shouldn't have, I know . . .

But the contents didn't mean anything to me. They were pictures, cuttings, squares of glossy, filmy paper cut from magazines and catalogues. There was a newborn wrapped in a white, satin-edged blanket from The White Company, and a chubby-thighed baby, asleep in her cot, looking comfy in a Pampers nappy. There was a curly-haired pre-schooler beaming as she sank her sharp white milk teeth into a triangle of Dairylea. There was a series of shots of a dark-haired girl who looked about seven, sporting an array of coats and bright hats and scarves, and cosy woollen sweaters, as she cavorted against an autumn woodland backdrop. There was a smug-looking teenager astride a pony at the Gleneagles riding school.

'Here!' called Pip. He'd been rummaging in some boxes under the bed.

He flung a swimming costume at me, and a grey nursing bra that had frankly seen better days.

When he saw the clippings in my hands, he frowned and pointed to the framed photograph of himself on the bedside table. 'Pippy. See?'

I told him he was very handsome. He smiled, as though I'd passed some sort of test, and dragged me out of the room to show me his trains.

He was still awake when she got in. She'll probably never ask me to babysit again.

But, oh Janey. What's going on?

31

Janey

'I'm not stopping – I need to collect Pip at twelve. Here it is.'
I handed the bag over with a hard stare.

'Oh *brilliant*, thanks. You're a star.' Her voice was too gushy.

'Why do you need an electric blanket suddenly? Are you really that cold?'

She grabbed my arm and pulled me into the hallway.
'Listen, Janey. James is arriving next week. I thought maybe
you and Pip could come over for dinner? I know you said you
were busy, but please. I'm asking you with a big *please*.'

'I don't think so, Hattie.'

'I know, I know the house freaks you out. But James . . . he'll
normalise it. He never lived here while any of the weird stuff
happened. He's exactly what we need. Don't be shy of him.
Come on, remember the fun we had?'

A short, bitter laugh escaped, and then this, 'You think I hate
this house because of a freaky music case, Hattie? Really?'

'What, then?'

'I really can't. I have to go.' I started towards the door.

'There's obviously something I'm in the dark about,' said
Hattie in a quiet voice. 'What is it, please?'

'I can't see James.'

'Why not?'

'What's the point, Hattie? What's the fucking point now?'

My voice sounded thin and melodramatic. *Language*, I seemed to hear my grandmother say.

But I sat down on the bottom stair, resting my elbows on my knees, suddenly tired of all the things I wasn't saying. Maybe I should take a leap of faith. Maybe it would be like a Narnian tale, and we'd hold hands and plunge through that dark pool into another world. Maybe we'd find our old selves there, and all that weary, intervening time would collapse into nothing.

Hattie sat down next to me. She wiggled one small, neat foot, nails painted the colour of cherryade.

I shuffled my feet in their dull black boots, so that the right was on a black square, the left on a white.

'Tell me.'

'Okay, if you really want me to.' I sighed. Why was my voice coming out like a nine-year-old? 'I was in Lower Five. Summer term. There was a party. This girl Laura Mallard, who I knew from the Saltire Youth Orchestra, invited me.'

Hattie looked surprised.

'Oh, I know. I wasn't a party sort of girl, really. But Laura had invited herself to stay over at mine because she'd cottoned on to the fact that Granny was clueless and wouldn't ask questions about the party, and she was right. Granny had no idea. The last party I'd been to had been a slumber party where we'd watched *Indiana Jones* and felt daring because we'd stolen two packets of Wotsits from the kitchen cupboard.'

'But this party was different?'

'This party was different. It was a student thing. Organised by—'

'Some students?' She shot me a teasing smile.

'J-james,' I said. My throat went tight.

'James? As in . . .'

'Your brother.'

'You mean the party was—'

'Here. Yes.'

'But the house was being let out. James wasn't living here.'

She shrugged, as though my story didn't add up, couldn't be true. She probably thought she knew about this house, every way in which it was haunted. Good old Janey wasn't supposed to come out with revelations, she was supposed to stay safely in her sidekick role.

I shook my head. Such awful thoughts.

'I know. I was surprised to see him too. I'd no idea we were even coming here until Laura walked me here from the bus. I was already half drunk. Laura had a bottle of cider, one of those huge plastic ones. She hid it in her cello case. Granny did, actually, question why she was taking her cello, and when Laura said we were going to have a music session at the party, Granny insisted I take my keyboard, too. I had to drag it all the way to the party, the bus driver nearly wouldn't let us on the bus.'

Suddenly, now, telling it to Hattie, it seemed *funny*. I felt a little flare of anticipatory relief . . . Telling this to Hattie *was* going to neutralise it, frame it as something else. I looked up at her, expecting to see her smile.

But she was staring at me in what could only be described as horror. As if she'd seen me for the very first time.

She stood up, shakily, holding on to the banister.

'Oh Christ, Janey. I've forgotten I've got to . . . take that . . . thing back.' She swayed slightly, her eyes fixed on the floor at her feet. 'I've got to go.'

About to lose my audience, I had to fast-forward. 'The room upstairs, Hattie. The noises you heard, when I came here for dinner with Pip.' My words were falling over each other. 'The night of the party, James found me up there, I was falling-over drunk and—'

She drew her coat around her. 'I'm sorry, sweetie. I really must dash. We'll do this another time. Promise.'

We'll do this another time. As though it was a manicure, or a trip to Harvey Nichols.

She walked towards the entrance vestibule, ushering me along – vaguely, charmingly – with an outstretched arm.

'Hattie. *Please*—'

She swung to face me. 'Where was Laura Mallard when all this was going on? She's the one that took you to the party and started you drinking. She should have been looking out for you. Where the hell was she?'

Suddenly I was so angry I could hardly breathe.

'Where the hell were *you*?'

She made a sound halfway between a sob and a laugh, and in a strange, childlike movement, placed her hands over her ears. 'Ramplings.'

'Why did you never – *never* – get in touch?' I persisted.

'Our letters must have—'

'*Fuck* the letters. You could have phoned me. You could have written from home during the holidays. I didn't even have your address. Nothing.'

Her gaze drifted over my shoulder, back into the hallway behind me. She made a strange noise, like the sound Pip makes when he's having a bad dream. For a second I wanted to put my arms around her.

'Hattie?'

Her eyes jumped back to my face.

'What?' she said, her eyes wild and caught. Then she

blinked, and the smile was back in place, plastered across her face: 'What is it, hon? Hmm? Because I really have to go.'

I reached for the right words, but they'd all gone.

'Nothing,' I said. 'Nothing, Hattie, nothing.'

And I walked past her, out of that wicked, endlessly beloved house. For the last time, surely, now. For the last time.

★

Pip wasn't happy when I arrived to pick him up from nursery. He'd been in the middle of painting when I'd arrived. 'Dend,' he insisted.

I glanced at his painting, stuck to the easel with tape – two slashes of black paint. 'You can finish your painting tomorrow,' I said. 'It's time to go home for some lunch.'

'Dend.' His hands, half-covered by the too-long plastic sleeves of the painting apron, clenched into small fists. We were heading into tantrum territory. Mrs Paxton came to the rescue.

'How about I put your painting safely over here and you can carry on with it tomorrow?'

Pip turned to her and nodded with a slow blink, as though, finally, he'd found someone who talked sense.

He wasn't impressed by his lunch, either, when we got home. I'd forgotten to buy the plastic white bread he preferred for his jam sandwiches and attempted to pass off a semi-wholemeal substitute. He wailed as I set it down in front of him.

'Come on,' I pleaded, sitting next to him. 'Just try it.'

Two tears, fat little globes, quivered on his lower lashes. He looked so *sad*.

'Oh, Pippy,' I whispered, and leant my forehead against his.

He screeched, pushing his feet against the table so hard that his chair tipped and almost fell backwards.

My phone buzzed in my pocket. My heart leapt: it must surely be Hattie, telling me she did want to hear it, telling me to come back.

But it was Steve. One of his classes had been cancelled. Could he pop down?

He arrived just as I'd got Pip down for his sleep. Guilty about the disappointing lunch, I'd given him a bottle of milky. He'd fallen asleep instantly, cheeks flushed, face set into a slight frown, as though unconsciousness was the only reasonable response to the proffering of wholemeal bread.

'What's up?' asked Steve as he came in. His forehead glistened with rain, as it had the first time I'd seen him.

All these struggles, I wanted to say. *All these struggles nobody sees.*

'Oh,' I shrugged. 'Pip's not happy with me.'

He drew me into a hug, and we swayed, slightly, there in the hall. How strange, to find myself there in his arms, at two o'clock on an ordinary Tuesday afternoon. It wasn't ordinary, though. Something was about to happen. I felt as though another world – older, realer – was pressing against this one, about to break through.

I thought of Hattie, in that other house, her hand outstretched towards the door.

'Tell me about it. Talk to me.'

'I just had a disastrous conversation with Hattie. Oh God, I don't know why I'm telling you.'

Because you've opened a door. You've opened a door and it's all going to flood through.

I drew away from him. 'It's all so pointless. And so long ago.'

203

He sat down on the floor, back against the wall, long legs stretched out in front of him, and held out a hand towards me.

'Come and sit down next to me. Tell me all about it. I'm listening.'

★

James had answered the door with his shirt tails hanging out of his jeans, a cigarette in one hand, hair rakishly dishevelled. He'd wobbled, standing on one foot as he hung on to the vast black door, and raised an eyebrow at the sight of Laura's cello case and my 88-key Casio keyboard.

The sight of him sent a sharp shot of adrenaline through me. Not just because I'd always been half in love with him, cherishing dreams of marrying him so that Hattie and I would be sisters, but because it meant the Marlowes were still here. I'd always thought the house had been rented out or sold after Renee and Hattie had gone, a theory borne out by the strange voice that had started answering the phone after a couple of months.

'Is Hattie here?' I gasped, almost tumbling over the threshold, and shoving my keyboard up against the wall.

'Nnnnnope,' he said, already turning towards the basement stairs. 'Come and get a drink.'

'Where is she?' I followed him down the stairs.

'Ramplings, presumably.'

I felt a dull throb of hurt in my chest, and in that moment realised how deeply I'd hoped that Hattie had never made it to Ramplings, that her mother had spirited her abroad somewhere, to Monte Carlo or Rio de Janeiro. That would be why she'd never got in touch.

He opened the door into the kitchen and I was hit with a wall of noise, and the heat of teenage bodies. James disappeared into the mass. Laura flicked her mane of long blonde hair and seamlessly joined a group of girls standing to the left.

I hovered where I was for a little while, unsure whether to tag onto Laura's group, who'd formed a closed circle, or to stay where I was, standing alone by the door. Or I could turn around, haul my keyboard away and leave.

Five boys, rugby lads, by the look of them, barged past me into the hall.

A couple of girls arrived, shrieking with laughter at a private joke and throwing their coats onto the kitchen dresser behind me.

Then I saw the drinks, all set out on the kitchen table – wine, cider, and bottle after bottle of spirits, glittering green and amber and ice white in the candlelight. Yes, I could get Laura a drink, and then I could tap her on the shoulder, and she'd have to let me stand beside her with the girls. I made my way over.

And then I stood. Because what on earth was I supposed to give Laura to drink? A gin and tonic, perhaps? That was Mum's favourite. I picked up the bottle, unsure how to actually make one.

Somebody appeared at my side. James.

'Er . . .' I said, waving the bottle in a questioning sort of way.

He took it from me, and sloshed several inches of gin into a glass, adding a trickle of tonic by way of an afterthought. Then he handed it to me with a nod. An approving nod, at the fact that I was drinking the hard stuff.

'What's Hattie been up to?' I shouted. The Clash was blaring from the stereo: 'Should I Stay or Should I Go'.

He looked at me blankly.

'Hattie? What's she been doing?'

He shrugged and glanced over my shoulder, scanning the faces at the other side of the room. I had to keep him talking. Taking a glug of gin, I stepped closer so I could talk into his ear.

'Are you at Edinburgh Uni?'

'Er . . . no?' He gave me a pitying look, as though I'd made an enormous faux pas. 'I'm at the Royal College of Music? I'm up for Pollock's eighteenth. You know Pollock, right?'

'Oh yeah,' I said. The name did sound familiar. 'Yeah. Jackson Pollock.'

He laughed, and looked at me properly for the first time. Little crinkles appeared round his eyes.

'*Great* party,' I said, suddenly infused with confidence. 'Really nice of your parents to let you have a party here.'

He snorted. 'Yeah, right. We got in through the back. The tenants are away touring for six months, and the catch on the kitchen window is busted.'

I was shocked. 'What about the alarm?'

'Nobody's ever changed the fucking code!'

'Oh yes. It's Hattie's birthday, isn't it?' I laughed and rolled my eyes, eager to demonstrate my insider knowledge of the Marlowe family.

James poured another inch of gin into my glass. 'Drink up.'

I smiled properly for the first time. He was being so *nice*. I could stick with him all evening and not have to worry about being a sad case on my own.

'Oh, there's Gary. *Hey! Gaz!*'

Gaz came over, and they started talking about a 'gig' they'd recently been to. I stood, nodding and smiling, and laughing when they laughed, until I realised that they'd completely tuned out of the fact that I was there.

I drifted off to find Laura, making four or five hesitant circuits of the kitchen, but I couldn't see her anywhere. My head was swimming. The gin, the sudden freedom from Granny and school, seemed to be loosening feelings I'd been trying to keep stuck down for a long time. I saw the door in front of me, a bright patch of light, and made my way up the stairs. Laura might be upstairs, and I did need to find her. But that needing somehow changed, with each wobbly step, into needing to find Hattie's room, needing to go in there and close the door, lie down on her bed, and pull the covers over my head.

But James caught up with me on the second-floor landing.

'Hey, why are you crying?' He pulled me in close to him, holding my head against his chest. 'I could hear you down in the kitchen, for God's sake.'

He smelt of cigarettes and gin, but underneath was the smell of Hattie. The lemon soap, the washing powder. Inexpressibly comforting.

The opening bars of Madonna's 'Crazy for You' floated up from the basement, and I melted against him. He started – oh God, he was kissing me – and in one fluid move, he opened the door of his bedroom and moved me backwards, still kissing, until we fell onto his bed.

There was no sheet on the bed, only a coarse yellow blanket stretched over the mattress. But there was a stale-smelling duvet and matching pillow.

'Sorry about the Danger Mouse covers,' he murmured into my ear, as he slid his hand under my top.

'Ha! That's okay. I've still got Paddington Bear ones,' I

said, trying to match his ironic tone and somehow failing. 'Somewhere at home. At the back of a cupboard.'

'The tenants must have left them.'

'Oh . . . Yeah . . . I would have left them too, if they were mine.'

It was okay. He would only want to have a bit of a roll around on the bed. Surely he wouldn't want to – dare to – have sex. I pictured Mrs White glaring over her spectacles as Hattie and I had giggled through the 'human reproduction' part of our textbook, with the bearded, hippy-ish-looking man and his soppy blonde wife.

Giggles were all very well, but when I looked down and saw James' *thing* then, thick and fleshy and very real, all of a sudden it occurred to me that I was out of my depth. Even with the gin swilling round my system, I knew that much.

He reached under my skirt, started pulling at the elastic of my pants. A terrible thought struck me: what if I smelled, down there? Nothing could be worse than that. I took hold of the exploring hand, kissed it sweetly and laid it against my shoulder. But when I let go it was back down there again, his strong violinist's fingers pushing the fabric to one side and feeling around. I remembered him proudly showing me his calluses, one exeat weekend not long after he'd started at Ramplings.

If we did it, though, that would surely mean we were going out together. James would get me back in touch with Hattie. Maybe we'd spend next Christmas together, singing round the tree and opening our presents. Renee could stay in Monte Carlo or whatever, and the three of us could keep house together, making cheese toasties and heating soup.

The blanket scratched my skin as he pulled my skirt up past

my hips and moved on top of me, pushing my legs apart with his knee . . .

And then into me. Every muscle tensed and I drew a sharp, shallow breath at the pain.

'Come on,' he muttered, pausing and shifting so that he could change angles.

And then he moved, and I knew that what I'd felt a moment ago hadn't been real pain. It hadn't been anywhere close.

I tried to find words. Maybe it wasn't too late to get him to stop. But he was making such strange grunting sounds. And his eyes were closed, lips drawn back over his teeth in a grimace. He hardly seemed like James any more.

I tried to think of him as he used to be – just back from boarding school with his violin case and a trunk of boy-smelling clothes, or rampaging around the forests of Glen Eddle in a cagoule – and when I found that I couldn't, panic rose up like bile in my throat.

It would be okay. It would stop soon. I held my breath as he gouged in and out of me, struggling with the waves of nausea. I pushed at his chest, but in the manner of a polite request rather than an imperative, and he gave no sign of having noticed. My mouth flooded with saliva and I managed to pull myself up on one elbow.

'James . . .'

His eyes opened, blank and empty. With one hand, he pushed me back down onto the bed. Lying there, my collarbone pressed under the flat of his hand, I thought of the grey, formaldehyde-drowned frog Mrs White had dissected in biology, its legs crooked and pinned to the sides, its cloudy eyes. I remembered how I'd cried for it that day.

The room started to spin, spinning off my thoughts, so that

I became nothing, nothing more than the pale ceiling above me, the sound of the headboard thumping against the wall, the waiting for it to stop. And then – because it didn't matter any more – the sound of my own sobs.

Finally, he shuddered and collapsed on top of me. I felt him pulse inside me before he pulled out and rolled onto his back. I lay there, frog legs trembling, and pulled the pillow over myself.

'Yeuch.' He stared at his hand, then wiped it on the yellow blanket, leaving a smear as red as paint. 'Blood.'

I couldn't say anything. My jaw was shaking. I closed my hand around it, held it over my mouth.

What was going to happen now? Was he going to shout at me, for getting blood everywhere? Or hold me, kiss me again, invite me for Christmas lunch? Which James was he going to be, now that we'd done this thing? Which Janey was I supposed to be? It seemed, in that moment, impossible that I could be any kind of Janey, ever again.

A voice came from outside the room. 'James! Where the fuck are you, mate?'

'Gaz,' he said, as if to himself. He reached for his trousers and yanked them on, the change in his pockets jingling as he stood up. 'There in a sec!' he shouted.

'We're out of fucking beer, you twat.'

'Hang on,' he called, fumbling with his zip, pulling on his Doc Martens. He moved towards the door, then turned around briefly, casting his eyes over the room, the bed, me. Then he left, slamming the door shut behind him.

★

'No,' whispered Steve. 'Oh God.' He was holding his face in his hands, against knees that were pulled up in front of him. I saw that one of his shoes had come undone, the end of one white lace muddy where he'd stood on it.

'I didn't say no.'

He lifted his head, dragging the hands down his face, skin taut between the splayed fingers.

'Jesus Christ, Janey. You were fourteen. You were off your face from drinking spirits for the first time. You were clearly distressed. Nothing you said or did – or didn't say – could've amounted to consent.' He spat out the words, enunciating each one with vicious clarity.

'Yes. But if . . .'

So many ifs. If I'd actually said no. If I'd pushed him off more forcefully. If I'd stayed downstairs in the kitchen. If I hadn't drunk so much.

'Look at me. *Look* at me, Janey.'

I managed to for a second. His eyes looked red and sore.

'He treated you like you were *nothing.*'

I exhaled, trying to let his anger ignite inside me, to let it touch that cold grey nothing. Then shrugged, and said quietly, 'It was a long time ago. But there's—'

A thin cry emanated from Pip's room. Silence. And then another, more insistent.

Go back to sleep. Back to sleep, baby.

'Mama! Mama!'

'Look, I'm sorry. You'd better go,' I said.

He stood up. 'I can't leave you.'

'I need to see to Pip. He's always out of sorts when he wakes up after his nap. He might get upset to find you here.'

'Will be you be okay?'

211

I nodded.

He put both hands on my shoulders and looked me straight in the eye. It was like an arrow hitting home. 'I'm glad you told me. I'll call you later, okay?'

Hattie

I should have listened to you. I know that. I should have stood there and listened to you telling me about James, and whatever it is he did.

Did *to you*. Because at fourteen, you were only a child.

I was aware, in a dull sort of way, that it would mean letting go of James. I mean the old James. The skinny boy in Superman pyjamas who used to read his Asterix comics to me when I couldn't sleep. Who sometimes let me sleep in his room, with his *Peter and the Wolf* tape playing at volume ten, when Mum and Dad were shouting at each other downstairs.

And maybe it would mean letting go of you too, the Janey I took with me when I left: giggling in biology, limping and mutinous in cross-country, sitting in my kitchen solemnly painting vinegar onto the ends of my hair, because you were worried I'd get a hairball and die, like Amadeus.

But it wasn't just that, I found that the person I've become couldn't listen. The nail polish, the perfect skin, the designer labels, the relentless common-sense attitude; it all started to slip and slide, like a cheap painting left in the rain.

And the person I've become couldn't stay to see what I saw. Not just you, standing there in front of me, with your arms crossed over yourself and your sleeves pulled over your hands. But blood, pooling on the tiles beneath you. Dripping off your hands and sliding down your legs.

And I could barely hear the sound of my own voice, let alone yours, over the sound of the crying.

I'm sorry, I'm sorry, I'm sorry.

I'm sorry for whatever happened. For whatever's coming. Sorry for it all.

32

Janey

Had it been the right thing, I wondered, to mention Pip's nursery parents' evening to Murray? I sighed as I surveyed the new 'My Family' artwork display in the nursery corridor: gloopy humanoids whose legs were fixed straight onto their heads, and a few monstrous-looking cats or dogs.

Pip's painting was a single blue line, bold at one end, scratchy and thin at the other where the brush had run out of paint.

What did it mean, I wondered? What had he been thinking? As though in response, I heard his shrill shriek emanate from the room upstairs where the special evening crèche was taking place.

He'd be exhausted by the time this was over – the crèche wasn't an ideal solution. Hard to believe that it was only a week ago that Hattie had offered to babysit any time I wanted. But there'd been no word from her after the James conversation, until she'd texted late last night, to say there'd been a change in her plans. She was going to London for a while. One of her clinics there needed nursing back to health. Apparently Ernie had had to fire the manager. 'I'll be in touch next time I'm up in Edinburgh!!!' she'd written, as though the use of exclamation marks might soften the blow, the implication that she'd gone for good.

I placed a hand against the wall and leaned there for a

moment, trying to draw some kind of obscure strength from Pip's blue line.

The front door opened and in came Murray, with – *what?* – Gretel in tow. I gave him a hard stare, which he ignored.

'Oh, hi,' said Gretel, as though vaguely surprised to find me there. 'The traffic was terrible. There were roadworks on the Mound so we had to double back and cut round the back of John Lewis, but then York Place was closed westbound. So we had to go down Broughton Street but it took forever. They've still got part of it coned off. And then I remembered I had to get lemongrass for the green Thai curry tonight – Murray doesn't like the red, it goes for his stomach – so we stopped at the little organic shop at the bottom of the hill. They didn't have any. Useless shop. So we'll need to go to Tesco on the way home. And then it was impossible to park. So we've left Trixie to park the car.'

I gave a nervous laugh, picturing Trixie working the clutch with an extended hind leg, checking the mirrors with earnest doggy eyes as she reversed into a narrow New Town parking space.

Behind them, the heavy red front door opened an inch or two and then swung back: someone was struggling to get in. Gretel stepped back on one six-inch acid green heel and watched. Murray, whose eyes had glazed over during Gretel's monologue, sprang to the door to admit a stooped, wizened old woman in a long black coat with silver buttons.

'Ah,' said Murray. 'Janey, meet Trixie, er, Gretel's mother.'
Perfect.

'Oh, hello!' I said, overcompensating. 'Pleased to meet you. How nice. What a good turnout.'
A good turnout? *Idiot, Janey.*

'Why is Gretel's mother called Trixie?' I demanded of Murray in hushed tones, as the two women inspected the artwork display.

'Why shouldn't she be called Trixie?'

'It doesn't sound very German. I thought she was called Mutti.'

'Mutti just means "mum" in German. And Trixie is short for Beatrix.'

'Doesn't sound very German either.'

He shook his head, his face screwed in impatience. '*I* don't know, Janey. Gretel's granny was English. Maybe she was into Beatrix Potter or something. What does it matter if her name's Trixie?'

Because I sent the woman a jar of bone-shaped dog biscuits.

And asked if she'd been fully vaccinated.

'Why did you say your house had a "lovely garden for Trixie"?'

'Because she lives in a retirement flat. I'm failing to see the issue here, Janey. Get to the point, if there is one.'

I cleared my throat.

'You should have told me you wanted to bring them tonight. It's a parents' evening, "parent" being the operative word. And what about the puppy, anyway? Where's he?'

'Bingo? He's asleep in his cage at home. Why the effing hell do you care?'

It could've tipped into a full-scale row, but just then Mrs Paxton came out of the Rainbow Room and ushered us in.

Having to sit on a tiny blue plastic chair seemed to calm Murray, or at least take the wind out of his sails. There were yellow ones for me and Mrs Paxton, and red for Gretel, who'd somehow managed to fold her legs gracefully to the side. She'd taken off her jacket to reveal a shift dress in a leafy pattern reminiscent of Miss Fortune's infamous green-and-olive number. I caught the eye of Trixie/Mutti, who was standing, hovering on Gretel's other side, and she looked away quickly.

'Pip is getting on so well,' began Mrs Paxton. 'A pleasure to have in the class.'

Murray nodded and made murmuring, appreciative noises, and Gretel flashed one of her girlish smiles at him. I was sitting close to her, one of her bare, tanned, slightly heavy arms just inches away from mine. I could smell her perfume and, underlying that, the faint, sherbet scent of deodorant.

It was amazing, the way she occupied her space in the room, the very opposite to invisible. She exuded the same air of entitlement, the 'nothing can go wrong' confidence that she had on the Thomas train.

'He seems very happy here,' I said with a tentative smile. Maybe there *was* no reason to be tense. Everyone was here because they wanted the best for Pip.

But Gretel turned to Murray. 'You said you were going to ask about his delusions.'

'Oh, er . . .' As Murray looked to Mrs Paxton for help, Gretel glanced back at me with a tiny triumphant twist of her mouth.

And here was the catch, of course, with her 'nothing can go wrong', golden-girl aura. My world could crumble around me, I could end up as a lunatic in a secure facility and lose Pip forever, and in Gretel's book, nothing *would* have gone wrong . . .

Mrs Paxton smiled wide enough to display two gold-capped molars, and screwed up her eyes to make it look like it was heartfelt.

'I take it you're referring to Pip's rich imaginative life? I want to reassure you that this isn't anything to be concerned about. His imaginary friend, this *Dend*, is nothing to worry about. In fact, we've all rather got used to having Dend around!'

So Dend had followed Pip to nursery. I began to feel sick.

'Is Dend much in evidence at home, Miss Johnston?'

'A bit.' I cast my mind back. 'But I'm not so sure it's a specific thing. "Dend" is just his word for friend.'

'Does he have any friends?' asked Gretel.

'Pip is a little shy,' conceded Mrs Paxton brightly. 'But this is entirely normal at his stage of development. He is learning to socialise with his peers. That is a big part of his learning journey.'

'So. No friends?' said Gretel.

'At this stage he plays mostly by himself . . .'

My heart contracted in pain. Pip sitting in the corner, or gazing at the window waiting for home time.

'But he does join in group activities when he's in the mood,' she went on. 'He likes music sessions, in particular. Although there has been some conflict over instruments. Dend always insists on having the tambourine,' she added with a delicate grimace. 'There's only one, and it is rather sought after.'

Murray shifted in his chair, clearly itching to offer funding for more tambourines.

'Just one more thing,' said Mrs Paxton. 'I'd like to make sure we have a joined-up approach to Pip's eating issues. I wanted to check, have you sought any advice about it? From health professionals, a nutritionist, anything like that?'

'Dr Polson told me not to worry,' I said. 'As long as he is eating something. And his milk is full of nutrients. He said the worst thing I could do was make a fuss.'

218

'Chuh!' This noise came from Gretel. 'That's because his NHS budget won't stretch to a proper referral. Murray, we'll organise something, yah? Get it fast tracked?'

For God's sake. I worried about Pip's eating. Of course I did. But he was doing okay, couldn't Gretel see that? His heart was beating, his lungs were breathing, his cheeks were pink. He could talk, and play, and run in the bright open air of the park, and laugh himself into a giggling heap over the slightest of reasons. He could open his eyes to look at me, and his mouth to tell me he loved me, and these things were all miracles.

Gretel didn't know what it took to keep a little life going, day after day, week after week, all the worry, and coaxing, and hoping. And the pleading with fate, in the darkest hours of the night, that no disasters would happen.

She had no idea.

I felt my fists tighten. Actually no, just my left fist. I released it and it tightened again.

Oh God. No!

My left hand reached over, grabbed the back of Gretel's chair and shoved. There was a loud crack as the plastic parted company from the metal legs, tipping Gretel to the side, then a flash of lime green as one of her heels flew into the air.

*

They insisted on coming back to the flat, the full delegation: Murray, Gretel and Trixie/Mutti.

I showed them into the sitting room, and took Pip off to his room to play with his trains. No way did I want him to hear this conversation. It took me a good minute and a half to prise him off me.

'Missed you, Mama,' he kept saying.

'Missed you, too.' Oh God, my nose was running. I was about to cry all over him. 'Now, see if you can make a nursery school for your trains, and I'll be back in a few minutes with your milky and a jam sandwich. Deal?'

Back in the sitting room, I tried to appease Gretel once again. She stood, side by side with Murray, in front of the bay window. Mutti was perched on the piano stool, looking as though she'd quite like to leave.

'I'm so sorry. I saw that the chair was about to break and I put out a hand to try and stop you falling.'

'You shoved me,' said Gretel calmly. She wasn't hurt: she'd landed in the story corner, and a large Winnie the Pooh had broken her fall.

'I don't know what to say. I'm sorry if it seemed like that. I misjudged the distance, or something.'

Murray sighed. 'I'll get to the point, Janey. Our lawyer says you haven't responded to either of the letters he's sent to you.'

'Well,' I said. 'You're having Pip stay over one night every fortnight, which is what you wanted. I assumed you'd have told me yourself if there were any issues.'

'We want to formalise the access arrangements,' Gretel cut in. 'Murray told you that already. We've some concerns about Pip, and we think it would be more balanced for him to spend more time with us. Say . . .' She glanced heavenwards and shrugged, pretending to search for inspiration. 'Friday to Sunday, three times a month.'

Murray turned around and faced the window. It had begun raining heavily.

'Balanced, how?' My voice sounded tiny in the room.

'Well, rather than spending most of his time with just one person he'd be—'

'No,' I said. 'He's only two. He would hate to be apart from me.'

'That's the problem,' said Gretel. 'He's too attached to you, your relationship is too exclusive.'

'He's *two*,' I repeated.

'As Murray says, we have a number of concerns,' went on Gretel, leaning into the words as though she was enjoying this. 'The parents' evening confirmed what we suspected: that Pip is introverted to the point of being reclusive.'

'Er, Gretel . . .' said Murray, shifting round to face us. It was quite astonishing, if you really stopped to notice. In the presence of Gretel, he lost his square stance, the deeper tones in his voice.

She flicked her hand to silence him. 'Then there's the eating thing. And he's having these delusions about invisible friends which are, to be quite honest, alarming. And then there's you.'

'What about me?'

'Pushing me off chairs. Calling Murray away from work because of some issue concerning a missing glove. I would say it's your own wardrobe you should be worrying about.' She looked me up and down.

'Okay, Gretel,' said Murray. 'Lets leave the personal stuff aside. Janey, I'm sure you could do with a break from one week to the next. Pip's wonderful, but he's a full-time job. We're here, and we'd like to be involved.'

'But you two work all the time,' I said, struggling to keep my voice steady. 'Even at weekends. How would you manage it? You'd have one foot in the office the whole time.'

'That's where Mutti comes in,' she said. 'She has agreed to care for Pip when Murray and I have to work.'

Mutti nodded grimly.

'No! He can come to you for the day. He can come every Saturday. And one overnight per fortnight. That's enough for him, honestly, he's only—'

'Take some time to think about it,' said Murray, with an 'I'm a reasonable man' sort of shrug. 'We want to do this all amicably, of course. I thought we could have a trial this weekend. Have Pip to stay for two nights, so he can acclimatise. He's been fine staying one night, after all.'

'He was sad, last time,' I said. 'He was sad afterwards, and he didn't leave my side for the rest of the weekend.'

'I've been looking into Saturday activities for him,' said Murray. 'There's a wonderful orienteering centre near Peebles.'

Orienteering?

'He's only two.' I shot a pleading look at Murray.

'And I've ordered a new bed for him,' said Gretel, as if that settled the matter, the plans couldn't conceivably be changed now. 'And a set of Rangers bedcovers.'

Rangers bedcovers?

'Mutti chose them. Her friend's grandson, who lives in Corstorphine, assured her. That's what all the little boys are into.'

Mutti shifted doubtfully on the piano stool, as though she wished she could retract her statement.

'We'll pick him up from nursery on Friday lunchtime,' said Murray. 'And bring him back on Sunday.'

The thought of being in the flat alone for two whole nights while Pip slept miles away, cold under Rangers bedcovers, well, it didn't bear thinking about. But what would happen if I refused? A further deluge of solicitors' letters, followed by a summons to the family court? My inadequacies laid out in court for all to hear?

'Please.' My voice shook. 'You can have him for one night this weekend. That's fine. And I'll work up to two, I will. But just not yet. Please.'

'Okay,' said Murray. 'Let's leave it at one night this weekend. But shall we say two nights the next time, in a fortnight?'

Gretel exhaled, puffing out her cheeks as though she was making a major concession. 'Fine.'

Wasn't it *me* who was supposed to be agreeing?

'Oh, and we're calling a meeting for the seventeenth,' she went on. 'We need to get a Parenting Agreement drawn up.'

'I've arranged a solicitor for you,' began Murray. 'Someone who used to work for us but has now moved firms. She's very good. Don't worry about the cost; it's all sorted. Please Janey, try to think of this as a good thing. Gretel and I can't wait to make Pip a proper part of our family.'

Gretel flashed him her spoilt-girl smile and gave an excited little wriggle of her shoulders, as though he was talking about a big present he was going to give her. I only just resisted the urge to smack her across the face. Mutti, last out of the front door, shot me a look of apology, as though from one prisoner to another.

33

Janey

The Jungle Jive crew had descended on my flat after this morning's class instead of going for the usual coffees.

Jody had a 'technique' she wanted to tell us about.

'This was in that book about mindful parenting,' she said. 'The one Paul recommended.'

She looked around the room expectantly, and Molly supplied the chorus of 'Oh, Paul's *lovely*.'

'He found it really helpful when Shona left. Some techniques to keep Elgin really centred and calm.'

'Oh, poor Paul,' murmured Molly. '*All* on his own.'

'Apart from Geoff,' added Cleodie.

'Sit down' said Jody. Cleodie, Molly and I sat down on my living room floor, on a big picnic rug that Jody had brought, and positioned our children in front of us.

Suddenly apples were raining down around us: Jody was tossing them from her bag.

'So, you take the apple, and you sit down alongside your child and look at it for a few moments.'

'Look at the apple, Cameron,' said Molly in a sing-song voice.

'See the way the light shines off it,' said Jody gently. 'Notice the colours – tawny red, green – and the way they merge into each other. The stippled effect, almost like an artist has used a paintbrush.'

'Notice the different textures, the rough woodiness of the stalk . . .'

'The little spidery black bit at the bottom,' intoned Molly.

Pip shrieked. 'Spider!'

'No no, Pip,' I said. 'Come on, look at the apple.'

'Lift the apple. Feel the weight of it in your hand. Pass it from one hand to the other. Think of at least three similes to describe your apple.'

'As hard as a cricket ball,' said Molly, which was a mistake because Cameron picked up the apple and threw it at the marble surround of the fireplace. 'As round as the moo-oon.'

'And I'm wondering – can you *smell* your apple?' said Jody.

I lifted our apple and sniffed, then held it in front of Pip's nose. He tried to copy me, but breathed out rather than in, propelling a little snail-trail of mucus onto its surface.

'Eww,' said Cleodie, who was leaning back on the heels of her hands. Rose was already halfway through munching her apple.

'And perhaps,' said Jody lightly, 'if we want to, we might take a little bite now. See how the skin of the apple might feel under our teeth.'

She lifted the apple to her mouth and rested her large, rabbit-like front teeth on the surface of it.

Pip gave me a baleful look and got up.

'Pip, come back.'

'Twains,' he called from the hall. Vichard jumped up and followed.

'Sorry, Jody,' I said. 'He's on to us, I think.'

'You get the idea, though?'

'I get the idea. Thanks.'

'The next step, if they still don't want to bite into it, is to cut the apple up and count the pips.'

I nodded and smiled. 'I'll get some plates and knives.'

But once in the kitchen I sat down at the table and put my head on my arms, just for a moment . . .

Recently I seemed to have lost the knack of sleeping altogether. Dropping off sometime between midnight and one, I'd be awakened by the dream at two, and lie awake for an hour or so afterwards trying to calm down and get back to sleep. Pip usually woke up about four, wanting a cuddle or drink. And then he woke up for the day around six. My eyelids had been drooping all day, and I was – shamefully, horribly – desperate to hand Pip over to Murray. He'd be arriving at five o'clock.

I jerked up when I heard a voice.

'Oh dear. What's wrong?' It was Cleodie.

'I'm fine,' I said, hastily sitting up and rubbing my eyes. Had I actually fallen asleep? 'I'm just so tired.'

'Jody wanted a basin of water to do apple ducking.'

'Hmm, might be better to do it in here.'

It was all I needed, a floor covered in water and a laundry load of wet towels. But if it would get Pip to taste an apple . . .

Cleodie drew up a chair. 'You must be knackered, looking after Pip on your own. I find Rose exhausting and I only have her during the day. They're such tedious people sometimes, toddlers.'

I blurted it out: 'I'm not sleeping. I keep having this dream.'

'What dream?' Cleodie's frog-eyes widened. The kitchen was quiet – and there was no noise from the sitting room either – they must've still been contemplating the way the light fell on the apples.

And I found I couldn't hold it in much longer, I had to tell someone and there she was with her unfazed expression and kind, froggy eyes. Blissfully unconcerned with the expectations and demands of parenthood, and all its unwritten laws.

'In the dream, Pip's lying there. Hurt. And there's a . . . a frightening thing.'

Silence again. But I could hear her breathing, even and slow. She didn't seem remotely shocked.

'What sort of frightening thing? A werewolf? A tax return?'

'A thing, an object.'

But suddenly I remembered her writing. I didn't want to end up in the latest sensational novel about a madwoman in the attic. Perhaps I should amend the dream, just as a precautionary measure. I said the first thing that came into my mind.

'A slotted spoon.'

'A slotted *spoon*?' she echoed. 'Like what you'd use to lift potatoes out of the cooking water?' She spoke as though the foodstuff in question was crucial.

'Yes, or vegetables, perhaps.'

The corners of her mouth went down and she nodded slowly.

'I can see that,' she said. 'I can see why that might be frightening.'

'It's not really—'

And then, from Pip's bedroom, Jody's voice: 'Ooh, naughty naughty, you *guys*, how did you get hold of that?'

We went through. Pip and Vichard were on the floor near his cot, playing with the trains. On the cream wall behind them, a black mess of scribbles. Most of them childish, indecipherable. Apart from one word, written quite clearly a few inches above the skirting board:

HELL

I stepped back as though I'd been hit.

'They must have got hold of this,' said Jody, holding up a permanent marker.

'Hell?' I said in a little, high-pitched voice.

Jody leaned closer towards the writing. She looked . . . could she possibly look . . . *smug*?

'This'll be Pip,' she said, gesturing carelessly to the scribbles. 'And this bit down here is probably Vichard. I'm *so* sorry. Oh, I'm mortified.'

'Vichard wrote "hell" on my wall?'

'We've been doing a wee bit of phonics work at home,' said Jody. 'He's tried to write "hello". That's what's happened.'

'He's *two*.'

Jody shrugged. 'I know. What can I say? Don't worry though, Janey. Children develop at such different rates, don't they. I've heard that it's better to leave phonics work till they're in primary one, really, because otherwise they get bored, you see. The gifted ones just get *bored*.'

I looked down at Vichard, who was stuffing one of the trains into his mouth and shouting 'Gah! Gah!'

'Pip, did you see what happened?' I grabbed his hand and pulled him round to face the wall. 'Who wrote this?'

Pip looked at me blankly, then at the wall, then pulled his hand away and turned back to his trains.

'I'm not angry, Pippy. I'm not angry. But who did this?'

Had someone – something – come in here and written that while they played?

'I really must see about getting him some of those Kumon lessons,' said Jody.

'Has anyone been in here, Pip? Apart from you and Richard?'

He shrugged. 'Dend.'

I moaned quietly. Jody took my arm and led me through to the sitting room. 'Make her some sweet tea, Cleodie,' she said. Cleodie ignored her and sat down on the sofa.

'I don't know what to do,' I said. 'He won't eat. He sees imaginary people. He keeps talking about this Dend.'

Jody rubbed the back of my hand.

'Imaginary friends are very common,' she said. 'I'm sure it's *quite* rare for them to be a sign of mental problems.'

I nodded, trying to hold back tears. In that moment, Jody felt like a reassuring presence. Someone who knew so much about phonics and Kumon teachers and mindful parenting should know what they were talking about.

'Now, Paul just raved about that family therapist they were seeing. Didn't he, Moll?'

Molly nodded vigorously. '*Raved.*'

'Just to get them over the whole transition. You know, Shona moving away with her human-rights barrister.' She shrugged. 'Geoff coming on the scene.'

'He'd see all of you, I expect. Individually, and then perhaps together for some sessions. Maybe for some role-playing work, or trust exercises. You and Pip. Murray and Gretel.'

Oh, she'd be delighted about that. Maybe they'd even drag Mutti along.

'I had a long chat with Paul about it and it sounds fascinating. So, for example, Gretel might be asked to act out a scenario from your point of view. Or Murray might be invited to take on Pip's role. Maybe crouch down on the floor when he talks, so he's physically occupying a smaller place.'

'We don't need a therapist,' I whispered. 'I'm tired. Just so tired.'

Cleodie stood up. 'Everybody out,' she said, clapping her hands. 'Come on. This lady needs a nap.'

Jody looked startled and opened her mouth as though to present an alternative, subtly better proposal, but shut it again when she couldn't think of one.

'I'll watch Pip and Rose,' said Cleodie, pulling me to my feet.

And in two minutes the house was quiet, except for the faintest sound of Cleodie reading Beatrix Potter in Pip's room. I sank my head into the pillows, eyes stinging with relief.

★

My three-hour nap meant I was feeling both spacey and wide awake when Steve came round later that evening. Murray had collected Pip and I'd sat and cried as though he'd been leaving forever with his little suitcase.

It was the first time I'd seen Steve since telling him about James and the party. I could still hardly believe I'd said all those things out loud, and I didn't know how it would affect things between us. Had I taken anything sexual out of the equation by leaning on him with my tears and confidences? Had I cast him even more firmly in the role of sensitive man, platonic friend? Was this a *date*? Not a date?

He touched me lightly on the arm as he said hello, in a way that gave me no clue either way, but felt somehow more intimate than a kiss would have done.

'Wow,' he said, when we went into the living room. 'This is the piano Hattie got you?'

'Isn't it gorgeous? I've been trying out some of my old tunes again but, well, I'm not much good any more.'

'Play for me. Play for me now.'

I sat down and held my hands over the keys, letting them find the opening chords for *The Trees of Glen Eddle*. He sat on the sofa, leaning back, one ankle crossed over the other knee. Somehow, having him watching me changed everything. I felt, for the first time in years, that energy flowing down my arms, the passion thundering into the room with each chord.

When I'd finished, arms weak and shaking, he was sitting up straight, eyes fixed on me.

'It's so beautiful. You're so beautiful when you play.'

'It was you,' I said, my voice choking in my throat. 'You made it like that.'

He shook his head. 'It wasn't me.'

I got down from the piano stool and sat down next to him. He swivelled round to face me, his arm trailing along the back of the couch so it was almost touching my shoulder.

'Why didn't you make music your career?'

I shook my head. It was so ironic.

'Dreams,' I whispered. 'Dreams again. It was a different dream back then.'

'More nightmares?'

I nodded. 'I wasn't sleeping well, I was averaging about an hour a night, in the week before my audition at the RCM.'

'The Royal College of Music? Really?'

'I actually started hallucinating, in the audition.'

I remembered, as if it was yesterday, the train journey to London, how the train had stopped at Peterborough station, and I'd fought the urge to grab my case and step out onto the platform, because it was the station nearest to Ramplings. How I'd felt nauseous from the cheeseburger I'd bought in the buffet car, its bright neon cheese seeping into the hexagonal cardboard carton. I remembered emerging into a world of noise and confusion at King's Cross station, the journey to the college by Tube, clutching my ticket so hard my fingers ached. In the college itself, the very air seemed rarefied, energised, charged with a sense of dreams within reach. After what seemed like hours, it was my turn. I found myself walking into a calm, almost unnaturally quiet auditorium, sitting down at the piano, breathing its smell: the smell of the lacquered wood, the crimson felt of the hammers.

'What happened?'

I'd arranged my music on the stand, smoothed my skirts just as I'd done now, and looked briefly up at the panel – two men and a woman, sitting in the front row of seats, holding notepads. One of them said a few words, and then . . .

'Something made me look across the room, and way at the back, in the back row of seats, I saw . . . Oh God, Steve. It was awful . . . It was something from my dream.'

'Okay.' He nodded.

'I started the first piece with the wrong chord. *Unbelievably.* I'd been practising it for months. It was like my fingers had forgotten what they were doing. I panicked, and started reading the music, trying to tell my hands what to do, you know? Instead of letting them feel their way, which they were more than capable of doing if I'd only been able to stop panicking. It was a total disaster. I had to stop halfway through the second page. I ran out of the room, out of the college, tried to find my way back to the Tube station. And I had a sort of panic attack.'

I'd sunk to my knees on the pavement, gasping for air, the world turning black. I'd cowered down by some railings, covering my head with my arms, the dirty, ashy smell of the pavement filling my nose. After some minutes, a waiter emerged from a little Italian café across the road and sat me down at a rickety table with a glass of water and two amaretti biscuits. Guiseppe, his name was. I pulled myself together and smiled, thanking him profusely, saying I was quite all right now, my good-girl St Katherine's persona reviving. He called me 'Bella', stroked a curl away from my forehead and scribbled his phone number onto a little scrap of paper, which he pressed into my hand, with an unpleasantly moist kiss, as I left.

'Could you have asked for another audition? Applied somewhere else?'

'No, I got into a sort of *thing*. If I even started thinking about having another audition, a panic attack would start. I applied for secretarial college, thinking I'd try again in a year or so. But when I left St Katherine's, there wasn't the support any more.'

Without the music staff at St Katherine's, nobody in the world had cared whether I had a career in music or not. Certainly not Granny, who was in the grip of dementia by that time, or my mother, who was doing a stint in a Broadway show and whose communications now took the form of occasional postcards.

Steve's fingers were within millimetres of my shoulder now, his other hand spread flat on the cushion near my knee.

'But it's *you*, Janey. It's like . . .' he shrugged. 'It's like how squirrels bury nuts or whatever.'

Squirrels?

'Or, you know, woodpeckers. Pecking wood.'

'Woodpeckers?'

He sighed, exasperated. 'It's what you *do*.'

233

I wanted to take his stray hand. I wanted to put it on my knee, or further up my leg. I wanted to pull him on top of me, feel the weight of him on me.

Suddenly he drew in a deep breath and stood up.

'Shall we go for a walk? Or maybe a drive? If I stay here any longer I'm going to . . .'

'Going to what?'

He sighed. 'We're just going to be friends, remember?'

'Oh, okay.'

★

1990s London receded in the shock of cold Edinburgh air outside. Steve drove northwards out of town, turning off the dual carriageway at the exit to South Queensferry, weaving deftly along unlit country roads. Finally, on a stretch of open land, he pulled the car up in a lay-by. There would have been a beautiful view in the daytime, fields sloping gently down to the coast. Now, the Firth of Forth cut a black swathe through the dark landscape, with the lights of Fife scattered beyond.

'So,' he said, pulling up the handbrake and switching off the engine. 'What's this dream about?'

His voice deepened at the end of the question, as though enough was enough.

'The audition dream? Oh, that was—'

'The one now. The dream you're getting now.'

'I can't. I—'

He sighed: the tiniest sigh, barely audible. It could have been impatience, or just an acknowledgement of the difficulty of it all. 'You have to get this out. This sleeping thing can't go on. Give me one word.'

234

'Oh God . . . I, uh . . . *hammer*.'

I dropped my face to my hands. What was I *doing*?

'It's okay.' There was a pause. 'It really is okay. I'm here. I'm listening to you.'

He spoke gently, but it felt like he was peeling my skin off, one strip at a time.

'In the dream, there's a hammer.'

Saying the word was easier the second time. I could feel myself sliding towards the edge. The unburdening. How would it feel to have told someone this? It couldn't feel worse.

'And there's Pip.'

There was a slight – ever so slight – change in the atmosphere in the car. His expression remained neutral, but I sensed an edginess in his stillness now, the pads of his fingers pulsing against the denim of his jeans. Out of nowhere, *Daphnia* flashed into my mind, revealed in the pale orb of the microscope field, its antennae still and its dark heart flickering. I felt again the shock of that secret life revealed. I could almost feel the heat radiating up to my cheek, and smell the faint scorching of the light.

What was this?

Did I trust him?

I love him.

My heart had decided. I was falling.

'It's dark, and he's curled on his side in a hollow in the earth, and he's cold because he's only wearing his pyjamas, and he's cold because he's dead. And beside him, next to his body, his soft little body, there's a hammer.'

Steve exhaled softly.

'And there are mounds of earth on the side, and I'm piling them into the hollow, sweeping them in with my arms. His

235

arm, and his little neck, are the first bits to be covered. And then I'm dropping soil over his eyes, and his nose, and his mouth and he's about to go under. He's about to disappear. And then it's like a massive, million-volt shock because I realise what I've done, and I'm scrabbling in the earth. Just scrabbling, trying to uncover him, but there's nothing there. Nothing there but earth. That's when I wake up. Oh Christ. Oh *Christ*.'

'Stop it, Janey. Stop it. You're hurting yourself.'

He held my hands, where they were clawing into my upper arms, and made them go still.

'It's okay,' he said in a low voice.

I slowed my breathing. He let go of my hands and just sat, staring ahead through the darkness towards the twinkling lights.

'Aren't you going to say anything?'

'It *is* only a dream, Janey.'

'But a dream where I've k-killed Pip! Why is it happening? Why?'

'Shh-hh. Stop panicking.' He let a pause fall. 'You must have thought about it yourself. What's your own take on it? Is it related to a memory, or anything like that?'

'I've never killed anyone, no, funnily enough. It's not a hobby of mine if that's what you're worried about.'

His hands flew up in a defensive gesture. 'All right. It's just, well, dreams aren't straightforward. The hammer, the earth, even Pip, could represent other, totally different things. With recurring dreams like this, your brain's probably trying to process something.'

'Hmm.'

'Often,' he added, 'it's some kind of trauma.'

'I was supposed to feel better,' I said, in a very small voice. 'I was supposed to feel better when I'd told somebody.'

He whipped round to face me.

'Don't do this,' he said. 'Don't put it onto me like this. I can't fix it. I can't fix it the way you want me to.' His voice was shaking.

Cold. Cold washed over me and through me.

'You're right,' I said finally. 'Actually, *I* was right, there wasn't any point in talking about it in the first place. Nobody can do anything. Could you just take me home, please. I'm tired.'

'I'm sorry,' he muttered. 'This is just all screwed up. I want to help you, and I want to listen, but my head's in a spin. I care about you too much. I want to . . . Jesus, I just want to . . .' He growled and brought both hands down hard on the steering wheel.

I wanted him to kiss me. To look me in the eyes and make love to me. Now that he'd stripped me down to this with his questions, I wanted him to spill back into me and fill those spaces, those ugly gaps, with himself, so that it wouldn't matter any more.

'But what – now you know about—'

'I don't care about any of that, Janey. That's not you. That has nothing to do with sweet, beautiful you. It's some fucking awful dream that's making you miserable. Most likely because of some fucking awful thing that's happened to you. I want to make it go away for you. But I don't know how. And all I'm left with is that I just want . . . *you*.'

I looked him straight in the eye and saw a fragile new version of myself reflected back to me. The dream seemed to shear away and dissolve, something that wasn't part of me

237

after all. And then, with each breath, then I could feel myself returning, like colour seeping into what had been black and white. Into my arms, my legs, my chest, my fingers.

'I'm scared, Janey. I'm scared, all right? I want you so much and I don't think I can stay here any more.'

'Stay where?'

'On the outside. The outside of you. You're pulling me. You're pulling me in.'

'Well' – it emerged as little more than a whisper – 'come in, then.'

'I can't do what you want me to do. You seem to think I can, I don't know, fix everything, or love you until it won't matter any more. But you're going realise that I'm just . . . I'm just . . .'

I managed the three words I needed.

'Let's go home.'

*

He drove with his face set into a frown, his breathing deep and strong.

He almost looked angry. Could he have misunderstood? I searched for words, to backtrack, to ease the pressure down a notch.

'Steve?'

But then, without taking his eyes off the road, he reached across and put his hand on my leg, his fingers squeezing the soft inner part.

By the time we turned into my street I was shaking, nerve ends charged to hurting point. Inside, he pushed me up against the wall to kiss me. He reached under my shirt for my waist, the bare skin of my ribcage, sending a million stars – soft, silent, white-hot stars – shooting down my body.

'How is it, how is it that you're never just one thing? One minute you're closed, all hard edges. Beautiful hard edges that push against me . . . here, and here . . .' He ran his hands down my sides, stopping to hold my elbows, my wrists, to trace my hip bones under the denim stretch of my jeans.

'And here.' He took my chin in his hand, tilting it upwards. 'And then I hold you in a different way and you're all softness, and curves, and . . . oh *God* . . .' He slid his hand under the waistband of my jeans, cupping the curve of my hip. Pulled me closer to him.

'Shall we slow down? Do you want to slow down?' he said into my neck.

'No. Definitely not.' I detached him and led him into my bedroom.

He sat down next to me on the edge of my bed as I pulled my jeans off, a friend again for a moment. 'Are you sure, Jay? Sure you want this?'

I nodded and opened my bedside drawer. 'Look, I've even bought some up-to-date condoms.'

'So you didn't entirely buy into the "let's behave ourselves" policy then?'

'Never.'

And then he was next to me, over me, but still too far, a million miles too far. I took hold of his hand, showed him where I wanted it. He groaned, and I felt his fingers slide into me. The fingers I'd watched that first day in the art class and wanted to touch. His body was finding its way home to me after all this time.

He drew in a long, slow breath with a catch in it, and opened his mouth to say something. But I seemed to be taking off his clothes, snatching at his belt and fumbling with his zip, releasing his hardness, pulling him onto me.

And when we came to the moment – the last moment before we changed from friends to lovers – he paused to look at me, as though to register it. Then without breaking eye contact, he moved and pushed into me. And moved and pushed, slowly, again, until I'd taken the whole of him inside me.

'Are you okay?' he said, stroking a lock of hair away from my cheek. 'You should probably breathe.'

'I feel like . . .'

'What?'

'I'm falling.'

'Let yourself fall. I've got you. I won't let you go.'

Something ignited in me, in my heart and my mind, and the world caught fire. I sank back on the bed, lost, utterly lost in the feel of him, and the deep pools of those eyes, taking me and giving me back. Taking and giving me back.

34

Janey

The next day, I couldn't stop singing. I knew I probably sounded like a demented Disney princess who'd found her prince, but all the same, it was as if something inside me couldn't help but soar free. I sang while I was putting on the kettle, while I was making toast and eggs for Steve. He was looking slightly crumpled, in yesterday's clothes and with a day's growth of stubble, and I couldn't stop touching him. I stroked his arm as I put his plate in front of him, with two golden slices of toast and two beautiful, pinky-brown eggs. Had anything ever been so perfect? I laid my hands on his shoulders and back, just to learn the shape of him, to feel how his muscles would move as he spread the butter on his toast or stirred his tea. I laid my cheek against the warmth of his hair, like I did with Pip.

It was like my nerves had grown towards the surface since yesterday, and were just under my skin where before they'd been buried deep inside. I imagined them unfurling, branching into a thousand little tendrils in that dark red space.

'So,' he said, as he finished his breakfast and sat back in his chair.

'So.'

'Back to bed?' he asked with a raised eyebrow and a twist of a smile.

I sighed luxuriously, stretching out my bare feet under the

table, feeling the cool of the tiles under my toes. 'Sadly not. Pip's coming back soon.' And Murray, blasting through the flat as if it was his own.

He gave me a smouldering look. 'Not sure I can wait until next time, though. *God,* Janey.' He sat up straight, suddenly, and reached a hand across the table. 'I want to be in you. Now.'

My insides clenched. I went to him where he sat, and pulled his head to my chest. His hands ran down over my back, fingers spreading as they found the tops of my legs, pulling me in towards him.

'Do you . . .' I pulled back and looked at him. 'Were you surprised by what happened?'

'I've been wanting to take you to bed since the first day I saw you.' He inched my pyjama bottoms down a fraction, bending to plant a kiss on the strip of warm skin he'd exposed. 'Wanting to touch you, your body, your skin, your hair. Not just to imagine what you'd feel like, under my hands, but to know.' His voice deepened. 'To know you from the inside.'

I exhaled sharply as he tugged me towards him again.

'But I had no idea I'd feel like this afterwards.'

'How do you feel?'

Do you love me? Do you feel like I feel? Can this really be happening?

He clasped his hands behind his head and stretched his arms. 'I feel bloody amazing.'

I sat myself down on his knee.

'Tell me about yourself,' I said. 'I want to know you inside out too. What about parents, school, where you grew up? Your dreams? All of that stuff.'

'If we've got time for all of that, we've got time to go back to bed . . .'

I looked ceilingward, pretending to evaluate. 'If you tell me five things we can go back to bed for five minutes.'

'Parents. Both dead now. Mum was a nurse. Dad worked for a frozen-food company. From Sheffield originally. That's where I was born. We moved to Edinburgh when I was eight because of Dad's job.' He shot at look at me. 'I was on a full bursary at St Simon's, if you were wondering. A Bursary Bum, as the other boys frequently reminded me.'

'Oh! That's—'

'No brothers or sisters. I was shy as a child, then one of those angsty creative teenagers, did my degree in art and art history, and that led me to teaching at the college. Dreams? To start painting properly again, have my own workshop and gallery, somewhere on the tourist trail, so commercially viable but still beautiful. Loch Fyne or somewhere.'

'And a tea room?'

I could run your tea room and bake cakes and scones and chocolate tiffin, and Pip could get a little fishing net and paddle by the loch side on sunny days.

'Yeah?'

'Scones are always good for a tea room. I've got a recipe I could give you.'

Jesus Christ. Scones are always good for a tea room?

His lips twitched. 'Er, thank you. Anyway, that's at least ten things. Does that mean I can have you for ten minutes?'

★

And later that evening, once Pip had been delivered back from Murray's, with a new art easel from the Early Learning Centre and an adult-sized badminton set (why?), I sang to

243

him too, in his bath, and while I was rocking him on my lap at bedtime.

But halfway through my second, heartfelt rendition of 'Make You Feel My Love' he gave a gusty sigh.

'Stop-it-I-don't-like-it,' he said, in a phrase I recognised from nursery. It was a form of words you were supposed to use (instead of shouting or crying) when another child pushed you, stole your breadstick or swiped your favourite toy. I wondered fleetingly whether it would work on Gretel: 'Stop trying to steal my child. Stop-it-I-don't-like-it.'

He'd only just closed his eyes when the doorbell rang. I tiptoed to answer it, willing him not to wake up.

Steve, please let it be Steve.

But it was Hattie on my doorstep, huddled in her coat with her hood up against the rain.

'Hattie! I thought you were in London. You look frozen. You're wet, come in!'

In the light of the hall I could see that she wasn't wearing any make-up, or maybe the rain had washed it off. Her skin shone smooth and clear, cheeks slightly flushed. She looked like she was about . . . twelve years old. So different from the flawless, hard-smiling Hattie who'd opened the door to me at Sutcliffe Heights on the day I'd found her again.

'I should have given this to you to start with,' she said, drawing a small black lacquered box out of her bag. 'When you turned up at my flat.'

'What is it?'

'A bunch of letters I never sent.'

'You came all the way over here and got yourself soaked through to—'

'Not exactly. Oh Janey. I've worked it out.'

My heart hammered in my chest. I put out a hand and reached for the wall, feeling the plaster, with its wash of cream paint, cool under my touch. 'Worked what out?'

'This thing about James.' She stepped forward and touched my arms. 'All that hurt coming from the upstairs room when we were trying to have dinner. The blood pooling over the floor at the bottom of the staircase. Oh Janey. I know he hurt you. That fuckwit brother of mine hurt you. And something else. There was a baby, wasn't there.'

★

I shook my head, gazed into her bright wet face, silently imploring her to leave it alone.

'Janey?'

'I can't. I just can't.'

But my nerves were singing, damn them, just under the surface of my skin. The things I'd buried the deepest were surfacing too.

It's safe to tell you things. It's just like telling myself.

35

Janey

It had been months before I'd faced up to what was happening, I told Hattie, while she sat on my sofa with a towel around her shoulders. Five, maybe nearer six. I'd never worked it out exactly.

The sickness had been bad all the way through, and late afternoon was the worst time for it. One particularly nauseous day, I had a lesson with Miss Fortune after school.

'How have you been getting on with your composition?' she asked, once I'd come in and sat down at the piano. '*The Trees of Glen Eddle*? Have you been thinking about those harmonies we talked about?'

'Yes, I still like the diminished seventh at the end.'

It wasn't like me to stand up to Miss Fortune, but I really liked the piece I'd written. It had come naturally, for once, and I didn't want to smudge it up with dissonant notes the way she'd suggested.

'Too obvious, dear. Too Disneyfied. Hmm. I wonder.'

She went over to her bookcase and drew out a folder with a couple of sheets of music.

'This is a wee thing I wrote a while back. Have a play of this and see what I mean. This could so easily have turned out nauseating and sugary. But it's a question of adding melodic surprises. And the whole character can be changed by a few gently discordant harmonies. They give it so much more depth. And intelligence.'

'*Blue Bear's Dance?*'

She closed her eyes briefly, and nodded. 'Play it and tell me what you think.'

Technically, it wasn't a difficult piece. I could pick out the melody easily enough with my right hand. My left hand reached for the harmonies, velvety dark underneath, and they made those top notes quiver and sing. Like tears about to fall.

On finishing, I went straight back to the start before she could stop me.

'Right,' she said softly after my fourth attempt. 'Now let's hear your piece again and put our musical thinking caps on.'

My mouth flooded with saliva. She followed me as I rushed to the yellow bathroom, and she hovered at the door, watching as I cowered over the toilet, my stomach wrenching itself inside out, again and again.

Afterwards, she took me back into the music room and motioned to me to sit down at the piano.

'So whose is it?' she asked. 'The baby, I mean.'

She moved round so she was standing behind me. I didn't dare look round to see her face. I just watched her shadow, dancing on the piano as she shifted her weight from one foot to the other. The room had darkened and the streetlight was shining in the window.

Suddenly, I just wanted to tell somebody. And Miss Fortune, for all her weirdness, was the one person who paid any attention to me. Somehow, I thought she'd appreciate the seriousness, the high stakes, if I told her.

'The father is James Marlowe,' I said. 'Hattie's brother, James.'

It felt strange to say it out loud. I hadn't said his name since the night of the party. My head swam at the sound of it in my mouth. Nausea surged again.

The shadow went still. Then it seemed to expand, growing around me till it was enfolding me.

'I see. An extension to the Marlowe dynasty.' Her tone – a parody of politeness – was devastating. 'But my *dear*, why haven't you got it seen to by now? Don't tell me you want to keep it?'

I closed my eyes, recalling the moment I'd realised I was pregnant. How I'd snuck into the library at lunch break to leaf through *The Human Body Explained*, a tome as large and uncompromising as a church Bible, but with full-colour images that could have been conjured from hell itself. Up till that moment, I'd almost been able to convince myself that the Regent's Crescent party, and my shameful behaviour, had never happened. But it had happened, because I was carrying a piece of it – of him – inside me. I'd dropped the body-bible with a massive thud and run to the girls' toilets to vomit.

And yet, as the weeks passed, I began to feel that I must have got it wrong, must have misunderstood the night of the party in some way. The real world began to reassert itself, where James was still boyish and brotherly, out there somewhere skimming stones in rivers or slithering along forest floors, where Hattie would soon return from Ramplings. The baby would be a girl, who would take after her aunt in all sorts of ways. I felt that she was headstrong, mischievous, the way she'd insisted on an existence, wriggling over from that strange, adult parallel world where nothing made sense and people weren't themselves. And I wanted to keep her safe in that spongy darkness, which is why I hadn't told anybody.

But how long would I be able to hide her? My stomach was hard and swelling by the day. Last week I'd had to steal Amanda Dooley's super-sized skirt when we were changing after hockey. I'd felt guilty at the sight of her, red-faced, trying to squeeze herself into mine, which I'd left in its place on her peg, the fabric torn where I'd ripped off the nametape. But I pushed away my guilt. Amanda's life – large as she was, and skirtless now – was paradise, pure paradise, compared to mine.

Because if the baby was as real as it seemed to be turning out to be, I wouldn't be worrying about my uniform for much longer. I'd have to leave school. I wouldn't even be able to do my exams. What would Mrs White say, and Madame Malo? Their faces curdled if you so much as missed a night's homework, so what would they say if you dropped out of the entire course? And then, having to actually *give birth*. To lie there stranded on a hospital bed with my legs apart, like that mournful-looking woman in *The Human Body Explained*.

'No,' I said. 'It's . . . it's a disaster.'

'And I suppose you just want nothing more than for this whole . . . disaster . . . to go away?'

I sniffed, and nodded, relieved at the thought that an adult might be able to take over, to say 'I'll take it from here, Janey, don't you worry.'

But suddenly I felt her breath on my cheek, and her hands on my stomach, over the place where I imagined the baby, floating in her own little universe in there.

And then, in a sing-song voice that was the most horrific thing I've ever heard:

'So, then. Nobody wants you. A little bastard.'

The word 'bastard' jarred horribly in her Morningside accent and I shuddered.

'No – body – *wants* – you,' she repeated, enunciating the words clearly, as though teaching them to a child, and gripping me a little tighter. 'They'll probably suck you out through a tube and sluice you away. Why don't you save everyone the trouble? Just ble-ee-ed your way out. Nature's way, and all that. For the best.'

But then she laughed.

'Come and sit down, Janey. Dear me, you look quite peaky. Not at all yourself today.'

I started bleeding on the bus home. I felt the thick wetness pooling underneath me, and when I slid my hand underneath the seat of my skirt, my fingers came up red. I got off at the next stop, afraid of bleeding over the seats.

Legs clenched together, I stood on the pavement shivering, and considered my options. Going home wasn't one of them. Granny was hosting the church vestry social tonight and had spent the last three days making quiches and lemon syllabub.

I realised I wasn't far from Regent's Crescent, and remembered James' drawling voice on the night of the party, boasting about the absent tenants, touring for six months, and the 'busted' catch on the kitchen window. And somehow it felt fitting: that's where this had begun, so maybe it was right for it to end there too.

Thankfully, no scaling of walls was required this time – the back garden gate swung open when I pushed it. James must have kicked it in for his guests' convenience. And he hadn't bothered to set the alarm, or to clean up. Broken glass crunched under my lace-ups, as I used the phone in the kitchen to call Granny and tell her, between clenched breaths, that I was staying at a friend's that night. And I had to sidestep past a cascade of dried vomit on the basement stairs.

My plan had been to go up to Hattie's room and wait it out,

but I only got as far as the first floor when I realised it was too late for that and made for Renee's en suite.

The next few hours were spent twisted on the floor, with strings and clots of blood sliding out of me. With each vice-like pain, I made myself focus on the short length of copper pipe that led from the base of the radiator into the floor, and the small unfinished patch of plaster behind it, grey with dust: two square inches of imperfection that Renee had probably never noticed.

And in the quiet moments, I noticed other things – how the streaks of blood shone a soft ruby red against the white porcelain tiles, and the way that the criss-cross of my handprints, on the curved enamelled edge of the Victorian bath, looked oddly beautiful.

By two in the morning it was all over. No anomalous traveller from another world, this was a human creature, with a tracery of tiny blood vessels under her skin, perfectly formed fingernails, and a whisper of fine dark hair as soft as anything I'd ever touched.

It was the sense of purpose that got me, that all these things should have been going on unseen – nerves, arteries, bone, muscle – cells reaching out, making connections, every single one with a meticulous purpose that didn't matter any more.

For a time – five minutes, perhaps, or an hour, or maybe even the whole of that night as it crept by – I managed to hold it all in my heart, the enormity of what had happened. She'd been a person. Separate from me now, but never separate. I cradled her in my hand, held her cooling body against my chest as I lay curled on the hard floor.

*

The lessons of the next day crawled past, the time punctuated only by my visits to the toilets every fifteen minutes or so to change sanitary towels. As well as the pains, I was shivering. My skirt and tights were still damp: Renee's tumble dryer hadn't finished its cycle by the time I'd had to leave to catch the bus.

'You're not looking so well,' said Mrs White at the start of biology. 'Why don't you pop along to see Mrs Potts. She'll give you something.' She patted my arm in a confidential way, as though to say 'women's troubles'. I thought of Mrs Potts's cool hands and nodded. The walk along the echoing corridor, with its marble floor and high ceilings, made me dizzy.

The smell of TCP assailed me as I opened the sick room door. Hilary Grogan was perched on the edge of a chair, holding a grey-cardboard sick bowl. Mrs Potts turned to me, and said, 'Janey, what can I do for you?'

Black came down over my vision.

'I called her a disaster,' I said quietly, as though I'd come about a grazed knee or a nosebleed. 'So Miss Fortune's killed her and now I can't stop bleeding.'

I registered the school nurse's mouth falling open before I collapsed into her doughy arms.

The next hour or so passed in a blur of voices, questions, phone calls, with an undercurrent of embarrassment about bleeding so heavily onto the smooth white sheets of the sick-room cot.

Granny couldn't be roused from her bowling club lunch, so it was Mrs Potts who accompanied me to hospital.

And it was Mrs Potts who held my hand while the medics asked questions I didn't know how to answer. The emergency procedure that they performed sorted out the bleeding. They told me so when I came round, as though I ought to have been pleased. There'd be no lasting damage, they said.

No lasting damage.

I closed my mouth, and my mind, against what I knew was coming next, and let the questions, over the next few days and weeks, flow over me, through me, around me. I imagined myself drifting, pitching, whirling, in a storm at sea, the roar of the water drowning out the sound of the concerned, and then increasingly insistent, voices.

How, what, who, when, where . . .

Granny was the only one who didn't ask me anything at all. She came to collect me from the hospital. I woke to find her standing at the side of my bed, her mouth a hard, gleaming line of coral lipstick, powder clinging to the downy hair on her upper lip. She unclipped her black crocodile handbag to retrieve a flower-embroidered handkerchief – I recognised it as one that I'd given her for Christmas, along with a rose-scented soap set – and dabbed it beneath rheumy, sunken eyes.

'Granny,' I managed.

'I suppose it's a blessing,' she began, then blew her nose loudly. 'A blessing, that your grandfather never lived to see this day.'

I looked down the bed at the humps of my feet underneath the blue hospital blanket, and wiggled them, thinking, for a moment, how strange that was: my brain wanted them to wiggle, and they wiggled. And what an odd word anyway: wiggle.

'I've spoken to the school. They've a place for you at Victoria House starting after half-term.'

Oh. One of the school boarding houses.

She shook her head, closing her eyes. 'I *told* Martina, I told her from the start. Children are one thing. For the sake of poor dear Michael I was prepared to take you in, and your grandfather was so soft in the head over you he wouldn't hear a word against the idea. But how I'm expected to manage a teenage girl – *on my own* – with the bridge club to run and the flower rota, and the Columba's committee?' She counted them off on her fingers, her rings jingling against each other with each jab. 'Well, I've no idea, I'm sure.'

She stared at me pointedly, as though waiting for me to rise up from my bed and insist on taking over the running of the Columba's committee.

'Wiggle,' I mouthed silently. 'Wiggle wiggle wiggle.'

'And now this, this *abomination*. The shock of it. I nearly took one of my turns when the school called yesterday. Lord knows what, going on under my roof.'

Nothing had gone on under her roof. Except there'd been a tiny life, growing in the darkness of my body as I ate cabbagey dinners, and did my homework, and slept in my little single bed under the eaves. A third heartbeat, fast and light as a bird's, in a house that had been as dead as a tomb since Grandpa had died. I closed my eyes.

'You can come back and stay in the school holidays,' she added, in a wavery, wheedling voice, as though she wanted *me* to comfort *her*. 'You're family at the end of the day and I'm not casting you out. Though Lord knows, it's about time Martina started doing her bit. Career or no career. Yes, it's up to her to sort this sorry mess.'

Sorry mess. Sorry mess. I remembered, with a start, that I hadn't mopped up the puddle of blood in the main hall, at the foot of the curving staircase, or the sticky footprints leading down the basement stairs.

★

'She was just a tiny thing,' I said to Hattie now. My voice seemed to be coming from somewhere else. 'But these days, they might have been able to do something. Maybe even then, if I'd got to a hospital. If I'd had any kind of antenatal care. I don't really know.'

And I'd been very careful, over the years, never to find out.

Hattie simply sat there, with nothing at all to say. There was nothing to say about antenatal care, or hospitals, or Renee's bloodstained bathroom. Nothing to say about James, or Miss Fortune, or Granny, or all the different ways things might've turned out.

She drew me into her arms, and held me, and rocked me, over and over again, like a mother would. And there in the silence, even as my heart broke all over again, love washed through me and around me: the love that I'd thought had disappeared all those years ago, but – I knew it now, as if it was written into my bones – had been there all along.

36

Hattie's Letters from Ramplings

Dear Janey,

Have you been getting my letters? Because I haven't been getting any from you. I'll try posting this in the village once my ban has been lifted. I'm suspicious of Matron's box.

I still haven't been sleeping and the girls in my house are still a nightmare. They called me a saddo today, because I cried in biology. We were doing life cycles, and it made me remember the day of the frog dissection. It shines in my memory, even though it was disgusting at the time. They're ages behind here, because they do so much music. Morning, noon and night.

The life-cycles workbook here is much less interesting than the one at St Katherine's. I miss everything about St Katherine's. Even Matron is awful, and has orangey bouffony hair like Miss Fortune.

Nothing strange has happened yet, but it still might. I still feel the buzzing in the air sometimes. And there's a spotty boy called Michael who's had a faint 'broom broom' noise coming from him the last couple of weeks. I have to sit next to him in history of music and it's quite distracting.

I just try to think about something else, like algebra or French verbs. Sometimes I whisper quelle dommage *and I imagine you laughing, and it brings me back to myself.*

The school play must be coming up soon. Hope you're practising your part! Who got mine, by the way?

All my love,
Hattie xxx

Dear Janey,

Mum has said I'm not allowed to talk about you, or St Katherine's, or anything to do with home. I knew she didn't like it, because she always pressed her lips together and breathed loudly through her nose. But I kept mentioning you anyway, even if nobody listened or said anything. Kind of like when your grandpa died and we agreed that we'd mention him at least once every day.

But last weekend when she visited for James' chamber choir thing, she said she was sick fed up of hearing your name and she didn't want to hear another word about 'the whole wretched business', whatever that's supposed to mean.

And nobody in school will talk about it either, simply because they are not interested at ALL.

It's as though I've got to pretend you never even existed. But it's like a great slice of me never existed either. I'm only half a person without you. Or maybe two-thirds, but not a whole person.

The only way I can keep you alive is writing these letters. Unfortunately I've got another village ban. I spilled Coke on Thomasina's bassoon and she fainted. But as soon as there's an exeat weekend I'll post them all.

Hoping that all is well at Granny's and St Katherine's.

All my love,

Hattie xxx

Dear Janey,

On Monday, Michael, the spotty boy I mentioned, stole Mr Parsons' motorbike and crashed it into a tree on the edge of the hockey pitch. He's done something to his spine and they're saying he's going to be paralysed from the waist down.

I went a bit funny when I heard, sort of curled up on the floor, right there in the lunch hall, with my hands over my ears.

Then Mum picked me up early yesterday and took me to see a doctor in London with a little blond beard – he looked a bit like Noel Edmonds. I had to sit outside in the waiting room for ages while they talked, and then Mum came out and I got sent in, and he made me strip down to my vest and pants so he could measure me and weigh me. And he asked me all these questions, to do with my headaches and my sleeping and blah blah blah.

He thinks I've been getting migraines, and says you can get visual disturbances with that, which might well explain why our faces disappeared that day in biology! I asked if migraines could cause you to think you were seeing things that weren't there, like maybe someone falling down the stairs. He just looked at me for a long time and said, 'The brain is the most complex of organs. We only understand a tiny fraction of how it works.' Then he asked me loads of other questions, then called Mum in again. He's prescribed some tablets for me to take, which we had to fetch from Boots on the way home. I asked Mum if they were for the migraines, because I thought he'd just said to take aspirin for that, and she muttered something about 'getting back on an even keel'.

I'm not going to take them. They're stuffed in the side pocket of my wash bag in with my dental floss and cotton buds.

How are you, my dearest friend? How's the piano coming along? Watch out for the METRONOME!!

All my love,

Hattie xxx

37

Janey

It was starting to look questionable whether we'd make the meeting, even though we'd been up since six. One measly 9 a.m. meeting with the lawyers and everything was falling apart. How did people – mothers – manage to get to work every day, wearing ironed shirts and clean suits, having deposited their properly dressed, clean and fed children at nursery? I thought of the job applications I'd posted the day before and despaired.

'Come on, Pippy. We must get you to nursery. Can I have my tights, please?' My coaxing voice was starting to wear thin.

Pip was jumping around in the middle of my bed, in the middle of a pile of clothes strewn across it. He'd taken my tights and pulled them on like a hat, so that the legs trailed down on either side of his ears, swishing slowly as he bounced.

I was wearing a dark-grey dress with a short black cardigan, the fifth outfit I'd tried on. My face was grey too. I'd hardly slept. I knew it was only a meeting with the solicitors but my stomach – or whatever part of my body produced adrenaline – seemed to be under the impression that I was facing a firing squad. The adrenal glands were somewhere near the kidneys, weren't they? I had a sudden image of one of Mrs White's photocopied worksheets, and then of the letters Hattie had given me, sheets covered with her tight little words. I'd fallen asleep reading them last night, and dreamed strange dreams about Ramplings, its turreted halls listing and sinking into an effervescent sea of Coke.

'I need my tights, Pippy,' I said, holding out my hand.

'More dam samwich,' said Pip. 'Dat one squashy.' He pointed to his jam sandwich, which was squashed onto the cream carpet by the bed. It would just have to stay there until I got back later.

'I'm sorry, darling, we have to go. You'll get a snack at nursery.' Pulling on the tights, I thought guiltily of the likely offering: cucumber sticks and raisins probably, served on dishwasher-faded blue and green plastic plates at ten o'clock. But I just didn't have time to make any more jam sandwiches, because it was after half past eight already.

'My tummy hungry,' Pip said as I buckled him into his car seat. His voice wasn't challenging me, he just sounded very tired. Tears pricked the back of my eyes. What kind of mother couldn't even feed her child breakfast?

'I'll speak to Mrs Paxton. Maybe they can make you a dam sandwich, hmm? I'll try, baby.'

But when we reached the nursery, Mrs Paxton took a hard line. 'I'm sorry, Miss Johnston, we can't make special snacks for the children unless there are specific dietary requirements. It's not a constructive use of the staff's time, and it sends the wrong message to the children.'

'But he hasn't had anything to eat.'

'Miss Johnston, I find that children will always eat if they're hungry enough. You'll have some lovely hummus and carrot sticks at snack time, won't you, Pip?' I fought down the urge to slap Mrs Paxton, but Pip just looked at her doubtfully and scratched his head with both hands.

Mrs Paxton frowned and peered at Pip's head, lifting the hair at his parting.

'Hmm. It seems we have an infestation, Miss Johnston.'

I looked closer. Two tiny creatures – they looked like tiny brown flies – were crawling around at the back of Pip's parting.

'Pip can come back to nursery tomorrow, once this has been fully treated.'

'But he must have got them here in the first place,' I said.

'Please, Mrs Paxton. I have a meeting with the solicitors.'

Visions filled my mind. Pip, gone every weekend from Friday to Sunday. Pip, being forced to do orienteering in a cold forest every Saturday morning instead of lying on the sofa in his pyjamas, watching *Thomas the Tank Engine* with me.

Some judge deciding that Pip shouldn't live with me at all.

The nursery hallway seemed unfamiliar suddenly. Like somewhere in a dream. The skin around my lips began to tingle.

'Miss Johnston?'

My eyes shot to the clock on the wall: 8.45.

I grabbed Pip and went back to the car, which had a parking ticket slapped onto the windscreen. How was it possible? I'd been gone two minutes at the most.

And I couldn't strap Pip back into his car seat – my hands wouldn't work properly. The harder I tried, the more clumsy and dead they became. I began to wonder whether I was awake at all, or just having a nightmare, one of those ones where something bad is coming and you can't run.

How long would it take to get there from here? I knew where McKeith's was, and I could picture the three New Town townhouses, knocked together and converted into offices. But how to get there? Somehow I couldn't bring to mind the streets that would take me there, streets I'd known like the back of my hand for all of my life. I looked past the nursery to the cars queuing at the traffic lights at the end of the road, and tried to remember which turning I'd take. It was left, wasn't it? But beyond that the streets simply dissolved into a grey blur in my mind.

Get a grip, Janey. Breathe.

I should call them and tell them I'd be late. I got my phone out, tried to find the solicitor's number, swiping at the screen with numb fingers.

The phone chirped and a text from Steve flashed up: 'All okay for the meeting? Best of luck. xxx'

I leaned back against the car for a moment and covered my eyes with my hand.

He'd been thinking about me, right at that moment. I hadn't been as alone as I'd thought. It almost undid me.

I pressed the telephone icon at the top of the message and exhaled slowly.

'Janey?'

'Pip has lice. I'm at the nursery and they won't take him.' And then, the words I'd never been able to say to anybody before: 'I'm panicking.'

'Don't drive. I'm on my way.'

*

And so it was that we ended up in the meeting room at McKeith's: Murray, Gretel and their solicitor; me, my solicitor, Pip (who refused to leave my side), Steve (who'd come armed with brown paper bags, and refused to leave my side either) and an unknown number of head lice.

I'd got my breath back now, and the feeling in my hands.

But itches had sprung up all over my body. Putting my head to one side, elbow on the table, I moved my fingers – casually, I hoped – through my hair.

It was the first time I'd met my solicitor. 'Pauline Gaunt' had seemed such a mature, responsible name, appearing at the top of her emails, but she seemed to be about eighteen.

'Don't underestimate Gretel,' I warned in low tones.

'Oh, Gretel's fine. She talks the big talk. But she's really, like, on it, you know?'

'What? You know her?'

'I worked for her when I did my seat in litigation here at McKeith's.'

'In your traineeship? When was this?'

'Oh, last summer.'

'So you've just started family law, then.'

'Yeah. Well, no, because I did a six-month stint during my traineeship.'

Murray's solicitor came in. She looked about twelve, with long, swingy hair.

'Hey,' she said when she saw Pauline.

'Hey, Holly,' said Pauline, and then added, sotto voce, 'Sorry I forgot to reply to your text, by the way. Did you see my cake on Instagram?'

'Mamma,' said Pip, pulling my sleeve. 'Where my pens?' I rummaged in my bag to try and find the colouring pens that were always loitering at the bottom. I produced a green one and a black one, and asked Pauline if she could donate a sheet from her notepad.

'So,' said Gretel. 'We want to put the contact arrangements in a formal document. But first, perhaps you could make some coffee?'

My head jerked up. She wanted me to make coffee now? But no, she was looking at Holly.

I found myself relaxing as Holly poured the coffee, and passed round some Danish pastries. Maybe this wouldn't be as bad as I thought.

Steve refused a Danish pastry but took an apricot, which looked like it was only there on the platter for ornamental purposes. He placed it in front of him on the desk and sat there looking awkward, with crossed arms and rounded shoulders. Gretel looked across at him, wrinkling her nose.

'So, basically,' Holly began, glancing at Gretel, 'we'd like these key terms to be set down in the agreement. Pip would stay with Murray and Gretel from Friday lunchtime to Sunday afternoon, three weekends out of four.'

Steve placed a steadying hand on my knee.

'No!' I said, in a small voice that sounded like a mouse. 'I've already said that's too much. I'll agree to one night per week, or two nights every fortnight. Any more than that and he'll be completely disorientated. He's only two. *I'm* his mother. He barely knows Gretel.'

Gretel sat back in her chair, looking sad for just a split second before she shrugged, with exaggeratedly wide eyes, as though to say, 'My point exactly.'

She would never know how it felt to be Pip's mother; anybody's mother. Maybe that's what I'd seen in her face, in that instant before she corrected her expression.

Holly frowned. 'Weeelll . . .'

'Dend!' shouted Pip, his limbs shooting out, rigid with excitement as though he'd been electrified. He was pointing to an empty chair to the left of Gretel.

I groaned inwardly. This was all we needed. A visitation from Dend.

Pip carefully took one sheet of the paper, and the brown pen, and placed them in front of Dend. Gretel smiled, clearly thinking they were for her, and reached out a manicured hand to pat Pip's head, but he darted away.

'I shared wiv Dend,' he pointed out to me, with an angelic expression, then reached up and scratched his head vigorously.

The imagined itches seemed to multiply over my body as Gretel held a whispered consultation with Holly, and I soon found I was fighting a terrible urge to scratch my crotch area.

With horror, I remembered Pip jumping on my bed with my tights over his head.

'You okay?' said Steve, his eyes concerned behind the black-framed glasses. 'You've gone a bit flushed.'

The door swung open and in came a man, of imposing build and with greying dark hair.

'Ah! Donald,' said Gretel, and she and Murray both stood up to shake his hand.

Oh no, not Donald Finlayson. He was a bit of a celebrity in the legal world. He had a regular slot on a morning TV show, giving advice to housewives who wanted to divorce their cheating husbands, or to tearful estranged fathers engaged in custody battles. He'd written the definitive textbook on Scottish family law. I knew, because I'd proofread it.

'Mine's a white with one, please Holly,' he said as he sat down. 'Now, Ms Johnston, three weekends out of four is our key stipulation, as I think you already know. There's also a week's holiday over the Christmas period, ten days at Easter and, er, a five-week block in the summer. And your undertaking not to take Pip out of Edinburgh without Murray's express agreement.'

'Outside Edinburgh? That seems very . . .' I shook my head uselessly. What was the word? 'Very ridiculous.'

I glanced at Steve, who raised his eyebrows and nodded.

'What if we want to go to Almond Valley Farm?'

Pip jumped up like a rocket. 'We going to farm?' He started bouncing. 'Now! Now!'

'Not now, baby,' I murmured.

'Dend come too?' He was pointing in the direction of my stomach.

I looked down. 'What?'

'Dend sitting on Mamma's knee. Silly Mamma.'

I shivered. So I was not only crawling with lice in unmentionable places, but had a ghost sitting on my knee.

Pip helpfully moved the pen and papers in front of me.

'That's a nice picture, Pip,' I said. It was a green swirly blob, which I recognised as a snot monster, one of his regular subjects. 'Is it Gretel?'

He tore it off the pad and scrunched it up into a ball.

Meanwhile, Pauline piped up. 'We won't agree to the "not going outside Edinburgh" thing.'

Gretel shrugged. 'We could extend the boundary to include Almond Valley Farm, and other attractions such as the Wallace Monument or the Falkirk Wheel.'

The itch in my crotch had become almost unbearable now. I remembered a magnified picture of a head louse I'd seen once on the internet, and suddenly thought I might be sick.

'Seems fair enough,' said Murray, leaning back in his chair. 'I think we can be pretty relaxed about the geographical restrictions.' Donald frowned; this wasn't Murray's usual hardball mode of negotiation at all. 'I mean, if we're doing five weeks in Barbados over the summer . . .'

'Hang on, Barbados?' I said. 'I thought you wanted to take him to Aviemore?'

'We can't,' said Gretel. 'Our holiday cottage was cancelled.'

I shook my head in bewilderment. Had they run out of holiday cottages in Aviemore? Was the next nearest one in Barbados?

'It was Annabel Masters' stepfather's holiday let, but then his niece, who was supposed to be backpacking in Thailand this summer, said she couldn't go because her boyfriend got a record deal . . . EMI I think it was. He's sort of a folksy-rocksy style but with a deep country twist, you know . . .'

And she was off on one of her monologues.

My phone vibrated in my pocket. It was a text from Hattie: 'How's the meeting? Hope you're giving them hell!'

'Gretel,' I said, as she was launching into a comparison of the best five-star hotels in Barbados. 'Please stop. Pip is not going.'

Donald looked over the top of his spectacles. 'There's no need to get excitable, Miss Johnston.'

My left hand moved across the table to Pip's scrumpled-up drawing.

No, please not now.

I watched in horror as my thumb and first two fingers formed an ominous circle, flexed against each other and . . . *ping.*

The crumpled ball shot right across the table, landing in Donald's coffee, splattering his white shirt.

I gasped. 'I'm so *sorry.*'

Gretel gave a slow tut and a sigh. Murray put his hands over his face.

Donald pressed his lips together as though he was trying to

suppress a sound, which escaped, like a hiss from a pressurised valve, as something like 'Fffffff . . .' Then he said, 'Holly, please phone Nadine and get one of my shirts biked over.'

Holly went off with a swish of her perfect hair.

Gretel, lounging back in her chair, said, 'Right, can we get this wrapped up? Janey, are you agreeable to the terms or not?'

Never had I wanted to leave a room so badly. My heart was thudding, and I was watching my left hand with no idea what it might do next.

Think, Janey.

If I agreed to three weekends out of four that at least would get Murray and Gretel off my back, and keep them friendly. But it wasn't right for Pip to spend all that time away from me, and with someone who had all the maternal instinct of a poison dart frog. And what about when Pip started school and I got a job through the week? I would hardly see him at all. And five weeks in Barbados, baking under a hot sun. Murray knew that Pip's eyes got itchy in the heat, and he got headaches that made him clammy and sick.

'I'm sorry. I just can't agree. Not to any of it.'

'Right', said Donald. 'Well, we seem to have reached an impasse then.'

I heard Murray whisper to Gretel. 'Maybe we could start with alternative weekends and see how it goes?'

'No, Murray,' said Gretel in a normal voice. 'This agreement sets the benchmark. What's the point of buying that blurdy house if we're not going to use it for family time? This is what *you* wanted.'

Murray laid his hands flat on the table. 'Shall we reconvene once we've had time to think all this through?'

My left hand lifted and the fingers folded and unfolded in a toddler's wave.

I grabbed it with my right hand and pressed it back on the table.

★

As we were walking out, Steve said, 'Is Pip with them tonight?'

My heart twisted. 'Yes.'

'Shall I pop over later? I could bring the new series of *Christiansen*. You probably need a glass of wine too.' He laid his hand on the small of my back, just for a second. We'd agreed not to be tactile when Pip was around.

I thought of the tights on Pip's head and the inspection I'd have to carry out later and shuddered.

'Maybe not tonight. I'm not feeling too well.'

'Yeah. About that. Maybe you need to speak to someone about, y'know, your hand? You didn't look well at all in there.'

How did he do this? Make me melt and also want to slap him at the same time?

I turned and looked pleadingly at him.

'It's not that. Pip put my tights on his head this morning. Before I put them on. Before I realised he had lice.'

He gave a low, resonant laugh.

'Well, why don't I make some dinner while you do whatever you need to do, and then we can catch up with *Christiansen*.'

Warmth seemed to radiate through my body. I could have cried. This man wanted me, even though I was a louse-ridden, partially possessed single mum, trailing an uptight middle-aged lawyer and his evil stepmother queen in her wake.

★

And later, he lay stretched out on the sofa while I worked out some Adele songs on the piano, his head resting on his hand, his arm making a V against the cushion. His shirt cuff was unbuttoned, the sleeve pulled carelessly up near his elbow.

'You're so effing talented,' he said softly when I'd finished. 'How can you not be doing this for a living? It's mad.'

I felt my cheeks turning red. 'I'm only playing around.'

'Play me something of yours. I want to hear *you*.'

I thought for a minute. 'Okay, well this one hasn't really got a name. It's about the sea, and a storm. I haven't played it for ages.'

But my fingers found the notes, even after two decades. The melody, hidden in some dark corner of my brain, found its way, pushing through the synapses and nerves and muscles, through the keys and hammers and wires, and into the space of the room. When I finished he came over and knelt on the floor beside me.

'I want you,' he said. 'I want to be in you.'

I took his hand and began to lead him towards the door. There were fresh sheets on the bed and Jo Malone candles on the dresser ready for lighting.

'No. Here.'

He caught me round the waist and leant me against the piano, sending a cascade of Chopin and Brahms off the polished lid and onto the floor. I felt the air cool against my back as he unzipped my dress, and pulled it down over my body. I stepped out of it, kicking it to the side, and in moments he was deep and hard inside me.

The more he filled me up – my body, my mind, my heart – the more I knew, beyond a doubt, that I needed him. He was finding all my emptiness. Changing it into something else. And then I couldn't think any more at all, only feel.

★

It was only later, when he lay sleeping beside me in bed, with his arm draped across my waist, that I remembered about Hattie's letters, still there on the bedside table waiting to be finished. I reached for them, careful not to wake Steve.

The tone of the letters seemed to soften a little as the winter gave way to spring, and it sounded as though Hattie was relaxing into her new life a little more, despite numerous, strongly worded complaints about the amount of music they had to do, and the food, the teachers' hairstyles, and the quality of the biology tuition. I could hear her twelve-year-old voice, funny and affectionate, and it felt cosy to lie there, safe in the warm yellow glow of the bedside lamp and read about her schooldays, with their echoes of the school stories I'd once loved – Malory Towers, St Clare's, the Sadler's Wells books. My breathing slowed to match Steve's and, once again, I nearly fell asleep. Until I reached the last two letters.

38

Hattie's Letters from Ramplings

Dear Janey,

I want to come home. I want to come home.

I was so lonely tonight that I actually went to see James. He's in Dartmoor House, on the other side of the woods, but visits by siblings are allowed between the hours of 7 p.m. and 8 p.m.

His room stank of sweat, and he didn't seem pleased to see me. He said he was busy working on a composition. I said, well that's good, and he said no it wasn't, it was f***ing atrocious.

I tried to tell him about being homesick, to get him talking about Edinburgh, and you, and Glen Eddle.

'Look, sis,' he said. 'This might come as news to you, but our family is f***ed up. Dad's so far up his own arse, with his bloody Broadway shows and his money and everyone fawning over him, that he's pretty much forgotten we even exist. And Mum's just as bad. She feeds off it. She needs it. People have got to want to be her, the woman married to the famous composer. If you want my advice, forget the lot of us, forget about bloody music, and get on with your life.'

'Forget music?' I said.

'Don't you see? It's a trap. That platform recital the other week: I was note perfect, and all Mr Foulkes could say was that I needed to put more of my own interpretation into it, that I had to find my own identity as a musician. I mean, what the

f***? *However many hours we practise, however many years of our lives we devote to this, we're only ever going to be Dad's children. We're never going to be good enough.'*

'Well, I'm certainly not going to be. I don't practise at all.'

'You're right, Hattie. You're so right. You're the least f***ed up of all of us.'

That's when it happened. He looked up to meet my eyes, and a fly, a black bluebottle, crawled out of his right nostril. It stopped to rub its legs together, then it buzzed and flew off.

And then. Oh God, Janey. Another one climbed out of his ear. He didn't sniff, he didn't brush at his face.

I wondered for a second if it had been real. If the buzz was something to do with this headache.

But something made me glance at the ceiling, and it was crawling with them. Flies. As I watched, they formed themselves into one black mass, buzzing and seething around a hatch set into the ceiling above his desk.

I grabbed his arm and told him to look, but they'd gone.

Maybe it's time to start taking those pills after all. I wish you were here to advise me. Or we could go to the library and look it up.

Wish, wish, wish you were here.

All my love,

Hattie xxx

Dear Janey,

There's no easy way to say this. My brother tried to kill himself last night. He climbed up into the roofspace, through the little hatch in the ceiling of his room, and drank a bottle of vodka and swallowed a load of pills. They found his violin there too. He'd burned holes in it with a cigarette.

They wouldn't have found him in time, except that I knew

where to look. When Mr Foulkes asked round at breakfast if anyone had seen him, my legs just kind of slid off the bench and started running like I was in a dream, out of the dining hall, straight through the woods, into Dartmoor House, past the games room, the music room and the laundry. Up the stairs and past the doors of the empty dormitories, my dream-shoes pounding on the rubber floor.

And a little song singing in my head, gleeful and sly: You know, you know, YOU know!

It's time to start taking the tablets. I'm going to have to start a new me, or I'm not going to survive. It's okay. I know what I need to do. Thomasina has asked if I want to join the lunchtime madrigal group. I think she's sorry she got me into trouble about the Coke. If I do that, I'll probably be able to make friends with them, and I'll be able to hang out in their dorm and look at pictures of Tom Cruise and spend hours doing make-up and perfecting my hair-tonging technique. They smoke out of the window sometimes, but I won't do that. Remember the horrible lines around Miss F's mouth?

So, my dearest friend. This is it. Goodbye. I'm going to put these letters away in a little black box. Remember that box with cherry blossoms on it that you always liked? I wish I could curl up in there, too, and go to sleep. And dream of the time when we were friends and talked in the fire escape, and made Shapiro plans, and wrote notes on each other's jotters, and walked during cross-country when we were meant to be running and, oh, everything like that. The time when my heart was in its right place.

I'm so sorry. I'm so sorry about it all.

Hattie xxx

39

Janey

We were standing in the queue to meet a life-sized butternut squash. Mr Greenfingers – a TV hero for the under-fives – had been visible when we'd first joined the queue forty-five minutes before, but he'd drifted away, bored, perhaps. Hattie had bought the tickets for the show – Mr Greenfingers and the Veggie Crew (LIVE!) – and we'd taken the train through to Glasgow, which had practically made Pip expire with joy. Hattie said that now she was back for good, she wanted to plan lots of 'memorable days' with Pip and me.

'You make it sound like we're all about to die.'

'No,' she said quickly. 'It's just that I've neglected you. I think you need some fun and some company. You're looking a little peaky.' She frowned and poked my arm.

'So you thought live vegetables might help.'

'Seriously, I'm worried about you. Have there been any more' – her face moved in closer to mine – 'incidents? With knives moving, or jars of jam?'

I couldn't help smiling at her earnest expression. I still couldn't believe the difference in her, since she'd come back. Today she was wearing a red and navy striped T-shirt, and jeans that were raggedy at the ends where the heels of her boots had caught.

'No.'

'And what about Dend?'

'Oh, Dend's still around.' I leaned down to Pip. 'Is Dend here today, darling? Or at home?'

'Dend is asleep I fink. Dend not like veggies.'

'He's got a rather active imagination,' I said wryly.

'Like me, you mean.' Hattie looked crestfallen. 'Is that what you thought, when you read them? The letters,' she added in a whisper.

It was the fourth time she'd brought up the letters since we'd left Edinburgh that morning.

'Of course not. God, Hattie, there's nothing imaginary about your brother trying to kill himself. I just wish I could have been there for you.'

'Were you shocked?'

'It was terrible to hear what happened to James. Really awful.'

I'd stayed awake most of the night, going round in circles thinking about James until my own head seemed to be buzzing. I tried to make everything add up: the boyish James I'd worshipped, the eighteen-year-old James with his casual cruelty and blank eyes, and in the middle of it all this despair. A despair over himself that I'd never known about. I wondered about what life had been like for him after the suicide attempt, about what help he'd had, or hadn't had, what resources he'd had to find to stick it out at Ramplings for another two years and then secure a place at music college. He'd got back on track, and had managed to live up to everyone's expectations for a few more years at least. But what had been the cost? Had he, like Hattie, had to construct a new version of himself, just to cope?

'No, I don't mean about James.' She shook her head. 'Were you shocked about my . . . abilities.'

I wasn't sure what to say. Did she *want* me to be shocked? Should I say something comforting and risk sounding dismissive? Or the truth: that I'd rather have the old Hattie – sensitive, unbalanced, mentally ill, whatever it was – any day over the shiny, unperturbable Botox Queen.

'I think you should tell me all about it.'

'Okay,' she said, nodding and frowning. 'Not here, though. Tomorrow night, your place? I'll bring wine.'

Pip got to have his photo taken with the butternut squash, and Mr Greenfingers even turned up just as we were leaving.

'Do you think you might like to try some butternut squash soup tonight?' I said in a coaxing voice, as I led him away from the mocked-up compost heap. Might as well ride on this wave of positive veggie vibes. But Pip looked at me in horror, glanced back at Mr Greenfingers and his eyes began to fill.

'Aw, Pippy,' I said, stooping to give him a cuddle. 'Don't worry.'

'Jaaaaaaam!' he wailed.

It seemed like a long way out of the concourse of the exhibition centre, tired families trudging ahead of us, with toddlers trailing from their parents' arms or being pushed in buggies overloaded with changing bags, rucksacks, coats and bags of veggie merchandise.

I stopped when I saw Steve.

He was just up ahead, walking next to a short, slightly built woman whose blonde hair was tied up in a careless twist. He was pushing a buggy. No, actually, it was a wheelchair. A child's wheelchair. And as I watched, he reached a hand down and stroked the top of a small blond head.

When they'd almost reached the doors of the concourse, they came to a halt. He stooped down to say something to the child, and then turned to the woman. They looked at one another for a moment, then he closed his eyes and drew her in towards him. He stood with his cheek resting against her hair, his arms tight around her. I could see the tendons of his hand, standing out with the force of the hold. And like this they clung to each other, perfectly still, as people moved around them, flowing past them to the exit.

It made me think of the moment when I'd held twelve-year-old Hattie, on the stairs at Regent's Crescent, after she'd shown me where the falling woman had landed. Locked in each other's arms. The still point as the world tipped and spun.

It seemed a miracle that I could reach for her, now. That she could hold tight onto Pip's hand and mine and lead us past them and out of there, into a taxi. Back to the station, and home.

★

He came over later. Pip was in bed and Hattie had gone. It had taken him five hours to respond to my sarcastic, furious text.

'What are you playing at?' I demanded, the shake in my voice robbing my words of all the power I'd hoped for. 'What is it? Another student you've got a bit too friendly with? Or have you got a whole secret little family tucked away?'

He sat down on the sofa and leaned forward, clasping his hands and resting his elbows on his knees. 'He's not mine.'

Breathe. In and out.

'Who is the woman?'

'Katya. She . . . We used to be in a relationship.'

I wrapped my arms around myself, trying to stop shaking. Grasped on to his use of the past tense and held on hard.

He walked over to the window and stood facing away from me, out into the rainy street.

'There was a disaster, Janey.' His shoulders curled in, just an incremental movement, and I realised I'd never seen him in pain before. This is what it looks like, I thought. I'm seeing him. I'm finally seeing him.

'What kind of disaster?' Suddenly, overwhelmingly, I wanted to walk over and place my hands on his back. I wanted to feel the warmth of him through the thin white cotton of his shirt. To stroke his shoulder blades where they jutted against the fabric.

'I met Katya at art school – we shared a flat and we just kind of clicked, you know? We were "just good friends", although I would have liked it to be more. She got together with this guy – a complete arsehole, but they ended up getting married. They tried for years and years to have a baby, IVF and everything. It worked in the end and they had a little boy – that's the boy you saw. Calum. The dad walked out on them when Calum was only nine days old.'

I thought of Pip at nine days old, the whorls of hair on his head, the scrunched-up red face when he cried. The way he used to sleep so deeply and still, as though he might quietly slip out of this life at any moment. How could anybody leave a newborn?

'I tried to help out.' He rolled his eyes. 'Good old Steve, the sensitive New Man.'

I was surprised. Somehow I couldn't see Steve doing nappies and warming feeds. He'd always seemed a bit awkward around Pip. And caring for a disabled child?

'At first, we were just friends. I was helping her out, that's all, collecting him from the childminder and that kind of thing, when she had to work. But we were good together, and we drifted into a relationship. I moved in with them. When Calum was . . . he was just two . . . Katya had to go to a funeral, so I was looking after him for the day. He'd had his birthday not long before and wanted to wear his new Spider-Man suit, so I helped him get into that. Then the phone rang.'

Those last two words – the way he said them – seemed to make the room darken. My hands felt cold with the wanting to touch him. I held them up to my cheeks.

'I went into our bedroom to answer it.'

I moved towards him now, and stood next to him. I could hear my pulse, pounding through the blood vessels in my head, distorting the sound in the room, whooshing his voice away as he tried to tell me.

'I knew that I should have closed the stairgate. I remember thinking it. But I didn't, because I was only going to be away a minute. But a minute was all it took. It was loud. Louder than you'd think. A thudding, sliding, thumping noise.'

'Oh God. *Steve.*'

'Such a big noise for such a small body. I ran to the stairs and there he was, on the wooden floor at the bottom, in a little red and blue heap.' He held his hands apart to show me how small he'd been. 'He didn't quite die. But he's . . .' He shook his head. 'Spinal damage. He can't walk. And there are other problems. His cognitive function seems to be impaired. They don't quite know the extent of it yet.'

He shrugged, and looked at me briefly before returning his gaze to the rainy street outside.

'Katya was incredible. She didn't blame me, or said she didn't. She said it could easily have been her. She said that parents take their eye off the ball all the time. They take risks sometimes, to keep the day moving along, to get things done. The relationship hobbled on for a while. But in the end it was impossible for us to stay together.'

I nodded.

'She's married again now. He's a great bloke, Martin. A joiner, self-employed. They live in Newcastle now. He's been amazing with Calum. Katya said I could stay in touch with Calum, when she asked me to leave. She knew I loved him. She sometimes calls me up when she's visiting her folks in Glasgow, to see if I want to meet up. But I've only seen him a handful of times. It's not really fair on the lad. Confusing.'

And today had been one of those precious times.

'I know I have it easy compared to Katya, and I really have no right to say it, but I always find it . . .' He gave a shaky sigh. 'Pretty grim, whenever I see him. When it happened, he was only little. He was so dependent anyway, just like any toddler I suppose. But as he grows physically bigger, his disabilities seem to grow too. The gap widens, you know?' He looked at me hard now, willing me to understand. 'All the things he should be able to do. It's difficult, seeing him. Afterwards, it takes me a while to get myself back together.'

'Of course,' I soothed. 'Of course it does.'

'Don't say it wasn't my fault.'

'Okay,' I said, and now I lifted my hand, and stroked the back of his neck with my cold fingers. 'It's okay, it's okay.'

The touch seemed to release something in him. He turned to me, and I pulled him in.

Waves of some unnamed emotion rolled over me, over and over till my heart felt it would burst. Pain, for his pain, palpably there under my hands. But in the middle of it all, a sharp bright shard of joy. This was *him*. He'd let me in.

281

40

Janey

'Poor guy,' said Hattie when I told her. She closed her eyes as though she was picturing it, as I had been all week since he told me, the thin Spider-Man limbs, the sound of a tumble and then the thud of impact.

We were sitting in the kitchen, with an empty pizza box on the table between us. Pip, mischievous in his pyjamas after an uproarious bath presided over by Hattie, had even tried a slice. It was still there on the edge of my plate, with a tiny, teethmarked half-moon taken out of it.

'I'm glad he didn't actually *see* the fall,' she said. 'Or maybe that makes it worse. Just to see that little shape, lying at the bottom. God, I don't know.'

'A bit like the falling woman,' I said carefully.

She blinked as though I'd caught her out, reached for the wine bottle and filled up first my glass, then hers.

'What was it all about? It wasn't just nothing. I know that now, after reading your letters and everything. Tell me, Hats.'

'Oh, it's just that house. It messes with your mind, that's all. As soon as this "retrospective" party thing is out the way I'm outta there, I tell you.'

She laughed and rolled her eyes. I said nothing.

'Did I tell you we had to cancel the Usher Hall? They couldn't sell enough tickets. So now it's just a drinks do at the house. I've managed to organise a couple of musicians, so they can come and perform some of his songs in the drawing room. Mum'll be livid, but it'll have to do.'

I reached my hand over the table and touched my pinkie to hers, as I'd used to do in lessons when I needed to get her attention. 'Tell me, Hattie.'

I could hear her swallow. The tick of the clock as the moments passed.

And then: 'I've got this thing. It's pretty weird.'

'It's okay,' I said. 'You don't have to tell me. But you know our old saying.'

'*Quelle dommage?*'

I tutted. 'It's just like telling myself.'

'Inklings,' she said loudly, with a shrug. 'That's what I used to call them. I've never said it out loud before.'

I nodded.

'I used to see things that nobody else could. It started while I was still at St Katherine's with you. That last term. When I got to Ramplings, they got worse. Clearer, I mean. Sometimes, the inklings were of things that were going to happen.' She shuddered.

'And you didn't tell anyone?'

'Mum knew I'd been getting these visions, or hallucinations.'

'The falling lady.'

'She was really freaked out. She thought you and I were egging each other on, with thinking the house was haunted and so on. She panicked. A full-blown Renee Marlowe panic. Nothing by half measures. So she decided to pack me off to Ramplings, as if that would ever have made any difference.'

'Really? You think she moved your whole family because of that?'

Hattie's eyes dropped down. 'Not the whole family,

remember. Dad had already gone. James was at Ramplings already.' She began playing with her fingers, squeezing the knuckle of each left finger with the thumb and forefinger of her right.

I cleared my throat. 'Are the inklings multisensory?'

She looked up and smiled. 'Multisensory. Absolutely. We should note it down in the Shapiro book.'

'More wine.' I stood up quickly, scraping the chair against the tiles. I pulled the bottle out of the fridge and glugged some into her glass.

'So what happened? They stopped, these inklings, after you started taking the tablets from Noel Edmonds?'

'Yeah. And started straightening my hair and everything. They did stop. Mostly.'

'Do you think it helped, you getting away from me?'

She traced a careful finger around the rim of her glass. 'You made me feel more myself than anyone else. More switched on. So yes. I think I was more prone to inklings when you were around.'

'Oh.'

'You know when you came back? That first day at my flat? I knew it. I knew it then, that the inklings would start again. You see, at Ramplings I learned that—' She broke off, tears wobbling on her lower lashes. 'I couldn't get too close to anybody. Because any strong feelings seem to set it off. Oh, the likes of Thomasina and that crew didn't have much effect. Even Ernie, bless him. It's ironic that I've ended up in a career that's all about appearances, and trying to stop the processes that are going on underneath. I started off loving it, the way I could help clients to feel better about themselves. But more and more I envy them, because none of them have as much to hide as I do. I want to scream at them to forget about their wrinkles and their saggy skin, and go home to the people they love. Because that's what I don't have. For me, the barriers *always* go up before I get too close. Because what if I see something? What if I see something about them?'

'Like you saw about me? The pool of blood and everything? Was that an inkling?'

She nodded, leaning down to pull a tissue out of her bag. She blew her nose loudly.

'That's how I knew about the baby. That you'd lost it. All that pain, echoing round the hallway when you were trying to tell me about James.' She closed her eyes and let the statement just sit there for a second. 'How were you, after it happened?'

It was a question nobody had ever asked.

'We were talking about you, Hats.'

'But tell me, how were you?'

'Well . . .' I paused for a moment, taking myself back to that time of my life that somehow felt like a dream, even now. 'There was an awful fuss for a while, of course. The police were involved, asking who'd got me pregnant, what Miss Fortune had done that day, what I'd done with the . . . remains, after . . . you know. There was a social worker with terrible bad breath called Barbara, even a psychiatrist, because I wouldn't tell them anything, I wouldn't even open my mouth. Until one day when I got tired of it all. I wrote a statement saying I'd been attacked by a man in the woods on Corstorphine Hill, that Miss Fortune had given me my piano lesson as usual, and that I'd thrown the baby's body in the river. Things quietened down after that. Though everything changed. For the better, in some ways. The boarding thing worked out quite well. I went back to Granny's for the holidays, to begin with, but by sixth form I was pretty much boarding over the holidays too.'

'Oh, Janey.'

'No, no, it was good. I liked it.'

I told Hattie how I'd enjoyed the feeling of company around me, without having to participate too much. I'd shared a sunny, L-shaped dormitory with a set of twins from Skye and a shy, studious Chinese girl. And I drifted towards 'the music crowd', a group of girls whose lives revolved around choir and orchestra. Unlike most of the St Katherine's girls, they didn't have boyfriends, or romantic crises, or heart-to-hearts requiring them to spend all night on the phone. Oblivious to their uncool A-line silhouettes, they didn't even bother to roll their school skirts up around their waists to make them shorter. They clattered back to the Victoria House every afternoon, rosy-faced with their violins, tubas and hockey sticks, and gathered to drink cocoa in matron's kitchen every night like a crowd of extras from Malory Towers. I sometimes slipped in to join them, perching at the end of the stout wooden bench with a glass of water (I never liked cocoa). Eventually, one of them would cut in with a line from the latest Chamber Choir piece and the others would put their mugs down and fill in the other parts, chins dipping earnestly with the beat.

What nobody knew was that I'd kept the baby alive, after she'd gone, gave her a little place of her own in my mind. In some older, sweeter, safer world, my belly kept growing, as though that horror of blood and pain had never happened. I let myself drift there at night, in the long grey nothing-hours after lights out, the only girl in the dorm who couldn't sleep. Didn't want to sleep. Because that was my time. Her time.

I remember waking up one Sunday morning in February and looking out the window, rubbing at the creep of condensation

286

with the back of my hand. The trees outside were still stark and bare, but a few snowdrops were starting to peep through on the grassy bank by the playing fields, and I realised that it was nearly spring, and she would've been born by now. I skived off church, saying I had a stomach ache, so that I could go back to bed and think about her, with her dark hair and tiny hands, and the curious, grey-blue eyes I'd imagined for her. All the next week I doodled during lessons, drawing baby clothes, a white cot with a heart carved into the side. The cellular blanket with a satin edge that she liked to sleep under.

A few weeks later I found a book in the Oxfam shop called *The First Year: Day by Day with Your Baby*. I learned when she'd begin to eat solid food, sit up, grasp at objects. I even filled in the blank pages at the back, writing down each small milestone as it should have happened.

She grew, she reached age one, took her first steps on cue.

And then, when she reached two and a half, it stopped.

It was a Tuesday afternoon and we were gathered in the gym hall, waiting to greet our French pen friends. I was looking forward to meeting mine, Celine. She'd seemed friendly in her letters: interested in music, and ponies and gymnastics, oppressed in a comical sort of way by her big brother. They lived with their mother in a big house near Paris.

Even as she walked over, I knew I'd got it wrong. It wasn't the nose stud, or the snake tattoo just visible where her top slid off her right shoulder. It was something to do with the slow blink when we stood face to face, the twist of the mouth.

I gasped then – I actually gasped – at the power of my own imagination. The Celine I'd written to disintegrated, as insubstantial as dust. I'd read into her letters what I'd wanted to hear, searched for the voice of the friend I'd been longing for.

Moments slid past. The September sunshine slanted through the high gym windows, warming the wooden floor, releasing a sweet gummy scent that reminded me of circuits, and Hattie, and one long summer afternoon when we'd been allowed to lounge on the crash mats watching Wimbledon instead of doing games. Madame Malo clapped her hands and started giving instructions. The three o'clock bell went. Nothing had changed, and everything had changed.

Because none of it was real. My baby hadn't grown into an adorable but mischievous toddler. She didn't like puréed apple, or Winnie the Pooh. She didn't have a mop of unruly curls that frizzed up at the back when she'd been sleeping, or eyes like the sea in winter. She was dead. Worse than dead. Had never lived.

Occasionally, in the months that followed, she'd pop into my mind, with a pouty face, her bottom lip sticking out, banging her feet because I wouldn't let her grow any more. And sometimes I'd hear a child shouting and laughing at the swing park, or having a tantrum at the shops, and my heart would contract, because it was her. And then it wasn't.

I got good at stopping such thoughts in their tracks, pushing them back inside that little room and locking the door.

But years later, when Pip was born and placed in my arms, she was there all around me. I saw her in his tiny fingers, furled around mine, before I shoved the thought away. And once, when he'd woken in the early hours for a feed, just a few months old, I'd gone to him, in that half space between sleeping and waking, and thought it was her pink round cheek against mine; her skin, velvet like rose petals.

'So that's it really,' I said to Hattie now. 'That's how it was.'

The room fell silent. I could hear the buzz of the fridge, and the tread of footsteps where somebody was walking about in the flat above.

'Sometimes . . .' I began, and then stopped, swallowing hard. 'Sometimes it still happens, even now. I just get this sense of her. Or I think I see her. It could be some random toddler at the play park or the coffee shop that sets me off, or one of those "miracle baby" articles about premature babies with their little woolly hats and all those tubes.'

'It's grief, I suppose,' said Hattie. 'When you lose someone, they're never really gone. Not in your mind.'

'What do you think happens to babies who never have a chance to live?'

She sighed, and fiddled with the bracelet around her wrist. 'What happens to any of us?'

'But, not to have any life at all.'

She wriggled on her seat. 'I saw something on TV once, with women who'd had miscarriages. It was on *This Morning* or something. One of the women said her baby's soul had gone back to the universe. To the earth and the trees and the sea and the stars. And, you know, that he would wait quietly to be born again, when it was the right time and place.'

'But not to her.'

'Maybe to her. Maybe not. *I* don't know. Or maybe' – her voice softened into a childlike tone – 'well, maybe his soul would go to heaven.'

I sighed. 'All alone. Have you seen how newborn babies get without their mothers?'

'Oh Janey, I don't know.' She clunked her glass down onto the table. 'I'm not exactly an authority on spiritual matters. Maybe other people would look after her. Dead family members. Maybe your grandpa.' She said it emphatically, as though to say, 'That's it, there's your answer'.

'Grandpa? He wouldn't have a clue! He'd try and teach her about photosynthesis or something, and forget to sterilise the bottles.'

'In heaven, the bottles probably come pre-sterilised.'

My heart tugged at the thought of a baby who would never need milk, in a sterilised bottle or otherwise.

But Hattie, my oldest friend Hattie, was here. She was warm, and impatient, and smiling, and here.

'You know what we need to do?' she said.

'What?' I leaned to rest an elbow on the table, missed, and sloshed wine onto my lap. 'Oh bugger. What?'

'I know you think this is all somehow connected, my inklings, and the stuff that's been going on with you. The stuff in the flat. But inklings, ghosts, whatever they are, don't buy jars of jam. This is someone trying to screw with your head. We need to do a Shapiro job on this flat. We have to escalate the investigation.'

'We'll definitely need more wine then.'

★

I'd been expecting to have a lie-in, but the doorbell rang at the crack of dawn. I pulled a dressing gown on and winced as I tugged a brush through my wild hair.

The light, as I opened the front door, sent a buzz of pain through my head.

'Gretel? Why are you here?'

She looked past me into the flat, an urgent look on her face. My legs felt weak suddenly.

290

'Is Pip all right?' Half a dozen scenarios had already run through my head: Pip lying crumpled in a heap at the bottom of a set of steps, Pip linked up to an array of bleeping machines in the Sick Kids Hospital.

'Where are his salopettes?' she demanded.

My brain went into 'do not compute' mode, struggling to think of a near-death scenario that would be alleviated by the prompt fetching of salopettes.

'W-what?'

'I told Murray to tell you to pack his salopettes. We're taking him skiing.'

'But he doesn't have any.'

She frowned, but in an amused way as though I'd said something funny.

'Surely he must? Gulliver has two pairs, and that's just for nursery.'

He bloody well would, wouldn't he, at his stupid forest nursery.

'Yes, but maybe that's because . . .'

She walked past me into the hall with an 'I'll sort this out' look, bashing me slightly with the corner of her enormous handbag. Maybe she thought that her presence in the flat would make salopettes materialise.

'He's also been going on about his "milky-bottle". To begin with I thought it was some glitch with his language, and that he meant a sports bottle or something. But no, Murray tells me he still drinks milk like a little baby.'

'Oh *God*, did I forget to pack his milky bottle? Oh no, you should've phoned. I would've brought it over.'

'Nicky Aitchison-Palmer's goddaughter had the same issue, she was also dependent on a baby's bottle until the age of three. Her teeth started to rot away at the front. The dentist suggested a fluoride supplement, or at the very least toothpaste with 1,400 parts per million of fluoride, which is what you find in adult toothpastes but not those ridiculous children's toothpastes which nobody should ever use. They can contain as little as 500 parts per million in some cases. But when the dentist found out about the milk addiction he just laughed, and tore off his mask, you know, the masks they wear, and said they shouldn't be faffing around with extra fluoride when the problem was quite clear and they should stop the milk immediately. When did Pip last see the dentist?'

She started marching towards the kitchen.

'No! Don't go in there . . .'

I wasn't thinking of the three empty bottles of wine, one lying on its side on the table, or the smashed glass in the sink. It wasn't even the post-it notes I was worried about: we'd drawn skulls in black marker pen on each of them and stuck them carefully on the 'hot spots', including the fridge door, the shelf where I'd found the strange jam, the table where my left hand had written nonsensical messages. The newspaper Hattie had 'prepared' was also fairly innocuous – she'd solemnly cut eye-holes in it, 'Just in case you need to spy on anyone unnoticed.'

No, it was Pip's Early Learning Centre easel I didn't want Gretel to see. It stood in the middle of the room, with an incident-room-style diagram drawn by Hattie in pen.

Around the edges were written names, some with little comments: Murray, Hattie (no!), Steve (too dishy), Jody (too stupid), Molly, Cleodie, Miss Fortune (demented), Mrs Paxton. Some had been circled, or linked up to other scribbled notes with arrows or squiggly lines.

But in the middle of it all was a stick figure with stiletto heels specially coloured in with neon-green highlighter, and its hands on its hips:

GRETEL: BITCH EXTRAORDINAIRE. CHIEF SUSPECT

Gretel stood for a moment, her hands on her hips in an unconscious mirroring of her stick-figure likeness. She made a sound that was halfway between a huff and a bitter laugh.

'I see now,' she said calmly. 'You're some kind of mental nutter. I am going to take your son away.'

She drew her phone out of her pocket and photographed the easel. 'You're an incapable mother,' she said as she drew nearer to the skull post-it on the fridge and leaned in to photograph that too.

'On what basis?' I snapped. 'Because I don't like *you*? Get over yourself, Gretel. Pip is fed and clothed and warm and happy. He's doing well at nursery—'

'Oh yeah – fed on jam sandwiches. Warm because Murray's paying for a roof over your heads. Doing well at the nursery which Murray pays for. Take away Murray's money and you are nothing. *Nothing.*'

'Murray's his father. I'm entitled to financial support.'

'Where are the furking salopettes? I need to get going.'

'I told you he doesn't have any.'

'Another pair of trousers then.' With a toss of her blonde mane, she marched out of the kitchen into the hall and Pip's bedroom.

And when I saw what was in there I closed my eyes and then opened them again, unable to process what I was seeing because it didn't make sense. Hattie and I hadn't even come in here last night.

But Gretel nodded, because she'd got what she needed now. This battle, or whatever it was, was surely all but over.

Because there was an object lying in Pip's cot, its black metal claw resting on the pillow, in the little hollow left by his head.

A hammer.

41

Janey

'It was awful,' I said to Steve later that night. 'She just looked at me and said, "I am going to *take. You. Down.*"'

I was lying in bed, face flushed, naked under the crumpled sheets. After a day of arguments, and frantic phone calls, and more locksmiths, I'd simply walked straight into Steve's arms when he'd arrived at my door. And this time our coming together had been different again. He'd soothed me, settled me, stroked away my nerves, quietened me with his hands and his lips and the movement of his body. Now, he'd made tea and brought chocolate digestives in, which I was eating from the packet.

'Dear oh dear.' He winced. 'Fighting talk. You'll have to take *her* down.' He aimed an imaginary gun at the door and pulled the trigger. 'P-ching.'

'Since there was only one glass on the table, she clearly thought I'd drunk three bottles of wine myself, and drawn the incident-room diagram on my own. And the hammer . . . God, Steve.'

She'd dialled Murray's number and spoken to him as though I wasn't even there. Like two lawyers discussing some troublesome case. 'Time for a change of tack,' she'd said. 'We've clear grounds to go down the social services route now.'

'I had to make up some story. I had to say that I'd been

hammering a nail into the wall to hang up a picture, and that Pip must have got hold of the hammer and thought it was a toy. It doesn't say much for my parenting skills but the alternative explanations look a lot worse.'

Intruders. Ghosts. Psychosis.

Steve shrugged. 'Maybe he did put it there. Maybe he did think it was a toy.'

'It wasn't there. It wasn't there when we left the house yesterday morning.'

But had it been? Could I be absolutely sure about that? I rubbed the heels of my hands against my forehead, trying to remember.

'I'm sure it wasn't. Do *you* think I'm going mad?'

'Course not. Could it have been Hattie? If you were both falling around drunk, she might've done it as a joke.'

'*No.* No, Steve, honestly. And Hattie doesn't even know about . . . the hammer dream, and everything.'

'Well, who does know?'

I looked at him, stroked him down the side of his face.

'Just you.'

He sighed, took hold of my hand and kissed it.

'I must have done it in my sleep. It's the only explanation. You know, I grabbed the phone off Gretel this morning, and *pleaded* with Murray to stop her phoning social services, but maybe I should have let them go ahead.'

'Jay . . .' His voice was soft now. 'You'd never hurt Pip. And she can't take him away from you.'

'She said she's going to request a court hearing. A children's welfare hearing or something. To decide who gets custody of Pip and everything.'

'That's not up to her.'

'Murray said he thought it would be a good idea! A good alternative to the social services route.'

It was a good, middle-class alternative that was safely in his lawyerly comfort zone. And hers. She'd played him so cleverly . . . he thought he'd talked her down, but she'd got her own way.

'No judge would take Pip away from you.'

'They might if they thought I was a "mental nutter".'

'But you're *not*.' He ran a hand down the side of my body, trailing his fingers into the dip of my waist. 'You're the perfect mum to Pip. You manage it all so well. He has a lovely life here with you.'

'Only because Murray's bankrolling everything. If he wasn't, if I had to work full-time, and pay for childcare, all the bills, everything . . . I have no idea how I'd manage.'

'He'd have to contribute. There'd be benefits and things. Tax credits and all that stuff. You're getting way ahead of yourself.'

'If she manages to sour things between me and Murray then it's bad news. One way or another, it'll be bad, bad news.'

I imagined myself, alone in the flat, night after night, seeing Pip only once a week, or every second weekend. Or maybe – because who knew where this would end – in some bleak room somewhere in the social work department, under official supervision.

'I hate it here without him,' I said. 'It doesn't even feel like home.'

'How about I take you out tonight. Away from this place. Anywhere you want to go. We could go for a drive. We could go for cocktails. We could go dancing.'

I thought for a moment. 'Anywhere at all?'

He nodded.

'I want you to take me to your flat. You promised to show it to me. No more excuses. I'm starting to think you're married, or a serial killer or something.'

He groaned and flopped onto the pillows. 'I told you, you'll need to give me warning so I can hide the body parts down the back of the sofa.'

'I could just wait outside while you do that.'

'And I'll have to do something with the buckets of blood in the fridge.'

'You said anywhere.' I elbowed him out of bed and threw his clothes at him.

*

I'd imagined his flat to be a light, airy studio with soaring ceilings, with boldly painted canvases vying for space on the walls, or standing half-finished on easels. I'd imagined having to step over the paint-covered sheets strewn across the floor, paintbrushes standing in jam jars.

So I was surprised when he took me to a compact box of a flat, six floors up in a modern apartment block right on the Shore, as he'd said.

'Make yourself comfortable.' He swung open the door and snapped on the lights. 'Back in a mo.'

I stepped from the hallway into a large rectangular room with a kitchen at the near end and a living area towards the back. It was empty other than two white sofas, a blue-glass coffee table and a flat screen TV set into the wall. A large picture window looked out across the river, over to the hills in the distance, black lumps against a duller black sky.

The walls were blank.

'Nice place,' I said when he came back, minus the leather jacket and wearing a different shirt. 'I like your blue coffee table.'

'Want some food?'

'Uh-oh . . .' I said. 'What will it be, caper sandwiches and beer?'

'Venison pâté and oatcakes? And I've got a nice hunk of Isle of Mull Cheddar.'

He poured me a glass of juice which I sipped as he set out the food on the pristine, granite-effect melamine worktop. I was trying to remember if a man had ever fed me. Murray certainly hadn't, that drunken night at Gleneagles. He'd fallen asleep straight afterwards, crossways on the oversized bed, and I'd raided the minibar for a little mouse meal of chocolate and nuts.

Steve and I ate at the breakfast bar, teetering on high stools. It felt like we'd sneaked into a show flat to have a picnic.

'So where are your paintings?' I asked.

'Most of my work's at the college.'

'Being such a visual person, though . . . I was surprised to see the blank walls.'

He shrugged. 'Haven't been here that long. I'll need to put something up.'

'When did you move in?'

'Two years or so.'

'Oh. Oh well. Best to get these things right first time, I s'pose. You wouldn't want to leave holes in the walls if you changed your mind. Not when they're so nice and . . . white.'

Nice and white?

He spread some of the coarse pink pâté onto an oatcake,

and it gave into two pieces with a soft, cracking sound.

'It's awfully quiet here.'

'It's a quiet block. It's half empty.'

'What do you mean?'

'They built this place at the end of the property boom, and lots of the flats never sold. The four floors above this one are all empty; they never got finished.'

'It's nice . . . I still think you should put up some of your paintings, though. We could hire a van and—'

'Janey.' He held his non-oatcake hand up in a stop gesture. 'Please. I haven't painted anything for a couple of years.'

'What? But—'

'Other than bits and pieces for work. Teaching keeps me busy enough for now.'

'Why aren't you doing your own stuff?'

He stared down at the worktop between us, silent for so long that I thought he'd ignored my question.

'Calum.' He put down his oatcake and brushed the crumbs off his hands. 'After Calum, I couldn't.'

I moved carefully off the wobby stool and round the breakfast bar to him. I pulled him close, cradling his head into my chest.

He stood up and pulled my hips towards his, pressing against me all the way down. With a long, shaky breath, he tugged my jeans down, finding me with his fingers. Then he lifted me onto the cheap melamine worktop, closed his eyes and pushed himself into me with a sound that was almost like a sob.

★

300

Later that night, lying in the cloudy white sheets of Steve's bed, in his empty white room, I found myself telling him about the baby I'd lost. He held me, my head against his chest, stroking my hair.

'I'm so sorry,' he said, the words humming through his chest wall into my ear. 'I'm so, so sorry that happened to you.'

'You don't seem surprised,' I said. 'About the baby.'

His ribcage rose and fell. Rose and fell again. I closed my eyes and it was like drifting. Drifting away.

'I always thought there was something. Something in your past that was very painful. Very current for you. I'm glad you could tell me. Whenever you're sad, tell me, and I'll hold you.'

I felt tears run down my face into the hair of his chest.

They weren't tears of sadness though, this time, but tears of wonder that I'd found him.

I twisted round, propped myself up on one elbow. I needed to look into his eyes to see that he felt it too – this channel of perfect communication that had opened up between us.

He reached up and cupped my cheek, wiping a tear away with the flat of his thumb.

'I'm here,' he said. 'I'm not sure there's anything I can say. But I'm here.'

And for a moment I was a child again, standing in the stream at Glen Eddle as the water rushed past, washing me pure and clean and cool.

★

I woke with a start. Steve was sitting beside me on the bed, watching me as though he'd been waiting for me to wake up.

'What time is it?'

'Just after one,' he said gently.

'What's wrong?' My thoughts flew to Pip again. Some kind of disaster had happened . . .

He reached for my hand and held it. My pinkie twitched against the grip of his fingers.

'I need to talk to you about something, and it's going to be hard for you. It's going to hurt you.'

'What?' Was it about Calum? Katya? Had he decided, somehow over the last two hours, while I'd been sleeping, that he was going back to them? I shouldn't have gone to sleep. I shouldn't.

'I know your Miss Fortune. I know Esme.'

What?

'How?'

'She taught me piano,' he said.

I wriggled further up onto the pillows. This wasn't such a big deal. He could just explain quickly and we could get back to sleep.

'Why didn't you tell me before?'

He pressed his big, bony hands more tightly over mine, as though he was trying to transfer strength to me. His face looked vulnerable, exposed without the glasses, his eyes black and fathomless in the half light of the room.

'Why didn't you say anything?'

'Because you first mentioned her in the art session. I felt it wasn't appropriate to say anything.'

I shook my head slowly. 'But the other things that happened *were* appropriate?'

You held me. You held me. You held me.

'No. I know they weren't. I was overwhelmed. There was this massive connection with you. Your life had been . . . been

302

shaped by her, too. It was obvious I couldn't be detached any more. I couldn't stay in the tutor role. It's why I had to say you couldn't come to the sessions.'

I pushed him out of the way, swung my legs out of bed, tried to stand up, but the floor seemed to sway. Maybe the whole, sad empty tower block was swaying, bending, in the wind that blew in from the sea.

'Janey? What's up?'

'I need some water.'

He followed me through to the kitchen, poured me water, cold from the tap. Then he poured himself a measure of whisky in a crystal glass and sat down on the sofa. I perched on the edge, the leather cold against my legs. I was only wearing a long T-shirt, one of his.

'Why didn't you tell me later?'

'It felt too late to tell you. And it's not something I find easy to talk about. Oh God Janey, I don't know. I should have. I should have and I didn't.'

'How did she shape your life?'

'It doesn't matter.'

'It does. You can't be a . . . a *blank* any more. You have to tell me about yourself. Or I'll have to go.' I shook my head, and repeated it more softly. 'I'll have to go, Steve.'

He sighed. Stared into the whisky, tilting the glass so that it caught the light.

'I started lessons when I was ten,' he said. 'They were offered as part of the bursary thing. My parents would never have paid for something like that. Dad didn't even want me to do them. He said I was "arty farty" enough already. But I liked the idea of the lessons because the heating at home didn't come on until seven, when my mum got home from work.'

303

And it had always been warm at Miss Fortune's.

'Oh, don't worry,' he said, seeing my expression. 'There were lots of latchkey kids in the 1980s. Not so much at St Simon's, but hey. My parents weren't bad parents, they were just . . .'

'Busy?'

'Yep.' He shrugged. 'They were busy trying to keep the bills paid, and they just kind of assumed I'd be okay. They used to laugh about St Simon's all the time, because the day they'd gone to look round they'd seen "smoked-salmon terrine" on the lunch menu. They put on posh voices – which they thought were hilarious – whenever they mentioned the school. They didn't know that the boys took the piss out of *my* accent whenever they deigned to speak to me.'

'I love your accent,' I said softly.

'I tried to lose it for a while, but the boys' private school accent never took. Maybe because I never felt like I belonged there. I always wished we'd move back to Sheffield, and I could go back to my old school and my old friends. My parents didn't realise. They didn't ever ask if I was, you know, *okay.* They never noticed my hands.'

'Your hands?'

'They were a mess. Hand washing and so on. It was OCD, probably, or some kind of anxiety disorder.' His voice was dismissive. Colder than I'd ever heard it.

I hesitated. 'Were you—'

'I was nothing special at the piano. But I think that worked for both of us. I only played for fun, and she never pushed me. I was eleven when she suggested I should stay for my tea. It was snowing, and she said I should wait until it had stopped, as the buses would all be backed up. So I stayed. A nursery tea, she called it. Toast soldiers, and egg-in-a-cup. Orange squash.'

'C-custard creams for afters?'

'You cold?' He slipped his arm round me and pulled my rigid body against him. I could feel the cage of his ribs down the length of my upper arm.

'It was an arrangement that just kind of stuck. Miss Fortune said I could walk straight to hers from school on a Thursday, and do my homework in the kitchen until it was time for my lesson to start. She got cream for my hands. She said it was important for pianists to look after their skin.'

'Cream.' I remembered the smell of Vaseline Intensive Care filling the air in the music room, and again my heart lurched into understanding.

'And then – it must have been a year or so later – it snowed again one afternoon. She wanted to listen to some piece by Debussy and she said we could go into her room, and lie down on her bed, as it was right by the window and we'd be able to watch the snow falling. I remember looking down at her feet as she kicked off her shoes. Her tights were inside out, and I was repulsed, totally, by the seam: the dark seam snaking over her toes. There was a counterpane thing on the bed, this heavy pink fabric, and it smelt damp when we stretched out on top of it. We lay there, watching the snow and listening to the music. The flakes were enormous, so slow, twisting as they fell. And they kept coming, coming and coming and coming, like the sky was made of nothing but snow, and it would never stop. It felt like everything would be buried soon, just buried and no one would ever know.'

The words emerged in a monotone, low and hypnotic like a prayer. I shifted, uncomfortably, on the edge of the sofa. But then he drew in a sudden, deep breath, and when he spoke again his voice was matter-of-fact.

'She didn't say anything when she saw that I was crying, just reached across and held my hand. And then, a few minutes later, she said I'd better be getting home.'

'Did it happen again?'

'Lying on her bed? No, but there were other things that were ... too close. Once in the school yard Mark McCrae rubbed dog shit into my hair, and when I got to her flat, she leant me over the bath and washed my hair, using this white rubbery shower hose which she attached onto the taps. And her Pears shampoo, which I smelled of for days afterwards. She dried my hair with a towel, and then drew it round my shoulders, tight under my chin. Then we sat in front of the fire and listened to Elgar's cello concerto.'

The cello concerto. All that storm and darkness.

'She never tried to talk me out of my moods. I liked that about her. But she was quite practical too. When she found out the boys used to take the piss out of my thrift-shop uniform, she went to Aitken & Niven and bought me a new blazer.'

'So did she ...'

'Oh, she didn't *abuse* me, nothing like that.' There was a long pause. 'It was just that she was ... I don't know. The only way I can describe it is that she was *greedy* for me.' He gave a shrug, a half shudder. 'Like she wanted me to be hers, her son, you know? I started going there most days after school, and it all became a big secret. I had to lie to my parents, and to the school. I made up a friend called Philippe, who went to the state school down the road and was supposedly helping me with my maths because he was some kind of fucking maths genius. And all just so I could go and sit in her music room and listen to Elgar.' He blinked and shook his head as though it was all unbelievable, as though it had happened to someone else, not him. 'I didn't have a single friend my own age.'

'How long did all this go on?'

'A long time, Janey. A very long time.'

Had he been in her flat while Hattie and I had had our lessons? The thumping from the back room. The table set for two. A crawling feeling came over me. This man. This man, who I'd trusted with my secrets, had been tucked into another layer of my life, hiding there like an insect all this time.

'Until when?'

'Sixth form, I guess. It started to fizzle out then when I got busy with exams and so on. And obviously then I left to go to art college in Glasgow.'

'So you're not still . . .' I shivered and his arm tightened around me, as though he was trying to strengthen me. 'In touch? With her?'

'I do see her. Yes.'

I felt it like a substance under my skin: the old horror seeping into the present.

'She's senile, though,' I said, grasping now for something that could negate the fact of his seeing her, or knowing her, and cancel out the betrayal.

'Yeah,' he sighed, letting go of me now and leaning back on the sofa. 'She's in a bad way. When I was round there last she was in her dressing gown – she'd run herself a bath, even though the carers are meant to do all that. She wanted to listen to some Tchaikovsky thing. She'd plugged her CD player into one of the sockets in the hall and balanced it on the side of the bath.'

'Oh.'

'I took it away with me, said it was broken. I'll need to get her one with a shorter flex.'

Suddenly I was irritated at the careworn, solicitous tone of his voice. Why was he talking about this like I'd be interested? Like we were somehow in this together? Did he expect me to say I'd pick one up from John Lewis next time I was there?

'I measured the distance between the socket and the edge of the bath.'

I shrugged, the insolent 'whatever' shrug of a teenager. I'd told him about what she'd done, hadn't I? About how her filthy black words had settled over my stomach that day. Over the place where my baby slept. Didn't he understand that I *hated* her?

'The problem is, it's impossible to eliminate all risk. The carer said that once she tried to heat her electric kettle on the gas hob. There were brown scorch marks all the way up the side.'

'So you see her all the time, then. Basically.'

Why did she have to spoil this – me and Steve – like everything else?

He shrugged. 'I go and see her a couple of times a week. Someone had to step in and sort out the care situation. That's the problem, when someone doesn't have family. They can slip through the cracks. She needs to be in a home, really.'

'Doesn't she have a case worker or something? Someone who can organise a home? It shouldn't all be down to you. Tell them it's not *safe* for her to live by herself any more. She seemed completely brain dead when I visited her.'

I'd *told* Steve. I'd told him I'd visited her. He'd sat there and said *nothing*.

'Oh, she was on those meds then. They decided to try her on them to calm her down a bit. Antipsychotic meds, basically.' He sighed. 'She liked to go on walks around the city: visiting her old haunts, remembering the old days, I suppose. I used to give her little jobs to do: posting letters, buying a magazine for me, or new drawing pencils, that sort of thing. It was a way to try and keep her engaged with the real world.'

I shrugged.

'But then she grabbed the man in the newsagent round the throat because they didn't have the magazine I'd asked for one day.'

'Why?'

'She gets these flashes of paranoia sometimes. Thinks people are conspiring against her. And hallucinations. She sometimes has hallucinations. They prescribed the meds after she attacked that poor man. But they were too much for her. Zonked her out completely. They tried something a bit different but that was even worse, so we had to take her off them again. But it's so hard, because it's basically not safe to let her go on her walkabouts any more. Not safe for herself or other people, really. So I try and take her out when I can. But it's not easy.'

'It shouldn't all be down to you. Tell them she needs to go in a home *now*, or you won't be responsible for what happens. Why should you be?'

I felt my hands clench in a rush of childish rage. I wanted to get him *away* from her. Away.

'You're not even family,' I went on. 'And she's suffering from severe dementia.'

Steve stretched out his legs and sighed. 'She's away with the fucking fairies, Janey. But she was like a mother to me, when I needed one. I can't give up on her.'

I shivered. 'I'm going back to bed. I'm tired.'

'Wait, Janey. Now I've started, I need to tell you the whole lot. We used to talk, Esme and I. We talked about pretty much everything. So I know – knew – a fair few things about you.'

Oh Lord. What a fool I'd been. Rationing out my secrets when he'd known everything all along.

'You knew about the baby. You've always known.'

'Yes.'

'No. Why would she have told you about that?'

He winced. 'Because it was *catastrophic* for her, the whole thing. You do realise that, don't you?'

I wrapped my arms around myself and pulled my knees up.

'The piano lessons just fell away, after the word got out. There were rumours that she'd hurt you. The St Katherine's parents cut her off, then there was the ripple effect to all the other schools. Edinburgh's a small place. So that was that. She was finished as a teacher. She'd been finished as a pianist well before that, of course. What with her various *misfortunes*.'

He gave a hollow laugh that made the skin creep on my arms. Was he referring to the car accident, or did he mean . . .

'Sorry, Steve. I really, really need to go to bed.'

'I need to ask you something else. The hammer thing, and your dream. It seems too much of a coincidence. Did you know something about it?'

'About what?'

But already, scenes were flashing through my mind like the stuttering images in an old film.

'The attack.'

I searched about, in my mind, for anything else he might mean. But no, he'd caught me. He'd caught me right in his trap.

I'd been pushing it away for so long. The night of the

310

carol service, December 1989. It had taken an effort almost more than I could bear, and had cost more than I ever had to give. I tried to find my anger again. Or even the panic. The superstitious fears I'd held on to. All the things that I'd attached to it – to her – over the years. Anything rather than remember the event itself.

'No, Steve. Not this. No.'

But I sank my head into my hands, and let it come back.

*

I emerge from the dark of the Marlowes' garden, through the alleyway and onto Regent's Crescent. If Renee's put her coat on, she must be going out. She must be going to see Hattie. If Hattie's gone to stay with friends, I'm going to find out who and where.

Further ahead up the street, is that her? A figure in a long coat, and why is she wearing Hattie's St Katherine's scarf and hat? And carrying her schoolbag? I can see the reflective strips. I helped her fix them on after last term's police road-safety talk. She isn't hunched against the rain, as Hattie would be: she hates the rain. No, she's striding along in a hurry.

I follow, the rush making me dizzy after crouching in the garden for so long. Streetlight slashes off the wet pavement, and I keep losing her, the dark shape up ahead.

She marches along Regent Road into town, crosses North Bridge, strides up the High Street. Where is she going? I'm exhausted, my chilblained toes aching in my damp school shoes. She makes for Lauriston Place, Tollcross. She's heading towards Morningside. Why would she be going to Miss Fortune's?

But that's what she does, moving steadily up the hill, and finally disappearing onto a side street.

I run to catch up, but when I turn onto Craigielaw Street there's no sign of her. Surely she's gone into Miss Fortune's flat, then? I'm confused. Is Hattie having a lesson? One final lesson before going away? But the curtains of the music room bay window are open and there's no sign of anybody. I wait, sitting on a low wall, studded with metal where old railings have once been removed. If she's having a lesson, why aren't they in the music room? My backside is numb from the cold wall, so I get up and push open the door into the tenement stair, taking care not to let my footsteps sound out in the stairwell as I cross the passage and out onto the back green. The kitchen window is easy to find: second along on the left. The curtains don't quite meet in the middle, and I peer through the tangle of spider plants on the windowsill, through the cups and plates jumbled on the draining board, and try to make sense of the scene inside.

The room is brightly lit, bathed in warm yellow tones like a cosy stage set. Music is playing inside – an aria from Madame Butterfly *– and Miss Fortune is attached to a kitchen chair. Strapped to it. With shiny black tape, spiralling from shoulders to waist, all along her thighs and down to her ankles.*

Her left hand – her good hand – is taped to the kitchen table, which has been pulled out to the centre of the room. The tape has been wound round the wrist, and looped round the tabletop three or four times. The fingers are splayed, each fastened down at the tip with a neatly cut strip of tape.

A fly caught in a crazy black web.

Her eyes are wide open and wild. Her cheeks are shiny, streaked with mascara.

She's staring at the figure seated across the table from her.

The figure rises suddenly. It's Renee, still wearing Hattie's school scarf, her face violently distorted, deep furrows etched into it like

*a Greek tragedy mask. She's holding something in her two hands,
something that doesn't make sense.*

*Miss Fortune turns away, tucking her head towards her left
shoulder. Her eyes seem to meet mine for a moment. I hold my
breath, but there is no moment of recognition. She can't see me in
the darkness.*

*Then Renee lifts the hammer high into the air and brings it
down on Miss Fortune's pinkie finger, one – two – three – four –
five – six times.*

★

What did I do?

I know that I stood, the wet leeching into my lace-ups from
the sodden flowerbed.

I know that I watched as Renee sat down again and lit a
cigarette. I watched as the smoke curled upwards, and Miss
Fortune sobbed, and Madame Butterfly's heartbroken aria
soared into the high-ceilinged spaces of the flat.

She waited a few minutes between each finger. It took
perhaps half an hour before she'd finished all five.

Plenty of time for me to fetch help. I could have knocked
on the door of one of the other flats, or found a callbox and
phoned the police.

Was I in shock? Paralysed by what I was seeing? I was only
a child, of course.

Or maybe I assumed Miss Fortune had done something
dreadful to deserve it, something to Hattie perhaps, and that
Renee was just a tigress, defending her cub.

But really, there has only ever been one answer. Thwarting
Renee – this new, terrifying Renee – would have meant I'd
never see Hattie again. And my twelve-year-old self did a cold,

hard calculation and decided that I needed Hattie more than Miss Fortune needed her fingers.

★

'Oh God. Steve. I could have stopped it.' I drew my hands away from my face, but I still couldn't look at him. 'I didn't help her.'

'You were twelve, Janey.'

'Do you know . . . why? What did Renee have against her? What had Miss Fortune done?'

He shrugged. 'Don't you know any of this? Emil Marlowe and Esme had a history. They'd met at Ramplings as teenagers, and it was all a bit Romeo and Juliet: his parents tried to split them up, but they couldn't do it. Only the car smash could do that, as it turned out. You know about that, yeah? While they were studying at the Conservatoire in Paris?'

I nodded. *The love of my life*, she'd said.

'I don't know all of it,' he went on. 'I know that Emil went to the States after the accident, and she moved back to Edinburgh and started teaching. I guess it was the only option for her, really. But he ended up moving to Edinburgh too, when he got married, and I think they started up again. There was a dynamic between them, despite everything.'

'Maybe,' I said, 'she thought that if Emil ended up with her, it would sort of redeem everything. Because they could build their lives around love, instead of being a glittering musical couple. It would be romantic, love winning the day.'

'Yeah, that's spot on, I think. And part of it was that she wanted to have a family. She tried to have children. Not that he knew.'

314

Dried-up, spinsterish Miss Fortune trying to get pregnant. I'd never known her at all, I realised now.

'In fact, Esme had just had her sixth miscarriage when Renee became pregnant with the lump of gristle that turned out to be James.'

Six. Six miscarriages.

'But Renee had a breakdown when James was a few months old. Some sort of postnatal depression. Emil shipped her off to an expensive "retreat" in Switzerland and moved Esme into his house to keep him company.' He broke off with an ironic laugh. 'He *really* was a piece of work. And she ended up looking after James. It all went on longer than anyone expected. Emil sent her packing as soon as there was talk of Renee coming back, which was just around the time James was learning to talk. He would have been two-ish? Two and a half maybe.'

Two and a half. She'd have seen him through the worst of his teething, maybe even potty-trained him. He'd have taken his first steps with her. I thought of Pip, his little legs stretching out and losing their baby softness as he learned to run, to jump, to climb.

'But it doesn't make sense. Renee would never have let her anywhere near Hattie, let alone hire her as a teacher.'

'Presumably Renee didn't *know*. Maybe she heard whispers, after she got back, or had her suspicions. Who knows. But when she did finally twig . . . Well, you saw what happened.'

'Why didn't Esme go to the police?'

He gave a short laugh. 'Renee said she'd come back, if the police started sniffing around, and next time it'd be her face. She said she had an alibi on hand. Some judge that lived next door to her who owed her a favour.'

315

I shivered. 'That may have been true. A favour is one way of putting it. The Marlowes all knew Lord Smythe was screwing his housekeeper.'

Steve poured himself another whisky – his third – and laid his head back against the sofa.

'It's crazy, crazy stuff. Phew.'

I sat back too. This wasn't so bad. Maybe, after all, I was glad that he knew.

'The lawyer doesn't think a criminal prosecution would stick, what with Esme's memory issues, though there's nothing to stop us reporting it to the police. And a civil case would have all sorts of problems, too.'

The air in the room seemed to go cold.

'What lawyer?'

'Oh, I sounded out a lawyer about it all a few months back.'

A few months back?

'I think it's a bit of a dead end, even with a witness now. They'd probably pull all kinds of holes in your evidence, with it being so long ago and given your age at the time. One option might be to have a conversation with Renee Marlowe. Appeal to her better nature. She could bloody well offer some compensation. It would go some way towards paying for Esme's care. Knowing there was a witness might, shall we say, focus her mind.'

I sat for some moments, aware of the sound of his breathing, which was rather fast. The faint, sour warmth of it against my cheek.

'Blackmail,' I said quietly.

'*No.*' He winced, and ran a hand over the top of his head. 'God, no, it's not *blackmail*. We'd be giving her a chance to make recompense. I mean, it was bad enough that he ruined one of her hands with his drink driving. Then she goes and smashes up her other one?'

I shook my head, feeling sick again.

'And it might help *you*, Janey. Put all this to rest.'

A few months back?

When, exactly, had he worked it out? When he saw the first 'Janey and Hattie' drawing? Had he twigged as soon as he'd heard our names connected? When I'd said Miss Fortune's name, after drawing the forest scene?

And of course. I'd panicked and gasped and rambled about how I thought I'd drawn myself holding a hammer. I'd given it all to him on a plate. All my secrets, without even realising. It was moments after that he'd drawn me into his arms. Held me that first time. Let all my hurt ebb into his arms.

I could feel it coming back to me now. Heavy, cold as lead. Pulling me under.

'You guessed.' It came out in a small, broken voice, as though I was pleading with him to say it wasn't true. 'You must have guessed I'd witnessed it, or at least knew something about it. That's why you befriended me. That's why you spoke to that lawyer.'

'What? No!' He slid an arm round me. 'I sensed that – perhaps – you knew something about it. Through Hattie, maybe. I wasn't planning to *involve* you. It just got me thinking, that's all. She was deteriorating so fast. She'd got so much worse over the summer. I'd started looking into care homes and found out how much they cost.'

Money. Money was somewhere at the root of all this.

Steve.

I remembered that first email from him, the pixels in his name dancing before my eyes. The sound of his voice, moving from gentleness to teasing to hard and back again. His eyes, feverish as he touched me, every time. Everything that made up 'Steve' flipped over like a deck of cards. The possible shapes of him, shifting so fast, a hundred different combinations that could have meant anything. Or nothing. I couldn't hold on to the meaning.

His arm felt heavy now, like a snake across my shoulders. I unwound it and stood up.

'Home.' I could hardly get the word out. My voice didn't even sound like mine. 'I need to get home.'

42

Janey

If Hattie was surprised to see me on her doorstep at 3 a.m., half blown over in the storm and the rain, she didn't show it. She took my coat off, peeling it from each arm as though I was a child. She led me down the stairs to the kitchen, fetching a towel to put round my shoulders. It smelt of lemon soap.

'It's finished. It's all finished. He's gone.'

He was never there.

I wasn't going to be able to stop it. The truth – the hot, corrosive truth – it was all going to come spewing out. I put a hand over my mouth.

'What's happened? Janey? Is it Steve?'

'Your mother. She tied Miss Fortune up and smashed her fingers with a hammer. I saw it happen. I saw it all happen through the kitchen window.'

Hattie frowned, but it was a frown of puzzlement. Not shock, or disbelief.

'You knew?' I said. 'You knew all along?'

She sighed, and closed her eyes briefly.

'I knew something had happened, that night, though I didn't know exactly what. The last day of term, right? That's what you're talking about?'

'Tell me.'

She sat with her head in her hands for a moment, a mirror

319

image of Renee at the kitchen table on that night. Then she got up, left the room.

She came back a few minutes later with her diary, the one I'd read, the one that had been sitting in the Woolworths bag in my box room for all those years.

She laid it on the table and opened the back cover, peeling the black leatherette covering away from the cardboard underneath. The flap came away easily, with a little splitting sound.

'Pritt Stick,' she said. 'It's lasted pretty well.'

Frowning, she eased two fingers into the space between the leatherette and the cardboard, and pulled out one folded sheet of paper. She gave a little laugh, as though in disbelief that the tiny rows of pencilled words were still there.

Thursday, December 14th
I'm alone in the house.

Mum's left me alone. One minute she was downstairs heating up a disgusting mushroom quiche for dinner, and then she was gone. I wouldn't even have known, apart from the slamming of the front door.

I wish I could rewind the last few hours. I've set off some kind of terrible trouble.

This afternoon, I went down to find her. She was packing things from the kitchen cupboards into boxes, and I held out my music case and said, 'What should I do with this?'

'Just box it up with the other things from your room, darling.'

I said I couldn't, because some of the music was Miss Fortune's own.

And I pulled it out and put it on the table. *Fun for Ten*

Fingers, the finger-strengthening book.

Mum picked it up, flicked through it, and the letter fell out. Just like it did when I first opened it, when I got home after my second lesson. It's been in there all along, the horrible thing.

The Letter.

17th October 1973
Dear Esme,

I am returning Blue Bear's Dance, *the piece you wrote for James' third birthday, which I cannot pass on to him for obvious reasons. You will be pleased to know that he is happy and settled. He calls Renee 'Mummy' now, and will have no lasting memory of your time here. I am sure you will understand why I must ask you not to contact us again. Please also stay out of the vicinity of Little Goslings Nursery. If you do not heed my wishes in this regard, I shall be referring this matter to my lawyers.*

Regards
Emil

Mum shoved it back into the music case, like it didn't matter, but her hands were shaking.

I asked her again if I could go to the carol service and she looked right through me as though I wasn't even there.

And now she's gone out. I'm in the house alone.

11 p.m.
I saw her come in – I was watching from the top landing, waiting for her, with her navy-blue silk dressing gown wrapped round me for the cold.

But she was dressed in my school uniform, which made me feel odd inside, like I'd gone over a bump on a fast road. And she was carrying my schoolbag.

Her hands, when she reached up to pull my hat off her head, were a reddish colour. I think that's right. I keep trying to remember. My head hurts too much to be totally sure. But I think that's right.

She's gone into the bathroom now. She's been running the water for the longest time. The pipes are making an awful racket, from all the hot water she's using. I can hear them through the wall. That's what it must be, that horrible, splitting, thudding sound. The pipes.

'Oh Hattie . . .' I folded the page up and put it back inside the cover of the diary. 'Poor Hattie. That was the TL from your diaries, then: The Letter. You should've told me.'

'I was frightened of it. Too frightened to talk about it. I didn't understand what it meant, not fully, but I knew it was probably enough to blow our family apart.'

I spoke in the gentlest of voices. 'So why did you show it to your mum?'

She sighed. 'I've asked myself that so many times. I think I was just tired, tired of holding all that power. I knew it was powerful because the inklings had started the day she gave it to me: the odd piano playing upstairs. Then the music case thumping around in the cupboard, as though the letter wanted to be let out. I thought maybe the inklings would stop if I, you know, handed it over.'

'But they only got worse?'

'Yes. Everything in my head seemed to get darker. I thought Mum, I thought she'd . . .'

'Oh God. You thought she'd killed her.'

'Well, she couldn't leave Edinburgh fast enough, afterwards. We weren't supposed to be leaving until after the weekend, but she bundled me into the car the very next day.'

'I don't understand about your diary. How did it end up back at school, in that box on my desk?'

'When I came out of the shower the next morning, Mum had been in my room, "packing up" the last of my things. I'd hidden my diary inside my history folder and that was gone, along with my other school stuff. She caught me going through the load of bin bags piled up in the hallway, and blew up at me, saying there was no way we were taking all my junk down south.

'I said there were important things in there that I had to send back to the school or I'd get in trouble: textbooks and stuff, and my script for the school play, marked up with my part, which I needed to hand on to Alice Simpson. But Mum said we were "done with that fucking school now".

'I was too shocked to reply – I'd never heard her swear like that before. And in front of Mrs Patel, too, but she just raised her eyebrows and pressed her mouth into a thin line, as though Mum was an unruly teenager. She marched me down to the kitchen and fed me breakfast, and said not to worry, she'd sort it. She was supposed to be taking all the rubbish to the dump, but she must have rescued my school stuff after we'd gone.'

'And sent it on to me, at the school, because—'

'If anyone would know what to do with it, it would be you.'

A sob caught in my throat. 'I'm sorry. I'm so sorry I didn't stop your mum. I'm so sorry.'

She took my face between her two hands, making me look into her eyes. 'Janey, I didn't stop her either. Nothing could

323

have stopped her. *Nothing*. Especially not a frightened little girl.'

'I could have phoned the police. Steve thinks . . .'

She shook her head. 'Steve? What's he got to do with all this, anyway?'

I stared down at the floor. It was so embarrassing to say it, that this was what it had come down to, the great, shining love that had been written all over my face. 'He knew everything. He's involved with Miss Fortune; he's basically like a son to her. He knew about you and me, and our lessons, about James, and the baby. He guessed I knew about the attack. He knew it all, all along. From the first day he saw me.'

I felt the thud of hurt about to fall again, as brutal as Renee's hammer. But Hattie reached across the table again and took both of my hands in hers.

'I'm here,' she said, simply. 'I'm here.'

43

Janey

The next few days were grim. Two versions of myself were fighting against each other. If I didn't want to hear from Steve, why did I still check my phone every five minutes? I erased all his texts with iron resolve, but couldn't – quite – erase his number.

I saw Hattie every day. She kept finding excuses to drop round: with a new kind of limeflower tea she'd found in Waitrose, or to borrow my calligraphy pen to write Christmas cards. She insisted that Pip and I go round to help put up her Christmas tree in the enormous drawing room. In those hours spent with her I would forget to check my phone, and even found myself laughing at the sight of her straining to perch Pip's Darth Vader figure on the top of the tree; he'd hidden Renee's antique gilded angel up his jumper.

In the end, Steve phoned at six o'clock on the Tuesday, just as I was trying to give Pip his dinner. Had he done it on purpose, hoping for a short, perfunctory conversation?

'Janey,' he said. My body loosened at the sound of his voice: my chest, my shoulders, deep down in my stomach, the places I'd been holding the hurt. And there was nothing, nothing but longing for him. Formed by his mouth, resonating through his jaw and the very bones of him, even my name sounded different: charged, somehow.

'What do you want?' I said, breaking up Pip's fish fingers with the side of his fork.

Pip shrieked. 'My! My do-it!'

My hand was shaking as I handed the little fork to him. He dropped it.

'Fok! Fok!'

I bent to pick it up, whacking my head on the edge of the table as I straightened up.

'How're things?' said Steve. His voice was odd, as though his jaw was tight. He could have been shivering.

'Are you cold?'

'Yeah. It's freezing. I'm just walking into Sainsbury's. Need to get some things for dinner. Red peppers. Mustard.' He paused. 'You okay?'

I hated the fact that he hadn't sat down somewhere – somewhere *indoors* – to phone me. I hated the fact that he was planning dinner without me, and I hated the assumption that *I* would be the one who wasn't okay.

'No,' I said. 'I'm not okay. Not in the slightest.'

If he had broken down at this point, wailed down the phone, begged me to come back, I'd have given in in a second.

'Thanks,' he murmured.

'What?'

'Sorry, someone just gave me a two-for-one voucher.'

'What for?'

'Diet Coke multipacks.'

'You don't drink Diet Coke. You're worried about aspartame.'

'No. *Yes.*'

Pip raised curious eyebrows at me. His eyes looked impossibly wide, luminous. I stroked a smudge of ketchup away from his chin. He smiled, revealing his sharp little milk teeth, white rows against perfect pink gums.

'You sound down,' he said. 'Do you want to talk?'

'Yes, I am *down*. Something to do with you using me for your *compensation* scheme.'

He said nothing.

'Yes,' I went on. 'It must have been such a bore to listen to all my little confessions. Even harder to bring yourself to touch me. To kiss me . . . to *sleep* with me.'

The hurt had nowhere to go. It was swelling higher and higher in my chest. I snatched a breath. 'For the life of me I don't know how you did it. All for the sake of money.'

Help me. Stop all this. Say you loved me.

'God, Janey. Is that *really* what you think of me?'

Silence.

Finally, he sighed. 'What a mess. What a bloody mess.'

Why wasn't there a 'sorry'? Where were the forthright, all-too-convincing denials I'd been half hoping for, half dreading?

'Yup.'

Steve. Steve, please.

'We should probably talk it all over.' There was a weariness in his voice that edged – ever so slightly – into distaste.

I shuddered. There'd been far too much talking over with this man. Too much cut-open honesty. I wasn't about to bleed more of myself out in front of him.

'No thanks. I think we're done. Goodbye, Steve.'

★

'All girls *together*!' cried Jody, punching the air.

I jerked back, nearly knocking over my caramel latte. I wished to God that I'd never mentioned my break-up with Steve, that I hadn't started crying in the middle of the Diddle-diddle-doo

327

song this morning. Or that I'd at least had the presence of mind to invent a dead aunt or other excuse.

'Men are obsolete,' she added. 'Or at least they will be, in a few years' time when they've improved the technology.'

'Except Richard and Cameron, of course.' Molly pulled Cameron higher onto her lap, as though Jody might suggest beginning the cull there and then. 'And Tom and Dave,' she added, ever the dutiful wife.

'A few of the best specimens will be retained, of course,' twinkled Jody.

Cleodie stretched her legs out, arching back against her chair, her sturdy, unshaved calves emerging under the hem of her skirt. 'But men are *nice* though, aren't they? To have around?'

'Exactly!' said Jody. 'When. They're. Around.' She jabbed the table with each word. 'Not when they blubber off with someone else and leave you.'

'Blubber off?' For a moment I pictured whales, fornicating and faithless, before I remembered that Jody had a whole lexicon of approximated swear words, for use when Vichard was in earshot.

'Well he has, hasn't he?'

'No. I finished it, actually.' I let out a shaky sigh. I held out a hopeful spoon of yoghurt for Pip, who batted it out of my hand with a contemptuous look. We'd been making progress, though. He'd eaten a tiny cube of pear last week, a triumphant dessert after his jam sandwich.

Jody shook her head impatiently, indicating that I was getting bogged down in mere technicalities.

'What did he do?' asked Molly, passing me another grey, environmentally friendly tissue. 'Did he have commitment issues? Was he seeing someone else?'

'No. He was just ... I think he was using me. Being manipulative.' I shrugged, trying to signal that there was nothing more to be discussed.

'Manipulative, ooh,' said Jody, sucking latte foam off a teaspoon.

'What did he do?' asked Cleodie and Molly in unison.

'Oh, he just wasn't the person I thought he was. I found some things out about him that were a little, er, worrying, to tell you the truth.'

'A nutter, then,' said Cleodie, with a gleeful eyebrow twitch. 'So was it him who was doing those screwy things in your flat?'

'Screwy things?'

'The weird things appearing in your cupboards and so on. Was that him, then?'

'Not unless he can walk through walls, no.'

Cleodie sprang upright. 'Have you ever left him alone with your keys, or your handbag?'

An image came into my mind, like a bubble popping to the surface: Steve catching me off guard with his embrace after the second art session, me scurrying off to the bathroom to clean the mascara off my face, leaving my handbag by my chair.

'No. Oh God, no I don't think so. If I ever did I was only gone for a minute.'

'He could have swapped your keys over. It's a classic conman trick.' She made a sweeping movement with her hand, as though to silence any dissent. 'I've been researching it for a bit in my novel. He'd most likely have gone for the back door key. The Back Door Switch. Was the key to your side door on your key ring? You know, the door from your flat into the tenement stair?'

'Yes – it always is.'

'When's the last time you used that key? If you're anything like me, you *never* use the back garden.'

She had a point. Pip and I, wary after the dog-poo incident, hadn't been out there since the summer.

'He could have switched that key, and switched it back at his leisure. Any tenement back door key would look the same: those old-fashioned long brass keys.'

She was right. Miss Fortune's, for example, would look exactly the same.

'He'd need to get into the tenement stair first,' I said weakly.

'Probably switched that key too. Or he could easily get someone to buzz him into the stair, saying he was the postman or something.'

I was about to say that no, Steve wasn't a conman who went around pretending to be a postman. He was an art tutor with a bit of a mixed-up past, who'd not been very forthcoming with me. But then I paused. Because *somebody* must have been responsible.

I turned to Molly, who'd put a sympathetic hand on my knee. 'But why? Why would he want to do those things?'

She shook her head sadly. 'Maybe he thought you'd lean on him, if you were frightened.'

Or if nobody believed me. If I thought I was going mad.

'It could be a way of getting control over you,' added Cleodie. 'Maybe he's just a damaged individual. The world's full of them, hon.'

Damaged. I thought of him stroking my leg in the car, the catch in his breath as he laid me down on my bed. I thought of his face, balled up with emotion as he drove himself into me, harder and faster and harder and faster, as though it might obliterate something.

Come back to me. Just come back.

Then I thought of Miss Fortune, of Steve making arrangements for her care, sorting out her financial affairs, thinking about settlements from Renee so he could get her into a home. He'd been like a son to her. He might be – oh God, of *course* he would be – a beneficiary under her will.

I thought of him carefully measuring all the electric flexes in her flat. The kettle with scorch marks in the plastic from the gas hob.

Jody tutted. 'Janey, hon, you look like you're about to be sick. Honestly, it's not worth getting upset over an obsolete man. I know! Let's have a girl trip to Buttercraig Lodge.'

Oh please, not Buttercraig Lodge. This was Jody and Tom's 'project' – a rot-riddled old house on top of a hill near Stirling. They'd been doing it up for a few years, splitting their time between there and their rented flat in Edinburgh. Last time at the coffee shop we'd had to 'ooh' and 'ah' over three photo albums of 'work in progress' pictures and I'd nearly lost the will to live.

'Well?' said Jody. 'Pip's staying at Murray's next Friday night, isn't he?'

'Yes, but—'

'Come up on Friday, we'll pamper ourselves all day, then you can stay overnight and we'll all get squiffy! I know a fabby private chef and I'll get her to come and make lunch and dinner for us. And there's a lovely mobile beautician in the village who does treatments: we'll all get manicures and pedicures.' She looked at me, and added in a low, confidential tone, 'Would you like a facial too, Janey?'

I smiled, wondering whether there was such a thing as an

immobile beautician, but Jody mistook my expression for enthusiasm. 'That's sorted then.'

'Does she use only organic products, though?' asked Molly. 'And products that are non-harmful to aquatic life?'

'C'mon Janey,' said Jody. 'What do you say?'

I searched my mind for another excuse. Then stopped, and mentally surveyed my life. Without Steve, it looked pretty bleak, my diary stretching emptily into the future. And I didn't even have the idea of Steve now, I realised. He'd melted away, somehow, over the last five minutes.

'Aww, don't worry, babe,' said Jody. 'We'll brighten you up a wee bit and you'll be beating them off with a stick. You're a couple of face peels away from a whole new future.'

★

And so now here we were, sitting in the lounge at Buttercraig Lodge, sipping cocktails, waiting for the air punching to begin again.

Cleodie was looking round the room with an air of detachment, as though she might be mentally taking notes for her novel.

I shivered violently, sloshing my non-alcoholic Woo-woo down my top. It was freezing. Half of the upstairs windows were getting renovated – that is to say, were not actually there.

The mobile beautician, a woman in her fifties with blue eyeliner and a frizzled eighties perm, had unfolded her treatment table in the middle of the lounge, its white towelling covering pristine for the first sacrificial victim.

'We're all girls together now,' said Jody. 'Apart from Vichard.' She patted his head, and he crawled away under the beautician's table, popping his head up through the face-hole.

'You can get it all off your chest. Tell us about Steve. Oh, but wait! That's the doorbell. That'll be Molly.'

She appeared in the room a moment later, carrying a blue plastic potty, with Cam trotting behind her, naked from the waist down.

'We're getting on so well,' she was saying to Jody. 'He's only had two accidents this morning. You don't mind me bringing him, do you? It's just we're really trying to get on top of it this week. Janey! How are you *feeling*? I've brought a brilliant homeopathic remedy for you to try. Arsenic something or other.'

'Great!' Jody was glowing with happiness now. 'We'll get on with some proper men-bashing in a minute. I'll be back in a sec.'

'Oops,' said Molly. 'That's Cam done a wee-wee. Well done, Cammie! Well *done!*'

'Isn't he supposed to do it in the potty?' I asked.

'It's important to praise him anyway,' said Molly. 'So he doesn't pick up any negative feedback surrounding the potty-training process. I'll go and find a cloth.'

Before long I was lying on the table with cucumber slices over my eyes, having all my make-up sponged off with cotton wool pads. I heard my phone ring from the hallway.

Steve?

I squashed the thought.

'Who's not got their mobile switched off?' asked Jody. 'Tut tut. Is that you Janey?'

'Er, yeah. Sorry.'

She sighed gustily. 'Janey, you need a wee mantra, hon. Repeat after me. Come on girls, everyone. *I do not need to speak to Steve.*'

'I do not need to speak to Steve,' they intoned. I mumbled and moved my lips convincingly, like I used to in church with Granny when they were reciting prayers.

'I do not need to know what Steve is thinking,' went on Jody calmly.

'I do not need to know what Steve is thinking.' I could hear the mobile beautician repeating it too in her thick accent, a gust of garlic-scented breath reaching me where I lay.

'What Steve is thinking is now none of my business.' Jody's intonation was light and almost musical now.

'What Steve is thinking is now none of my business.'

Yes it bloody well is.

Jody paused, before finding further inspiration. 'Steve breached my trust and broke into my home.'

'Hang on. I never said that,' I said. God, what would the mantra be if Jody knew the whole story?

Steve may have been planning to electrocute an old lady.

My phone rang again.

'I'll answer it,' said Jody, darting into the hall.

'No!' I pulled myself upright on the table.

She came back in, holding the phone out. Her voice was quiet. 'It's the nursery.'

'Miss Johnston.' It took a second to recognise it as Mrs Paxton's voice. She sounded different. 'We've been trying to call you. There's been an incident.'

'What incident? Is Pip hurt?'

'We've no reason to think that,' she said carefully. I sank onto a chair. My legs seemed to know what was coming before I did. 'The children were playing in the basement area this morning. Jill was taking George to the toilet, and Hayley had to take another child inside because he was having an athsma attack.'

'What about Pip?' I managed.

'There was a bit of a panic, because the athsma attack was quite serious. So the children were left alone for a few moments. Just a very few moments. But unfortunately nobody noticed Pip had gone until the end of playtime.'

'Gone?'

'I'm sorry, Mrs Johnston. We don't know where Pip is.'

44

Hattie

My heart lurched horribly when I heard the phone ring. I should've paid attention: my body knew to be on edge, even if my mind didn't yet.

It was Mum, phoning from the car.

'We've just left Harrowdean.' She spoke like it was the ancient ancestral seat of the Marlowe family, not a spanking new gated mansion near Maidenhead paid for out of James's 2006 bonus. I thought maybe I'd get an instructional speech about how hospitable James and Simone had been, but she was only thinking about the party.

'Is everything ready for this evening?'

'Yep. The caterers are here.'

'How many are we catering for?'

I paused. 'Er, I told them to cater for twenty.'

'Twenty!'

'We haven't had too many RSVPs, Mum. I think a lot of people are away.'

'Nonsense, Hattie. Please tell the caterers to double the numbers. What will it look like if we can't feed our guests?'

'I can't tell them to double the numbers, Mum. They've already prepared the food, they've just brought it in from their van.'

'From their *van*? The lobster thermidor?' Her voice was shaking.

'We didn't go for the lobster thermidor in the end. Remember, Mum? We went for the miniature fish pies.'

'Fish *pies*? But that's entirely inappropriate. The Simpsons are coming.' Clearly there was some reason why the Simpsons and fish pie combination was an abomination but I didn't have time to fathom it just then.

'Er, no, they're not coming, Mum. They had another engagement.'

'What engagement?'

'Their granddaughter was singing in the school carol service.'

'School *carol* service?' She sounded old, then. Like one of those old people who can't quite believe how far the world has gone to pot.

'She had a solo or something. Listen, Mum, I have to go now. Lots to do. See you later.'

'We'll be there by five. Make sure it's all sorted by then.'

I made my way up the stairs, threading fairy lights through the banisters and fixing them on with special fixings. I'm not sure what I was thinking about just at that point. I was probably hoping Mum would drink so much she'd forget about the menu. Or thinking how James would most likely settle down with the whisky decanter and get smashed too, with Simone spending most of the night checking her phone before disappearing upstairs.

So I was sitting on the stairs, between the first and second landing, fiddling with one of the fixings, when it happened. A shape, black as a raven's wing, shearing down the edge of my peripheral vision. I whipped my head round just in time to see it drop out of my line of sight. But when I stood up to look down onto the floor of the hall below, there was nothing there but the tiles, swimming in my vision as if they'd lost their solid substance and turned to water.

I told myself it was a migraine and went to my room to find my pills.

Janey

Murray was talking now. He was on the end of the phone but he seemed far away, his words strange and drawn out. He'd told me that he was at the nursery, but he could've been talking from another planet. Or was it me on another planet? A strange, underwater world where nothing was quite reaching me.

I looked around myself. Yes, this was happening. Cleodie was driving my car. We were driving from Stirling back to Edinburgh because Pip was missing.

Missing.

'Janey,' Murray was saying.

Jaaaaayyyyneeeeee . . .

'Are you listening? I know it's hard to take in. But they're not sure whether Pip was taken or whether he somehow managed to open the gate and wandered off. But one of the pre-school children said he saw Pip leaving with a woman. He described her as a "granny" with a long black coat. You'd better talk to the police.'

I almost laughed with relief. 'Mutti! That must have been Mutti. Remember she wore that black coat with silver buttons to the parents' evening? Did she think she was collecting Pip today?'

'No, Janey,' he said gently. 'Gretel and Mutti are in Glasgow today for a charity lunch.'

'It is,' I insisted. 'It's bloody Mutti. Tell the police to find her. Now, Murray.'

'You're not making sense.'

'It's Mutti.' My voice broke up in my desperation for it to be true. 'Who else could it be? Who else would take him?'

'Janey? The police want to talk to you now. I'm handing you over.'

I nodded.

Detective Sergeant somebody. I tried to answer the questions. To concentrate on what he was saying. Something about any relevant information . . . circulating descriptions . . . CCTV operatives.

I looked across at Cleodie and out of the window at the road signs going past. Yes, this was happening.

He was saying something about dog handlers now. And an item of clothing.

'Mutti,' I croaked. 'I think Mutti's taken him. Please . . .'

Something about lines of inquiry. Following up all leads . . .

I thought of how I'd watched Pip wake up this morning, his eyes wide and luminous from the instant they opened. He'd held out his arms to be lifted, relaxing his little pyjama-clad body onto the contours of mine as I carried him through to the kitchen. I thought of his demand for 'milky' murmured into my ear with a gust of sweet, sleepy breath, his absolute trust that I'd meet all of his needs as they presented themselves.

It struck me then that I should lock them down, those moments. Fix them into my memory so they couldn't slip away. They might be the last ones. I tried to remember dropping him off at nursery, the exact moment when I'd kissed him, when I'd turned round to wave goodbye, and found I couldn't.

I couldn't.

Had I, then? Had I dropped him off at all? Had I been in such an absent-minded hurry this morning, thinking about driving to Stirling, that I'd rushed out of the flat and simply left him there in the hall, bewildered in his coat and boots? Or had I left him standing on the pavement as I'd shoved money into the parking machine near the nursery, and just driven off without taking him in?

No. Because he had been at nursery. The policeman had said so. He'd been there, and he'd been playing until . . .

Pinpricks of light were bursting into my vision.

Then Steve's voice: *Stop fighting. Let yourself float to the top.*

I couldn't float. I couldn't. But one thought did, bursting to the surface in a bright clear bubble. Something from Emil's letter:

Please also stay out of the vicinity of Little Goslings Nursery.

And then Steve's words:

She likes to go on walks around the city: visiting her old haunts, remembering the old days, I suppose.

I forced my lips and tongue around the words. 'It might be Esme Fortune.'

They prescribed the meds after she attacked that poor man.

'She's off the meds now.' It came rushing out. 'He told me. She's off the meds. Please find him. God, please find him.'

The policeman had to ask me three times before I registered what he was saying:

'Do you have an address?'

Hattie

I got Janey's text and realised what all the butterflies had been for.

'Pip's gone missing from nursery.'

I texted back: 'WHAT??'

'Cleodie is driving me back. It might just be Miss Fortune.'

What might just be Miss Fortune?

I dialled Janey's number. She told me that she needed to keep the phone line clear.

'I want to help. Please Janey, how can I help? What can I do?'

'Just stay there. I'll phone you if I need anything.' And then, in a voice that sounded like she was twelve: 'Try and have an inkling, Hattie.'

Janey

Murray phoned me back. It could have been a minute later or twenty.

'They've tried Miss Fortune's flat. They rang the buzzer and got a neighbour to let them into the stair so they could check round the back, but there was nobody in. They're trying to get her carers on the phone, but there's some possibility she may be away. The neighbour said that her son was round yesterday. He mentioned something about a trip away, cancelling the usual carers.'

'Her son? She doesn't have a son.'

'*Fuck*, Janey.' I heard his voice crack for the first time. He was on the verge of tears. 'I don't know what to do. I don't know what to do.'

His panic, somehow, calmed me. It didn't matter if he fell apart. I was Pip's best chance. *I* was.

Keep floating.

As we drove south, a thought kept intruding through the blur. *Norway.*

If Miss Fortune had him, where would she have taken him? I tried not to think of cold, grey swirling water as we drove over the Forth Road Bridge. I tried not to think of canals.

Fjords.

Stupid. How would an ancient, demented woman smuggle a toddler out of the country to the Norwegian fjords?

Argenteuil ... blossom ...

And suddenly I realised. The evening-class fliers I'd seen in the nursery, with their little Monet thumbnail: a line of trees along the Seine, the shadows cutting across the water. 'A Riot of Light'. Miss Fortune would've left them there. It would have been one of the 'little jobs' Steve had given her.

I could see her face in my mind now – that knowing snarl when I'd got my fingering wrong or forgotten the name of some key composer – and my childhood terror flared up, as real as it had ever been. It was as though she'd led me to him. Right into his arms. Into his trap.

But underneath the panic there was something else. Something from that lesson when she'd talked about Argenteuil, and Grieg, and I closed my eyes.

Sunday afternoon walks in the park with the other love of her life.

The love of her life had been Emil. But the *other* love hadn't been a man. It had been a little boy. A little boy of two and a half, with dark hair, and a smattering of freckles over the bridge of his nose, who loved to feed the ducks.

'Inverleith Park,' I said to Cleodie, who nodded and pressed her foot harder on the accelerator.

45

Janey

Inverleith Park. She was there, sitting on a bench, shielding her eyes from the low winter sun, holding the string of a red helium-filled balloon. And Pip. He was crouched at the water's edge, crumbling fragments from a muffin. He waved when he saw me. It took all the resolve I had not to sweep him up against my chest and squeeze to feel the life in him.

When I sat down next to her she didn't look at me, but waved an empty Costa bag over my lap.

'Would you believe it, we got here and I realised I'd forgotten the bread. So we popped into a coffee shop to get something. Mr and Mrs Duck and the ducklings would be so cross if we came with nothing. Jamie seems to have been to this . . . *Costa* before, but I must say I can't think when. They gave him this balloon.'

Jamie . . .

I remembered the day, just a few weeks ago, when I'd knelt before her in the music room. How I'd hurled my Marlowe questions at her, trying to summon her out of *Cash in the Attic*, or whatever other world she'd escaped to in her head. How she'd come alive, briefly, at the sight of Pip. She hadn't said 'Janey' at all. That small, strangled noise of distress had been 'Jamie'.

'I know Renee has sent you, dear,' she said now. 'But please don't ask me to give him back. Please don't ask me. Please don't.' She pulled her thin tartan skirt further down over her knees, and I saw that she'd forgotten to put on her tights.

She was an old lady, that's all. An old lady with varicose veins, and legs blue with the cold.

'It's okay,' I said softly. 'Renee's not here.'

'It's just that . . . No,' she said, frowning. 'That's not right. I haven't seen Steve, have I?'

She searched my face, seeming to think I would know.

'Which is a nuisance, dear. He usually keeps me right. I meant to ask him. I meant to ask him, before he left, who was collecting Jamie today. I didn't know, so I came just in case.' There was a shiver in her voice.

'Okay.'

'If you see him, ask him about my blue pills, would you?'

'I will.' I nodded towards Pip. 'When does he usually have his bath? Perhaps we should be getting him home.'

'Oh, seven on the dot,' she said firmly, as though any other time would be preposterous. 'As soon as piano time's finished. Emil plays the piano in the drawing room, little songs and what not, for James . . . when he's at home. Is he home at the moment, dear?'

'I'm not entirely sure.'

'Emil won't let Jamie play on the Steinway, though.' She tutted. 'It's one of the things we don't agree on. What's it there for if not to be played? When I give Jamie his little lessons, we have to use the upright on the top landing. He just plays a few notes, up and down, but his touch is just beautiful. And I know he's got a good ear. He loves the *Carnival of the Animals*. And the Chopin nocturnes, at bedtime. He lies with his wee head on my lap, and his thumb in his mouth, just gazing out of the window as the evening falls, and, oh, my dear, sometimes

344

I can hardly breathe. For the love, you know. It gets you in the chest.'

'I know. I know how that feels.' If I didn't get my arms around Pip soon I'd stop breathing myself.

'I brought this with me.' She drew some folded manuscript paper out of her handbag. '*Blue Bear's Dance.* I thought I might get a chance to play it for him today.'

'Maybe another time. But, you know, it's getting late.'

'Just ten minutes. Please?' Her voice was thin, almost lost on the wind. She sounded much younger. It struck me that she'd have been younger than me at the time she'd lived at Regent's Crescent, playing mother to James. All that love she'd felt, with nowhere to go in all the years that followed.

'It doesn't seem fair,' I said.

'It was never going to be fair. And I did it anyway. I've been such a foolish, foolish woman.'

'Did what?'

'Gave up my heart. To that little scrap of a child. Gave up my heart.'

It was the almostness that got me, then. The drab December trees where she'd always dreamed of blossom. The scum-covered pond that should have reflected the trees, and the endless sky. The crowds she'd never played for. The man who'd never quite loved her. The six babies who'd never lived. And the little boy: the warm, breathing, growing boy who'd never been hers.

'I'm sorry,' I said. 'I'm just so sorry.'

A gust of wind caught the Costa bag, which scuttered out of her lap onto the ground. As she bent to pick it up I called softly to Pip, holding out my arms. He hopped across and draped himself over my lap, lifting his feet off the ground and stamping them down again. I curved myself around him, buried my face against him.

'Mamma.' He climbed up on my lap, muddy shoes scrabbling against my jeans, arms round my neck, sticky hands in my hair.

'Oh, Jamie,' said Miss Fortune in a whisper. '*Beautiful* boy.'

Out of all this, there was one truth that I could say.

'I lost a baby once, too.'

She turned to me then, and her old face seemed to crack across the middle.

'Oh my dear.'

I put my spare arm around her thin shoulders and drew her towards us.

Hattie

I'd got her text of course, the one saying that Pip was safe. But still. The sight of Janey, Pip and Miss Fortune, lined up on my doorstep, was a bit of a shock. Not what I was expecting at all. Not least because Mum and James were due any minute.

Miss Fortune was crying: silent, slow tears. Janey was babbling, actually pushing the old woman over the threshold, telling me about the police, and how they'd been planning to just take her home because she wasn't going to make a complaint in the circumstances, and it was a matter for social services. They were creating a referral. They couldn't get hold of Steve. She was telling me how she couldn't just *leave* her.

'Please, Hats,' she said. 'Just for an hour or so and then I'll come and get her. I'll take her home, or she can stay at mine or something. I'll keep trying Steve. He'll know what's going on with the carers and everything. But I have to take Pip to Murray's. He's been frantic.'

She looked at me and shook her head. 'I can't show up at Murray's with her in tow, Hattie. I just can't. They'll use it against me . . .'

Then I realised. She'd forgotten about the party. She'd forgotten that Mum and James were about to show up. Why should she have remembered, after everything with Pip that afternoon?

'Where's Steve anyway?'

'He's leaving,' said Miss Fortune, sniffing back her tears. And then, softly and sadly, to the tune of 'New York, New York': 'He's leaving to-day . . .'

I took hold of her hand.

'Off you go,' I said to Janey and Pip. 'Go, go . . .' and I flapped them out onto the street.

Janey

Murray opened the door and snatched Pip up into his arms, burying his face in the crook of his neck. His back heaved as he held on and held on.

Gretel appeared behind. Her nose wrinkled briefly at the sight of me, pink-eyed and tousle-haired, holding on to the end of Pip's balloon.

'Have they arrested this mad old woman, then? Who is she anyway?'

'She's an old teacher of mine.' I faced Gretel and kept my voice low and calm. 'A music teacher. She's very sadly suffering from dementia and didn't know what she was doing. The police said it wasn't a matter for them. Social services are going to take it from here.'

'So you've been slinging accusations around about Mutti when all along this was one of your nutter friends.

Unbelievable. Mutti got a huge shock when the police turned up at the Rhino Watch Lunch. You owe her a big apology.'

'Where Bingo?' shouted Pip and wriggled out of Murray's arms.

'Come through,' said Murray, recovering his wits and leading me into the kitchen, an enormous extension to the back of their property. The back wall consisted entirely of floor-to-ceiling glass doors giving out to the patio and long, striped lawn. He opened a cupboard and then stood looking into it as though he couldn't remember why he'd opened it in the first place. He'd aged since the last time I'd seen him. His nose looked beakier than ever, thread veins standing out on his cheeks. His hair a little wild, the grey showing more than usual.

There was a large metal cage built into the far corner of the room. I started when I saw Pip open the door and climb into it.

'That's Bingo's cage,' said Gretel with a sigh. 'He's still with the dogsitters. We haven't had time to collect him yet.'

'Tea?' said Murray, finally remembering why he'd opened the cupboard.

'Don't start getting all cosy,' said Gretel. 'Tell her.'

'Tell me what?'

'We're going for full residence,' said Gretel. 'In light of today's debacle, we really have no choice. We can't tiptoe around your feelings any longer, not when Pip's safety hangs in the balance.'

Until recently, I might have almost thought she had a point. Not any more. Something had changed in my thinking, crystallising with my encounter with Miss Fortune at the pond.

'Pip's safety is not hanging in the balance. If you want to

blame someone, blame the nursery. They're the ones that let him walk off with a stranger.'

'Ah, but she wasn't a stranger, was she?'

I walked over to the cage. 'Come on, Pip. Let's go home.'

'Going for a residence order would be a last resort,' said Murray in a tight voice. 'But I am concerned, Janey. I know this situation today wasn't all down to you, but I think you need to take a step back and get yourself on an even keel. I mean, all this business about hammers, and slotted spoons and so on, come on. I know you'd never *actually* harm him, but it's a sign of stress and I think you need to get some proper help. In fact, I'm going to have to insist on it.'

He'd missed the sharp look from Gretel.

'Slotted spoons?' I said.

'Yes. Gretel said you'd confided in her about the intrusive thoughts you've been having.'

I stared at Murray. As if I would confide in Gretel. But . . . Cleodie.

Cleodie, with her too easy, frog-eyed friendship. The instinct that had made me pull back, mid-confession.

It all fell into place.

'So Cleodie is . . .' I turned to Gretel and shook my head. 'I don't know how you've done it, but you're using her as some sort of spy.'

'What?' said Murray. 'Gretel, who is Cleodie?'

'I'll tell you later,' she said.

'Tell me now.'

She turned on him, quick as a snake. 'This is your *son*, Murray! Your only *son*! You can't expect me not to do my homework – *your* blurdy homework in fact – on something as important as this!'

349

'What else have you done?' I demanded. 'Apart from getting her to befriend me, the poor pathetic single mother? What else did you pay her to do?'

An image flashed into my mind. Pip being sick in Cleodie's sitting room the first time we went for coffee. Me grabbing the changing bag but leaving my handbag unzipped by the side of the couch. And later, of course, I'd slept the afternoon away while she minded Pip and Rose in the flat. Her gleeful description of 'Back Door Switches'. She lived in a flat identical to mine, on the next street, backing on to the same patchwork space of shared back gardens. From her kitchen window, she'd have been able to watch and learn my routines. Pip's pirate magic lantern switching off at 7.30 p.m. The bathroom light snapping on at 2 a.m. every night, after I'd woken from the dream. And the juicy gossip from the art class – including a full account of my meltdown over the hammer picture – would have flown freely from Jody once Cleodie had wormed her way into that set.

'You told her to shake me up a bit, didn't you? Just little things, to unnerve me. Moving things around in the flat. The knife appearing in the fridge, and so on? Yes?'

Gretel just looked at me, eyebrows raised, mouth pushed out in a 'so what?' pout.

'It was to see how you'd react under pressure. We do it all the time with our trainee candidates: take them away for a week and observe how their decision-making skills are affected in different situations. Think of it like that: a robust vetting process.'

'A *vetting process*? To be my own son's mother?'

'It's the modern world,' said Gretel. 'Get used to it.'

'It's not the modern world, you delusional bitch. You were

350

trying to get your hands on my son because you're a spoilt cow who thinks she can get whatever she wants. Well, not this time, Gretel. Not this time.'

But as soon as the words were out, I found I was on the verge of laughing. My heart felt like it had been released and could soar into the sky.

Because if it was Cleodie who'd done all this, it hadn't been Steve.

★

I drew my phone out of my bag and dialled his number.

'Where are you? I've been trying to get hold of you.'

'*Janey.*' The phone gusted and crackled, as though he was walking in the wind. 'I'm on my way to Waverley station. My phone was off, sorry.'

'Where are you?'

'I'm off to Newcastle.'

'I'll meet you at the station.'

I drew Pip gently out of the cage and led him out of the house, raising a hand in acknowledgement to Murray.

'Balloon, Mummy.'

I made a loop in the end and slipped it onto his wrist, and he walked with his face upturned, watching as it bobbed along above him.

A taxi passed by and I flagged it down: quicker than driving and parking. As we rumbled along, over the cobbles, down the Mound, I became aware that two stories were running in my head at the same time, each demanding the whole of me, each making the other impossible.

Steve loved me. He was the only man who'd ever seen me. Who'd ever 'got' me. I'd lose half of myself if I lost him.

351

Steve was a damaged man who'd lied to me, who I could never trust.

Both of them couldn't be true. They couldn't run on the same track. I was hurtling, hurtling towards the point when my world would simply split in two.

I seemed to hover outside of myself for a moment, watching myself sitting there in the taxi with Pip clutched to my side, waiting to see what I'd do.

Would my hand reach forward and tap the glass? Would I tell the driver to stop, to turn around, to take me home?

But, no.

Steve was waiting on the concourse by the train information displays. He looked cold, hunched down inside his jacket. A wheely suitcase stood by his side.

'You're leaving for good.' It didn't need to be a question. I could already see the answer in the closed-off look on his face.

'Yeah. Katya and Calum are on their own again. Martin's left.' He shook his head. 'God knows what that was all about, some kind of argument. I'm not getting involved. But she needs support. I'm going to stay with them for a bit, at least till she sorts herself out. I can take Calum to day care, and pick him up when she's got late shifts. Help with the physio side of things. Then, I don't know, maybe try and get a job teaching in Newcastle so I can be near them.'

'What time's your train?'

He looked at the clock up on the noticeboard. 'Till half past. Walk me to my platform?'

Stay.

All the agonising, the racing to get here, and I still wasn't quite brave enough to say it.

We walked through the concourse and over to Platform 2.

Pip, now in his element after realising he was in a train station, trotted happily alongside me, and insisted on walking right to the end of the platform until the concrete stopped and there was just the grey sky above us and the track stretching ahead of us, all the way to England. All the way to Steve's new life.

I gathered up my courage. 'It wasn't you. It wasn't you who broke into my flat and did those things.'

His face creased in disgust. 'For God's *sake*, Janey.'

'It was Cleodie. On behalf of Gretel.'

'You're kidding.' His voice softened. He reached out a hand and touched my arm. 'That's shocking. Really shocking behaviour. Have you spoken to Murray?'

I nodded. 'I've just come from there. It's been quite a day. Miss Fortune took Pip on a little unscheduled outing from nursery.'

'What?'

'She was very confused. But also kind of lucid, in a weird way. The police have created a referral or something. She's going to need to go into a home, Steve. Or have more carers at least.'

He nodded. 'That should be happening.'

'Does the council even know you've gone?'

'I just had to leave a message with social services. It might take a while to filter through.'

'She was kind of stuck, back a long time ago. I wanted to say sorry for what I did. For not saying – doing – anything about Renee. But Miss Fortune caused Renee to find out, you know. About the affair. She planted one of Emil's letters in Hattie's music case.'

'God. *Why?*'

I shook my head, thinking of her small life, enclosed within the four yellowing walls of the music room, where she'd smoked, and dreamed, and listened to the music she'd once been able to play. Where she'd taught an endless stream of pupils who didn't care.

Maybe she just wanted to make herself known. To stand up and say, 'Here I am. This is me.' To stop being invisible.

'I can only be me if there's you,' I said simply.

'Not true, Janey. You could never not be you. You just *are* you, and you're incredible. So incredible. You just need to start believing it.'

'How much of it was true?' I blurted out. 'With me, I mean. I can't separate out what you knew, and what you didn't know, and whether what you seemed to feel for me was real. Or something I imagined.' The words choked and disappeared as I ran out of breath. 'So please, just tell me. How much of it was true?'

'All of it.' His voice was low. 'You got to me, Janey, like no one else ever has. I felt this massive connection with you from the start. I didn't fully trust it at first. I thought maybe it was because of the shared history. But as time went on, I realised it was just because of, well, you. Just you as you are. And then it was too late. I was hooked. And I couldn't tell you about Esme in case it changed things between us.'

'But did you ever . . .'

Did you ever love me?

'Say it,' he said softly.

I shook my head.

'Why do you never say what you're thinking? You see, this is what you do. You want me to fill in all your gaps. All the things you can't say, or do, or believe. Love was never going to be

354

enough for you, Janey. That's the whole problem. I can *never* do what you want me to do.'

With a groan, he lifted his hands to his head. They closed into fists, scrunching his short hair. Then he looked up.

'It's like you want me to love you *into existence*. Nobody can do that, Janey. Nobody.'

I nodded. I shouldn't really be surprised at the hurt. Of course he was never going to stay.

The train was arriving now, moving smoothly up the platform with a hiss of brakes. Coming to take him away from me.

He gripped my upper arms, as though holding me together, holding me up. I felt the charge all down me.

'Just promise you'll stay strong, Janey. Just keep being yourself.'

Out of nowhere, anger shook me so hard I could hardly speak.

'You can't just *leave* me! Stay with me. *Stay with me.*'

'I need to get on the train,' said Steve.

'You've got another minute or two.'

'I should go.'

He lifted the handle of his suitcase. I needed him to hold me. Just one more time. One more time to last for the rest of my life.

He placed a hand on my shoulder. 'Take care, Janey.' And he turned, walked up the platform towards his carriage.

I could go after him, I thought, as I watched him. How late would be too late? When he stepped up onto the train? When the doors shut? When the guard blew the whistle? When the train actually pulled off?

'Mummy!' A gust of wind caught Pip's balloon, and the

loop I'd tied round his wrist slipped off. The balloon lifted and lurched away. In a split second I read Pip's impulse to run after it: towards end of the platform and the track. I grabbed him, catching him under the arms, yanking him backwards.

'My balloooooon!' he wailed.

'Pip, calm down.'

His feet scrabbled on the concrete, every fibre of his little body consumed with wanting that balloon.

I held on and held on. He collapsed onto the ground, back arched in a full-blown tantrum.

'Pip, Pip, calm down.'

Steve was still walking.

Look back. Look back.

'I hate you, Mummy! I hate you!'

Just look back.

'*Hate* you!'

And he was stepping onto the train now, pulling his bag up behind him.

I sank down onto my knees and folded Pip tight in my arms, as he fought and kicked and struggled. As my own heart fought and kicked and struggled.

You just are *you, and you're incredible.*

You got to me, Janey, like no one else ever has.

I can never *do what you want me to do.*

And then I thought of Miss Fortune, shivering on a bench in the park, pulling her thin skirt further down over her knees.

I just had to leave a message with social services. It might take a while to filter through.

I looked up into the sky, up, up. Pip's balloon was just a little red dot now, dancing on the wind, being buffeted in a northerly direction, towards Leith, towards the Firth of Forth, Fife, the cold, blue mountains.

Pip was growing quieter now. He got onto his knees and circled his arms around me, his face wet, his breath hot against my neck.

Somehow in the struggle, the truth had come free.

The train was leaving now, the windows sliding past, making the ground seem to slide beneath me.

Wrenching together all my courage and my strength, I lifted Pip and I turned away.

And I said goodbye, then. I said it into the sky, as far as the eye could see, said it to the Steve who had never existed anywhere except in my heart.

46

Janey

Pip had fallen asleep in the car on the way over, and I was holding him in my arms as I walked up the steps to the Regent's Crescent house. A man dressed like a butler pulled open the door just as I reached it.

'Hello,' I said. 'Is Hattie here?'

'Please come up,' he said. 'They're in the drawing room.'

I was slightly annoyed, if truth be told, that Hattie hadn't suggested keeping Miss Fortune here for the night, then I wouldn't have had to drag Pip out of the house again like this after giving him his dinner and bath. But she hadn't replied to my texts. What could she be doing that made her so busy, too busy to get back to me after the day I'd had?

As if on cue, my phone bleeped. 'Don't come back. Miss F asleep for the night. Will call in the morning. x'

The time on it was two hours ago: 5 p.m. A bit early to be going to bed surely.

With the next step – the third step on the staircase – I remembered Renee's 'retrospective' party. He'd be there, wouldn't he? James.

I wobbled to the side, legs suddenly weak under the weight of Pip. And I thought of my fourteen-year-old self, off my face on gin, wobbling up these steps on the night of that other party. The heft, the weight, the consequence of each of those steps that night.

So there they were, seated around the room in silence.

Hattie.

Renee.

James and – what was her name again – Simone?

The Cartwrights, a couple I remembered from years before.

Lord and Lady Smythe, the Marlowes' neighbours.

And Miss Fortune, her hair askew, with a pillow crease along one cheek.

'Janey! Pip!' Hattie got up, came over. 'Are you okay?' she whispered, pulling us into a hug. 'Didn't you get my text? I had her asleep upstairs, but she woke up when the Cartwrights came in.'

'Janey,' said Renee, with a bitter little twist of her mouth that was presumably meant to look something like a smile.

What should I do? Shake her hand? Kiss her? I felt my body begin to move forward.

What was this? Could it be that I still had an urge to please this woman, after everything? I stopped. Stilled myself. Simply nodded. 'Renee.'

James got up.

Hattie had spoken of his drink problem, his suicide attempt. I'd been expecting a skeletal, yellow-skinned wraith of a man. I hadn't quite reconciled this with his job as a top banker, but maybe he was one of those thin, glittery-eyed types that kept going by snorting coke in the toilets.

But no. Six feet tall, he'd filled out into, well, a man. His features had thickened, his eyes a bit piggy in a fleshy, tanned face. A smart suit and an expensive watch.

'Janey.'

There was nothing in his eyes. No awkwardness, no guilt. Did he even remember what had happened?

'This is Simone,' he said. She was petite and tanned in a simple pale-grey shift dress and dangly earrings.

I wanted the haunted, yellowing wraith back. Even the arrogant shit of an eighteen-year-old who'd used me and chucked me away without a thought. Something – *something* – that I recognised. Because how could I make sense of any of this, if James didn't exist any longer . . . if he'd just *gone*?

A uniformed girl with a tray stepped forward hopefully. 'Have a drink,' said James.

He lifted one of the champagne glasses and held it towards me. I glanced down at his hand: smooth and tanned against the white cuff of his shirt, the long violinist's fingers less pronounced now that they'd thickened with the onset of middle age.

'Hattie,' I whispered. 'Can you take Pip for a second?'

I left the room, made for the nearest bathroom and vomited it all up. The anger that had been lodged inside me all these years, safely dammed up by the things I'd told myself: No, no, it was nothing. And it was mostly my fault.

Even now, with James in the next room, part of my mind was working to minimise it. I thought of the news I'd been watching just last night. A sixteen-year-old gang-raped and tortured in a derelict London tower block. A twelve-year-old who'd committed suicide after years of abuse in a Midlands care home. A man who'd murdered his wife and her toddler by setting fire to their home, just up the road in East Lothian. I'd turned it off in the end, because what could you do? How would you ever handle it if you could see it all: a trail of human misery stretching on and on, as far as the eye could see or the mind could imagine.

But none of that changed what had happened to me. It didn't make it *nothing*.

All I had was the truth. *My* truth.

I pulled myself up, looked in the mirror. I'd aged about a hundred years since this morning but I stood up straight, and nodded slowly to myself. To all my old selves. It was time to take James on a tour of the house.

Hattie

It's hard to remember exactly what happened next. The counsellor said it might help to write it all down. I need to get my head around what happened, incorporate it into myself, accept it as part of my story.

Janey had run out of the drawing room. I was holding Pip.

The atmosphere in the room had changed.

Mum turned to the Cartwrights. 'Marian and Kenneth,' she said. 'How was your Monte Carlo trip? What's the weather like at this time of year?'

'Oh, well, the hotel's not what it used to be,' said Marian. 'Gone downhill, you know. The towels used to be so fluffy but really now I'd have to describe them as quite hard. And the new egg chef seems really quite incompetent. Gave Kenneth a duck egg instead of a goose egg on the last morning.'

'And it rained,' added Kenneth, who seemed anxious to downplay the trip.

'And did you see the Williamses out there?' went on Renee.

'Yes, but George is not doing so well.'

A discussion followed about George's failing health. He

had Parkinson's disease, apparently, and was finding it hard to grasp small items, like his keys.

Then Miss Fortune piped up, 'Oh, how dreadful for him. I too have very limited use of my fingers since Renee here smashed them with a hammer.'

There was total silence for about three seconds until Marion gave a polite, tinkling laugh and Kenneth and the Smythes joined in. Renee raised an eyebrow and made a twirling motion at the side of her head. The guests were happy to accept that Miss Fortune had gone loopy. The alternative didn't fit in with their world, which centred around socialising with the old Edinburgh set and quaffing champagne in Georgian drawing rooms.

Janey came back in then, and asked James if she could have a word. From where I was sitting I could see her leading him up the stairs. My skin prickled. Why would she be taking him up to the bedrooms?

But then the musicians came in – a pianist, a tenor and a soprano – to perform some of the songs from Dad's musicals.

The soprano sang 'Once Upon a Summertime' and everyone said 'Ahhhh . . .' and clapped.

I heard the stairs creak in the hall, and looked round again to see Janey leading James downstairs now. He looked as though he was wobbling a bit. Hanging on tight to the banister. He'd probably drunk too much already. I felt a pang then, as though I should follow them down, but it didn't seem like a good idea to leave Miss Fortune and my mother in a room together.

The pianist started up the opening bars of 'Vienna Serenade'.

During the applause that followed, Miss Fortune leaned

down and drew something out of her handbag. She handed it to the pianist. 'Do play this, dear. I do so want to remember Emil *properly*.'

The pianist studied it for a moment. The soprano peered over his shoulder at the music on the stand, the dark blobs and slashes of ink on heavy cream manuscript paper.

'Ooh,' she said. 'I've never seen this arrangement of the *Dark Side* theme before. It modulates into E flat minor. Interesting.'

'This is not the *Dark Side* theme.' Miss Fortune winced over the words as though they tasted sour. 'This is *Blue Bear's Dance*. See?' She gestured towards the title at the top of the page.

But it was indeed the *Dark Side* theme that rang out through the drawing room as the pianist played the opening bars. I did a quick bit of mental maths. Judging from the letter that Dad had written to Miss Fortune, returning the manuscript, she'd composed this, his hit melody, about fifteen years before he even sat down to write *Dark Side*.

Mum knew it too. It was written all over her face. She rose and walked out of the room, and I followed, the sleeping Pip still in my arms. In the hallway below, James was emerging from the basement, heading towards the front door.

Janey stood at the top of the basement stairs, a dark shape, just watching.

'Where are you going?' Mum's imperious tones rang out through the hall.

'Get Simone. We're leaving.'

'You can't *leave*!'

'I said we're leaving.'

There was mud on his shoes, as though they'd been out in the garden.

Miss Fortune was singing now, her voice drifting out from the drawing room.

'*My laddie, oh my laddie, when you lay your head to sleep . . .*'

Simone appeared behind me.

'Get the *fucking* bags, Simone,' said James. Then added, to me, 'This is a fucking nut house.'

Renee followed Simone up the stairs, as the climactic bars of *Blue Bear's Dance* rang out from the drawing room.

'*What do you dream, my laddie?*'

This next part is important. It's hard to remember it clearly because it's been burning its way through my brain for nearly three decades now. Burning too dark to be contained in what was then the future, in this vanishing point of a moment.

Mum reached the top of the stairs. Instead of following Simone into the bedroom, she dragged the stool over from by the upright piano, and positioned it in the mid point of the balcony landing, underneath the cupola, black as black. And she climbed on to it.

She caught my eye, and waved: a sad but inconsequential sort of wave. It was a gesture I'd seen a thousand times, when leaving for primary school on dark winter mornings, or boarding the Ramplings train at the start of a dozen miserable terms. I'd seen it not long ago, at Newark airport, glancing back as I'd walked through the barriers to catch my flight home.

And then, for one moment, I felt it all. Howling emptiness, pressing up against the walls of her mind, finding and filling every room and passageway so there was no room for anything else. It was unbearable to feel it for a second. How must it have been to carry it for decades? A lifetime?

I saw how it was that she'd anchored herself to this life

with outside things. Things that she thought the rest of the world cared about, that would give her substance through their eyes. Being married to a famous composer helped, not just because of the money – her family already had plenty of that – but because of his passion, his creative spirit, his moods, the way he drew both men and women to him. And there'd been the beautiful houses, the travel, the influence with people who mattered, the parties that were talked about for months afterwards. Two pleasingly photogenic, almost-talented children who she'd never quite managed to love. This house had always seemed so imposing, so solid in its Georgian stone, but I saw now that it was only ever a glittering stage set, paper thin.

And now it had all gone, disappeared along with the last echoes of *Blue Bear's Dance*, and there was nothing to stop her from falling away.

In the inklings, she'd fluttered, her hair streaming behind. A black bird diving to earth.

Now she dropped like a stone. She dropped like the nine-stone lump of flesh and bone that she was, and when she hit the bottom she crunched, and split.

47

Janey

The funeral took place on a blustery Tuesday the week before Christmas; unseasonably mild, but misty grey. In the circumstances it was family only, which meant just Hattie and James. Simone hadn't stayed. She'd said she had some work thing: a new project in Madrid, and that she didn't know when she'd be back. She'd turned her back on all this horror and gone off to find the sun.

'I think she's had enough,' said Hattie when she came round to mine that evening. 'James has been drinking like a fish since it happened and she can't be arsed to see him through all that again. The doctors told him the last time that his liver would pack in if he didn't stop. I'm trying to make him get help. A clinic or something. Residential therapy. I phoned up a few places yesterday and they sound good. But the truth is when he gets like this he doesn't *want* to stop.'

'Does he have anyone else – friends – who might be able to help? To talk to him?'

She looked at me. 'I keep thinking of the flies, the flies crawling out of his nose. I thought I'd saved him that time, but I hadn't, I'd only delayed the inevitable. I'm going to lose everyone, Janey. I'm losing them to the inklings.' Her voice was rising now, with a hysterical edge to the words.

I put my hand over hers. 'You're not. You're *not*.'

'It's all come true, Janey. The falling woman. I saw the

future. It was all tied up in me like a horrible black knot. You should stay away from me. You and Pip.'

'I don't think you *were* seeing the future.' I paused. 'Hattie, have you thought that maybe you were just seeing your mum's thoughts? She'd been envisaging committing . . . doing something like that for years, and that's what you saw. It was an obsession for her, the thought of ending it all, throwing herself down those stairs, a huge emotional black hole that pulled on everything in that house. Twisted it. You would have felt it on some level. You saw her crying on the landing that night, didn't you? You wrote about it in your diary. Maybe some trick of your senses made you see what you knew intuitively, played out in physical form.'

She frowned.

'All of your inklings could be explained that way.'

'The music case?' demanded Hattie.

'You'd picked up on Miss Fortune's emotions. She'd put the letter in your music case and she wanted you to notice. She was *consumed* with wanting you to notice. That's why it started banging about. They do say, don't they, that teenage girls can, well, be a focus for strong emotions, channel them, kind of thing.'

'Like a poltergeist.' She said it with a gusty sigh.

'I don't know about that. But think about it: the boy at Ramplings who was paralysed in the accident, he'd been obsessed with motorbikes for weeks before it happened. Even James, with the flies, you know, just before he . . .'

'Hmm.'

'And what you said about those noises, on the night when your mother attacked Miss Fortune. How you thought it was the pipes, from the hot water she was running?'

367

'Oh yes,' she said dully. 'I see what you're getting at. Maybe I was hearing the thoughts that were inside my mother's head that night.' She shrugged and looked me straight in the eye. 'The sound of steel splitting bone.'

'You were picking up on their thoughts, not their futures. Because, Hats, nobody can see the future, can they? I think it's much more likely to be an extreme kind of empathy.'

'*What?*' She looked embarrassed.

'Such an emotionally generous little girl, you were.'

'If I was so empathetic, why didn't I do something? Why didn't I help her?'

'She'd had two years in a psychiatric clinic, or whatever it was. What do you think *you* could have done?'

'Maybe not then, but since Dad died I've only seen her, what, four or five times.'

'She chose to live in New York, Hattie.'

Her big brown eyes were shining with tears now. She gasped in a short breath, trying to hold in a sob.

'But every time I look at you, or little Pip, I can't bear it because what if I see something?'

Like Pip in a pool of blood, X-rays with black masses invading the lungs.

I waited for a rush of horror, a chill of terror, but it didn't come. The mother in me stepped forward. Or the friend I'd been back then, loyal and unafraid, stronger than I'd remembered.

'So what if you do?'

'Do I tell you?'

'Tell me. Don't tell me. I don't care, as long as you're here.'

'I thought it was some kind of demon,' she said, a tear escaping down her cheek. 'A devil. Some wickedness in me, making me see those things.'

'No, no,' I said, in the gentle, rocking way I spoke to Pip when he'd had one of his nightmares, and was trying to convince him – or myself – that monsters didn't exist. 'No, no.'

'And then I told myself it was some kind of mental imbalance, some kind of hallucination thing that I could block out with medication. But maybe you're right, Janey.'

She looked at me like she was *pleading* with me to be right.

'Maybe it was just my heart. I locked it away for all those years. And I couldn't hear it. Not until I got you back.'

A little bit awkwardly, I put my arms around her.

'Help me, Janey.'

What could she want from me, from Janey who jumped at the shadows in her own bedroom? Janey who couldn't fall asleep without *Christiansen* because she was afraid of nightmares? Yet I was strong. For her, I was strong. I was more than myself. More than myself because of the me I was in her.

'I've been carrying this around for *so long*.' Her voice tightened as she tried to control a sob.

I thought of my twelve-year-old self, who'd held Hattie on the stairs all those years ago. How I hadn't needed to *know*. I just needed to be.

Now – here and now – I could feel the muscles of my arms, tight with holding her. The breath, going in and out of my body without a sound. My feet, aching a little where my shoes met the floor. And just like an old favourite song, once known but long forgotten, I found I knew the words.

'You can put it down now, Hattie. You're not on your own any more. You can put it down.'

48

Janey

Miss Fortune hadn't seen the fall. The pianist and the singers must have heard the commotion coming from the hall, the howling from Hattie, on her knees over her mother's body. But they kept going, working through Emil's greatest hits as Miss Fortune smiled and tapped her foot, and the Smythes and Cartwrights wondered what in God's name was going on. I'd taken Pip in there, still asleep, and laid him on the couch beside Mrs Cartwright, before going downstairs again to crouch awkwardly with my arms round Hattie until the ambulance and the police arrived.

Murray, of all people, had taken Miss Fortune away that night, after a desperate phone call from me. He arranged an emergency place at a care home, and paid an eye-watering sum up-front for her to stay there until the care situation had been sorted out.

But when I phoned the care home, the day after the funeral, they said she was home again now so Pip and I went round to visit. I was glad to see Mabel when she answered the door. The flat seemed a bit brighter, too, and less musty-smelling.

'How is she doing?'

'Aye, nae too bad today. She's bin at the piano.'

Sure enough, a little chinking noise was coming from the music room. We walked in to find her sitting on the piano stool, picking out the top line of Shostakovich's Second Piano

370

Concerto with the fourth finger of her right hand.

She flung up her arms when she saw us. 'Jamie!'

'Pip,' said Pip with a frown.

She laughed knowingly.

'Pip, then,' she said with a wink. 'Sit down next to me. Do you see this little fairy dancing on the keys?' The fourth finger picked out *Incy Wincy Spider*.

'Would you like to try?' She budged up on the stool and Pip climbed up carefully, first pulling himself up to kneel on the cushion of the stool, and then rotating round and unfolding himself to a sitting position. His legs looked so little, his shoes dangling only a few inches below the bottom of the seat. There was a purply bruise on his shin, just peeping out over the ribbed cuff of his sock, from where he'd fallen over one of his trains the day before.

He lifted his hands to the keyboard, and stretched them out like two little stars.

'Very *good*!'

Pip dipped his chin, trying to hide a smile.

'So,' I asked Mabel, 'did everything get sorted out with the care schedule and everything?'

'Aye, I feel terrible about that day wi' all the bother.'

'What do you mean?'

'Did you no hear? She hadnae bin taking her medication, and she got out and went off wi' a wee kiddie. Ended up goin' into emergency care. There was a mix-up at the agency, that's why I wisnae here that day.'

'You? You're from an agency? I thought you were from the local authority.'

'No, luv. I'm from *the agency*.' She spoke slowly and clearly, a voice for speaking to those with mental deficiencies. 'That

Steve, when he had to go away, he increased my hours, ken, up to four hours a day. Eight till ten and five till seven. Because he wouldn't be able to keep track of things from Newcastle an' he was worried about her. It was to start the next day, but the agency sent me to Mrs Marquez three doors down, and poor Esme here was on her own for a day and a half wi' no meals, and nobody tae give the medication.' She shook her head and looked down at the floor. 'It's no wonder she went walkabout, poor soul.'

'But the council? Steve, he said he'd tried to tell them he was leaving and just had to leave a message.'

It might take a while to filter through.

She shrugged. 'He probably wanted her reassessed. He wants to get her into a home I think. Anyway, I'm here for now. I'll see she's all right.'

'I'm so . . .'

'Mummy, Mummy, my finger is spider!'

'And now let's pretend to be gorillas, stomping all over the keys!'

A cacophony broke out, punctuated by peals of laughter from Pip, and happy gasps from Miss Fortune.

'She's so *different* today,' I said.

'She has good days an' bad days,' said Mabel. 'But that Show-pann seems to perk her up. You were right about that. I've bin playing it for Mrs Marquez and all. And the ladies at the day-care centre. We play it in the afternoon, while we're putting out the tea and biccies, and then I put on Rod Stewart for something a bit more cheery, ken. "Maggie May" an' that? That's my favourite. Played it for Esme too the other day, and it got a smile out of her.'

And that, I thought as I left with Pip, just went to show, the ways in which a person could surprise you were pretty much endless.

★

'So it's all sorted now,' I told Murray. 'Really, I can't thank you enough for stepping in that day.'

Murray waved the thanks away and turned to fill the kettle, splashing droplets on the starched cuffs of his work shirt. 'It's easy to do things like that when you've got money.' He didn't say it boastfully; his money was simply a fact to him.

He switched on the kettle, set mugs on the counter, and then turned to face me, his hands clasped behind his head.

'So, everything's underway,' he said with a suppressed, nervous excitement, the same sort I'd seen in him when a big corporate deal was going down.

'What's underway?' I said.

'I'm buying Gretel out of her share of the house.'

'So you've broken up?'

'Of course. After her behaviour, there was no other option.' He shook his head, and I saw the muscles in his cheek tighten as he clenched his jaw. 'It was appalling, the whole thing.'

I felt a little rush of warmth. He was on *my* side now. Mine and Pip's.

'Did you get to the bottom of it? Why she did it, and everything?'

'Cleodie, it turns out, is one of the PIs the firm uses.'

'A private investigator?'

'Yup. She's the only female one on the books, apparently, and Gretel had used her a couple of times before. A woman can blend in better, in certain situations. She saw from her

373

invoice that she lived near you and spoke to her about doing a bit of extra work.'

'And Rose?'

'Search me. Maybe she *is* her niece. Maybe she just borrowed her for Friday mornings.'

I shook my head. 'How did Gretel even persuade her to *do* all this? I mean, isn't it basically illegal?'

'Hmm. Well, it was something to do with her novel-writing aspirations. Gretel offered her enough money to give up the day job for a whole year, and also promised to set up a lunch with an aquisitions editor at one of the top London publishers.' He shook his head. 'Someone she went to university with, apparently.'

'Jesus.'

'I'm sorry,' he mumbled, looking downwards like a little boy.

I wasn't going to let him away with it that easily. 'Sorry, what was that?"

He flipped back into lawyer mode and spread his arms expansively.

'It's my fault,' he said loudly. 'I wasn't in control of the situation. Which is unforgiveable, given that Pip became involved. I'll admit it, Gretel drew me in. She's a very charismatic individual.'

'She's certainly very something.'

His face dropped and he looked at me in confusion, like Pip when he couldn't fit his trains together or find the right jigsaw piece.

'I didn't really know her at all.'

'Oh, Murray. It's not your fault.'

He began pouring the tea. 'From now on, my only consideration

374

is what's best for Pip. And Janey, I've got a suggestion for you. A proposal, if you will. For you to think about.'

'Oh?'

He placed the two mugs on the table, then turned back to the counter for Pip's juice and a packet of Hobnobs.

'So, as I said, I'm buying Gretel out of her share of this house, and I'd like it . . . No, I'd *love* it, if you and Pip would move in.'

'What? I don't understand.'

'Think about it, Janey. It's a big house, plenty of room for all of us. You could rent out your place and invest the money for the future. You'll have the run of the place during the day when I'm at work, and, well, we could spend evenings together. Weekends. No back and forth for Pip. No worries about contact, and residence. No more lawyers, or hearings or any of that gubbins.'

It was what I'd always wanted. What I'd dreamed of, those lonely days and nights in the flat. To be a proper family.

He put the juice and biscuits down on the table, and positioned himself awkwardly behind one of the kitchen chairs, leaning his weight on it like it was a lawnmower, or a Zimmer frame. But his brown eyes were kind and steady as he held my gaze.

'And Janey, who knows? Who knows what might happen. There's always been something between us. Chemistry. That's why we're here, after all, isn't it?' He dropped his voice to a murmur. 'We made Pip.'

I looked at my feet. I could barely remember making Pip. Though I did remember the months of flirting in the office that had fuelled it.

'You're, well, I think you're awesome.' His face reddened

with his use of the borrowed teenage word. 'It feels right with you. Comfortable. It feels like home. When I see you and Pip, when I used to come on Fridays, I always just wanted to kick my shoes off and relax. I never wanted to go home. Never. I just wanted to stay there. With the two of you.'

I thought of those Friday afternoons, the times I wanted to rub his shoulders, stroke his hair, the way I could watch them for hours, him and Pip playing. The way that Murray felt like family because of our DNA tangled up in the boy I loved so unspeakably much.

'If – *if* – anything like that happened, we could take it slow. Very slow.' But for a moment he looked as though he wanted to undress me there and then. My pulse quickened, a little buzz of adrenaline. Could this really happen? With Murray, in his thousand-pound suit, in the cold hard light of day? Away from the befuddlement of the client dinner at Gleneagles, or the cosiness of the flat on Friday afternoons?

'And if it didn't, we'd still have Plan A, to live here as a family. Not as a couple, but as partners. Co-parents. We've worked well as a team, so far. Gretel notwithstanding,' he added swiftly, in a low-voiced disclaimer. 'Nothing's going to change that. I really believe we could make it work.'

For a moment the idea felt like sliding into a hot bath on a cold night. There'd be no more waking up in the dark, alone in the flat except for Pip. There would be no reason, any more, for my heart to speed up when I opened the door into a room. No more constant, underlying dread of another little surprise waiting. There'd be Murray pottering around, or snoring from his bedroom, or at the very least about to arrive home from work soon. There'd be the warmth from the Aga, and Bingo asleep in his basket.

376

'What if we met other people?'

Who would I meet, though? I thought of all the men out there, single, separated, and divorced, adding their profiles to dating websites, hanging around in trendy bars. None of whom were Steve. Or Murray, for that matter, with eyes that looked like Pip's when he smiled.

He shrugged. 'If that happened . . .' he cleared his throat. 'If you and Pip wanted to move on, move out, well of course I wouldn't stand in your way. You'd still have your flat, your own place to fall back on. We'd set it up so that we could unwind the financial side of things easily. But we'd have tried our best for Pip. Don't you think he deserves a shot at a proper family?' He smiled, his expression sad and hopeful in equal measure. 'Don't you think *we* do?'

★

I phoned Hattie and asked her to come over that night, because that's what friends did, wasn't it? They talked over each other's men situations and sorted them out. It felt a little strange though – unpractised – and I could almost sense our twelve-year-old selves sitting beside us, ready to giggle at any romantic outpouring.

'So what is your man situation?' asked Hattie, pulling her face into a serious expression.

'I still have feelings for Steve. And I was kind of thrown today. To realise that he did look after Miss Fortune. He didn't abandon her.'

'What about you, though? Didn't he abandon *you*?' Then she added, 'That was quite good, wasn't it? I sounded a bit like a therapist then.'

'Remember at the train station, though. He said, "It's like you wanted me to love you into existence." Oh God, Hattie, I think he's right. I wanted too much from him. More than he could give.'

Hattie sat thinking for a moment, surveying her nails. I heard her breath, moving heavily in and out. I wondered what she was about to say. Perhaps she'd had one of her inklings. Perhaps she'd seen a dark aura emanating from me, one that reached out towards men with desperate, grasping tentacles.

She looked up at me and delivered her pronouncement. 'What a twat.'

'What?'

'We all need loving into existence, Janey. That's what love *is*.'

I thought of Pip, whose gastronomic repertoire had now expanded to include plain pasta, and whose waist now proudly filled out all his age-three trousers. I thought of the Brahms Intermezzo I'd nearly mastered, practising on Hattie's cherrywood piano into the evenings while Pip slept. And the tiny creature who I'd held, in trembling hands, and kissed, over and over, whispering words of love that would have to make do for a lifetime never lived.

'I don't know.'

'Sounds like he was afraid you'd love *him* into existence. You'd make him grow an actual spine.'

'Harsh, Hattie. A bit harsh.'

'You can go on thinking he's a tortured creative soul if you like. But he'd better watch out if *I* ever run into him.'

She huffed and I was reminded of her giving some boy from St Simon's short shrift because he wandered off during the eightsome reel when he was supposed to be my partner. ('It's okay,' I'd whispered, tugging on her sleeve. 'He had sweaty hands anyway.')

'I keep coming up against this longing for him. I keep thinking I've done it, that I've moved on, and then suddenly I'm back there again. Back where I started.'

'It might just take time to let him go.'

'But this "letting him go" is like a staircase that should lead somewhere, somewhere in the open where I can breathe. But just when I think it's opening up it winds steeper and darker and tighter.'

She sighed.

'Then maybe it's because you're going the wrong way.'

'What do you mean?'

'Maybe you should try going down the staircase.'

'I don't understand. Do you mean try and get him back? You just said he was a twat.'

'What I think doesn't matter. What *you* think probably doesn't matter all that much, either. You have to feel your way, with something like this.'

'I can't pin him down. I can't understand exactly who he is or what he's going to do. I think he's one thing, and then he's something else.'

'People *aren't* just one thing. You can't grasp them, and keep hold of them. They change, they're a little bit different from one day to the next, with one person to the next. I hate to sound like Miss Fortune, but think about music. A note can change, depending on what other notes you put in front of it, underneath it, behind it. People are more like a tune, really, than a single note.'

'He couldn't say that he loved me. He couldn't say it.'

'But what about you? Where are *your* feelings in all this? Do you love *him*?'

'Oh God, Hattie. I can't help it. I've tried to stop, but it slams into my chest every time I hear his voice, or see his name on a text. It's like my body, every part of me, is saying *yes*, even though my mind is trying to be sensible.'

Hattie flumped onto the table and rolled her eyes. 'Well then? It hardly takes a love expert to know what *that* means.'

'But I don't know if I can trust it. Things aren't always what they seem to be. When I think about how he sat right by me while I did those drawings and didn't say a *thing*, when he knew all along. All the time he knew.'

'He knew what? He knew what the drawings were about, did he?'

I looked at the table.

'So what *are* the drawings about, Janey? Are we going to talk about this now?'

I met her eyes, just for a second, before looking away again. Her expression was steady, and frank. Too frank. This friendship business was hard going.

'Have you still got them, Janey? Have you still got the first one?'

So I fetched it from its shelf in the box room: that first drawing I'd done with Steve, with those few lines of spiky writing underneath, listing to one side of the page as though the words were being dragged down.

'Are you sure this is a skipping rope?' she asked.

'I think so,' I said. 'What else could it be?'

'It's just that it starts in the middle of you, and joins on to her tummy.'

'What? No, that's just because my hand was jerky when I was drawing it. The line goes through my hand, see?'

'It goes across your hand but it starts here.' She pointed.

'And don't you see? The other figure is so *small*.'

There was a long silence, in which I struggled with myself. Of course, part of me had always known. But that part didn't know how to find words, and fought them down, even when they tried to form.

Then she whispered, 'What were you going to call your baby, Janey?'

'Hattie,' I said at last, when I could speak. 'Of course I was going to call her Hattie.'

49

Janey

The sun shone low in the sky that Christmas Eve afternoon, slanting through the basement window at Regent's Crescent and onto the worn kitchen tiles.

I'd come to talk to Hattie. Not the girl sitting next to me, but the other Hattie, that small voice who'd somehow got lost in the middle of all the noise. She'd been so many things, over the years, to different people. To Granny, she'd been an 'abomination'. To Miss Fortune, she'd been a ruthless reminder of her own miscarried babies. To Mrs Potts and other well-meaning people, she was 'never meant to be'.

To me, she'd become an imagined version of everything she might have been, had she lived. I'd tried so hard to guess, with all those sad cuttings from magazines, supplements and catalogues over the years. Whenever I'd come across a picture of a baby, or a little girl, that made me think of her, I'd been overwhelmed by the need to cut it out and keep it. To keep it safe in my blue cardboard folder. Because if I simply turned the page I'd lose her all over again.

I'd explained all this to Hattie, my dearest friend, who'd been sitting by my side at the kitchen table, listening as it all poured out. Pip was curled up in the window seat, fast asleep after the excitement of seeing Santa at Dobbies that afternoon. And now it was time.

I took the pen in my left hand.

'Are you there?' I said.

My hand felt warm. And this time, when it moved, the movement seemed to come from somewhere inside myself, like a river that had finally found where to flow.

HERE

'Hattie?'

HERE

'I want to know what you would have looked like, whether your hair would've stayed dark or grown lighter, whether your eyes were green or grey or blue.' The words came out in a rush once I'd started. 'I want to know what you would have *felt* like, sitting on my knee. Whether you'd have been sturdy, or thin and spindly like Pip. If you'd have been one of those contented children – a good sleeper – or edgy and wriggly and curious. What things you would've liked to eat. What games would've made you laugh. I'll never know you. Not in this lifetime. Makes me yearn after another lifetime. Another chance. And it makes me feel so guilty, that this lifetime isn't enough, when Pip's in it.'

I glanced over at him, curled up on the windowseat. Still fast asleep.

'And you never knew *me*. You never even knew what I looked like. Or how much I would've loved you.'

YOUR VOICE
YOUR HEARTBEAT

'I want you to stay with me.'

THE TREES OF GLEN EDDLE

'I want you to stay.'

LET ME GO
LET ME GO
LET ME GO
LET ME GO
LET ME GO
LET ME GO
LET ME GO

No.

I would fly apart into a million pieces if I let her go.

I wrapped my arms around and held myself. I gathered my old selves into me. The Janey who'd hidden from love all these years, only to let Steve in and then lose him. The Janey whose nightmares and panic attacks had ended her music dreams. The Janey who'd miscarried alone in a cold marble bathroom. The Janey left shaking and bleeding by James. The twelve-year-old Janey stunned at the loss of Hattie. The bewildered eleven-year-old kept away from Grandpa's funeral. The six-year-old who'd waited, stomach churning, on Sunday nights, for her mother to call. The four-year-old who'd felt who knows what when her mother left to follow her own dreams.

And then I cried for that other girl who'd never quite had a place in this world. For my little Hattie. I cried for her lonely place on the edge of my consciousness, existing only as a shadow of what could have been. I cried for the petulant two-year-old who liked apples, the one-year-old with the velvet pink flushed cheeks, for the mischievous toddler who threw biscuits at Murray and drew spiky pictures. And as I cried, they flew off like petals in the wind. I tried to grasp after them, but they spun and spun around me, away from me, until I was crying for the thing in the centre of it all. The scrap of a human being who'd gripped my finger, just once, as I cradled her on the bathroom floor. The creature who'd offered, within the span of her tiny body, more heartbreak than my fourteen-year-old heart could hold. Who I'd wrapped in my white Aertex PE shirt, and buried, in the grey light before dawn, by the cherry tree in Hattie's garden.

*

'Remember the tune thing,' said Hattie, when the room was quiet again. 'It's such a sad thing that happened. Sometimes terrible things do happen and there's no fixing them. There just isn't, and it seems like a great dark hole torn out of your life. But it's part of your tune, you see? *She's* part of it. Little Hattie. And your tune's beautiful.'

I couldn't speak. I just sat there watching the light playing against the kitchen wall, the slow dancing shadow of the clematis that had grown across the window.

'Well,' I said finally. 'If I've got a tune, God help anyone who has to listen to it. I lost the key and the timing a looong time ago. Miss Spylaw would put me in detention for "wilful deafness" like that time with the chime bars.'

Hattie shook her head. 'You just don't listen. If you did, you'd hear it. And you'd hear where it's going.'

I thought of all the ways I'd changed, since Hattie had come back. No, not changed, just become more myself. She'd briskly pulled aside the curtains, on those shadowy corners of my mind, without even knowing it. She'd laughed along empty corridors and thrown open doors to long forgotten rooms.

Then I remembered one of those first, nerve-racking lessons with Miss Fortune, and my relief when Hattie had arrived for her five o'clock slot, bringing the chill of the October afternoon in on her clothes. Miss Fortune had made me finish off a tune for her, made me find the key. 'The root chord,' she'd said. 'The home chord. The tonic. Melodies behave just like us. They always find their way back home.'

★

It took ages to get Pip to sleep, what with the nap he'd had at Hattie's, and the long, reassuring conversation we had to have about Santa. In the end I suggested a 'Santa Lite' option, where the presents would be dropped down the chimney without the need for a home invasion. Pip had nodded in relief and finally closed his eyes.

When the flat was quiet I sat on the couch wondering what to do. Everything was tidy, the presents were wrapped, and there was no food to sort since Murray was hosting Christmas dinner at his house. He'd even invited Hattie, as though she was some elderly spinster aunt with nowhere else to go. He was paying his Latvian housekeeper triple time to cook dinner and clear up afterwards, so that we could sit around playing with Pip's new toys, laughing over board games, or dozing by the fire into the evening.

It was a glimpse into a life that was mine for the taking, a life of comfort and warmth and ease. There'd be no more moving around for Pip at the weekends and all his things could stay in one place. There'd be pancakes on Saturday mornings. Long walks with the dog on Cramond beach, or in the Pentlands, stopping for Sunday lunch in a country pub somewhere. Perhaps a tentative coming together, as a couple. All the quiet happiness that would go along with that. And when Pip grew up and left, Murray and I could travel the world, see all the places you were supposed to see before you died. We'd have dinner together in New York and Rome. See the opera in Vienna or Sydney Harbour.

It wasn't as if I'd ever really settled in this flat. At best it had been an uneasy, temporary home. What would it feel like to pack up all our stuff? To empty out Pip's toy cupboard, our wardrobes, the bookcases, and pack all the contents into boxes? It wouldn't take long. I could probably do it in an evening if I wanted to. Murray could come down and help. I could imagine him rolling up his shirt sleeves and getting stuck in, telling me to throw out this old thing or that, because he'd replace them with new ones.

Boxes, though.

A memory comes into my mind.

Boxes piled in the hall, being taken out of our house, one by one, by two big men I've never seen. One of them's called Jim Strachan and the other one is called Honey. They're putting the boxes in a white van. I'm watching Mummy, who is fluttering around, pointing to boxes and running her hands through her hair. I'm watching through bars, which are the banisters in the stairs. I'm sitting there with my Mickey Mouse suitcase on the step below, pretending to be on a bus. And then all the boxes are gone.

Now Granny's arrived, and she picks up my suitcase. She looks cross.

She says to Mummy: 'Do you really have to go straight away?

387

You should come and get her settled in at least.'

'We need to get there by five to pick up the keys.'

'Where are we going?' I ask.

'It's so exciting, poppet,' Mummy says, taking both my hands in hers and jiggling them up and down. The freckles on her face are standing out against the white. Under her eyes the skin is purple and bruised, like the skin on Grandpa's turnips.

'Where are we going?'

'You're going to Granny's, and I'm going to London, poppet. Remember?'

I picture a soldier in a furry black hat. Christopher Robin going for tea with the Queen.

London Bridge is falling down, falling down, falling down.

'Will you be back tomorrow?'

'Not for a while. You're going to stay with Granny and Grandpa.'

I struggle with the impossible.

'But it's okay!' she says, eyes wide. And she leans in close. 'You'll be able to see me on the television!'

I nod in relief, finally understanding. Understanding why she can be doing this. Mummy will come on the television every night, instead of the news. She'll talk to me, and read my bedtime story, which she hasn't done for a while actually. I've been waiting since last Christmas to find out the ending of 'The Magic Porridge Pot'. And I want to find out. Will the town be drowned in porridge, or not?

'Will I be in the telly too?' I ask, wondering how I'll be able to talk back, how she'll be able to see me. Or will I be invisible?

'Oooohhh,' she says, laughing and hugging me tight. 'One day, darling. If you work hard, and follow your dreams.'

I'm confused.

'Stay, Mummy.'

Granny takes my hand in hers. I hate it. It's rough and smells of onions. She's been making mince again.

Wood and clay will wash away, wash away, wash away.

'Come on, Janey. Your mother's in a hurry.' She gives a sharp little nod like a pecking chicken. 'Goodbye, Martina.'

Granny doesn't like Mummy because her voice is too loud, 'too showy for her own good'. My voice is quiet, so she doesn't mind me. I keep my singing in my head.

Mummy's eyes fill with tears. The green part looks greener, shiny, and the white part looks a bit pink. She looks pretty when she cries.

Silver and gold will be stolen away, stolen away, stolen away.

She glances at her watch. 'So you don't mind waiting here for—'

'Waiting for the letting agent. I said I would do it, didn't I? Come on now, Janey, let's go up and fetch the rest of your things.'

Granny walks me up the stairs. But at the turn of the stairs I stop, and look back at Mummy through the dark wooden struts of the banister. I watch as she half lifts, half drags her suitcase over the threshold, and bumps it down the front steps, lifting one hand in a backwards wave.

Look back, look back, look back.

But she's gone, and the door slams shut behind her, echoing off the blank walls.

And I'm an empty girl in an empty house. Nothing but Granny's hand to keep me there, to keep me from floating up, up, away into nothing.

★

I went to bed, and I didn't turn on *Christansen*. I lay there, listening to the sound of my own breath, shushing in and out like waves on the beach. The tide, coming in gently.

389

For the first night in months I didn't dream.

In the morning I woke to the sound of my own voice, saying his name. Always the name on my lips, since the first day I saw him.

50

Janey

'Play on swings first?' asked Pip.

I pushed him gently, the creak of the metal chains loud in the silent morning air. There was nobody about – nobody at all – until he appeared, rounding the corner from the main road.

Steve.

He made his way quickly along the street, up the short front path to Esme's door, drawing keys out of his pocket to unlock it. He was wearing a black parka jacket, his head hunched down into the greyish fur of the hood. He looked about twelve years old, legs skinny in his jeans.

He'd come to see Esme on Christmas day.

'More swing, Mamma,' demanded Pip.

We played for another ten minutes before crossing over the road, walking up to her door as Steve had done. One of the net curtains hadn't been pulled all the way across, and I could see the two of them. She was sitting in her armchair, and he was opposite, on the sofa, sketching her.

He'd started drawing again.

He answered the door, and when he saw me, he put his hands on the top of his head, and exhaled, long and loud, as though he'd been holding his breath.

'Hello,' I said. 'We came to say Happy Christmas to Esme.'

'She's in here,' he said, ushering us along the hall and into the music room.

'Jamie!' She stood up when she saw him. She looked so comfy today, in a long-sleeved navy jersey dress, and a silk scarf with grey and green leaves on it.

'Janey and Pip have come to see you, Esme,' said Steve. I liked how he said it in his normal quiet voice, not the loud booming voice most people seemed to use around her.

'Merry Christmas!' I said. 'I thought I could play some carols for you, if you like?'

'Way in a manger, little lord manger,' began Pip, in his reedy little voice.

'A-way! A-way!' sang Miss Fortune. 'A lovely major fourth, if you listen carefully with those little ears. A-way!'

'You're not in Newcastle for Christmas?'

Steve sat down in one of the flowery armchairs. 'Martin's moved back in. God, what a relief. It was never going to work, the three of us living in the house like that. But I'm going to see Calum one Saturday every month. I'll go down on the first train and let Katya and Martin get out for the day, have some time together. They're both into cycling.'

'So, you're back?'

'Just got back yesterday,' he said. 'Wanted to scoot out of the way before, y'know, Christmas day.' He grimaced. 'They hadn't found a replacement for me at the college yet, thankfully, so I'll be going back there next term.'

'And you've been drawing?' I nodded at the sketch pad, lying on the arm of the sofa.

He reached for it, and made to close the cover, but I put a hand out to stop him. The sketch showed Miss Fortune playing the piano, head tilted slightly to the side, eyes closed, the skin between her eyes pinched into parallel frown lines.

'That's her Rachmaninov face,' I said.

392

He smiled. 'Yup. The second piano concerto.'

'It's amazing, how you've made her hands so full of movement.' I shook my head. 'How do you do that?'

He pulled the pad away with a gentle tug. 'It's only a sketch. Just playing about, really.'

'How has she been?' I inclined my head towards Miss Fortune.

'Yeah, not too bad. Looks like we'll be able to get her a place at that independent-living place near Musselburgh. She'll have her own little apartment, but communal eating facilities and whatnot, and trained staff on hand all the time. Murray's been brilliant, by the way.'

'Oh, the copyright infringement thing? Have the other lawyers agreed on a figure yet?'

'No, but *Blue Bear's Dance* is going to make life a lot easier, put it that way. For her and for me, frankly.'

He did look more relaxed today, his face more boyish and the lines less pronounced.

'So what are you doing for Christmas lunch?' I asked.

'M&S finest. Nine minutes in the microwave.'

I couldn't leave them here, with the smell of microwaved vegetables wafting round the flat, him sketching images conjured from decades before.

'I wonder, could I tempt you with jam sandwiches on the beach? Pip and I aren't going to Murray's till three, so we were going to go and build Christmas sandcastles. You could sketch the beach, and the sea. It'll be beautiful today.'

So Steve fetched Esme's coat, and her black clippy handbag, and bundled his art things back into his bag. I drove them to Yellowcraigs beach, just down the coast, where the sea shone cobalt blue under the December sky. Just a few skeins of cloud drifted overhead, though it looked as though rain was gathering over the hills on the Fife side.

Wrapped up in our coats, we walked along the sand without talking – though Pip was still singing 'Away in a Manger' – our feet sinking into the drifts until we reached the foreshore, where Miss Fortune stopped. She stood, gasping from the exertion, with her hands on her hips. 'So lovely – to see – Kirrin Island again!' She nodded across the sea to Fidra Island and its storybook lighthouse nestled white beyond the grassy crags. 'Shall we play the Famous Five, Pip?' It was the first time she'd called him Pip.

She reached down, pulled off her shoes, and set off across the sand in her tights. Pip looked at me for permission, his eyes wide and urgent, then scrabbled to remove his own socks and shoes, and went after her, stubby little feet smacking across the ridged, wet sand.

'God, his feet are going to freeze.'

'They'll be fine.'

I spread out the picnic rug, and took out Tupperware containers with Pip's jam sandwiches and the cheese and tomato ones I'd made for me. We'd stopped at a petrol station for crisps and chocolate 'to make them go round', as my grandmother would have said.

We sat in silence, listening to the water swishing back and forth. I waited for him to speak. I knew it would come, the same way I knew the tide would keep moving up the beach.

'So I've realised a few things recently,' he said. His voice was light, but there was a very slight shake in it.

'Oh?'

'I really like you, Janey. My feelings for you are really quite strong.'

394

'So why did you go? Why did you go to Newcastle?'

He shook his head, as though despairing of ever finding an answer. 'I dunno, Janey.'

I waited.

'I suppose,' he said quietly, 'I'm used to being on the outside. That's why I spent my teenage years holed up with Esme in her flat. It meant I could opt out of everything: school, friends, my own family. And then later, with Katya and Calum, and Martin. I'm always the one looking in. You were different. You wanted me inside.'

I nodded.

'And then somehow you didn't. You pushed me away, just when I'd finally found what it took to open up to you. Not only that, you seemed to think I was some kind of monster.'

'It was a shock.'

'Oh, I know I arsed the whole thing up. Completely. The way I told you. I can see that now, but it still hurts. That you could think of me that way.'

'Oh no, look, they're heading towards the water.'

He sprang up and jogged out towards Esme and Pip. In a moment they were all walking up the beach, Pip skipping in anticipation of the picnic. He flumped next to me on the rug, and I rubbed his freezing feet with wads of napkins before popping his socks on. I bent and kissed them, holding one snug foot in each hand, feeling the soft little bones flexible under my grip. He shrieked and rolled away.

'Jam sandwich?'

I gave him one from the box and he sat, knees bent up in front of him, holding it with both hands in front of his mouth, face earnest as he closed his teeth carefully around the pointy part of the triangle.

Steve picked a cheese and tomato one. 'Mmm, su-perb,' he said, to no one in particular. 'Can't have a picnic without cheese and tomato.'

'Me try?' said Pip, turning.

Steve handed the sandwich to him. 'Don't take too much, yeah?'

Pip turned the sandwich round in his hands, looking at each of the edges. Carefully, I looked away, far, far away out to sea.

'Mmm,' he said after a moment, indistinct through a mouthful of sandwich. 'Can't have picnic wivout teese and mato.'

I glanced at Steve, who raised an amused eyebrow at me but said nothing. We sat eating, to the sound of the wind, and Miss Fortune humming along to 'Away in a Manger' as she nibbled at a Wispa. Pip kept throwing sideways glances at Steve. When he'd finished his sandwich he crawled over to his bag and pulled out his sketchbook.

'Er . . .' began Steve.

'No, Pippy,' I said. 'That's Steve's work, sweetie.'

But he'd pulled it out and opened it up. A few loose sheets fell out: the portrait of Miss Fortune at the piano, a picture of a path winding through winter woods, half finished.

And there was one of me. He'd sketched me, in watercolour pencils. I was lying on my side on the sofa, in my flat, curled around Pip, who was sleeping. The throw was draped over our legs, and I was wearing my green cardigan. My head was resting on a cushion, one or two stray curls lying across its velvet sheen. My left arm was tucked around Pip, and I was holding something in my hand, cupping it as though it was something precious. The tendons on my wrist stood out, ever so slightly, with the effort of holding it in just the right way.

It looked like jewellery, or a bunch of keys. Silver, shining, white to silver to black. I looked closer. A handful of musical notes. The beginnings – the merest whisper – of a tune.

I drew in a deep breath and held it.

'Mama and me,' said Pip nodding. Then he turned to Miss Fortune. 'Play sea castles again?'

'Stay out of the water!' I called as they wandered back down the beach.

'They'll be fine,' said Steve, who was putting the sketches back in his bag and closing the clasp.

I gathered my courage. It had to be now.

'Are you in love with me?'

He frowned, and his face clouded over.

Oh God, he was going to say 'What does love mean?' He was going to say it was just biology, a pattern of learned responses. The pain bit in again. I was going to have to leave. I was going to have to walk off this beach, drive home, drop him and Miss Fortune back at her flat, and wrench him out of my life.

Then he spoke, quietly, the breeze whipping his voice away so I could hardly hear it.

'There's this *yes* inside me, when I see you. Or hear you. Or even just when the thought of you crosses my mind. In fact I think it's always there. It's all through my body like a heartbeat. Like a rhythm, behind everything. Newcastle was all wrong. *So* wrong. I can't fight any more. I had to come back.'

'So?'

'It's always you. It'll always be you. You're so deep inside that it feels like you're all through me. Like it was always going to be you. From the moment you came into Esme's music

397

room that first, rainy Thursday night, and I hummed along to your playing in the back room while I was doing my maths.'

'You're rewriting the past,' I said, with a wry little smile.

'Some things are so strong that they do. They just do.'

He held out an arm, and it looked kind of lost, just suspended there, waiting for an answer. I wriggled over the rug and curled myself into that space, the space within the circle of his arm that was only ever meant for me. With his left hand he lifted my chin, and pausing, as though one world was about to tip into another, he moved his lips to mine.

51

THREE MONTHS LATER

Hattie

I'm so proud of Janey today. She'd played down her new job, said she was just an administrator for this new music charity. But it seems like she's basically running the whole thing. They co-ordinate musician volunteers and have them perform at old people's homes and schools for children with special educational needs and that kind of thing. Today was their annual lunch for the Scottish Alzheimer's Trust, and there was a string quartet and the most amazing contralto – a sixth former from St Katherine's – who sang 'When I Am Laid In Earth' from *Dido and Aeneus*.

Janey chose the music, organised the venue and the food.

But the music, it was one of those occasions when the music somehow transcends everything. One of the old people was actually crying with joy. She was gasping and moaning. One of the carers patted her arm and offered her a biscuit, but Janey walked straight over and put her arms around her. Where does she get this from? This confidence? She does something for people when their feelings become too much. She holds them. Contains them, using nothing but herself. It's like what she does with Pip and it just astounds me every time.

I was sitting there thinking about all that when he came up to me, a big man with dark hair and a goofy sort of face.

A *lovely*, goofy sort of face. 'Hi, you're Janey's friend, aren't you?' he said. 'I'm Paul.'

'Oh, Jungle Jive Paul?' I said. 'Alzheimer's Paul, I mean.'

His lips twitched, but he kept his face straight and solemn. 'Er, Alzheimer's Paul, yes.'

'Congratulations on the, er, lunch thingy. The event. And congratulations on hiring Janey. She's the best.'

'She's incredible. This passion she's got. She's taking us to a whole new level. I mean, look at this, today. Look, do you mind if I join you? Just sit here and talk to you for a bit? I'm a bit tired of all the – you know – dementia chat.'

'Isn't Geoff here today?' I asked. It was a bit direct, perhaps, but there was something about him. Something that made me want to cut through all the crap and the small talk as quickly as possible. Why waste time dancing around the whole silly Geoff thing when, well, when there was so much other stuff to do.

Paul rubbed his chin slowly. 'Ah. You heard about Geoff, did you? God, this is awkward. Yes. Geoff was, um, just someone I came up with. Jody was getting a little bit intense. I needed a little space, shall we say. Geoff was just . . .'

'Your imaginary friend,' I supplied.

He exhaled and sat back in his chair. 'Exactly.'

'Entirely reasonable in the circumstances, I'd say.'

That's when he smiled.

Physical attraction. It has always felt a bit too inkling-like for comfort. Stomachs fluttering and blood surging and all that. But this time I was, well, curious about it, and about what it might be trying to tell me. About Paul. About myself, standing there at the edge of my future. It had taken Janey, with her trailing sleeves and her stubborn grey eyes, to make me see: I didn't need to be afraid of what I could feel.

'Look, I'm not sure ... I don't usually ...' He shook his head, appealing to me to understand, and somehow I did.

'It's okay,' I said. 'Neither do I.'

'It's awfully hot in here. Would you like to go for a walk?' The little questioning lift of his eyebrow seemed achingly familiar, yet entirely new. As though I'd been waiting the longest time to meet him.

'I'd love to. But first I should probably introduce myself properly.'

I held out my hand and it tingled as he reached out to touch it.

'I'm Hattie.'

Janey

One sunny day in spring, we drove up to Glen Eddle: Hattie, Steve, Pip and I. We left the car in the car park and made our way along the forest track towards the bridge over the river. The boys went on ahead, Pip skipping along in his wellies to keep up with Steve's easy, long-legged strides. They seemed deep in conversation.

'Pip doesn't seem so shy these days,' remarked Hattie.

'He and Steve always seem to have a lot to talk about. They discuss ideas for paintings and stuff. Or at least Steve goes on about his at length, and Pip nods carefully and then says something like "blue wocket" or "doggie on twain".'

'Does he still talk about Dend?' she asked.

'Dend? No, Dend hasn't been around much recently, now I come to think of it. Only at night-time, maybe. Pip makes me say goodnight to all of his cuddly toys, and then Dend, and then him. It's a bit of a ritual.'

Hattie paused. 'I wonder if Dend was a sort of, well, an inkling. Pip could see that there was . . .' Her voice trailed off before she began again more confidently. 'Another child in your family. He could see her playing on the edges of your mind.'

Oh Hattie, with your inklings and all that worry and angst.

I nodded slowly. 'Maybe. Yes, maybe.' I'd learned to deal with Hattie's inklings as I did with Pip's frets and worries, giving them my full and careful attention, but not *too* much. And afterwards, coaxing her back into the here and now.

'I love the cherry blossom. Thank you.'

She'd collected it that morning from the tree in her garden, and had brought it with her in a little hooped wicker basket.

'And thank you for . . .' I shook my head.

For coming back. For bringing me back.

'Silly,' she said, bumping her shoulder into mine and keeping her eyes fixed on the path ahead. There was no need to put it into words, because we both knew all the ways in which we had saved each other.

'Here we are. Here's the old bridge.' Her voice was full of delight, as though she was amazed it was still there, waiting for us.

We threw the petals into the clear cold river while the trees sighed around us, and Pip laughed and splashed with the stones at the water's edge. Steve sat on the bank beside him, sketching a scene a bit like the one I'd attempted in the art class. He'd drawn in the first strokes of the mountains, steep on all sides, cradling the forest, the past and the future.

The last of the petals twisted and fell, and began their unknowable journey downstream. And now that I'd let go of the daughter that could have been, might have been in another lifetime, I was able to accept her for what she was: a tiny, lost, loved thing who never had a chance to live. I could fold her inside my heart and let her just be that, as my heart beat on, carrying me through my life and all the things that were to come.

When the light began to fade, we walked back to the car, Steve and Hattie each taking one of Pip's hands and swinging him along like a giant grasshopper, his squeals ringing out in the quiet of the woods. We took our wellies off and packed our things away into the boot.

I was ready to go home now. Home was the flat, with Steve's canvases stacked in the hall waiting to be sorted through, his easel in the kitchen, and half of my wardrobe filled with his clothes. It was the comfy armchair by Pip's bed – he'd moved into a 'big boy' bed now – where we read stories every night, and the tide of Duplo that encroached over every available floor space over the course of the day, to be gathered back into its boxes each evening. It was Bingo's basket in the corner of the kitchen, ready for his 'sleepovers' when Murray was away on business. It was evenings spent at the kitchen table with Hattie when she came over, with tea and flapjacks, and the laughter in her voice, and all the layers of myself – childhood, girlhood, womanhood – held safely there in every conversation.

Home was Pip, it was Steve, and it was Hattie, and most of all it was a quiet place inside me where I could let myself be loved.